SOMEWHERE STILL

DENITTA WARD

WELBOURNE PRESS

PUBLISHED BY WELBOURNE PRESS

∾

All rights reserved.
Copyright © 2017 Denitta Ward

FIRST EDITION

Somewhere Still is a work of historical fiction. Apart from well-known actual locales and some actual events that figure in the narrative, names, characters, places and incidents are the product of the author's imagination or are used fictitiously. Any resemblance to current events or locales, or to living persons, is entirely coincidental.

PRINTED IN THE UNITED STATES OF AMERICA.

ISBN-13: 978-0-9993018-1-4

Library of Congress Control Number: 2017912479

∾

Cover design by Frina Art
Photo credits: Nicole Jenkins

WELBOURNE PRESS

*For Patricia Diane Ray
in memory of
a woman who could Charleston like no other,
Virginia Todd*

∼

Sign up for the Denitta's newsletter at www.denitta.com

Find a Reading Group Guide to Somewhere Still and a peek at Prohibition Cocktails, the nonfiction companion to Somewhere Still at the end of this book.

SOMEWHERE STILL

PART I

I think the girl who is able to earn her own living and pay her own way should be as happy as anybody on earth.

— Susan B. Anthony

1

When he's the right one, you'll just know, and you should settle for nothing less.

Jean sighed as she mulled over one of her mama's many old-fashioned rules. She sat at the kitchen table, considering what it meant to be seventeen, stuck somewhere between child and adult, in the place where childhood rules no longer applied and new ones had yet to take hold.

She breathed in the stale air, the mentholated ointment mixed with eucalyptus, and could tolerate it not a second longer.

Reaching over, Jean opened the window and took in a deep breath, hoping to catch a faint hint of the lilac, a bit of springtime after a cold winter. Instead, a gust blew in from the Kansas City stockyards, and the pungency of the musk and muck made her eyes water. She shut the window firmly.

Settling back in her chair, Jean opened her favorite extravagance, *The Parisian Monthly*, and turned to the tale of a doe-eyed girl lost on the streets of Paris. Having read the story before, Jean knew an enticing man was to soon follow and the thought made her feel prickly and restless. She turned the page and saw an ad for women's delicate lingerie, which only made the itchiness worse.

Jean set the magazine on the table and cast her eyes out the window considering whether she could sneak outside for a stroll before her mama woke up.

"Would you read me the news? I can't stand not knowing what's going on in the world," croaked Mama's feeble voice. Jean quickly shoved the magazine under yesterday's newspaper. Mama was awake and asking for something already.

Maybe I'll get out tomorrow. Jean held back a sigh. She'd been cooped up for weeks fetching pills, making meals that went uneaten, missing school. Across the room the slight woman with thinning ashen hair let out a cough and covered her mouth with a threadbare blue handkerchief.

Consumption. Tuberculosis, the doctor called it. Not uncommon in the city, he had said grimly, offering no cure. The days weren't so bad, but at night the coughing fits would set in, waking people in the apartments up and down the hall. Jean sighed. No matter how much she chaffed at the rules and demands her mama made every day, no one could replace her wisdom or her love, now or ever. Jean would be willing to sit a hundred more days in that stale air if only something could make her feel better. She would give anything to cure that cough, but no cure could be found. Jean rose from the chair and took the few steps over to the bed.

She tenderly kissed her mama's cheek and unfolded the day-old newspaper, scanning the headlines.

"Sure. I'll read you the headlines and you tell me what you want to hear, okay?" replied Jean, raising her voice to assure she'd be heard over another coughing fit.

Jean had read most of the stories aloud the day before, but her mama didn't remember so well anymore. She was losing weight by the week, all bones and angles and raspy coughs, and had taken to the bed, not quite here and not quite there, but always wanting something.

"Jean, get me the tea. Can I have you read to me? What about some water? Why don't you help me sit up?" Mama demanded, "I'm thirsty."

The words burst harshly from her lips, but Jean knew that deep down, Mama simply needed reassurance that she was paying attention, still mattered to someone.

How lovely Mama had been in her youth, and how strong, always there with a pocket handkerchief to mop up Jean's tears when she missed her Poppa, always working hard, tatting lace, making a living so that Jean could have a better life.

Jean took a violet-sprigged handkerchief from her pocket and tenderly wiped away the beads of sweat on the pale woman's forehead.

A glass of water stood on the round table next to the bed, along with a fresh cup of dark tea flavored with a dash of honey. Mama had forgotten that the drinks were beside her.

Jean picked up the teacup, careful not to spill into the delicate saucer, and took a tiny sip to make sure it was not too hot. She blew on the tea to cool it, watching ripples form in the amber liquid.

"Now don't go drinking my tea," Mama said. "I told you I'm thirsty. You're gulping it all. No manners."

"Oh, I won't," Jean assured. "It's cool enough for you now."

Jean placed the teacup gently into her mother's hand. Those once-strong hands had fed her, diapered her, held her when she woke from a nightmare – and now those hands trembled and felt so cold.

"Stop staring," Mama said. "Ladies don't stare and you'll catch flies with your mouth open like that. When are you going to read the paper to me?"

Jean, suppressing a sigh, studied the paper, looking for a headline that might captivate. Police had started breaking up bathtub gin parties, and the papers would often name names and provide all the details, but this week the big news was about the city's Milk Wars. Local dairies were fighting against big ones and now the high society Consumer League ladies were sneaking around inspecting the dairy barns in their silk dresses, declaring that the dirty barns spread typhus.

"'Dirty Dairies Declared Deadly.' Or maybe this one, 'Ale Cures

Ailments,' read Jean. "Oh, now this is a good story. A group of men are trying to get beer declared medicinal. Says it'll cure the common cold, if they'd only be allowed to have a drink. Why are people so against it? Hard to believe liquor was important enough to go amending the whole Constitution."

"Beer as medicine," the grey-haired woman said with a wheezy laugh, "what will they come up with next? Druggists working as bartenders? Probably get them a lot more business. Men do like their drink. Now, would you get me my pills or maybe a glass of beer so I can be cured?"

"I'll get you a beer the day I get one too. It's gotta be something for all the fuss made," laughed Jean, tossing her long dark hair as she flashed an impish grin.

Jean and her best friend, Francie, had giggled about such things together, too, as they shared dog-eared pulp magazines, with their stories of rakish men, illicit gin joints and brushes with the law.

Mama smiled back at her, and for a moment, Jean felt hopeful, as if everything were the same as it had been, when they'd made easy jokes together.

"Now, I've told you about that. There's to be no drinkin'. Makes a girl lose her judgment. Men notice such things. Those kinds of men don't need thinking about . . .," and with that the coughing began.

Mama cleared her throat and continued, "You think there are all kinds of opportunities waiting out there, but ladies still carry the burden of consequences. You hear me? The burden of consequences."

Jean nodded. She had learned to sit very still during these lectures, which were occurring daily since the last doctor visit.

Her thoughts flew back to when Mama had been well. They had been like two best friends, sometimes even matching their outfits and the buckles on their shoes.

Jean missed the days when they had secretly climbed to the rooftop and slept outside together in the summer, under the moon and stars. Mama had whispered stories about the stars, and in the morning, they'd tell each other their dreams. In the winter, they had run to the rooftop when it snowed to make snowmen and angels.

Now, Mama kept instructing all the time, as if she needed to make sure Jean knew everything about being a grown-up as fast as possible. Jean had trained her face to appear engaged and attentive as her mama talked on, but let her thoughts sail out the window into the city streets.

Someday she'd get out into the world, be a working girl, maybe, somebody. As much as she loved her mama, Jean didn't want to grow up to be like her, alone with no man to help her, coughing and wheezing and lecturing. She envisioned herself like the lady on the front of this month's pulp magazine, wearing a fringed dress that showed her knees, carrying a beaded purse that dripped with money and casting heavily lidded eyes in the direction of a man in a fancy woolen suit.

"Are you even listening?"

"Of course. The burden of consequences," parroted Jean, giving the newspaper a shake.

"Oh, now, how about more tea," Mama requested, her voice a thin rasp.

Jean furrowed her brow as she rose from her chair and put the tea kettle on to boil, the newspaper still in her hand.

"It'll be just a minute. Listen to this. You'll like this story," said Jean, taking a seat on the bed and tracing a headline with her finger. "There's a new hotel that opened on Petticoat Lane. Says it has a dining room built like Pompeii and the lobby has green marble shipped all the way from Italy."

Jean sighed, imagining a dining room filled with columns and toga-clad women.

Exciting life happened in Kansas City, and someday they would air out this mentholated room and she'd go find it.

"That hotel's opened already? Miss Abby told me it would open soon. You go see and tell me all about it," Mama offered, with the hint of a smile.

Jean's eyes widened at the possibility of being set free for even an hour or two. The look on her mama's face was eager and encouraging, something Jean had not seen in weeks.

"Go and see it? Really? Oh, I'd love to," said Jean, her face flushing.

"Well, go. Good for you to get out some."

"Today? Could I just walk in like I was somebody, do you think? And what would I wear? Should I just wear this?" Jean asked, wrinkling her nose just as the copper tea kettle began to boil. She looked down at the scratchy twill dress sewn from two flour sacks, a plain brown homemade shift with no ruffles or lace.

Jean took the porcelain tea cup from the bedside table and, stepping towards the hot plate, poured the hot water into the cup. She reached for the tea box, but it was empty. She felt a jolt of disappointment as she pried off the lid and looked inside. Twining's Earl Grey was her mother's favorite, and Jean took care to reuse the teabags one, two times, or even more if she could, until the little bag finally broke loose or failed to turn the water even a pale amber.

"Mama, the tea is -- " Jean began, shaking the teabox upside down.

"I know, Jean, I know. I meant to say I just want some water," Mama said, forcing a smile. Jean blew on the hot water until it was cooled. Her eyes misted as she handed the cup to Mama.

"I'll get some more of your favorite tea," Jean promised, "soon, soon."

Jean knew that any money spent on an extra, like tea, meant less money for the next month's rent.

"Well, now, about that hotel, that Empire," Mama began.

Jean walked to the wardrobe bureau, the wooden floor creaking beneath her bare feet, as she thought about the big hotel with its tall windows. Opening the wardrobe's mirrored door, she surveyed her slim choice of dresses.

"I can't, Mama. I can't just frolic down to somewhere called the Empire. The Empire. What would I wear?" Jean asked.

"Real fancy people there, you know. But, that dress you have on is nice enough just for a look. Wouldn't wear that to go in there asking for a job, of course," her mama paused, waiting for a response but getting none. "Now there's a thought. Work. I was thinking a hotel might have all kinds of opportunities for a girl who wanted work and all."

Mama lifted her teacup and added softly, "Work might be a good thing for you, baby girl."

Jean's eyes widened. *Is she teasing? Work? It would be too good to be true. Work equals money. Money. A welcome change from the scrimping and pinching we've done for months. But who would tend to things here, and what about school?* Jean puzzled.

Jean had completed almost three years of St. Patrick's High School before her attendance lagged, what with the doctor appointments and sleepless nights. Her girlfriend Francie had brought over assignments, but it seemed pointless to scratch out math problems, calculate angles and read textbooks about tiresome ancient people. Working would be a relief.

"I could work," Jean began, "But who'd watch after you?"

Jean's enthusiasm wilted at the thought of her mama alone all day. It just wasn't possible.

"Don't give me a thought. I can take care of myself. I'm fine," replied Mama, her voice trailing off as the coughing began again and her frail shoulders heaved.

Blood stained the violet-sprigged handkerchief, and Jean quickly replaced it. She boiled water and washed a stack of handkerchiefs every day, but they had grown so threadbare and, with no money for more, she'd have to find fabric to cut new ones soon.

She glanced around the room to see what she could use, and her jade green eyes lit on her own favorite nightgown. If she made it calf length, instead of floor length, she could use that material for new, good cotton handkerchiefs for her mother. She'd have to wait until her mother fell asleep though or Mama would protest.

As she handed her mama the soft blue handkerchief, her favorite, from the stack of three hankies she had washed and folded the day before, Jean put a hand on her mama's forehead. The fever was back, but it wasn't too high yet, Jean concluded.

"Just a minute, Mama," Jean said as she picked up the soiled cotton cloth ever present by the bedside, "let me rinse this out."

Their home was not much more than a bedroom. No proper kitchen, just a hot plate for cooking and a wooden icebox. Jean and Mama had braided a bright rag rug for the room, so their feet could be warm when they stepped out of bed on chilly mornings. The braiding had been easy and fun, but the challenge had been getting it to lay flat.

With Mama so sick now, Jean felt grateful for the time they'd spent in getting the apartment as snug and cozy as possible with their limited money. Jean mused for a moment about how different their lives might have been if her father had lived to see her grow up.

She stepped into the apartment hallway, leaving the door ajar. She took a deep breath as she walked down the hallway and knocked gently to make sure the bath wasn't occupied. Though she told Mama that no, she didn't mind sharing a bathroom with the neighbors, it was an embarrassment sometimes and there wasn't an ounce of real privacy.

Jean dampened the washcloth with cold water then rinsed it and wrung it out just so. Cool wet cloths helped cut the fever and Jean had learned to have one at the ready. There had been a few times Jean had wanted to flee the sickroom. She needed to breathe in some fresh air and get away from the pills, the smell of mentholated liniment and soiled linens, but to even think that felt selfish and wrong. She'd made a kind of peace with all the daily tending Mama needed.

Jean did the washing, made the soup and toast, helped Mama change out of her nightgown and together they'd fallen into the rhythm of care-taking. Mama was all she had in the world. Poppa had passed so long ago and Jean had been a tiny thing then.

"You look so much like your father," Mama sighed as Jean stepped back into the room. "Dark thick hair, and those big green ocean eyes of yours, and your pretty mouth, like a rosebud opening to bloom. He was part Lakota Sioux, on his mother's side. That's where you get that pretty hair. And those eyes, they're from my mother; she was dark Irish."

"Oh, Mama," Jean said.

"You're so much like your father, Jean," Mama said. "He took care of me so well when I was big with child. I got so sick at first, and he brought me cold compresses, just like you're doing now."

Jean smiled ruefully and pushed a lock of her hair behind her ear with the tip of a finger. She had grown used to Mama's reveries. She didn't think she looked a thing like her Poppa, that sturdy soldier who had died when she was only six years old, but it made her mama happy to think so, and Jean felt ready to appreciate anything that made Mama feel better.

She remembered Poppa as a tall, strong man, who carried her up on his shoulders and told her that someday, if she kept growing so fast, she would touch the sky.

Mama's face had grown red from exertion and fever, or maybe memory, as she talked about him.

"Let me just cool you off and then you know what? I just might go see that hotel today," Jean said.

She picked up the tiny metal pillbox from the stand, opened it, took out two tablets and laid them by the water glass. Not a cure, the pharmacist said, but they helped Mama sleep.

"There you go. You take these now?" Jean asked, offering the tablets.

"Ok. But get me the envelope by the door, baby girl. There, there on the table," Mama whispered.

Oh, not again. Jean knew the envelope held twenty-two dollars and fifty cents, their last money from Mama's job. She fought back the small fear that landed square in her stomach every time Mama asked for the envelope. Jean knew the envelope never held enough and that the request meant more of the repetitive stepping and fetching she'd been doing the last several weeks.

Her mama would ask for the envelope, count out the bills and coins, put it all back in, and hand it back to Jean, a stern grimace across Mama's face. Not five minutes later, Mama would ask for the envelope again, count out the bills and coins, put it all back in, and again ask Jean to set it back on the corner of the table. Jean had learned there was no telling her mama 'no' when it came to fretting over the money.

Jean got the envelope and handed it over, knowing what would come next. But instead of the pensive counting and silent moving of lips to form the numbers "one, two, three," her mama riffled through the envelope and brought out one silver piece.

"Go down and see that hotel. Do some shopping. Take this fifty cents. I could use today's paper, some tea and don't forget milk. You'll have plenty of change. Go, go on now."

Jean looked at the fifty cent piece in her mother's thin hand, but she couldn't bring herself to reach for it at first. She didn't want to waste one of their last, precious coins.

"And don't give me that look, missy. We can afford it. I have enough for next month's rent for sure," said Mama, straightening her frail body and giving The Look, the look that said hitch up your britches and get on with it.

Rent. Ten dollars. There's only money for barely two month's rent, even if that were our only expense. Jean forced a smile as she took the silver piece and tried to shrug off the little nagging worry always at the edge of her mind - the thought of how money spent could ever be replenished.

I'll just make the best of today. Maybe I'll go by the hotel then visit Francie and together we'll go the store, worry about tomorrow, tomorrow. She loved her mama but a few moments of light and air and sunshine would be refreshing.

Jean twisted the hem of her simple brown dress. For Petticoat Lane maybe she needed something fancier. She pulled a pale pink scarf trimmed in lace from the bureau drawer, one her Poppa had sent when he was stationed in France. She knotted the delicate silk to hold back her ever-wayward hair and slipped on her shoes.

"Come here, let me straighten that scarf for you," offered Mama. "I like the way that green lace at the edge sets off the color of your eyes."

"You do such beautiful tatting," Jean said. "I always was all thumbs with the delicate work."

Jean let her straighten the scarf, even though she could have done it for herself. Mama always enjoyed brushing Jean's long hair, but her arms had grown too weak now. Jean knew Mama still wanted to take care of her the best she could.

"While I'm out, how about I get that tea box refilled with your Twinings Earl Grey," Jean said, as she sat down on the edge of the bed. The tea was an indulgence but its hint of citrus and spice, and the idea of it sailing on a big ship from England, always brought a smile.

"Now, that would be a treat," said Mama, retying the scarf.

"Lean forward and I'll plump your pillow," said Jean. "And I'll buy us some peanut butter. We'll have sandwiches for dinner, too," Jean offered.

Mama had not taken solid food for days and had barely sipped on tinned soup, but Jean hoped that she would get her appetite back soon. Jean hoped so hard that someday everything would be better again.

"That'd be nice," said the frail woman, handing Jean the envelope as she eased back onto the bed pillow. "Go on. Don't forget the key. You lock the door, promise?"

"I will. I promise. You worry too much, Mama," Jean said as she gave her mother a quick peck on the cheek. Her mama's face was cooler.

"You sure you're okay?" Jean asked, as she picked up the damp cloth from the nightstand and placed it gently over her mama's forehead. Jean didn't mind the caretaking so much as the uncertainty. Not knowing which might be a good day or how bad the coughing would be at night, how bad it could get. She looked at her mama carefully, searching her face for any sign of pain.

"Anything else? I won't be gone long," Jean reassured her as she tucked the cover around her mama's shoulder.

"Just a sip of that water. I'll be fine. Just need some quiet," said Mama, her eyes shutting as she swallowed the pills. Jean held the cup to her mama's lips as the thin woman took a sip. She set the glass back quietly on the bedside table, then picked up the front door key.

She pulled the apartment door shut, taking care to lock it quietly.

The apartment walls were wafer thin and the neighbor lady complained when doors slammed but she was generous with her Slavic cooking. She tiptoed past the Ivanovic's door, taking in a deep breath to savor the smell of the pierogies. Today's pierogies were potato and onion, most definitely. Jean's mouth began to water as she made a dash down the two flights of stairs.

"Good afternoon, Otis," said Jean to the doorman as she opened the apartment house door. Perhaps it was too fancy to call Otis a doorman, but it made Jean feel special to think of him that way. A doorman meant safety from whatever might lurk on the other side of that door. Besides, a working girl would have a doorman.

Truthfully, the apartment house was undeniably shabby, but the landlord let Otis live in the basement in exchange for taking care of things, mopping floors and such. Otis was friendly, with brown eyes that saw much, and kind lips that stayed quiet about it. He always took an interest in the residents' comings and goings.

"Miss Jean, you look very right today," said Otis, pulling his lean frame straight as he rose from the front step and slipped the book he was reading into his back pocket.

Otis was constantly talking philosophical-like. Mama said he always carried with him a book. At first all they saw was the Bible but lately he'd taken to reading some book about meatpacking. He was a fixture at the Stover building, sitting on the front steps smoking his cigarette with one hand and holding a book in the other.

"Not seen you smile in 'most four weeks now. This morning the sunshine glows right into you, helps you shine your light. You going out?" Otis asked.

"I am going out, finally. I really think I need to find myself some work," Jean confided. "I'm almost an adult. Practically anyway and --" Jean stopped, feeling the cardboard patches in her scuffed shoes. "Well, I think it's what I need to do."

"I expect that's about right, Miss. A'most grown now and able to do for yourself. Just know opportunities are waitin' for you. You take right good care of things here," he said, gesturing towards her third story window. "God takes notice of such things. Finding work. Yes, I'll pray on this."

Otis stubbed out his cigarette and carefully placed the cigarette butt in his shirt pocket. He never littered, and Jean didn't know for sure if he was naturally neat, or if he simply knew he would be the one who would have to clean up the stoop. Jean had noticed how careful he always was and it made her careful, too. She didn't want to make more work for anybody.

"You pray for everything, Otis," teased Jean. "But I'll take your prayer as my hope."

"Prayer is powerful, don't doubt it, but hope don't pay the bills, I know that," said Otis, extracting another cigarette from the pack. "Your mama, she's ready for you to go out into the world?" Otis asked as he pulled a lighter from his pocket and struck the flint wheel.

"Big world out there, Miss. You real serious about working? Get up every day, do a full day's work somewhere?" Jean nodded as Otis took a drag and continued. "Miss Abby. I know she can help out some with your mama. Needs to fill her days anyhow. Be a favor to Abby to take care of someone again."

Otis's grown daughter, Abby, had moved back in with her father over the winter after the Spanish Flu epidemic swept through the city, leaving her house empty in a way that could never be filled again. People said Abby could birth babies and cure ills. She seemed normal enough, except for her heavy, sad eyes that spoke of burdens a mother should never bear.

"Mama being alone is a worry, Otis. Every fifteen minutes she needs something and her coughing is ..." Jean's eyes dropped, ashamed at how harsh her words sounded. "She just needs -- and we, we got nothing put aside."

"You're worried, aren't you Miss Jean? Don't worry so. You ever need, then Miss Abby and I can help. We know there might be some hard times comin'. But, you're a good girl. Smart. Wits and that smile will carry you. Trust in that," Otis said, flicking ashes into a small metal ashtray he carried in his pocket.

"Thank you, Otis. I just need a start so Mama won't . . . you know," Jean replied, forcing a smile.

"I hear that the new hotel is open. Empire Hotel. Owned by a Mr. Whitcomb. Mr. Randall Whitcomb. He owns half the town, they say. I think it's more like thirty percent in reality. But I hear it's fancy like this cowtown has never seen. Kansas City's coming up in the world, I do say. They say Mr. Whitcomb has an elevator that runs on electricity even. Fast, too. Paper says it travels over 500 feet a minute. I hear it'll have a little seat in there for a girl elevator operator to sit on when she gets tired of standing up," said Otis. "Right fine for a girl, I'd say."

"A girl? Really, a girl elevator operator?" asked Jean, pressing her hands against her skirt. "Do you think I could do that?"

"I hear that a girl could. 1921. Things are changing now that women can vote. Guess they can work too. Even do a man's job like elevatorin'. Measured steps of progress, they say. If you're interested, take yourself down to the Empire. Talk to the doorman there. My cousin, James. Plays ball for the Monarch team, works there off days. He says Mr. Whitcomb wants everything modern in that hotel. So modern even to have a little gal operating the elevator. Like they do in New York City. Wouldn't that be something?" Otis looked pleased to share this tidbit.

"James is his name and he's there now?" asked Jean brushing a strand of hair into her scarf.

"Working today," Otis nodded. "Might want to go, see if he'll have a word with you."

"Oh, thank you, Otis, I will," said Jean. "Maybe Abby could check on things upstairs, too?" Leaving Mama for even a few hours was a worry.

"'Spect she will today. Don't give it another thought," Otis said, taking another drag on his cigarette. "Might use that fine scarf to cover your nose today. The smell of money is strong."

Jean muffled a laugh as she pulled the scarf's tail over her face. "Thank you, Otis," she said, her head inclined.

2

Jean could feel the sun's warmth on her back as she walked toward Eleventh Street. Otis was right, the smell of money was strong today. The air was crisp and the wind blew in the smell of the stockyards over at the West Bottoms.

The paper said more than two million cattle would come through the yards this year, most destined for the packing houses or rail station. All the cattle, hogs, and sheep sent a stench through the town at certain times but that stench meant jobs, and jobs meant money, and money meant ease of mind.

Jean put the odor out of her mind. *Nothing to worry about if there's nothing you can do,* Mama often said. Jean's heart lightened with each step away from that sickroom. It had been weeks since she'd had a free moment, a moment not consumed with worry.

Mama wasn't getting better, wasn't going to get better, the doctor had said, but what did doctors know, anyway? Still, until Mama got better, Jean had no choice but to figure out how to make do on her own. She looked around the city street imagining what kind of girl might work in a stylish building on Petticoat Lane.

Women in the city didn't really work unless they were the immigrant women in the garment factories or the millinery shops. Her mama had been lucky to find work tatting, making lace for rich women's dresses, but it was a skill Jean had never learned, with all of its fuss and precision. It hadn't seemed important to learn a trade, not until recently, when the doctor gave his grim prognosis.

Jean knew that Mama tried to keep her spirits up, not let on that things were bad. The doctor wouldn't say if it were weeks or months, but he hinted that it may not be long before Jean would be all alone in the world, with no family, no money, no Mama. Jean kept up a cheerful front during the day but often had to excuse herself after dinner for a few minutes alone.

She wanted to be a brave girl and not let anybody see her sad. She wanted to stand up straight and tall, and never let the weight on her shoulders show to anybody.

Mama joked that Jean had taken too much interest in primping in front of the bathroom mirror lately and Jean didn't dash her lighthearted thought with the truth: the reflection in the mirror was just a lonely, scared girl with tear-stained cheeks.

Whatever happened with Mama, whether that doctor might be right or wrong, Jean knew she had responsibilities now, to find work, make her own way. Every penny she made would ease Mama's burden. Jean hadn't let herself think, really think, about the goodbye part, the part that the doctor implied could be coming.

A sweet mewling roused Jean from her sad reverie, and she turned in time to see a flash of pepper fur as the tiniest kitten she'd ever seen sped past her chasing a mouse almost as big as the kitten.

For a moment, Jean considered turning around and going straight back home to her mama. She squared her shoulders. She had to stay strong. Jean knew grief from losing her Poppa so young; it was unfair that Mama could be taken from her too. The only family she ever had seemed on the verge of disappearing.

No, she couldn't think about the sad thoughts. She pushed her sorrows away by focusing on the practical, the here and now things that she could change. A job, work. A paycheck.

I'm practically an adult. It's time to take responsibility, Jean thought. Even if it meant putting herself out there with fancy people with expectations, people who never had to share a bathroom with their neighbors or count their pennies to buy tea, people whose lives filled the society page.

I can do it. Nothing to be intimidated about. Just because some people have money doesn't make them any better than us, even if they put on airs otherwise.

Jean had seen the ladies who visited the department stores on Eleventh Street, the Harzfeld's and the EBT - Emery Bird Thayer Dry Goods Store. They carried themselves with such assurance, all draped in packages and furs. Jean wished she could buy one of those furs for her mama. Maybe with a warm fur coat, she wouldn't have such a harsh cough.

Jean had once shopped at that dry goods store with her mama. They needed to dress up just to walk along Petticoat Lane, her mama had instructed. Without a man in the house, Mama had learned how to size up a crowd and make her way in the world, lessons Jean took care to learn by example.

Mama told her that Eleventh Street got the nickname Petticoat Lane because the well-dressed ladies took over that street, scuttling from one shop to another, taking tea at the EBT, socializing and making sure they were seen with the city's very best.

"You can tell a lady by her shoes," Mama had said then. "Good, sturdy, pretty shoes help a woman walk proudly in the world, with her head up, not looking down at the ground for loose change. And the cut of the cloth – Oh, Jean, if I had time, I'd make you a dozen pretty dresses."

Jean smiled and remembered the ocean of lace parasols and swish of long skirts as they walked along the sidewalk. They'd made their way through the department store's revolving glass door and Mama had studied the lace on one of the dresses hanging on the rack, running her fingers over and over it so her hands could memorize the pattern. Then Mama had taken her to the very center of the store. It had been Jean's first elevator ride and Mama insisted that they take the brass elevator to the very top floor.

What she recalled most vividly was the imposing figure of the elevator operator, a man with white gloves and a firm smile. He was all business and the first man who had called Jean a lady, though she had been barely a schoolgirl.

Jean's stomach quivered with memory and the idea of running an elevator herself and seeing all those kinds of people who'd visit a hotel. *The President might even stay there. I could meet just anyone.*

Excitement overtook her as she raced the last block toward Petticoat Lane. She felt the cardboard loosening in the sole of her left shoe and slowed her pace to a prim walk. *A lady, a working lady, can't be seen running.* She put her hand up to adjust the silk scarf and self consciously looked up and then down the street. There was the hotel doorman smiling at her. He'd seen her running like a child. *Rats! Oh well, I'll just pretend he didn't.* Jean tossed her hair, nonchalantly pushing aside her youthful transgression as she passed by the hotel's big picture window. She tried to steal a look inside.

She could make out a shimmering light from a chandelier. The luxury of it made her palms tingle and a flutter build up in her stomach. She delicately patted her pink scarf back into place. Flushed from running, she didn't have to pinch her cheeks to make them look red with rouge.

"Good day, Miss," said a male voice. The doorman. The words startled Jean. Strange men didn't talk to her on the street. With a quick intake of breath Jean deliberately chose not to appear flustered.

"Oh, yes, good day, sir," she replied.

"May I get the door for you?" he asked, extending his gloved hand towards the arched doorway. Jean felt her confidence melt away as she registered the formality in his voice. Then she remembered that Otis had said his cousin, James, would be the doorman. She took a little confidence in that small connection between her world and the bright, luxurious world she hadn't entered yet.

"Thank you, I want to, but I don't know if I should go in yet. I have a question for you first, James," replied Jean.

"Very fine, Miss," he said formally, laying his gloved hands back to his sides as a smile edged across his chiseled features. "But, Miss, how do you know my name?"

"Oh, I'm sorry. Otis said that. I live in his building and he told me. His cousin, he said. I mean, Otis said his cousin James worked here at the best hotel in all the city and played ball for the Monarchs. That was rude of me not to be properly introduced," fumbled Jean.

"That's okay, ma'am. It's true enough. Otis and I are family, cousins, and you must be Miss Jean," the man said. Jean's eyes widened as James nodded. "Yes, Otis told me. He said you may be coming down this way, what with looking for work and all. He asked me to keep an eye open for you."

Jean's mouth hung in surprise, aware now that the adults in her life had conspired to set something in motion days, if not weeks, before. *Maybe I can work here, maybe it's all arranged.*

"Oh, yes sir, I am looking for work. I do want to work here. I do," Jean burst out. She looked around nervously, realizing she was standing on a public street talking to a stranger, and a colored man no less. Jean thought of people as people, regardless of the color of their skin, but she had been chastised many a time by others who thought differently. James read the apprehension on her face and turned to the side to look down the street.

"Guess it may not be right to stand and talk like this. You just bend down and fix that strap on your shoe and listen," he suggested.

Jean looked at her scuffed shoes. A strap had come apart. The shoes were shabby hand-me-downs from the lady Mama worked for, but they once had been good quality. Ragged didn't begin to describe them and now they were broken, too. Jean bent down and tucked the strap back into the side of the shoe.

James took a glance her way and whispered in a low voice, "Mr. Randall Whitcomb, he owns this hotel and the society ladies tell him they all want a girl to run his elevator. First place in Kansas City with a girl transportin' guests. Has to be someone tiny, like you, because elevators can carry only so much. Have to leave room and weight for the guests and their big luggage. Has to be a girl not afraid of people, smilin' and friendly, but knows to be quiet, too. Can't be scared of strangers. Maybe a man or two in the elevator sometimes. Can't be scared of that."

"I'm not afraid. People who go to a hotel, they've got to be the most interesting people in the world," Jean replied, projecting her voice upward. She'd spent enough time fiddling with her shoe. She couldn't fix it anyway, so she stood up straight. Her mama had made her walk around their little room for hours with a book on her head to get the good posture of a true lady.

As she rose, she noticed an older man in a long black overcoat, a newspaper under his arm, approaching. Beside him strode a younger man with thick dark hair, a strong, square jaw.

He looks like he owns the world. She took a step closer to the hotel door as the two men approached and flashed a nervous smile. The older man brushed by, giving her no notice. The younger man hesitated for a second and smiled at her, not the way men so often did when she walked by herself or with Francie, but with a look of genuine kindness.

As they neared, James sprang to action and pulled open the brass door, "Sir, good day to you both."

The older man gave a brief nod but said nothing. The younger man didn't hesitate to reply, "Morning, James. You playing any ball this week?"

"Sir, yes, sir. I do play this week and next. Home games," James smiled.

"Well, good luck. I'll be sure to catch your games. Know what this is?" asked the young man, flipping a silver shoe buckle into the air and then tossing it to James. "Found it just down the street."

"Thank you, sir. I just may be able to find its owner," James replied, holding his gaze on the man and resisting the urge to acknowledge Jean, "And it would be an honor to have you at my games, sir," James said as the men entered the hotel.

He checked that the brass door closed firmly behind the two men. "And that, Miss Jean, is Mr. Randall Whitcomb and his son, Elden. Elden Whitcomb, a fine man."

James's voice rang firm with knowledge and conviction, but Jean barely registered his tone. Jean felt grateful to him for not mentioning who the owner of that buckle might be. She stood, mouth slightly agape, staring at the closed door thinking about the way the young man, Elden, with his easy smile and new woolen suit had filled the space as he strode down the sidewalk.

She looked down at her broken shoe strap with embarrassment. As she looked up, she caught James also studying the tattered bit of leather.

"So here you go," said James softly, handing her the shoe buckle. "Get yourself ready. Get your shoes fixed. Wear your Sunday best and know what you're going to say. Think on this. Now, do you want to take a peek inside?"

"You've been most helpful, James," said Jean, hiding her humiliation behind a warm smile, "With them in the lobby I'm not ready to go inside but I'll be back and I'll think on this, like you say."

As she started down the street, her mind swirled with possibilities. *Think on this? What is there to think on? I've got to do it, put my mind to it and get this job. But what do I say? Francie. Francie can help me figure out what to say and do. Mama taught me how to fit in with those people, all 'please' and 'thank you' and curtseys. And always smile, she says. Smile. Oh, his smile. He looked every bit as elegant as his name. That boy, Elden. Elden.*

She repeated the word over and over in her mind as she hurried toward Francie Nowak's house. She felt so happy, she wanted to skip, but if she didn't walk carefully, her shoes would start flapping. Jean started thinking of all the things a good job could buy: rent money, new shoes, and her mama's favorite tea. Her friend Francie would scarcely believe this good fortune.

Francie's family lived on Strawberry Hill and practically ran the Catholic parish that had given charity to the fatherless Jean with the working mother.

Years before, Francie's mother arranged for Jean to enroll in parochial school, with the hope that Jean and her mother would join the church. And they did. But the rituals and sacraments washed over Jean, who focused more on the time spent with Francie. She'd learned to mimic Francie's genial manners and the kind way she talked with the nuns.

"Hey, Francie," Jean called through the screen door as she stepped onto the Nowaks' covered porch. Two dogs and a boy in sailor shorts shot out of the front door and down the steps followed by a toddling baby wearing a graying cotton diaper and a toothless grin.

"Hey there," said Jean, stooping to pick up the toddler, "Want me to carry you?" The little boy nodded and lifted up his arms. Jean gingerly picked him up and balanced him on her hip. The child cooed as Jean felt a warm wetness stream down her hip.

"Oh, dear, I think you've wet on my dress," Jean muttered, shaking her head. "Francie, can you help me with this sweet boy?" Jean called through the screen.

"Hey, Jean!" said Francie opening the front door. "Oh, there's our boy. Did you see Adam go by, too?" Francie asked, lifting the child away from Jean. "Oh, look at that, you're wet. Come in and we'll clean you up."

"Adam's on the lam. He went by with the dogs. I just need a washcloth then we're out of here, okay? I have a lot to tell you," Jean said in a rush. She'd learned that if she didn't pull Francie out of her house quickly, they'd both get consumed in all the childcare and housekeeping it took to run the Nowak clan.

"Come in and clean up while I get Adam and tell Grandma I'm off duty," said Francie. "All seven kids were mine until mom and grandma got back from church. I'm due a break."

Jean entered the wood frame house and looked around the living room, ever a jumble. Francie's grandma had moved in right before Christmas, making the home even tinier. Francie, her grandma, and the littlest girl slept in what was the dining room. The boys were up in the attic and the middle girls, all three, shared one bedroom.

Francie's poppa worked nights in the railyards and her mother helped by taking in sewing and piece work that inundated the living room with scraps and bits. She had plenty of work even though she'd taken care to give Jean's Mama all of her lace-making orders.

"Go on in the bathroom if Mary ever gets out of there. Just knock on the door and say 'move it along'. Tell her she can stare at the mirror all she wants; it still won't change her nose any," said Francie, sounding like the exasperated older sister that she was. Jean knocked loudly on the bathroom door, ready to repeat words she'd said many times before, to little avail.

Finally cleaned up and with an afternoon of freedom ahead of them, Jean locked arms with Francie as they walked down the street. They made an unlikely pairing, with Francie at 5'10" towering over Jean's 5'2" frame.

Jean eagerly chattered about the possibility of working at the Empire as they walked into the corner grocery store picking out tea and peanut butter. Jean told Francie about watching her broken shoe buckle flipping casually in the air and back into Elden's palm as the gorgeous man greeted the doorman.

"You can't imagine what I was feeling. Thought I might up and crumble into the sidewalk with embarrassment," Jean laughed nervously. "I won't get work unless I look like I deserve it," Jean said to Francie, taking the Earl Grey tea tin from a shelf.

"So some new shoes then, I guess?" offered Francie when her own laughter stopped. Jean stood silent for a moment. Francie didn't know the depth of Jean's money woes. There was no money for something frivolous like new shoes.

"Oh, no, I'll just borrow Mama's. It's not like she's going out tomorrow or anything," replied Jean, feeling immediately ashamed. Francie patted her hand.

"It'll be okay, Jean. You'll need a new dress for certain though," suggested Francie. "Let's go to the sundries shop next. They have beautiful fabric."

"Fabric? I can't sew a stitch and there's no time either. I'd look like a scarecrow in a silk gunny sack if I tried to sew a dress," said Jean. "Remember when I made that nightgown for you?"

Francie giggled, fully aware of Jean's lack of cultivated domestic tendencies. When Jean had decided to make a nightgown for Francie's birthday, she had started with small, even stitches, but by the time she finished, the stitches had gotten so big that Francie had poked two fingers through a stitch when she'd pulled the gown over her head.

Jean was glad to hear the laugh; she didn't want to have to confess how little money sat in her pocket, certainly not enough for dress fabric.

Emboldened, Jean continued, "A homemade dress? Oh, no. No. That's not going to be me. I'm more like a modern girl with real clothes, well, someday maybe. And then I'll have on lipstick, too. Just so. Like a modern girl."

"Modern Jean, the career girl," Francie said.

"What do you think ladies wear in those fancy hotels?" Jean asked.

"I do know they don't wear homemade dresses with great big stitches," Francie giggled, bobbing her dark curls in agreement. "If you work there, you might get a uniform to wear, but you know my mother would gladly make you any dress you want, though you know the price that comes with. She'd eventually expect a little conversion in exchange."

"Is she going to bribe me with candies again to get me into church?" Jean asked playfully. Francie's mother was not above sweet-toothed bribery to save her brood's souls. Pocketfuls of penny candy had made Francie a regular at Sunday Mass from a young age and no doubt contributed to her rounded curves now that she was a teenager.

"Think she needs a refill of her candy stash for your brothers?" asked Jean pointing towards the store's confectionery counter.

"Always," replied Francie. With their thoughts on sweets, the girls wandered to the penny candy section to debate the choices.

"Wait! Forget candy, look at this," said Francie, her eyes lighting on a *Ladies Home Journal* displayed on the counter. On the cover were girls – *Sweet Nothings*– it read. Francie opened to a random page.

"There's the modern girl," said Francie pointing to a picture titled 'The Influence of Beauty'. Pictured was a girl dressed in a slim chemise of gossamer chiffon, her bobbed hair falling in soft, short waves. *That is the modern girl. That can be me.*

"I can pin my hair up and make it all gentle and soft like that, too," said Jean.

Francie pulled out a quarter from her thin coin purse and handed it to Jean. Jean tried not to clutch it too tightly. A quarter felt like a lot of money, heavy in her palm.

"Which candy?" Jean asked.

"Forget sweets. You buy the magazine. I'll go find hairpins," Francie offered.

The girls took their purchases to a bench outside the store and paged through the magazine. The titles of the articles alone were exciting: "Why You Must Have Beautiful Well-Kept Hair to be Attractive", "The Women's Voters Birthday", an advertisement for Victor Talking Machines - as if there should be music in every home.

"Music in every home," Jean said. "Can you imagine having a Victor talking machine right in your own house?"

"Amazing," Francie replied. "I never thought of it before now. Of course, Jean, the way you sing and dance, you always have music, wherever you go."

"Francie, what do you think I ought to wear to the hotel?" Jean asked. "I can't get anything new and this brown dress won't do."

"If only we wore the same size, I could lend you my best Sunday dress," Francie said.

"That's it! Oh, Francie, thank you," Jean said. "I can wear old Sunday dress."

"The dotted swiss one with that pretty lace hem that your mama made?"

"What do you think?"

"It will be perfect. Do you want me to come to your house in the morning and help you fix your hair?" Francie asked.

"You have school but I'll pin up my hair before bedtime," Jean said. "And I'll let you know every single detail about that hotel, too."

As Jean gave Francie a hug goodbye, she felt enveloped in the sweet, spicy scent of rosemary. Francie loved rosemary, and she often placed a sprig of the herb inside her blouse.

Jean headed home with her magazine and hairpins. She could smell the scent of Otis' sweet tobacco as she neared the Stover building, home. Otis was sitting on the stairs out front, thumbing through the *Kansas City Star*.

"Otis, I met James and the hotel really does want a girl elevator operator. How did he know to tell you? And the Whitcombs look like royalty, I swear. And I'm going to do it. Tomorrow," Jean gushed as she approached the front door. "I'll dress nice and use my best manners. I know I'll meet all kinds of people. Do you think I really could, Otis?"

Otis tamped out his cigarette, put the butt in the little metal ashtray he kept in his shirt pocket and cocked his head up at Jean. The afternoon sunlight glinted off the silver of his graying hair.

"Might be a right wonderful job to have, Miss Jean. I knew James would do right by us. Now, have you given some thought to what you'd say to this Mr. Whitcomb?"

Jean looked chagrined. She'd talked with Francie about everything, everything but the most important part.

"Well, I guess I'd go in and ask to see him and tell him straight off that I want to be his elevator operator," Jean said tentatively, her voice thin and her brow scrunched.

"Direct, direct is good but sometimes you have to dress things up a bit. How about you leave a card for Mr. Whitcomb with your name and tell the front desk clerk you want to meet him. Look sharp because the man, he'll tell Mr. Whitcomb everything you do and say and how you look," instructed Otis.

Jean nodded as Otis continued. "If the man asks what you need to see Mr. Whitcomb about, you tell him it's to discuss a business opportunity. But don't say any more. That will get his attention and then he can't just forget to tell Mr. Whitcomb."

For as kind and straightforward as Otis seems, he sure is smart, thought Jean. "That's what I'll say, Otis. Thank you."

Otis was a brilliant man, one to be listened to, Mama had once said, and Jean had taken a shine to him right away. From a young age she'd enjoyed long afternoons sitting on the porch steps listening to his stories of the South and how he taught sharecroppers' children in Atlanta.

"Oh, you would have figured it out. You're a force, girl. You have spunk. Now get on up to your mama before she starts to worry on you," said Otis, rising to open the door for Jean.

Jean gave Otis a smile as she made her way upstairs to unlock the apartment door. She heard a mewling sound and looked down to see the little pepper-colored kitten. The kitten rubbed against her ankle, and she bent slowly to pet it, being careful not to frighten it away.

"Whose little kitten are you?" she asked. "Did you catch that mouse you were chasing? I'm after something good, too. I'm chasing a job to feed me, and you're chasing a mouse to feed you."

The kitten purred as she petted its soft belly and smooth, sleek back. A little puff of dust flew off the kitten's back, and it seemed to snuggle into the gentle caress. When Jean started to pick it up to cuddle it close, the kitten yowled and scratched at her with its tiny claws. Jean let go, and the kitten scurried out of reach.

"Come back," Jean called softly. "I'll find some milk for you. Don't you want a friend?" Jean watched as the tiny kitten disappeared down the hallway.

Jean slowly and quietly opened the door. Her mama was sleeping, the washcloth still on her forehead. Jean quietly put away the groceries and plugged in the hot plate to put a kettle on to boil, her mind on walking into the Empire tomorrow and finding work.

She retrieved her best dress from the wardrobe and shook it out. The yellow dotted swiss had faded a bit along the princess seams. She'd borrow her mama's brown leather shoes and maybe even her silk stockings. *It'll be fine. I'll make do,* Jean thought. *It's not like I have a choice, anyway.*

Jean looked over at her mama, sleeping quietly, not even making that rattling sound as she breathed. Jean poured two cups of tea and put one on the bedside table. She took the washcloth from her mama's forehead and gently pressed her fingers to her mama's brow, letting out a sigh of relief when she found that the fever had broken. Now she could start thinking about the future.

She took a seat at the kitchen table and opened the package of hairpins. She wound tiny strands of hair around her finger and pinned them into little circles, then took out a nail file and shaped her nails into ten perfect ovals while she puzzled over how to make a calling card. A nice calling card would get some attention. *What to do?*

Mama had one fountain pen and she liked nice writing paper, Jean knew. *Where is the pen and is there any paper left?* She cast her eyes around the room; *ah, yes, there, in the closet.*

Jean quietly opened the closet door and stood on her tiptoes to look at the shelf above. One cedar hat box lined in pink satin. The box always held their most important things. She took it delicately off the shelf and laid it on the foot of the bed.

Lifting the lid, she smiled and shuffled through the papers – a letter from Poppa, a marriage license, a birth certificate and behind that six perfect sheets of light blue paper marked with the Crane logo. Underneath was nestled a fountain pen.

"Oh, Mama, you saved me," Jean whispered, looking over at her mama who let out a little snore.

Jean took the pen with its black ink and elegant paper to the table and was struck with a blank mental slate: *What to write? What exactly is on a calling card?* She'd seen one somewhere. *Where was that? The magazine. The ad for Crane stationery, which page?*

She fluttered through the magazine. There it was. A calling card was simple – just a full name written in fine script. She carefully folded the writing paper into fourths and hardened off the edges with the side of the ink pen. She tore it with care, chose the most perfect piece and folded it into half again.

She picked up the ink pen and wrote out "Virginia Mae Ball" using the fancy capitals for the V, M and B, like she'd learned in penmanship class.

She remembered how the letters had looked so elegant when the teacher had drawn them on the blackboard. She was glad she had paid attention that day. Jean held up the sheet – perfect, but plain. Plain ugly. She tried again and compared the two. The second try was definitely better, but it needed something more. She'd seen a pretty mark in the magazine and even the name of the mark had sounded special: the fleur de lis.

Jean opened the magazine again and flipped to the story on Paris fashion – there it was. The mark was regal. That's what the card needed, right at the center. With a few quick strokes, done. Enough, but not too much. Perfect.

Jean then quietly got out the iron and shook out the cotton dress she'd chosen. She carefully ironed the pleats and laid it over the kitchen chair when she'd finished. Readying herself for bed, she knew she would barely sleep, already filled with anticipation and a rising apprehension.

By daybreak she gave up any pretense of trying to rest and rose to prepare for the day. She plugged in the hot plate and then raced to the bathroom eager to pluck out her hairpins and see the mass of soft curls. *Enchanting*, Jean thought as she admired her reflection. She zipped up her freshly pressed dress, collected the hairpins and hurried back to the apartment as her Mama was waking.

"Can I borrow your shoes today?" Jean asked as soon as her Mama's eyes had opened.

"Well good morning to you, too. What did you do to your hair? Looks nice," croaked Mama, her voice raspy with sleep.

"You look like a fairy princess, Jean. Watch out for the frogs!"

"What frogs?"

"Jean, in the story, the princess kisses the frog so he'll turn into a handsome prince, remember?"

"I do remember, Mama," Jean said. "But I always thought the princess would have more fun with a talking frog than some prince who'd boss her around and make her curtsey to his parents."

"You may be right, Jean," Mama said. "Don't settle for a prince. Hold out for the talking frog."

They grinned at each other for a minute, but then Mama had another coughing fit. Jean saw that her blue handkerchief was dotted with blood, and she quickly replaced it with a clean, plain one.

"I think I'm getting a job today, at the Empire. Like you said yesterday. Otis and his cousin are helping. You slept through dinner or I would have told you everything. So, you like my hair?" asked Jean shaking her curls.

"Beautiful, you're beautiful, Jean, my little princess. So you're going to be the elevator operator, are you?" asked her mama, propping herself up on the bed pillow as she suppressed another cough.

"Now how did you know that, Mama?" Jean asked, turning her head in wonder.

"Oh, that Otis. His girl, Miss Abby. Now that she's come back, we've talked. Helps me think things through. We'll get you settled in a job soon," said Mama.

Jean's eyes widened as her mother continued.

"Yes, Abby. She arranged things with James, a second cousin, there at the hotel. Don't give me that look. I can still take care of things for you. Now, actually getting the job, that's all up to you. But you will. You, there with the curls and that lacy yellow dress, you're a beauty. And wear those fancy stockings today."

Jean stepped to the bedside, kissed the top of her Mama's head and handed her a porcelain plate with one piece of toast on it. She set a cup of tea on the bedside table.

"I'll be back by lunchtime and tell you everything," Jean said, opening the chest of drawers and picking up elastic bands and the delicate stockings. They were light as butterflies.

She collected the hand-drawn calling card from the kitchen table and took it with her down the hall to the shared bath.

Jean rolled on the hose, admiring their silky glow. She ran a comb over the top of her still-wavy hair and then stood on her tip toes and felt around the towel shelf for the lipstick she'd secreted away several weeks before.

She'd spent a full nine cents on lipstick, an indulgence strictly forbidden by her mother. Lipstick was for tarts, her mama always said. Lipstick was for modern girls, though, Jean knew. With only the tiniest pinch of guilt, Jean drew on bright red lips. She pinched her cheeks to make them rosy. Jean caught a quick glimpse of her handiwork in the mirror and gave herself a smile.

As she left, she looked for the little kitten she'd seen earlier, but it was nowhere to be found.

3

The white-gloved doorman stood sentry outside the Empire Hotel, opening the door with a slight bow for each of the ladies who entered. He looked twice when he saw a young woman striding down the walk, the picture of confidence. She bore little resemblance to the child of the day before.

"Good morning, James. How are you today?" Jean called out as she approached the door.

"Fine and you, Miss? May I get the door for you?" James asked.

"Yes, please. I'll be going in today," replied Jean.

James pulled the door open and Jean stepped into the lobby. She had never seen any place so elegant – green marble columns, mahogany walls, parquet floors, soaring ceilings, deep velvet chairs and a wide winding staircase. *Definitely how the other half lives, as Mama says.*

Clusters of well-dressed women were gathered in the lobby, sitting in groups of three and four, heads together, clucking among themselves. Jean stepped through the doorway and stood reviewing the tremendous space.

"Good morning, Miss. How may I help you?" said a voice. Jean looked around, surprised, searching out the voice in the dimly lit lobby.

The hotel's front desk was tucked discreetly in the corner. Jean had not taken in the entire room yet nor even seen the tall, bespectacled man standing at the desk. She had hoped for a few moments to get her bearings, but no luck.

Jean stepped forward towards the desk, "My name is Virginia Mae Ball and I've come to see Mr. Whitcomb. Mr. Randall Whitcomb."

"Do you have an appointment?" asked the desk clerk, pulling his glasses down to the tip of his nose.

"Oh, no, but I believe he will see me. It's a business matter. Please give him my card," said Jean.

Her neatly filed fingernails shone as she offered the card to the desk clerk. He held the card out at arm's length and cocked his head to the side as he read. "Hmmph, don't see many hand drawn cards here," he observed, not hiding his disdain. "Made this yourself, did you?"

The aloof man shook his head and Jean felt any semblance of confidence melting away under his withering gaze.

"Just have a seat, Miss. I'll see if Mr. Whitcomb is currently available, if you would be so kind as to wait," he said, pointing to one of the velvet chairs near the cluster of women.

"Certainly. Thank you," Jean said with more authority than she felt. Jean regained her wavering confidence. "I believe he will see me," she assured.

Maybe the handmade card wasn't such a good idea, she thought, gingerly taking a seat on the edge of an enormous circular bench covered in red velvet and buttons forming diamond patterns. She edged her hand along the stitching. *Money. This feels like money.*

Jean shut her eyes and took in a deep breath, rehearsing in her mind what she would say to the man. Her thoughts were broken by the chatter of the women, so loud Jean couldn't help but overhear.

"And so I just told Randall it's time to bring this city up to date. How hard could it be to hire a lady?" said an elderly hummingbird-sized woman to two ladies sitting on an adjacent sofa. Jean tucked those words into her mind. Maybe the hotel was ready to hire her, a lady. Me, a lady. *What a fine word*, thought Jean.

"Now we'll see how progressive he really is. Hiring a lady to do a man's job. We'll just see what he's made of," replied one of the ladies, her lips pursed and her wide-brimmed hat bobbing with the nod of her head.

"And what kind of pull his wife really has," laughed the third, then she dropped her voice to a sotto whisper. "Did you hear about the baby? People say Katherine got the girl a position at the Emery Bird to keep things quiet. She protects her men from everything. Look, there's Mrs. Katherine Whitcomb now. No circles under her eyes today. Guess she's not on one of her benders," the woman said wrinkling her nose.

Jean watched as the third woman tipped her head back and mimed taking a drink. Two of the women tittered and one looked on, disapproving.

Jean followed their gaze to the lobby door where a raven-haired woman wearing a stunningly modern drop-waist dress was entering the lobby with the flair of royalty. The woman's eyes flitted across the lobby and a smile spread across her face when she caught sight of the three women on the sofa laughing together. Jean heard the swish of silk and caught a scent of lilac as the woman breezed by.

"So good of you to come today," said the woman they'd identified as Katherine, addressing the hummingbird lady. "I hoped to arrive a bit sooner, but I was feeling a bit fatigued from my travels. We're just back from New York, you know. But I had to come and catch up with the League. I heard you've spurred them to get out to the dairies. Do let's go on to the Pompeii Room. They're expecting us."

With that, Jean noted how graciously the lady named Katherine extended her slender hand to help the birdlike lady up from the sofa. The lady tottered delicately to her feet.

"Come now, ladies of the Kansas City Consumer League, let us gather," the elderly slip of a woman pronounced, raising her voice to address the entire lobby. The group of women quieted as she continued. "Mrs. Whitcomb has offered to escort us to the Pompeii Room where we will convene our meeting. Come along now."

Jean watched as the lobby emptied and Mrs. Katherine Whitcomb led the group through a doorway beyond the grand staircase. She wondered what it would be like, to wear an elegant dress with matching wrap, and to eat lunch in such a grand place, with other ladies. Someday, maybe she would be walking into that Pompeii Room.

The clerk returned before Jean could gather her thoughts. "Miss, your card has been reviewed. Regrettably, Mr. Whitcomb is not available at this time. But his assistant can see you now. He only has a few minutes, however."

Jean felt her heart sink; an assistant may not have any authority to hire her, but she had to at least try. "Fine. Thank you," said Jean, hiding her disappointment at not being seen by Mr. Whitcomb himself, and summoning her courage as she rose.

"Please follow me," the clerk replied, making the briefest of bows.

Jean followed him toward the grand stairway as a sweet thought came to her, might Mr. Whitcomb's son be the assistant? Could she bear to stand before such a striking man, ask for a job, and not stumble over her words?

Jean could feel her heart thumping wildly and with each beat, her courage slipped away. She hesitated as the desk clerk, oblivious to her plight, led her to the sweeping staircase. Jean hurried behind him and looked fearfully up at the dozens of marble stairs that circled upwards. She couldn't imagine ascending that behemoth without tripping over her feet.

Fortunately, he continued on to the elevator on the far side of the lobby, and pushed a button. The brass elevator door opened revealing mahogany paneled walls inlaid with almond scroll work. The clerk opened the inner door and gestured for Jean to enter. He secured the outer door, closed the interior brass folding door and pushed first a locking lever and then the button marked with an eight.

The elevator engaged with a clicking sound and then glided

upward. How it moved was a mystery to Jean but she recognized the feeling it made in the small of her stomach.

"Mr. Whitcomb's office doesn't often take visitors," said the man, seeming to fish for information. Jean did not respond. The man persisted, "So you have business with Mr. Whitcomb?"

Jean knew she should say "yes," but was certain her voice would come out like a mouse squeak. Instead, Jean tilted her head toward him and nodded. That small gesture seemed to appease the man well enough. The elevator came to a stop and the man opened the doors. Jean felt a rising panic and her palms began their fearful tingle.

"This way," the man said. Jean followed him down a hallway, elegant with embossed wallpaper and a dark wainscoting. He stopped in front of a wood paneled double door and knocked twice.

"Enter," said a deep voice from the other side. The clerk opened the door and walked in. Jean thought for a minute she might faint. But thinking of fainting and being a person who up and faints are two different things entirely. Jean wasn't a fainter. A fainter would never have a homemade business card or have to worry about paying rent.

Jean took a deep breath and stepped across the threshold onto the plushest carpet she'd ever felt, butterflies still colliding in her stomach.

A stout man stood looking out a floor to ceiling window that gave a view of the entire city. His hand held a gold pocket watch. He checked the time and slipped the watch into his waistcoat pocket. Turning into the room, he put one hand on his hip and faced Jean.

This portly man was definitely not Mr. Whitcomb's enticing son. Jean felt an edge of disappointment mixed with relief. She glanced around the room, checking whether Elden might be sitting there by the fireplace or at the desk in the corner. *No such luck*, thought Jean but with that realization she could feel her pulse rate slowing.

"Mr. Green, this is Miss Ball. Miss Ball, Barnard Green, Secretary to Mr. Whitcomb," the clerk said handing Mr. Green the thin writing paper Jean had offered as a card.

"Please ring when I may escort her back down, sir," he said, turning to leave the office.

As the clerk pulled the door closed behind him, Jean felt the weight of the responsibility she had to take on. She quelled her fears and seized the opportunity, taking three steps toward Mr. Green.

"How do you do, sir? I am Virginia Mae Ball," she said giving a small curtsey and not giving through to the anxiety quivering in her belly.

"Mr. Whitcomb is in a meeting but you've met him I take it?" asked the portly fellow.

"Met?" replied Jean, "Met," she repeated, buying time. "No, not formally. Mr. Whitcomb and I have crossed paths, of course, but we've yet to be formally introduced."

What she said was not wholly untrue. She had crossed Mr. Whitcomb's path, although it was on a sidewalk and not socially. Jean felt pleased she'd come up with that truth so quickly.

"Yes, yes, of course," said Mr. Green. "And now you have business to discuss?"

Jean began to talk before the man could pose more questions. "I understand the hotel needs an elevator operator. I'm the girl for the job. I can do it. I'm friendly but I'm discreet." Jean knew she should stop talking but the words kept spilling out. "And, and I'm the right size," she concluded, immediately wishing she could take back those last few words.

"Elevator operator. Yes, we had ..." began Mr. Green. Before he could complete the thought, the office door burst open and a distinguished looking man crashed into Mr. Green's office.

Without even a cursory greeting, the man slammed the door and leaned back on it, facing Jean, eyes shut.

"May Jesus help me! Those women are hellacious. That old one is a tiny Lucifer in lace. Now they want a donation for some whorehouse for unwed mothers. Want to teach them to type or some such nonsense. And they have my own wife telling me to hire more ladies. Says it's time. Says it's the right thing. What do they know about right? Right or wrong, I'm still the man in charge here," said the man, jutting his thumb towards his chest, "and I'll decide what the right thing is."

Mr. Green cleared his throat. The man opened his eyes, stared directly at Jean, and stood up straight.

"I'm ... I'm, yes, I see. Mr. Green, I don't believe I knew you had a meeting." The man put his left hand to his brow and rubbed the crease on his forehead.

"An unscheduled meeting, Mr. Whitcomb. We have a young lady interested in the new elevator operator position you and I had spoken of last week, sir. Miss Virginia Mae Ball," said Mr. Green offering Mr. Whitcomb Jean's handwritten card.

Jean ducked her head, her cheeks burning scarlet, at the man's words and the shabbiness of her well-intended effort. She had lost all momentum and had no idea what might come next.

The elder businessman cleared his throat and put a hand up to adjust his tie.

"Pardon my earlier words, please. Business can be challenging these days, Miss Ball," said Mr. Whitcomb, pulling down on the edges of his waistcoat, and taking the card from Mr. Green.

"Yes, sir. Mama says every challenge is an opportunity," Jean said softly. Hearing no response, she looked up at Mr. Whitcomb.

Thumbs locked on the pockets of his vest, he stood nodding at her. Jean took this as an encouraging sign and continued, "And, as I told Mr. Green, I understand the Empire Hotel needs an elevator operator. I'm your girl. I'm friendly and discreet and I need the work."

The words just sprang from her, unbidden and Jean shifted uncomfortably from one foot to the next. Her mother's shoes felt uncomfortable, and she could feel a blister forming on her left heel.

"Well, you certainly waste no words. If everyone I did business with cut to the heart of things like you, my life would be much simpler," chuckled Mr. Whitcomb.

"But I question your premise, Miss Ball. Why do you expect I'd want a lady running my expensive machinery, a public elevator no less? Have you any idea what that equipment cost me? And besides, my ladies usually work in the laundry. Have a seat, please," he said gesturing to one of the leather chairs across from the desk.

This may not be so easy, Jean thought with more than a sliver of dread, then she remembered what Otis had told her about girl elevator operators in New York City and pieced those thoughts together with what she'd overheard from the women in the lobby.

She might be young, and she might be inexperienced, but she could do this work. She knew she could. All she had to do was convince one man that she had the nerve.

Jean took a deep breath to steady her thoughts. She hoped that this man wouldn't notice the sweat forming on her brow.

"Thank you, sir," she said, remembering her manners as she took a seat. "This is the newest hotel in the city, Mr. Whitcomb. Everyone knows its modern here, the most modern place in the entire Midwest. In New York City all the best hotels have female elevator operators now."

Mr. Whitcomb cocked his head, assessing the girl sitting before him. "Just got back from New York myself. Can't say you're wrong. Women get the right to vote and now they want the right to take over bit by bit. Happening all across the country I hear, or so they tell me," his voice resigned. "So what would one have to pay a lady like that?"

Jean knew she needed seventy cents a day to make do. She had scratched out the math over and over. Fourteen dollars a month would pay for rent and food, with two quarters left for unexpected, like new shoes maybe once in awhile, or a few cents for a magazine or candy.

"Ninety-five cents, sir. A day," Jean said, lifting her chin and trying to hold her voice steady, knowing her mama would chuckle at her gumption.

"No. Come now, I pay my best doorman that and he's a man with responsibilities," said Mr. Whitcomb, narrowing his eyes as he settled into the high-backed chair across the desk. Mr. Green stood quietly by the window watching the exchange.

Jean summoned a courage that had been building inside her from the moment her mama had suggested she look for work. The money. She needed a job. They needed the money, the security.

"Well, what do you think it's worth to be the first hotel in the city with a lady shepherding guests to and fro?" countered Jean.

Even as she asked the question, the queasiness in her stomach eased a little. This banter was not so hard. Maybe Mama was right, every challenge was an opportunity.

"Eighty cents," he replied.

"Ninety-two and I can start tomorrow," Jean said quickly, the words flying out before the thought was even fully formed. She heard Mr. Green chuckle softly and saw him shake his head.

Mr. Whitcomb cast a glance at Mr. Green, who raised one eyebrow and tilted his head, as if to give assent.

"Ok, but you'll start Friday and we have to make it ninety. If I start paying the staff with pennies, my accountant will pitch one of his fits. And, don't get your hopes up. This is only on a trial basis."

"Yes, sir," said Jean, unclenching her fingers from the folds of her skirt. She'd rubbed a couple of the polka dots flat without noticing, and she hoped no one else had noticed her nervousness.

"So Friday then. Well, Mr. Green, meet our new elevator operator, Miss, Miss . . ." said Mr. Whitcomb as he turned over the handwritten card in his hand and read, "Miss Virginia Mae Ball. Please welcome her to the Hotel Empire family. She'll work the 8 a.m. shift, nine hours a day, weekends off. And have her see Mrs. Velmar in housekeeping for a uniform. Then get down to that Ladies' League meeting in the Pompeii Room and tell them I have an announcement."

"Yes, sir. And you want her to see Mrs. Velmar? Today, sir? For Friday?" Mr. Green asked, eyes wide.

"Yes. Mrs. Velmar. Before Miss Ball leaves here today she needs a uniform so she looks like the help and not like--" his eyes dropped to Jean's feet and he stopped himself mid-sentence. Jean followed his gaze to where it rested.

Her stockings. The elastic band had broken on the left side. The stocking had slipped down to the ankle and puddled in a bunch. Jean's face burned with shame. First a homemade calling card, now this. Maybe she was not cut out for high society, Jean worried. She wanted to salvage what she could of her dignity, though.

" -- not like a waif, right? I know," said Jean, finishing his thought, "but I'll do my best, you'll see," she said, smiling with a certainty she did not feel.

"Yes, well, go on now. Report to the front desk Friday, eight sharp," he replied, shooing her away with his hand.

"Thank you, sir," she said, dropping a little curtsey. "Ninety cents a day," she uttered under her breath as she followed Mr. Green out the door, ignoring the pool of hosiery at her feet.

Twenty cents extra every single day, four dollars more a month than we need. Four dollars! Miraculous to think they'd have that kind of money. *A working man's wage.*

Mr. Green didn't speak until they reached the elevator. "You'll find Mrs. Velmar on the basement floor. Can't miss her. Afterward, you exit at the lobby. Go on," he said pointing to the open elevator, "I have to get to the Pompeii Room straight away."

Jean entered the elevator as the man reached in and pressed the button to the basement floor. "There's no magic to it. Pull the doors shut and turn that lever. Off you go."

"Thank you, Mr. Gr ..." Jean began but he was gone. She bit her lip and tried to recall exactly what the clerk had done to make the elevator move. She pulled the two doors firmly shut, turned the lever and pushed the button marked with the letter B.

A feeling of pride filled her as the elevator began its descent. *At least I can hitch up my stockings in private.* She had just finished the final adjustment when the elevator door opened and she was met by a wide woman with jowls and a scowl.

"I'm Miss Ball. I'm looking for Mrs. Velmar. I've been told she's in charge of uniforms," said Jean, intimidated by the woman's dourness.

"'Zats right, and so vhut?" said the woman. Her accent was as thick as a winter goulash.

"I'll be the elevator operator starting Friday, at eight in the morning and Mr. Whitcomb would like me to be fitted for a uniform," she explained.

"'Zat right?" asked the woman, crossing her arms.

"Yes, ma'am," replied Jean. "Do you know where I can find Mrs. Velmar?"

"Me," said the woman pointing to her ample chest. "Uniform. Right. Eight. Friday. 'kay," nodded the woman.

"Should we do measurements?" Jean hesitated.

The woman cocked her head at a dramatic angle and studied Jean head to toe, then narrowed her eyes. "Nie, nie! Friday. Go," she said, her head shaking back and forth as she shooed Jean back into the elevator alone.

Jean had no idea what might happen when she showed up on Friday. She had a job, definitely, but she clearly had no hope of a uniform. Without a uniform she feared she wouldn't look like the help but, instead, like a lost little matchstick seller.

She headed back home, full of hope but wondering — with more than a degree of trepidation — what the future might hold.

4

On Friday Jean woke up at seven, late for her, as she was used to being up and making breakfast before her mama had even thought of stirring.

Today the world opens up. Jean stretched and couldn't help but smile. She had a place to be and something to do, something that would fill the pantry, pay the landlord, and give them extras like they'd never imagined.

Her mama lay snoring softly and Jean remembered the delight she'd seen on her mama's face as she recounted the meeting with Mr. Whitcomb. It was like nothing Jean had ever seen. Pure pride.

Jean rolled quietly out of bed, hoping not to wake her mama, and made a quick breakfast of tea and bread with strawberry jam. Mama had made that jam in better days. She set a plate by the bedside for her mother.

Miss Abby was coming in twice a day to check on things, so Jean had no worries about leaving for a few hours. As she started out the door, she caught a glimpse of the little kitten she'd seen the day before. Even though she was in a great hurry, Jean thought about what it felt like to be really hungry.

She went back into the apartment and splashed a tiny bit of milk into a saucer. She didn't want to waste milk or money, but the milk was getting old, and a little splash surely wouldn't be missed. Jean carefully placed the saucer by the door and then pressed her hands along the front of her yellow dress with the lace her mama had stitched so carefully, smoothing the material. From the corner of her eye, she saw the kitten starting toward the saucer, and she wanted so much to cuddle it, but she still had a little scratch from last time. Besides, she had no time at all today.

She bounded down the apartment house stairs in her best dress and the polished leather shoes she'd borrowed from her mama, though she had gently declined, without explanation, the offer of the silk stockings.

"First day of work!" she called out to Otis who stood on the front steps with his smokes.

"I reckon so, Sunshine. Miss Abby and I are proud of you. You make your mama proud, too, Miss. And I know that for sure your poppa is watching over you from heaven today," he replied with a wave.

"Thank you for your good advice," she said. "Everything you told me helped me get this job. I know I got this job because of you, Otis."

"You earned this opportunity, Miss. I know you'll do fine," Otis called out after her.

~

"First day of work," she said to James when she reached the front of the hotel.

"Yes, I heard, Miss. Best of luck today," James said, smiling as he pulled the door open for her.

Jean didn't pause this time to survey the lobby. Instead, she headed straight to the front desk. The hands on the lobby clock read 7:38 a.m. and the desk clerk looked up at her expectantly.

"You are Miss Ball, yes?" asked the man behind the desk.

"Yes, Virginia Mae Ball. The new elevator operator," she replied brightly.

"Early," he observed glancing up at the clock. "Good. Mrs. Velmar has your uniform finished. Got it done last night. She's in the laundry." The man extended his arm in the direction of a far hallway.

"Yes, sir," replied Jean.

Jean started to walk down the hallway but saw no door marked laundry. At the end of the hall was a stairwell.

Laundry must be in the basement, she thought, venturing down the stairs tentatively. She could smell detergent and felt a burst of humidity as she reached the bottom stair. Jean felt suddenly grateful that she would be operating an elevator instead of working in the wet heat of the laundry room. The whir of washing tubs and the sound of women's voices came from a narrow hallway to the left. *That has to be it.*

She knocked on the door. No answer. She knocked again. Nothing. Polite knocking was clearly futile. The motors of the washing tubs drowned out any chance of being heard. Jean pushed hard on the door, hoping it not rude to barge in. A waft of humidity hit as she entered. She could feel her cute curls going limp.

"You Virginia?" asked a round woman wearing a long white apron.

"Yes, ma'am," Jean replied.

"Here for the uniform?" the woman queried, setting aside her laundry basket.

"Yes, ma'am," said Jean.

"Here you go," said the washerwoman, reaching over to a hook and handing Jean a garment on a wooden hanger. "Put it on. Mrs. Velmar will sew up adjustments. Got just a few minutes, so skedaddle," the woman said pointing to a canvas curtain behind her.

Jean took the hanger and ducked behind the curtain. The hanger held a grey wool skirt that would barely graze the top of her calf – short by any standard, but below the knee so it was still arguably respectable.

The skirt was paneled; each panel was cut slim through the thigh and billowed into a soft wide scoop at the bottom. The hem almost looked like rounded flower petals. The skirt was accompanied by a white linen blouse with long sleeves, puffy, like something European, Jean mused. The outfit was set off by a vest made of wool in a rich maroon with gold brocade trim and epaulets like French soldiers wore.

Jean put on each piece of the uniform and looked down at the outfit. She wasn't quite sure if she looked like an organ grinder's monkey or a sophisticate. *As long as there is no hat, I'll narrowly escape the monkey look,* she thought.

Jean came out from behind the curtain and there stood the wide woman from before, Mrs. Velmar. Somehow, just from seeing Jean standing in the elevator, this woman had concocted an outfit that actually fit – more or less. The elastic in one sleeve cut into Jean's wrist. *I'll tug that out bit by bit. No need to tell this lady there is a single thing wrong with her handiwork.*

"This is so nice. Can I see a mirror?" asked Jean.

"Nie. No mirror," replied Mrs. Velmar taking Jean by the shoulder and turning her around.

"You made this so quickly and it's so elegant," complimented Jean, as she was being twirled.

"'Zat right, " said Mrs. Velmar nodding and then reaching up to take Jean's face in her two rough hands. "Face o' fancy 'otel. Good. Look nice, be nice," explained Mrs. Velmar.

Jean had never considered an elevator operator as the face of the hotel, but now thinking about it, Mrs. Velmar was right. Everyone would see her first thing in their day. First impressions matter, Mama had always told her. *This job is going to be a big responsibility.*

Jean smiled her brightest smile at Mrs. Velmar, "Thank you," she said.

"'Zo sweet, 'zat right," instructed Mrs. Velmar. "Wait, last thing first."

The woman reached behind a willow basket and pulled out a hat. It matched the maroon vest perfectly and had a row of gold brocade trim, but could have just as easily fit onto an organ grinder's monkey as on an elevator operator. Jean tried not to let her disappointment show.

"Now go," pronounced Mrs. Velmar pointing out to the basement hallway.

Jean smiled weakly and nodded. She twirled her way up the basement steps, choosing to forget she could be mistaken for a street performer's mascot, and let the gray skirt swell like a tulip around her knees. *Positively enchanting*, thought Jean. As she rounded the corner by the lobby desk she stopped short.

How will I ever run an elevator? She smiled at the man behind the desk who looked away and busied himself with papers.

Reaching the elevator, Jean punched the arrow pointing up and waited. She heard its gentle arrival and then opened the door. A brass cage with a handle on the side prevented her entrance.

What did that man do? Jean tried to remember. *Just pull*, she recalled, *easy enough*. She entered, closed the doors, and tentatively pushed the brass button for the third floor, a test run. *Flawless*, thought Jean with a new confidence as the elevator glided upwards.

When she returned the elevator to the lobby, her first guest was waiting, a tall man in a dark suit. She opened the cage door and there he was, filling the doorway.

The young man who'd been with Mr. Whitcomb that first day. The man who had sported a broad smile and an aristocratic tan. The one who had spoken so easily to the doorman and who had acted like even James was a somebody. Jean's heart quickened.

Elden made a small sound with his throat and Jean realized she'd been staring. She felt a tingle arising from her midsection.

He's going to actually step into this small space, so close to me, Jean thought. She nervously adjusted her hat.

"Going up?" she squeaked.

"I don't care. Which way are you going, doll?" the young man gave her an easy smile as he slid his blue eyes sideways at her. Jean felt her hands go sweaty and her nerves made his words jumble in her head. *Doll*, Jean thought. *He thinks I'm a doll.*

"Oh, I'm no doll. I'm Jean. No, I'm Miss Ball. I mean, Virginia. But you can call me Jean," she replied, more flustered than she intended.

"Doll. Ball. Ok, Jean then. Miss Jean. It is Miss, right?" Elden said, taking off his hat. Jean's eyes locked on his thick, wavy hair, noticing how the darkness contrasted with his sea blue eyes.

"I said, it is Miss Jean, right?" he repeated, a smile playing across his lips.

"Miss Jean?" Jean replied dumbly. "Oh, me. Yes, I'm Jean."

"So I heard," he laughed. "I mean, you're single, right? Those League Ladies wouldn't have been able to force a married woman on Pops anyway. Hiring a girl is a big enough step, Pops said. Eighth-floor. You take me on up there, okay, doll?" he asked, pointing skyward as he entered the elevator.

"Jean. You can call me Jean. Really," she repeated, realizing her name was the only thing that had yet to come out of her mouth. "A doll is a – " she began but knew she didn't have the words to explain the difference between her circumstance and that of the modern girls who danced and dashed about from one party to the next.

The young man looked at her earnestly and Jean felt a tingle rising across her chest, her words lost.

"I did it again, didn't I? Mother is always on me about my language. Says I sound uncouth, calling girls 'dolls' and such."

"Oh no, I think you're quite couth, in my opinion. Any man in a suitcoat can't be totally unmannered," said Jean, blushing as she pushed the eighth-floor button with efficiency.

"Couth. Couth. That's a new one. I like it. I'll use that one on mother next time she's hounding me. And my name's Elden, by the way, Elden Whitcomb, Kansas City Whitcombs."

"I'm Jean Ball, of the 'life is a ball' Balls," said Jean, easing her tension with a small joke. Elden smiled.

As the elevator arrived at the eighth floor Elden reached over and hit the first-floor button.

"What?" asked Jean, the tingling having quickly turned to something a little intimidating.

"Just going for a ride, Jean," Elden joked. "Let me run this thing. You have a seat there. I'll be the elevator man. You rest there in that monkey hat of yours," he said pointing to the elevator chair.

Jean gave a nervous laugh. She hadn't played in a long time. She pulled open the tiny chair and took a seat, tugging off her hat with a measure of embarrassment,

"Okay, if you know what you're doing."

"Well, don't assume that now," Elden said, with a grin as he reached up and jimmied with the elevator cage door. The elevator went past the third floor and then made a halting lurch before it reached the second, stopping between the floors.

"Oh no, I've done it now," said Elden, his voice rising with urgency and eyes widening in alarm. Jean felt her stomach sink as she registered the fear in his eyes.

Broken. Her face grew pensive; the elevator was at a dead stop. Jean stood up fearing her first day on the job would be her last.

"Oh, no. This isn't good. What do I do?" Jean bit her lip and put her hand to the brass control panel.

"You're stuck with me now. We could starve away in here." Elden smiled as he ran a hand through his thick hair.

"This isn't funny," said Jean. Her cheeks were crimson as she fought back the tears welling in her eyes.

"Don't look so worried, Jean. Couple of days, we'll be okay, then it's ... I don't know ... guess we'll have to start eating lint out of our pockets," said Elden grimly as he reached out and took Jean's hat from her hand.

"Maybe some of your monkey friends can drop in for entertainment," he said gesturing to the tiny trap door in the elevator ceiling. "I hear monkey is good eats." Elden twirled the hat in a circle on his finger and then put it back on Jean's head. He shrugged his shoulders as a cocky grin spread across his face.

It was only then that Jean realized he'd stopped the elevator intentionally and he'd been teasing. She raised an eyebrow up at him and sat back down on the tiny chair, crossing her legs and turning her back to him.

"Oh, look, see here, maybe I didn't have the cage quite shut," said Elden, noting her consternation, "Guess I should pull it closed?"

"Oh heavens, you clown," said Jean as she stood up and yanked the cage door shut. The elevator lurched to a start and headed on its way.

"Capable, aren't you? Impressive," said Elden, his dimples showing as he smiled.

Jean was proud of how she had handled that, her first mini-emergency on the job, and was flattered at his attention.

"Thank you," she beamed, relieved the elevator hadn't truly been broken. "You want the eighth-floor, right?" Jean pushed the number eight button efficiently.

Elden dropped his gaze toward his feet. "Sorry if I scared you. I guess I can seem cavalier, huh? Mother says I don't take things seriously enough."

"Oh, don't call yourself cavalier. That sounds like something bad. Having a sense of fun, that's a good trait," Jean replied, feeling competent and forgiving. "Tell her you have the good sense to have a sense of fun is more like it." Elden looked at her, charmed, and didn't say a word.

The elevator arrived back to the eighth-floor. Elden pulled open the doors and stepped out. "Well, good day, Miss Virginia Ball. 23-Skidoo, Monkey Hat Girl," Elden quipped, his eyes twinkling.

"'Skidoo, Mr. Elevator Man," said Jean, as she pulled the brass door shut. *He is magnificent.*

She could feel her heart thumping and sensed a thrilling warmth spread across her bodice. Elden, the most handsome man she'd ever seen, had talked to her like she wasn't just a hired girl. He seemed to even like her, maybe.

Her immodest thoughts were quickly put aside when she got back to the lobby. Two fine ladies were waiting for her. Well, they looked fine at first glance but then Jean looked again. They were actually far from fine. Both were spattered with mud and in stocking feet, carrying their shoes.

"Hens! He turned the hens on us. Son of the devil," said the first lady.

"Excuse me, going up, ladies?" asked Jean. The ladies were deep in conversation and didn't seem to hear her.

"Hens? Roosters. They were a troop of fighting cocks, I swear," said the second lady, brushing the dried mud from her skirt, "and accidentally left the henhouse open my eye. It was deliberate, plain and simple. He didn't want us to see his dairy. I'm sure it wouldn't have passed our inspection."

"I'm sure it was as foul as those fowl. Foul things. They rushed in so quick I didn't realize what it was until it was on me. One pecked my stocking and gave it a big hole. Look," said the first lady pulling up her skirt and showing her stocking. The delicate silk had a huge hole that could never be mended right, Jean observed. The elevator gave a gentle ding.

"Floor, please?" asked Jean. The ladies, absorbed in their conversation, didn't respond. Jean stood there, trying to look inconspicuous but unsure of what to do next.

"Didn't know my old fanny could move so fast. Did you see how he laughed at us when we climbed up on the fence?" asked the first lady.

"Then when he yelled 'You may think you have the right to vote, but you don't have the right to snoop. Get out of my barn.' I was so scared I almost soaked my britches. What a horse's rump!" said the second lady.

Jean's eyes were wide with disbelief at the tale unfolding before her, but the ladies still didn't seem to have noticed her as they recounted their adventure. "Well you with your, 'The hounds! The hounds released from the Gates of Hell!' didn't help any," said the first.

"All I could think of was the hounds that guard the gates and do the devil's bidding, what with the flapping and the sound and the smells. It was chaos, like the chaos of Hell," said the second with a note of proud melodrama in her voice.

"Well, do you want to write this up for the League report or shall I?" asked the first lady.

"Oh, you do it. And let's you and I forget the part about me and the Gates of Hell though, okay? The ladies would never let me live that down," said the second.

"So true," agreed the first.

"You ladies must be with the Consumer League," volunteered Jean, not realizing it may be unseemly for the help to engage guests.

Jean's mention of the Consumer League finally distracted the women from reliving and retelling their harrowing escape.

"Oh yes," said the second lady noticing Jean for the first time. "You know the League's work, dear?" she asked patting her hair in an unfettered attempt to regain her dignity.

"Of course, everyone does," said Jean with enthusiasm. "I know they're working on the dairies now. Do you know how many children died last year from typhus? It's so sad," said Jean, parroting what she'd read once in the newspaper.

"Eight. Eight little ones from bad milk in the last year," said the first lady without hesitation.

"You are pretty well-informed on this. Do you happen to know any of the League women?" asked the second, aware that the tale of their misadventure could quickly spread.

"Goodness no, not me. But it's in all the papers. Well, the facts are in some stories and the gossip is in others, but I piece it together to get the full picture," replied Jean. The ladies laughed loudly.

"That's right," said the first lady, reaching out to give Jean's hand a pat. "That's how it is."

"So, may I take you up now?" asked Jean, reminding the ladies of her duty.

"Of course, where are our manners? We were prattling on and this lady has work to do. Yes, up, please. You must be our new elevator girl we had Mr. Whitcomb hire," the first lady said to Jean. Turning to her friend she added, "I'm so glad Mr. Whitcomb might be listening to what we League Ladies say after all."

"Yes indeed. Forward-thinking man," said her friend. "I think we got his ear but good after that trip to New York. Katherine said he couldn't believe the jobs women do there. Man's work, like this," the second lady whispered to her friend, "We'll all make progress if we work together. Measured steps," the lady concluded with a satisfied nod.

Jean wasn't exactly sure what the women meant but it sounded important and she was glad they approved of her working a man's job.

"People notice when we women step out and take on new things," said the first woman, addressing Jean, "You do well and it lifts us all up. Lifts us up," she added, gesturing to the elevator panel and laughing at her tiny joke.

"Now let's get on, Ethylann. Four, please. We're staying in the Governor's Suite. I love the benefits of being the one who organizes the fundraisers, don't you?" said the second woman.

"Well, we really do need to stay in the suite to get things ready for the party tonight. We are raising money for the League's work after all," said the first.

"Yes, I know. And I do think we were right to rent the hotel's Main Dining Room. It's just so elegant and it has the best dance floor," the second lady said, adding in a hushed whisper, "and I think we'll have the right bartender for it, too. Mr. Whitcomb has the best gin, you know."

Jean tried to absorb what she'd heard – a social group of ladies who could afford to rent out a whole dining room and they'd have a bartender? She wasn't sure which fact struck her as the more implausible.

The elevator came to a gentle stop. Jean cleared her throat and announced, "Floor four."

"Thank you, dear. Remember, whatever you do, watch out for life's wild roosters. Never know when one might rush you. We hens have to watch out for one another," advised the first lady with a hardy laugh.

"That's right, Mrs. Parker. That's right," said the second lady, shaking out her petticoated dress as she stepped into the hall.

The two headed down the hallway, heads tipped together, laughing. Jean smiled as she deciphered the innuendo and tucked away the thought that she should tell Francie about it later.

It was well after twelve noon when the front desk clerk rang for the elevator and told Jean she had twenty minutes for lunch. She ran back to the apartment and burst in the door, eager to show off the elegant uniform. The blister on her foot had burst, but she paid it no mind. She ran as fast as she could.

"Hi, Miss Fancy, don't you look nice," her mama, resting on freshly plumped pillows, said with admiration. "Come catch me up. Let me see that hat. Isn't that something." Jean had not seen her mama glow like this in months, eager to hear every detail. Jean shared the story about the uniform fitting and then all about the encounter with the two League ladies, leaving out the references to their bartender.

"And Mama, there's a boy. The owner's son and he, oh, he," Jean began then stopped, unable to think of just the right words. "He made me laugh, Mama and -- I had so much fun. I think I want to work every day, and his eyes were, oh," Jean stopped, remembering those playful blue eyes. Suddenly, ordinary words were not adequate. She could feel the color rushing to her cheeks.

Her mama coughed and put the pale blue handkerchief to her lips, hiding a smile. "Well, work is good, Jean. But a girl needs some time to dream. Don't be that girl who works every day. Their lives become their work and then what do they have?" Mama asked. "Now, are you minding your manners? Polite to those ladies? Rich, stylish ladies over at the Empire, so Miss Abby tells me."

"The ladies? Oh, right. But it's the men, the men who run things, Mama. And don't worry, I'm not a child. You taught me how to behave. I have to get back to work now," said Jean, leaning over to plant a light kiss on her mama's cheek.

Jean liked the sound of those words "get back to work." They felt good to say and it felt extraordinarily good to see the pride in her mama's face.

5

The afternoon was a blur for Jean. There had been a bunch of ladies, their fine leather luggage being ferried by the bellmen, and they were followed by businessmen with serious faces. None were particularly chatty, but Jean enjoyed watching the guests and getting a sense of who they were by how they carried themselves and what they carried.

In late afternoon the elevator was called to the eighth floor. Her heart began to thump loudly. She hoped the door would open and there would be Elden. But when the brass door pulled back, it was the other Whitcomb, Mr. Whitcomb, looking very much like a boss, refined and stately in his impeccable woolen suit and shiny black shoes.

"Good afternoon, sir," said Jean, hiding her nervousness behind a friendly smile.

"Miss Ball, I hear you are working out well. And how is work finding you?" he asked. Jean smiled at his compliment. And she had never considered how work was finding her. All she'd ever worried about was finding work.

"Lovely. This is the loveliest place I've ever seen. I'd live here if I could," rambled Jean.

"Some people do you know. Eighth floor apartments. Business men can stay when they are in town for extended visits."

Jean was awestruck. "Brilliant. That's brilliant!" she said, as if discovering the idea for the first time, which she was.

"Well, now show me how you operate this contraption, Miss," said Mr. Whitcomb stepping into the elevator. Jean felt suddenly nervous though she had run the machine a dozen times already. It wasn't complicated but there was a touch to it. She pulled the cage door firmly shut and pushed the button to start. The elevator gave a lurch as if setting into gear.

"Whoa there, miss," said Mr. Whitcomb taking a step toward Jean as he regained his balance. Jean automatically ducked to the side.

"Almost fell on you, didn't I? Better me than a guest I suppose. Let me show you how to ease into the start. People like an easy start. Builds confidence in the place to have things run smoothly, you know. It's all about the appearances," he instructed.

Mr. Whitcomb took Jean's place at the controls, clearly comfortable with the machinery. He brought the carrier to a gentle stop and re-started it. "See just that little touch there on the lever, nice and slow. Have you tried out the chair yet?" he asked pulling down the mahogany seat that folded up against the button panel.

"Well, yes, but I wasn't sure if I should," Jean answered meekly.

"You think you can stand all day? Every day? Wife tells me that leads to veins in legs, unsightly things," Mr. Whitcomb replied, "Can't have that."

Jean blushed at the mention of ladies' legs. That was not something to discuss, especially with a man and a boss at that.

"So, first day of work. Any questions? Anything I can tell you about this place you haven't already heard?" asked Mr. Whitcomb pleasantly.

"There is one thing, sir. It's payday. When is payday?" She had meant to ask at the interview but it seemed so inappropriate to talk of that after she had bargained for more money.

"Now that's a good question," replied Mr. Whitcomb, tilting his head as if in consideration, "I pay the maids every day. They tend to work close to the bone, you know. My professional staff, I pay on Tuesdays. Used to pay on Fridays but I found the Saturday crew would show up whiffing of hooch and looking haggard around the edges. No need to tempt temptation, I say. I'll pay you on Tuesdays, too, though I doubt you'd have that temptation problem, no?" he concluded with an eyebrow raised.

"I wouldn't. No. That sounds fine. Wonderful," said Jean, relieved at the implication she would be kept on. She summoned her courage and asked, "So on Tuesday, I'm paid for today through Monday then?" asked Jean.

"Of course," replied Mr. Whitcomb. "I'll have Mr. Green make a note of it."

As the doors were opening, he casually added, "Big fête tonight. League party. If you come run the elevator nine to midnight I'll pay you a quarter more for today."

With that, Mr. Whitcomb stepped off the elevator, not waiting for a reply. Jean's mind raced – this was too good to be true. More money. Of course she'd work.

Jean stuck her head out of the doorway, "Yes! I will!" she called out to the lobby as Mr. Whitcomb walked away. He turned toward her and nodded.

Jean's cheeks flushed. She ducked back into the elevator and quickly pulled both doors shut. *A quarter extra! And here I am, screaming like a fishwife across a hotel lobby.* Her cheeks burned with shame. Decorum. *Carry yourself with dignity,* her mama had drilled into her. *Mama would give me an earful over that little scene.*

Jean's shift was almost over. She'd go home, tell Mama all about seeing Mr. Whitcomb again, have dinner, then come back. Instead, she went home and, finding her mama asleep, immediately pulled off her own shoes and collapsed onto the bed, exhausted from the day.

I'll rest a minute and then make a peanut butter sandwich. Instead, she fell quickly asleep lying beside her mama. Jean awoke with a start from a car horn making a terrible "ahoooo-ah" racquet in the street below.

It was already dark outside. Immediately filled with dread that she had overslept, Jean glanced at the clock on the bedside table. 8:51 p.m. She had less than ten minutes to look presentable and get back to the hotel. She sat up and reached down for her shoes. Her feet were so swollen and they ached as she crammed them in.

She grabbed her monkey hat and glanced over at her mama, still sleeping. The tea. Jean turned on the tea kettle and then poured the almost hot water into the tea cup. As she quietly set it on the bedside table, she glanced at the clock, 8:54 p.m.

Jean ran down the stairs with a little limp, not bothering to lock the door. Jean ran the few blocks back to the hotel, stopping to catch her breath at the entrance and gather her dignity before walking calmly through the ornate lobby. She surreptitiously caught a look at the clock over the front desk, two minutes to spare.

Jean took in a deep breath and surveyed the lobby. It had been transformed. Candles were lit over the fireplace mantel and at the lobby desk. The place felt magical and the air smelled of roses. She could hear a twinkling of piano keys streaming from the ballroom, inviting dancers to the floor. Jean felt her pulse race, taking in the excitement, joy, at the loveliness of it all.

It'll only take a minute to glimpse what's going on in there. She quietly made her way through the lobby, down the hall, and toward the ballroom. The room itself was breathtaking.

Eight white Italian marble columns soared thirty feet in the air ending in gold laurels that held up a domed ceiling. At the dome's center was an exquisite bronze medallion shimmering with all-electric lights. Tall cathedral candelabras cast in bronze graced each corner of the room.

Although it was breathtaking in its beauty, it was completely vacant save for tables strewn with half-empty dessert plates, coffee cups and used silver. The sounds were coming from a room just beyond.

Jean crept through the empty room in the direction of the music toward the smaller dancing parlor. She stood to one side of the entry and poked her head around the corner. Ladies were everywhere in long dresses, some smoking with long cigarette holders.

The men wore waistcoats. One was so fat he waddled like a penguin. Others looked elegant and the whole crowd was like something that stepped off the pages of a magazine.

The piano player, a colored man, tickled the ivory keys and began to sing out in a rich voice, "Ain't We Got Fun". Ladies grabbed their men's hands and led them to the dance floor for the fastest foxtrot dancing Jean had ever seen.

I could do that, if someone would ask me to dance, Jean thought, imagining herself swept onto the dance floor. Jean didn't want to pull her eyes away from the scene. Fascinating.

It was then she noticed a young man walking right towards her. Elden. She pulled herself out of the doorway and crushed up against the wall. A potted palm hid her from view. The young man walked right by her and didn't say a word.

It's this monkey grinder outfit. I probably blend right into the walls. Jean adjusted her hat and listened for more footsteps. No one else was coming. It was past time to get to her work station.

Jean hurried back through the ballroom to the lobby. There, by the lobby fireplace stood the young man, his tuxedo jacket tossed over one shoulder and bow tie dangling loosely around his unbuttoned collar.

He picked up an oversized Faberge-style egg sitting on the mantle and offhandedly tossed it in the air. Jean watched him with interest and a slight feeling of dread as she watched the precious bauble bounce into the air.

He shouldn't touch the hotel things like that. That probably cost a month's wages and it's so fragile.

She turned away before Elden could catch her staring and quietly called for the elevator. It landed with a gentle chink. She opened the elevator cage and entered. *It had been such an eventful day and it could be a long night.*

Jean pulled down the wooden seat, taking a moment to gather her thoughts. She bent to adjust the piece of cotton she'd stuck in her shoe to protect her blister, and she didn't hear anyone approach the elevator but suddenly there he was. Elden Whitcomb, smiling at her. Jean straightened up as fast as she could.

"Hey, doll, it's you again," said Elden. "Good of you to work this late for the League Ladies and all. Special night. Ladies raised lots of money to help them raise their hell."

Jean laughed remembering the image of the two League Ladies she'd met, all fretful about the Hounds of Hell.

"Sounds like they do a lot of that – I mean, do a lot of good, here in town," she offered, holding her voice steady as she took in his elegance, grateful he had again broken the ice.

Jean heard a crashing sound come from the lobby and Elden's eyes cut sharply to the left. "Well, speaking of raisin' hell, brace yourself. Here comes the city's original hellcat," said Elden rolling his eyes skyward as he tipped an imaginary drink glass to his lips.

He quickly pulled his hand down as a couple approached the elevator. It was Mr. Whitcomb with a woman who seemed to have forgotten how to put one foot in front of the other. Katherine Whitcomb. Elden took the lady's arm from his father and smiled lightly at Jean.

"Glad you are working tonight. Eighth-floor, please," said Mr. Whitcomb to Jean, as Elden steered the woman into the elevator and leaned her against one of its mahogany walls. He affixed her hand around the brass rail that ran the perimeter of the elevator.

"Sh'work tonight? Sh'work here? We don't 'please' the help," slurred the woman indignantly, eyes narrowing.

Swaying unsteadily, the fringe on the hem of the woman's dress danced around her bare knees. Jean had never seen a dress so short or someone so short on personal faculties.

Jean pushed the number eight button and melted into the corner of the elevator.

"Lots a money tonight, baby. Lotsa dough for the League," said the woman, her words sliding together.

"You did well, Katherine. You put on a very, very nice event. You were the belle of the ball," Mr. Whitcomb assured her quietly.

"Dansh, dansh, dansh with me then," and with that, the woman started to move to music only she was hearing. Mr. Whitcomb looked over at Jean. Elden looked away in embarrassment.

"I will, Katherine, as soon as we get to the apartment."

"You devil, devil," said the woman, wagging a finger sloppily in front of her face, "I know what you want in that 'partmet." Mr. Whitcomb flushed at the implication. "Here take my shooo-wes, take my shoo-wes," she said, unsteadily lifting a slippered foot towards Mr. Whitcomb.

"Let's keep these on for now, dear," said Mr. Whitcomb.

The woman's face darkened, "I said shoo-wes. Now," she demanded. Jean could not believe anyone could speak to this dignified man with such disrespect. She braced herself for his response. *This will not be pretty.*

"Of course, Katherine. I'm sorry. You're right. These shoes need to come off. You've been on your little feet all night. Your poor feet," Mr. Whitcomb said.

Jean had never seen a grown man cater so. Mr. Whitcomb knelt down and took off first one shoe then the other and slipped them each into his suit pocket. Jean could scarcely believe the hold this woman must have over him.

"Thazbetter," she said with a tight pout and nary a thank you. Jean stole a look over at Elden who appeared to be ignoring the little exchange. "Don't you look at him. He'sh a Whitcomb," the lady slurred loudly in Jean's direction and then turned her nose up and away from Jean.

Jean's eyes grew wide, unsure of where she could hide. The moment was broken by the soft ding of the elevator reaching the top floor. Elden quietly positioned himself in front of Jean as Katherine Whitcomb took her time navigating deliberately out of the elevator.

Mr. Whitcomb turned his head back to Jean as he stepped out, "Goodnight," he said with finality. Elden stepped out of the elevator and whispered to Jean conspiratorially, "Hellcat, see? And she calls *me* uncouth, doll."

"Yes, sir," said Jean, her voice shaking as she shut the brass door. Rich people were more complicated than she'd imagined.

She was grateful for the elevator door to close and to be whisked back to the lobby where three couples were waiting to go up. The women wore beaded dresses that showed their bare backs, Jean noticed as they entered. Two were smoking with long black cigarette holders. The men's eyes were red rimmed and one of them held a tall stemmed glass filled with an amber liquid.

"Floor, please," said Jean as the group entered.

"Oh look, it's the girl from our rooster-frenzy morning, the day the cocks went wild, Ethylann," said one of the ladies. Jean remembered this lady as the one with a better sense of humor, all splattered with mud and talking of dairy farms and typhus scares.

"Good evening," said Jean with a smile. "Four, right? The Governor's Suite?" Jean asked, pushing the number four button.

The lady giggled, "Good memory."

"Better than I could do right now," said the man holding the glass. "One more of these and I won't be remembering my own name." The party of six laughed as if he'd told a wildly funny joke. Jean tried to remain inconspicuous.

"Fourth floor. Have a nice evening," she said, opening the door to their floor.

The group exited, with one of the men holding another up with both arms. "Help me here with him," he said to the man holding the amber drink.

"Not a chance. Might spill this," said the man, holding his glass high. "My medicine, you know." And with that, the party-goers' laughter could be heard as they made their way down the hall.

When the clock struck midnight Jean's first workday finally ended. As she walked through the dark street after the end of her shift, her mind raced through all the things that had happened over the day and she tried to recall them in sequence: A job, a uniform, then the most handsome man ever, and extra hours and pay of a dollar fifteen, a party put on by ladies with style and fancy missions in life, and her boss; no, Elden's parents, who may have their own set of troubles.

She felt a thrill remembering it all. Life had suddenly become quite fascinating and she couldn't wait to share it all with Mama and Francie.

6

"Here are the receipts for the rent. I paid everything up through July," Jean beamed, holding the tissue thin receipts so her mother could see.

Jean had worked every week, five days a week since the day she started and had earned more than forty dollars. She'd paid June and July rent with money to spare after stocking the pantry.

"And I got you two tins of the Earl Grey, and some sugar and those thin cookies like Poppa used to buy you," Jean said in a rush.

"Oh, Jean, you didn't need to do all that," her mama said softly, eyes dancing. "Now, did you get some new shoes for yourself? I've seen how you soak your feet every evening after work, and I know those shoes have blistered you."

"I'll do that next payday, Mama," Jean said. "Don't you worry about me. My feet just needed to toughen up, is all."

"If you say so."

"I'll put the money all here in your pay envelope. You want to count?" Jean looked over and saw her mama's face relax.

"Oh, baby girl. I'm so proud. Look at you. Just look at you. Your Poppa would be so proud. No, no, I'm not counting right now. So, why don't you get on out today? It's your day off after all," her mama said, trying to suppress a cough.

"Miss Abby told me there's a celebration in the city park. She said maybe you should go with Francie for a picnic. Just get me my pills and put a sandwich by the bed, okay?" asked her mama as the question ended with a coughing fit.

"And I got you the medicine, Mama, that one the doctor said might help more. Opens up your lungs. Remember?" Jean asked, casting a hopeful smile her mama's way.

"He said it would clear this cough up, didn't he?" Mama asked. "Yes, I recall he said just that. But those were too expensive for us, baby girl. Too expensive and we told him 'no thank you,'" Mama recalled.

"You told him 'no thank you,' but I went back to see him last week and told him you meant, 'yes,'" Jean beamed. "It'll get you feeling better quicker."

Jean unfolded the paper revealing ten blue tablets. The doctor called them lung pills and the druggist said it was quinine, iron, potash and phosphoric acid. A modern cure.

"That is just what I need, baby girl. Just what I need," Mama said softly. "If I promise to take one, will you promise to get some dreaming time today and go to that celebration, Jean?"

Jean nodded, grateful for the suggestion. Mama was right, it was a day to celebrate. And with Miss Abby coming in several times a day to sit with her mama there were no worries keeping her at home.

The city's first zoo had opened on a stretch of empty land south of town and the founder had dedicated an entire park in front for the public's use. He named it after himself, Swope Park, and today they'd have bands playing there until dark, followed by fireworks.

"I'd like to go. It'd be nice to get outside. Maybe you can come too?" asked Jean.

"Too much for me. Can't walk far in one stretch. Need my sleep," declined her mama, "Let that medicine work."

Jean nodded, the medicine would take a week to work, the druggist said. "Ok, if you take the medicine, I'll get outside today," Jean bargained.

Jean felt a mixture of sadness and relief. Mama was plainly not feeling better but a free day in the sunshine would be a wonderful respite.

"Let me fix you something then," Jean offered as she reached for the white bakery bag on the table. Taking out the loaf of bread, she cut two slices of bread and carefully spread the peanut butter, not too thick. She put the sandwich on a plate by the bedside. "Anything else?"

"Lock the door on your way out," rasped her mama, covering her mouth with a handkerchief as the coughing began.

Jean leaned down and saw blood on the blue cloth. "You sure you feel well enough to be alone?"

"Course. You worry too much. It's nothing. Let me rest, would you? Miss Abby will be by in the next hour or so."

"Okay, you know what you need," said Jean as she placed a kiss on her cheek. Not hot today, barely even warm. *That's probably a good sign.* Jean slipped the key onto her necklace, a gold chain with a jade flower.

The necklace was her one constant. It held her first memory, her strongest memory of her Poppa. Poppa, all dressed in his military uniform, had fixed the clasp around her mama's neck, then leaned in close and gave Mama a kiss.

"You come back home to me now, promise," Mama had said, cheeks flushed, and Poppa, standing there so majestic had replied with such certainty, "I promise."

Even as a tiny child it felt like a moment to hold on to. Jean knew it was a moment she'd hold forever after the telegram arrived and her mama sat on the bed clutching the little flower necklace and reading the yellow piece of paper again and again. Her mama's eyes had again filled with tears the day she gave the necklace to Jean, the day she told Jean about her illness. The day Jean swore she'd never take it off.

Jean set a little saucer of milk outside the apartment door, and the little kitten appeared to sip it. She bent and petted the kitten, delighting in its soft purr.

"You're getting bigger," she said. "Will you let me hold you?"

The kitten flicked its tail and ran off again, so Jean locked the apartment door and skipped down the steps two at a time. Once outside she ran to Francie's, excited to tell her all about work.

Francie agreed to meet her at one o'clock by the fountain in the center of the new park. Barely noon with the sky already dripping humidity, Jean hurried on to the park and took a seat on the edge of the park's grand fountain, finding a dry spot so as not to dampen her cotton dress.

The fountain's dedication plaque said it was sponsored by the Consumer League ladies. They had put in fountains all over the city and said it was to give the horses and dogs some place to drink so they didn't sully the water supply. Now that she'd met a few of them, Jean thought that a few of the ladies really just liked putting up plaques congratulating themselves for this or that.

She gazed up at the fountain - five maidens sitting at the feet of what looked like a Roman God. She couldn't imagine what it cost. Hundreds and hundreds. *Imagine all that money and work just for something pretty.* She couldn't resist slipping off her shoes and resting her feet. She gathered her skirt and dipped her toes into the cool water.

"Hey, my horse has to drink out of there! Grimy toes could give him the runs!" said a voice behind her. Jean quickly jerked her head around.

Was the fountain not for people? But Ewwww, what if a horse had gulped and spit in the water?

She turned to give the schoolboy a scolding for frightening her so, but held her tongue when she saw that the vocal complainer was none other than Elden, standing behind her with not a horse in sight.

"Fooled you," he smiled, leaning down and flicking water across her bodice.

Jean's eyes widened and she quelled the nerves she felt tickling across her palms. *We're just two people in the park*, she thought. *I can try to just be myself here, not his father's worker.* She smiled and gave a playful splash back.

"Elden! For a second I thought you were a schoolboy who needed a lesson in how to talk to a lady."

"No, no. By all means, if a lady wants to soak her feet in horse spit, she should always feel free."

Jean laughed and her nervous thoughts dissipated. "Well, now you've just up and ruined it for me, Elden. And my little toes were having such a divine swim," she said in a tone of mock elegance. She lifted her feet from the water and gave them a shake, sprinkling water droplets onto Elden's tailored pants.

"Sorry," she said with an impish half-smile. Elden reached down and playfully flicked her again with water,

"All in fun, kiddo," he replied. Jean giggled. He was so comfortable. She wished she could banter so easily. "Here with family today or just enjoying the view of old Bacchus' cod sack by your lonesome?" asked Elden, pointing to the statute in the center of the fountain.

"No, not family," she replied blushing, "Not family. Friends. And who's Bacchus?" She had a good idea of what a cod sack might be, but her knowledge of Roman gods was not similarly endowed.

"Old Bacchus. God of libation, relaxation, and intoxication – my favorite three temptations in the world," Elden said flashing a charming grin, "Learned about him at Wentworth. They love to teach about dead things there."

Jean laughed at his cavalier statement. Everyone knew Wentworth was the best private school in the State. The society page was always full of which boys were offered admission, which had graduated, and what companies they'd gone on to run. Jean's eyes brightened as she took in Elden's handsome confidence and worldliness.

"You here with your parents?" asked Jean, vividly recalling the stumbling Katherine Whitcomb and unusually obsequious Mr. Whitcomb.

"No, the gang. Parents think parks and such are for commoners, which is fine by me," said Elden. "There, over there's my gang," he concluded gesturing to a group of boys across the park who were watching Elden with interest.

"Elden, Elden, come on!" "Who's the dame?" the boys hooted in the distance.

"You go on back with them, that's okay," said Jean lowering her eyes, embarrassed by the attention.

"But I came over because I didn't think I'd see you again and then there you were. And now I don't know when I'll see you next," said Elden. His sea blue eyes shimmered with sincerity. Jean looked at him closely, wondering if his intentions were as sweet as his words.

"But you surely know where to find me," Jean smiled and raised one eyebrow at him.

"Oh, not at the hotel. I mean. Not like that. I'm sorry," he gulped, mistaking her look for one of disdain. "I just meant not as an employee. I have a car. I mean, well, we all eat. No, we eat dinner. Can I take you out? Not today, of course. Maybe I should meet your parents?" Elden's words came out in a rush and he stopped, dropping to her side with a husky sigh. "I'm not doing this well, am I?" he ended, endearingly.

Is he asking me for a date? He barely knows me, but he's so sophisticated and he is the boss' son, and he has an automobile and maybe, maybe he even likes me a little.

Jean looked at him with her sweetest smile, "I'd be thoroughly charmed," she said. She'd read in the magazines that was the right thing to say.

"Great! Friday night, six o'clock then," he declared, a little too loudly.

Jean let out a tiny gasp. This was a date. A real date. A boy had asked her out to dinner, well – had asked her out anyway, maybe out to dinner. She couldn't quite tell.

"Six o'clock, sure, Friday," replied Jean quickly.

"Okay, doll. Jean, I mean Jean." He turned and broke into a run after taking a step back.

Before he reached the waiting group of boys, he turned and shouted over his shoulder, "Wait, I need your address!"

Jean felt as if every person in the entire park stopped and stared at her. "The Stover Building on Eighth," she said in her quietest voice that would carry all the way to him.

"An apartment?" he shouted back with a note of incredulity that echoed across the park.

"Well, of course," she shouted, not realizing there might be a difference between renters and owners. Jean turned back to the fountain, unable to keep the smile from her lips.

~

Francie found Jean sitting by the fountain, lost in thought. She quietly sat down her picnic basket and tapped Jean on the shoulder.

"Anybody home?" Francie called.

Jean looked up, startled. "He found me and he asked me out," she said without even giving Francie a 'hello.'

"Who did what?" asked Francie, taking a seat on the fountain's edge.

The entire story spilled out and ended with both girls squealing in delight, then bending their heads together to discuss the possibilities.

"I'll come do your hair for the date, all right?" Francie said. "We can put it up in a chignon with the sides rolled up. And Jean, let's cut down my yellow silk dress for you to wear."

"I couldn't, Francie," Jean said. "It's your best dress. It's beautiful."

"Oh, please do, otherwise it will sit in my closet doing nobody any good," Francie said. "It's too small for me now, but I couldn't bear to let it go. I could let it go for something this important. My mother can stitch it to fit you in a heartbeat. She's the best seamstress in Kansas City."

"Would she really? I would love it," Jean said.

"You'll need shoes," Francie said.

"Oh, how I wish I could afford some buttery leather dancing

shoes, but they're so expensive," Jean said, adding conspiratorially, "Francie, one of us needs to start dating a cobbler, and soon."

Francie and Jean giggled together. Jean grinned, and Francie reached up and patted her hair into place, tucking a stray wisp back into the bun at her neck. "Have you ever thought about cutting your hair, into one of those fashionable bobs?" Francie asked.

"Oh, never," Jean replied. "Mama calls my hair my crowning glory."

"Yes, and on your wedding night, you can let it all down and it will be a velvety waterfall, just for you and your husband to share," Francie said.

"Stop it, now, I'm nervous enough," Jean said. "Here I get one tiny little date, and you already have me married off to this fellow."

"You never know, Jean," Francie said. "With your dark hair and those flashing ocean green eyes, you could go anywhere."

The sound of laughter rolled toward them, and then they looked up in astonishment as two dozen white doves flew up into the clouds. The sun sank lower on the horizon.

As afternoon turned to evening a band played, speeches were given and then the glow of the fireworks on the park lawn dimmed in comparison to the glow in Jean's heart.

7

*J*ean counted the hours until Friday afternoon and had to make a concerted effort to engage the lady visitors as she worked, her mind filled with thoughts of what she would wear, what she would say to Elden on Friday evening.

It was all she could bring herself to talk about in the evenings with her mama, after the obligatory conversation about the day's aches and visits from Miss Abby. The days of the week seemed to drag along, not keeping pace with the mounting anticipation in her heart.

She raced down to the time clock on Friday afternoon and found herself stuck behind the wide Polish woman, Mrs. Velmar, who could sew anything but had never figured out the simple time machine. The woman stood contemplating which direction the card would best fit. Not that there was a choice. Jean pushed the hair from her eyes, tapping her foot impatiently.

"Rush, rush. With you now, always ze rush," teased Mrs. Velmar as Jean plucked her timecard from the metal bracket.

"It's Friday," Jean replied hurriedly, as if that were explanation enough.

"The Friday, the 'Zaturday. That iz not news. Makes no difference.

You, you remind me of królik. Królik, alwayz hop, hop, hop around, heart goes the pitter-pat, quick, quick, you know, yes?" Mrs. Velmar had tucked her hands up like rabbit paws and pushed her teeth out as if they were bucked.

"A rabbit?" Jean questioned. "I remind you of a rabbit?" She almost laughed out loud, remembering how this woman, now impersonating a bunny, had been so intimidating on her very first visit to the Empire.

"Ze rabbit. Królik! Zat right," nodded Mrs. Velmar, her rabbit grin breaking into a smile. "Fast, fast to want to go. Pitter-pat, pitter-pat. You has pitter-pat, me think?"

"Maybe," Jean said coyly, as her cheeks turned pink. Had she really been so anxious, so obvious? Jean wondered.

"Królik must always be careful. Not so much the pitter-pat, yes?" said Mrs. Velmar, finally punching her card.

"I'll try to hold off on the pitter-pat," Jean assured as she punched out and tossed her card into its slot. "See you next week!" She could hear Mrs. Velmar's "zat right," echoing behind her as she bounded up the basement steps and headed for home.

Jean had just put her hand out to open the apartment door when Francie swung the door open wide, a hot curling iron in hand and a red checkered apron tied over her school uniform. Francie's chestnut hair hung in long ringlets, singed in place.

"I brought you the yellow silk dress, and your mama says it's absolutely perfect and I'm going to curl your hair. Now don't say a word. Just sit down," Francie directed, leading Jean into the apartment and shepherding her to the kitchen chair. She crimped and curled and burned Jean's hair into submission.

"Jean, don't forget your city manners tonight. Napkin goes in your lap. Chew each bite at least thirty-two times and leave at least one bite of everything on your plate so this boy doesn't think you're ill-mannered," instructed her mama, propped up in bed with two pillows, "And where are you going exactly? Be home by nine sharp and don't be late. I'll worry. And don't talk about religion or politics, of course. And ..." Mama prattled on, not waiting for Jean to respond.

"Enough, Mama. I know all that. Please no fussing over me," said Jean. Francie laughed and gave Jean a wink. It was 5:55 when Francie finally declared Jean suitably attired.

"We have a special surprise for you," Francie said. "Your mama and I have been saving up for a long time, so don't even think about saying anything but thanks."

Jean's mother reached under the pillow and handed Jean a white box.

"Oh, you shouldn't," Jean exclaimed. She took the proffered box and untied the string that held it shut. Lifting the lid, she saw the most beautiful, buttery leather dancing shoes she had seen in all her life. She took them out of the box and held them close to her chest, hugging them tightly.

"Be careful," Francie said. "Don't muss your dress! Do you like them?"

"Oh, Francie, you know I do. Thank you," Jean said. "Mama, thank you."

"I had a little bit of lace left from when I felt better, and it was so lucky, Jean," Mama said. "Francie's mother needed the lace for one of her dresses, a really expensive dress she made for one of the society ladies. Francie made up the difference, and now you can dance all night with your beau."

Jean's eyes filled up with tears of gratitude. She knew that her mother had given up one of her few real treasures to afford a treasure for her.

The shoes fit perfectly, and when she put them on her weary feet, she suddenly felt as light as air. She gave Francie and Mama a hug and sprinted down to the lobby where she was met by Otis, who held the front door open for her.

"You look sharp, Miss Jean," Otis admired.

"I'm going out to dinner tonight, I think. At a restaurant!" Jean gushed.

She remembered eating in a fancy restaurant with white cloth napkins once with her parents, the night before her daddy had left for the big war. And since then, she'd only visited tea shops with her mother to celebrate an occasional birthday. Dining out without a very special reason was unheard of.

"Out to dinner, is it? Well, now, you should get out. Your mama's so proud of you getting that job and maybe even tickled about you meeting a young boy," said Otis with a wink. "Miss Abby told me about that. We all need you to find your way now, you know. It starts by you getting out of that apartment."

"I know. It's going to be wonderful, too. Mr. Elden Whitcomb has asked me to dine," Jean said trying to hold back any affectation.

"Elden Whitcomb is it? Mr. Whitcomb's boy?" asked Otis, putting a cigarette between his lips and striking a match. The match didn't light but dropped from his hand. Jean stooped to retrieve it and lit it by striking it against the sole of her shoe.

"Where did you learn to do that, Miss Jean?" Otis asked.

"Some things just come naturally," Jean grinned.

"I hope you have a mighty good time with that Elden Whitcomb," Otis said. "Make sure he treats you right."

"Oh, Otis, thank you," Jean said, blushing a little. "Do you know Elden?"

"Know of him, Miss Jean. Nice young man. Now, some say he may have a few wild oats to sow but he'll be a good businessman one day. People smart. You just be sweet. Be your sweet self," Otis took a deep drag on the cigarette, as a long, red car pulled up to the edge of the sidewalk. "Remember, you are a lady, and you deserve to be treated like a lady by a true gentleman."

Otis put his cigarette on the edge of a window ledge and sprang to action, like a protective father. He strode out to the waiting car, passing in front of Jean to get there first.

"Mr. Whitcomb, I presume?" Otis asked the young driver, with an air of formality.

"Yes, sir," said Elden, getting out of the car and coming around to the sidewalk.

"Here for Miss Ball, sir?" asked Otis.

"Yes, sir, if that's okay." Elden looked nervous around the edges.

Otis reached for the car door handle but Elden interceded, "Sir, thank you. I'll get the door for her, if I may."

"Yes, sir, Mr. Whitcomb," responded Otis with the slightest of smiles. Maybe this Elden wasn't as wild as his reputation. Most boys with such a car would have just pulled up and honked its' obnoxious car horn and then waited, all packed in there with their raccoon coats and fancy shoes, not bothering to get out of the automobile.

"Good evening, Jean, *ma jolie mademoiselle*," Elden greeted Jean.

"Thank you but really I have no idea what you said," blushed Jean.

"I said you are a very pretty lady. Beautiful. Full of beee-u-tee," said Elden, stretching out the word for full emphasis. "It's French."

"Oh, thank you," Jean giggled. She could feel her heart picking up its pitter-pat pace, and she couldn't help but think of Mrs. Velmar.

Elden opened the car door. "You can sit right up here with me, not in the back. It's safe. This is a Revere, came out last year. Seats six. Can you believe it? The gang loves it and the top goes up and down," Elden bragged. "Oh, but your hair, Jean. It looks so nice," he paused and then pointed upwards. "The convertible top. I can put it up for you, if you want," he offered.

Jean thrilled at the notice of her hair. "No. It's wonderful. This is fine." She scooted into the front seat. Otis stood on the sidewalk, observing watchfully and Jean noticed Francie hanging out the apartment window also scrutinizing every move. Elden looked away as Jean pulled her feet into the car. *Good. A boy shouldn't stare at a young lady's ankles. Only ne'er-do-wells are obvious.*

Jean waved up to Francie as Elden went around to the driver's side. Francie waved back with a fury and mouthed "What a car!" Jean delighted in giving her a good impression.

The city streets were no longer always filled with horses and the Model Ts and wooden wheel cars were nothing like this.

Elden jumped over the car door into the driver's seat, not bothering to open the door. Otis shook his head as Elden jerked the auto out into the traffic lane, not bothering to check for cars.

"How long have you been driving? This is a great car," Jean admired, electing to ignore Otis' doubtful look.

"It's a roadster. New. Lots of fun. I've been driving for years now. Couple anyway. City's grown so fast and dad needs me to run here and there all the time. I like to get out of the city, too. Sundays are made for driving. I just go and go - gotta get out somewhere, you know. Like to go out where the fence posts fly by like matchsticks," Elden said with a laugh, his foot heavy on the gas.

The roadster picked up speed, and as it did, the expression on Elden's face looked free and wild.

"You get out much, to the countryside?" he asked.

"I can't even think of what's outside of the city limits. We just don't leave town," Jean shook her head in wonder.

"You all never get out? No picnics at the lake? Anything?" asked Elden.

"No. No way to get there. Some people just don't drive," Jean added, knowing most people could never dream of owning a car, especially not one like this. She wondered how anyone could be so insulated not to know that. Maybe rich folk really were different, like her mama seemed to believe.

"Your Pops, he doesn't drive at all?" asked Elden.

Jean realized she'd let this conversation go too far. He needed to know there was no Pops, although she halfway feared he'd turn the car right around and drop her back at her doorstep.

"You're lucky to have both of your parents, Elden," Jean sighed, weary of always having to explain away her father's absence.

"Lucky? No, I'd never say that. You have met my parents, right?" Elden asked with a mischievous grin.

"I'm on my own almost, see? My poppa, he passed when I was small. The War. Mama, she's frail, bedridden now. Not getting better," explained Jean, trying to keep her voice free of any emotion.

"Almost on your own? How so?" he asked.

"I work. I'm taking care of my mama. We do fine, really," replied Jean, brooking no pity.

"No one telling you what to do?" asked Elden, looking for the bright side.

"Mama tries, believe me, but not really, no. There's no one telling me what to do. Not a soul but me and my conscience," said Jean, and it was true.

Elden let out a low whistle and shook his head.

"So that's how you came to work for Pops, I guess. Girl on her own. That's where the push came from the League Ladies then," Elden deduced. "They want to change the whole world, Dad says. Even want girls to learn to drive."

"I suppose," Jean replied, "Those ladies seem to know their minds. And it's such a nice hotel."

"Yeah, the hotel's alright. It keeps Pops out of trouble and Mother as happy as can be expected. I guess it's okay."

"Seems better than okay to me. And tell me, where are we going tonight?" Jean asked as the car turned off of the busy street of Broadway.

"There, there it is," said Elden pointing to The Savoy Hotel just on their left. The Savoy housed the nicest restaurant in the city, the Savoy Grill, and it had only just started letting women dine there, too.

Everyone knew that if a place was named "Grill" that was code for "Men Only," but the Savoy had up and changed all that, scandalous as that was. It had been a big to-do in the newspaper when that happened and some men still boycotted the place.

"The Savoy Grill?" asked Jean, "Are you sure?"

"What's not to be sure about?" replied Elden as he opened his car door.

"The Savoy Grill," whispered Jean to herself.

She knew it was the finest place in town. Presidents even dined there when they came to town. A wave of worry grew in the pit of Jean's stomach as she looked down at her borrowed frock.

Carry yourself with dignity. Better to underdress than overdress, thought Jean, recalling two lessons her mama had drilled into her since childhood, not that Mama ever had an occasion to overdress.

Elden got out of the car and tossed the key to the uniformed man standing sentry outside of the restaurant.

"Don't put too many miles on it, my good man," Elden quipped, as he opened Jean's door.

"Of course, Mr. Whitcomb," said the doorman with formality. "I'll park it in the customary location." Elden nodded and offered Jean his arm as the man opened the door to the restaurant. Jean gasped.

The lobby was filled with white Italian marble and in the center of it all was a huge dome skylight, with glass in shades of pale green that filtered to a yellow-golden color at the edges. Jean felt like she was standing under a display of constant sparkling fireworks that didn't move at all.

"Pretty, isn't it? Art Nouveau, you know," said Elden. "Hey, remind me to show you the telephone booth here that a salesman locked 'ole Houdini into. Couldn't get out. What a stitch! Bet he never comes back to Kansas City. Or, if he does, at least he won't stay at the Savoy."

Before Jean could respond, they were greeted by a man in a tuxedo jacket.

"Mr. Whitcomb, we have your table ready, sir," directed the maitre d'.

"Number Four?" asked Elden.

"Yes, sir."

"You're going to like this place, Jean. We always get the booth reserved for the Presidents. Some call it the Presidential Booth, but we just call it Number Four. In the know, you know," Elden said smartly.

Jean was swept into the main dining area and took in its entire splendor. The room was filled with history and elegance. The walls soared to the sky. Each held a huge mural way up towards the ceiling height, larger than life, depicting something from the West - pioneers in a covered wagon, huge runs of cattle forging the river, life along the Santa Fe Trail. An oak bar ran the length of one side of the room and it was topped in pure leather dyed banker green. Drink wasn't legal but at some places people apparently just looked the other way, Jean surmised.

Jean took a seat in a cozy, high-backed booth covered in soft leather and Elden slid in across from her. There was real linen on the table and Jean had never held silverware so heavy.

Elden ordered a beer for himself and, for both of them, exotic food Jean had never heard of - Buffalo Steak and Prairie Chicken, tastes Jean had never dreamed of experiencing. It was more food than she could eat in a week.

She tried everything, on her plate and his, and exclaimed over each bite but declined his offer of a sip of beer. Elden was amused by how new everything appeared to her.

They talked about his family, his people he called it. His mother was from a Strawberry Hill family, immigrant stock, though her people had moved away before Elden was born. His father's people, well, they were Kansas City Whitcombs from way back, you know, Elden had said.

Jean didn't know but nodded anyway. They talked through the main course and dessert – fresh strawberries with whipped cream – as well. She couldn't eat another bite.

"In France, you wouldn't be allowed to take home the leftovers," Elden said. "The chefs worry that people will guess their recipes. Here in the States, though, we can box things to go. Would you mind taking home some of what we can't finish?"

"Oh, thank you," Jean said, flustered. It felt as if Elden had read her mind; she so much wanted to share a taste of those strawberries with Mama. The leftover buffalo steak and chicken would help stretch their food budget, too. Jean didn't know if Elden knew how much he was helping her, and she blushed when she thought that he might know how little money her family had, when his family had so much.

Jean began to worry that this dinner had to be costing a fortune. Elden signed the check when it arrived without letting Jean glimpse the total.

So this is what's it's like to feel like a kept woman, Jean thought. *Like one of the women in the pulp magazine who dallies about, going from parties to shops to fancy restaurants.* Jean sighed contentedly, relishing the feeling of being cared for, protected. A feeling she'd not had for years, if ever really.

"You're like no other girl, Jean. So sweet and true," Elden said as he left her at the apartment house doorstep. Jean trembled a little, wondering if he would try to kiss her, and if he did, what she should do.

Elden looked into her eyes and held both her hands. As he bent toward her. Jean felt so nervous, she stepped on his foot, and he ended up kissing her cheek. He laughed, a deep, full-throated laugh, and she thrilled at the sound of it. Elden handed her the little brown paper bag that contained the strawberries and left with a huge smile on his face.

The evening had been perfect, something right out of a storybook, Jean couldn't help but think as she floated up the stairs.

The kitten met her at the door, as if waiting up for her. Jean knelt at the door and put a small tidbit of the buffalo steak into the kitten's saucer, just for the joy of knowing that the kitten's tummy, too, would be full tonight. She quietly unlocked the apartment door, taking care not to rattle the knob as she gave it a turn. Her stealth was for naught; Mama was wide awake, having anticipated Jean's return.

"And, so? Tell me! Was it beautiful? Is he nice? Where did you go? Did you leave a bite of everything? Was it perfectly elegant? Oh, Jean, you look like a princess standing there. Come sit. Tell me everything," chattered her mama, sitting straight up in bed and saying more words in a minute than she had in weeks. Jean barely knew where to start.

"It was beautiful, yes. Nice, undoubtedly. Delicious, elegant, princess – oh, yes." Jean said, sinking onto the bed. "Mama, I brought strawberries! He said we shouldn't waste the leftovers."

Jean loved the light in Mama's eyes as she nibbled on the strawberries, fresh and delicious, dotted with sweet whipped cream. She kept chattering happily as Mama tasted the chicken, the buffalo steak, and the fruit.

"He talked to me like I was a friend, like Francie and I talk, Mama," Jean said. "Just like Francie and I do. And it was the Savoy Grill and he ordered everything. I've never seen such a place."

"The Whitcombs must have more money than the Rockefellers," she continued. "And we sat in the booth where Presidents sit. Number Four. And there was stained glass all gold and cream and green with long pieces and little triangles filled with color, and the silver was like something the Queen herself would use."

Jean tried to find the words to describe every exquisite detail. "And we were waited on by a man who seemed to know Elden. He spoke to him with such deference but Elden was kind and polite back. There's not a pretense about him. He's so smart and he knows how to drive and he has his own car, a Paul Revere or something, and we tooted the horn on the way home and it made that big noise. And the steak covered the whole dinner plate and I ate a chicken that wasn't really chicken but it tasted like chicken," Jean laughed.

"Miss Abby came in and told me about that car, too. She watched you leave. Said he was a gentleman, opening the door for you and all," Mama interjected.

"And it's beautiful. And he said I was beautiful," sighed Jean as she fell back on a bed pillow.

"Did he now? Well, my girl is beautiful. And deserves the good things. Don't you forget that," Mama said, reaching out to stroke Jean's hair.

"Oh, and afterward I asked Elden if I could keep one of the menus and he just smiled and said of course. And he got one for me and do you know what dinner must have cost? I can tell you it was more than my ninety cents a day," said Jean, referring to her daily wage.

"Lots, lots more than that," she concluded and dissolved into giggles, "Just look!" Jean sat up straight as she slipped a piece of paper out of her pocket and handed it to her mama. It was the Savoy Grill's menu, printed with all of its fancy writing capturing gastronomic delights neither member of the Ball family could even imagine.

"I'll never forget this night, Mama. Just never," Jean said, her eyes shining and face filled with light. "We laughed so much but I was nervous. Look, my hands are still shaking. It was so exciting and he wants to go out again and show me his favorite place in the whole world and I said of course, but only if Francie comes, too - with Harold." Harold was Francie's beau, well not exactly her beau, but a neighbor boy who wasn't terribly offensive, as far as boys go.

"Then he said, 'Sure, sure, doll, if you think they'll be comfortable. I don't know them, but the more the merrier!' and I reminded him I'm no doll," Jean continued, "He said it would be on a Sunday morning and I should bring a sweater along for the ride. We'll have the top down, and he'll have his cook fix a picnic. His cook! Mama, the man has his own cook. I can't believe it. Won't that be fun?"

Jean fell back on her pillow and waited for a response, but heard none. Jean looked over and saw her mama, the menu resting across her chest and a smile on her thin face, fast asleep. Jean smiled.

Mama looked happier than she had been in months. No, years. Jean pulled the coverlet up over her mama and got herself ready for bed. She saw that one strawberry remained, untouched, and as she cleaned up, she set the strawberry on a porcelain saucer as a treat for when her mama woke up again.

As Jean waited for sleep, she recalled the dinner, Elden's laugh, the way he had ordered a beer like a man and had driven so fast, so wild. He had a gusto, an embrace of life she had only read about in magazines and had imagined.

She lay in the dark trying to get to sleep. It felt too magical, too wonderful to be real. He had stepped from the pages of some magazine story and swept into her life in a roadster convertible. A fantasy come true. And she fell asleep to the blissful sound of pitter-pat.

8

"Oh, gosh, I'd love to go, Jean!" Francie said gleefully when Jean invited her for the Sunday outing with Elden. "We have early Mass anyway. I'll make sure Harold goes, too. He'll come if I ask and tell him there's fancy food and he'd get to ride in a car. He'd do it just to impress his brothers," Francie giggled.

Like Francie, Harold had brothers and sisters and extended family spilling out of every room of his house too. "Good Catholics," Mama said. Not that they knew any bad Catholics, so Jean wasn't sure of the distinction.

"You'll come over right after Mass then?" Jean asked. She had recently attended one endless Mass with Francie and it was there Jean realized Harold was smitten with Francie. He'd been waiting at the church steps and she'd seen him casting around searching for something as they came up the sidewalk in front of the church.

His eyes lit up like fireflies when he spied Francie, and he had bounced down the stairs to take his place beside her to walk into church. It was cute how eager he was and she was happy to walk behind them, thinking about the possibilities between the two of them. Harold had led Francie to her own family's pew before leaving her to take a seat with his parents. Such tradition in the church, Jean had mused.

Jean always found the service itself confusing, what with the ups and downs and crosses and everything in Latin and then they'd all lined up, which took forever, with the wafers and the wine.

Afterwards they'd passed around the basket of money. She had brought a nickel from the money envelope at home and felt it was a huge investment, as she offered it to the collection plate but then Francie had whispered, "Thump the bottom when you toss it in, Jean, and it sounds like you've dropped in more money," so maybe it wasn't so much after all.

Jean had done as Francie said then Jean gave her a pious smile as she handed the basket on. She had shot Jean a sideways grin, acknowledging their inside joke. Francie could make even the simplest things fun and the hardest things bearable.

Francie assured her she was free the next Sunday and that Harold would be sure to come, too. Then the girls discussed every detail of Jean's dinner date and chattered on about the possibility of a Sunday drive down a country road and a picnic laid out under the shade of a tree.

"I have to get home to Mama and make her lunch but I'll let Elden know it's on. Next Sunday," Jean said as she gave Francie a hug goodbye.

Jean walked slowly home, thinking of how quickly everything had changed. She had a job, and now had a boy who liked her, a boy who could take care of things, and she herself was making enough to take care of Mama now instead of the other way around. Life had certainly taken a turn.

But Mama, she thought. *She's not getting better.* The very thought of her mama put a weight on Jean's heart, knowing the burden of what was to come one day, that there was no turning back and no hope for a cure.

The idea of death, grief, frightened Jean. She'd seen what happens when grief comes into a home and takes hold. It had happened when she was little, after her Poppa died.

Months and months went by before her mama would smile, take her hand and walk to the park, say happy words to a little girl who was not even five years old. Jean pushed away the thought of what was to come. This last time, the doctor had been clear. It was a matter of time and Mama had hung on with a tenacity that surprised even him, he had said.

Just these past few weeks, Mama seemed to let go a bit and rest easier. After Jean started at the Empire, Mama actually seemed relieved, not worried so much. Then when Jean had gone out on a date with Elden, she heard her mama laugh for the first time in months and months.

Maybe Mama's seeing that I'll be okay, thought Jean, *that I can stand on my own.* These thoughts made Jean proud but couldn't eradicate the shadow of sadness in her heart. It all brought back the loss of her Poppa, so strong and true, how hard it had been to see Mama so sad. How unfair it is to lose someone. *I'll get her more of the lung pills today.*

Jean stopped in at the pharmacy and ordered the pills. Another ten. *Maybe, just maybe this would be enough to drive out the consumption. Just ten more.* It was a hope, one Jean held close.

As she climbed the steps to the apartment and fitted her key in the door, Jean resolved to be more patient, more tender with Mama, to try harder to make her smile. She caught her breath at the top of the stairs and straightened her skirt, determined to look neat and prim, so her mama would feel proud of her.

"Mama, I'm sorry I'm late, but I got to talking to Francie, and......"

But her mama was gone when Jean got upstairs. Gone gone. Not packed up and gone, but still. She was gone somewhere and it wasn't anywhere she could be found. Jean put her hand to her mama's cheek. It was cold, like marble cold.

"Oh no, Mama," Jean sobbed, pulling her hand away. *I shouldn't have gone to visit Francie. I didn't have to go. What do I do? Get the doctor? Get the neighbor? No, she needs a doctor. Otis, he'll know what to do.*

Jean ran down the stairs shouting, "Otis, Otis, Otis!"

"Oh, honey, no," said Otis reaching out to put his hands on Jean's quaking shoulders. "No, young'un, no. I'm sorry. So sorry. But no, child, I can't go up there with you." Otis shook his head, sad-like. "Colored man in a white woman's apartment. She passed on and me there with a little girl? Colored man - this city - can't do that. I'll get Miss Abby, honey. She can help. She'll be right up with you," he said, guiding Jean toward the stairs.

Why does this have to be so hard? He knows Mama and me and can't even come up to help. Nothing about that feels fair. But Abby, at least Abby knows things. She'll know what to do. She'll take care of us.

"'Lo' now child, what are we to do here?" Abby murmured as she entered the small room. Abby approached the bedside and carefully looked at Jean's Mama. She reached out and put a wrinkled hand gently to the lady's cheek, "Yes, she's passed. She's gone over, child."

"No," Jean cried out. "Please make her better, Miss Abby. Fix her. Make her better."

"She's safe now, don't you worry," Abby said. "You get two coins now, what for her eyes. We close them for her 'cuz she sees all she needs in heaven now. That's all she needs to see."

Jean fumbled two coins from the pay envelope and handed them to Abby. Jean couldn't breathe, couldn't speak, couldn't cry. She couldn't figure out how two coins would cure this, but she wanted to try anything. When she saw the coins placed on her mama's eyes, she laid her head down on her mama's chest and hugged her as hard as she could, willing her to come back to life.

"Let her go, child," Abby said.

"No," Jean replied. "We have to wake her up, Miss Abby. Help me wake her up."

She held on to her mama and tried to send so much love that her mama would wake up again, but it didn't work. Miss Abby quietly gathered towels and water.

"We need to wash up the body," Miss Abby said.

"She isn't a body, Miss Abby," Jean said in a plaintive voice. "She's Mama."

Jean reached for her necklace and tightly clutched it, till the edges made indentations on her fingers. Now she had no one, no one at all, anywhere in the world, no family. She hoped Miss Abby would tell her what came next.

"Come back, Mama," Jean said. "Wake up, Mama. I didn't mean to be late with the medicine. I'm sorry. Please wake up, Mama. Please wake up."

Miss Abby hugged her then. Jean took comfort in the sweet cinnamon smell of Miss Abby's warm embrace. Jean felt like she was in a haze, and nothing made any sense without her mama there.

Miss Abby called on Francie to come right over and Otis and Miss Abby took care of the practicalities and funeral arrangements. Jean was too sad, too sad to sleep, too sad to eat, too sad to think.

Even with Francie by her side, she felt truly alone. Francie took care of the practical things, the worldly things as Francie's mother called it.

Francie went to the hotel and spoke directly with Mr. Whitcomb's assistant. She arranged for Jean to have a full week off and, at home, she rallied parish members. They brought in plates of food to nourish the body while Jean's spirit healed. But Francie couldn't bring herself to talk to Jean about the sadness, the deep things that sat in a hard place in Jean's heart and cut off her air.

Francie was quick with an offer of a muffin or a foot rub but couldn't seem to find the words that would help make things right. For all the times Francie had made the hardest things bearable, Jean found that even the smallest things suddenly felt too hard for her.

She stumbled into the hallway and leaned against the wall, taking deep breaths. The kitten appeared at her ankles, mewling and rubbing her. Jean slid down the wall and sat on the floor. The kitten leaped into her arms, quivering. Jean's tears fell on its soft fur, but it stayed there in her lap, and the two of them sat in the hallway together as the sun began to sink low in the sky.

"We're out of milk," Jean said. "I didn't think to get milk."

The kitten snuggled close to Jean's chest and purred in her arms. Jean would think about things like milk later, when she could think again.

∼

The days leading up to the service were a haze. Jean's fog began to clear on the day of the service itself, when everything moved in slow motion and it was as if she could feel, really feel in her heart, the meaning of everyone's words.

The service itself would be small – Francie's family, church members, Otis and Abby, a few neighbors, and an old school friend of Mama's who now ran a manicure shop.

Her mama had no living sisters or brothers, so the family pew in the tiny chapel seemed barren and cold. Jean took a seat in the front pew and numbly watched the minister make his way to the pulpit. She felt a hand on her shoulder. Firm, a male hand. She turned. It was Elden seated behind her.

"I'm so sorry, Jean," Elden said, gently patting her shoulder twice. Jean thought she caught a faint scent of liquor as he leaned toward her but pushed that thought away. Jean nodded as the service began.

When the service ended and the chapel emptied, Jean was the last to enter the vestibule where the mourners had gathered. She looked around for Elden but he was gone. Lydia, a round woman who smelled faintly of Ponds lotion, was the last to leave.

"I'm sorry, Jean. Your mama was a good friend. I wish I would have known how sick she was. Didn't know she had the consumption even. Took her fast. I'm so sorry." Jean nodded, recalling the stories her mama had told of Lydia, the girl destined to make it on her own.

"Now, you need to come see me, Jean. We have a lot of talking to do. A girl can't go through this alone. I've done it myself and I know what it's like. It'll get bad and then better and then it'll turn itself around and sit down beside you and hold you right down, too. That's the grief. That's its way. And that's when you come see me," she said, patting Jean's hand and then reaching into her tapestry handbag.

"None of us can do this alone. You've had too much loss for a girl so young. So here's my card. Lady Lydia's Salon, right there on Petticoat Lane, you know," said Lydia, offering her a cream colored business card. Jean read the card. The shop was around the corner from the Empire.

"I'm working at the Empire," volunteered Jean, grasping for a sense of normalcy. "I'll come over for a visit when I get back to work maybe."

"You must. You must come. You come to say hello and put your feet up. And you come whenever that grief comes and you just can't shake it. Promise me that," said the lady reaching out to roundly embrace Jean. "Your mother would be pleased to know we could look out for one another now." Lydia dabbed her eyes with a handkerchief, then gathered her handbag and kissed Jean goodbye.

Francie walked back to the apartment with Jean and offered to spend the night. And the next night and the next. After almost a week of tea and tears and more tea, Francie gently told Jean that the only lasting cure for grief was a return to things routine.

"I just can't, Francie. I can't go back to work and pretend everything is the same," said Jean, dreading having to put her key in the lock and open the door to an empty apartment each night.

"You have to, Jean," said Francie as she picked up her boar bristle hairbrush. "Go back to work and I'll stay here through the weekend with you. I promise."

Francie separated Jean's chestnut locks into three sections and began to brush. "And look up Elden, too. It was good of him to come to the service, you know. And we're getting out with him on Sunday. I already told him we would go," said Francie evenly, always looking for a practical cure.

Jean flicked a look over her shoulder at Francie. Jean's mouth was agape and she was unsure of which emotion she was experiencing – anger, sadness or maybe a flicker of hope.

"That's right, I did. And it's too late to put a stop to it, Jean," continued Francie, straightening Jean's head and drawing the brush through the locks. "I talked to him after the service and said it would do you good. You know your mama was too sensible to want you sitting around here all blue and teary-eyed anyway. We'll just go out for a ride on Sunday and get you back to the land of the living. Harold's coming too. Now close your mouth up. It's done and it's the right thing to do," Francie finished, setting down the hairbrush.

PART II

Sometimes it's the small decisions that create destiny.

— Hayward Parker

9

Sunday morning Jean woke up, her mama's favorite blue hanky wrapped around her fingers. She lay in bed, ignoring the light peeking through the window, and not holding back the tears.

The tears were still coming at night and in the small hours of the morning before the sun had fully risen. Jean wondered if she'd ever know what it was like to feel normal again. To smile.

"Miss Jean, Miss Jean," a soft voice called from the hallway. "I was to check on you now. Francie told me. She gone to her church and said you was to be up now," continued Miss Abby. Jean, squeezing the handkerchief tight, gingerly rose from bed and opened the apartment door.

"Oh, good, you're up," said Miss Abby, choosing not to acknowledge the tear-stains on Jean's face. "I brought you a tea and your favorite nut bread and Mrs. Ivanovic made your favorite, an egg with onion and sausage," the woman said gently pushing the door open further. "

You get dressed and out front by ten, I was to tell you."

Miss Abby put the tea cup and platter of sweet bread and savory sausage and egg on the kitchen table and turned to Jean.

"But, Miss Abby, I can't. How do I – " began Jean, wanting to ask the secret of continuing on. She laid the blue hanky on the counter and took a seat at the narrow kitchen table.

"You do. You just do. Sorrow don't bring them back," whispered Miss Abby, anticipating the question as she took a seat across from Jean.

"My babies, I cried and cried then cursed my Lord until I'd doomed both me and Him to the fires of Hell several times over, and it didn't change a thing. It hardened my heart for a while, no doubt. I couldn't bear to hear a baby cry, wanted to stop mothers in the park when they were sharp-tongued to their children. Wanted to shake them and yell 'Don't. They may be gone tomorrow and all you'll have is your harsh words.' Overcome, I was. Finally I grew exhausted from the sad."

"And then what happened, Miss Abby? How did you go on breathing?" asked Jean, her eyes riveted to Miss Abby's face, searching for an answer.

"Breathing was all I did do for awhile and it wasn't because it was my choice. One morning, daybreak, I was sitting at the kitchen table and I had my talk with God. Told him I couldn't do this anymore and He had to fix it or I'd fix it myself. It was dark in my heart, Miss Jean. My heart. Can't tell you how dark," the woman continued, a look of seriousness on her face that bespoke of a grief like no other.

"And then?" asked Jean, desperate for a grain of truth to make things bearable.

"Then I asked God for a sign. A sign that my babies were alright, were somewhere still being cared for in His world. Not here of course, but in spirit. Told him I needed the sign right now."

"And?"

"A cloud had covered the sky all morning, everything was gray and wet and sad. But as I said the words 'right now,' the cloud separated to let a single beam of light through. It came through my kitchen window and landed right on my cheek. Right on the place my baby girl had kissed me last. And I knew. Right then I knew a truth that I hold to this day," Miss Abby said softly.

Jean's eyes filled with tears as Miss Abby continued, "Can't know why things come about, Jean. Ain't meant to know. But my babies are alive, in spirit. Sometimes I can still feel them. When I'm doing good. For others. When the sun shines on you just so, you know then. You know they is okay. They is somewhere. You get yourself some sunshine, Miss Jean," counseled Miss Abby, reaching out to the pale child. "You need to get yourself some sunshine."

Tears streamed down Jean's face, holding the sadness that Miss Abby had once felt. Miss Abby picked up the blue hanky that sat on the kitchen counter and offered it to Jean.

"You gonna be okay. You need to find your sunshine. Promise me you'll get out today?" she asked as Jean reached for the threadbare cloth.

Jean nodded as she dried her eyes.

"I best let you get dressed. I'll let myself out," Miss Abby said softly.

Jean took a bite of the warm bread, letting its cinnamon sweetness fill her mouth and following it with the entire cup of chamomile tea. She felt the sun radiating through the window and her mouth formed a tiny smile.

Jean tucked the hanky, her mama's hanky, into the pocket of her summer dress, tugged on the pretty shoes gifted to her and, holding close to those little parts of her mama, she headed outside.

As she placed a saucer of milk in the hallway, she added a tiny scrap of egg and bread. The kitten lapped up the milk and gobbled the egg, but simply sniffed at the bread. Jean laughed at its puzzled expression.

"Do you want to come visit, or do you just love me for my milk and egg?" she asked the kitten, but it ran off again before she could give it a good cuddle.

Outside, Jean leaned up against the entry's wrought iron railing, careful to dust it off first, and waited for Francie and Harold. She watched as they approached, heads bent together in conversation.

Harold looked up at Francie with puppy eyes and Francie didn't seem to even notice. Jean had seen ladies in the hotel chattering on and smattering their hands around trying to impress a man. Some men didn't even seem to care. Others seemed to care a little too much. It was sad just to watch.

But Francie and Harold were different. They were a well matched couple, she observed. He wore knickers with a Fair Isle slipover sweater and two-toned white and tan shoes. Harold can almost pass for fashionable, Jean mused. Francie wore her sensible grey cotton dress with white cotton tights, always looking ready for a parish meeting with her family's priest.

"Hi, Harold, Francie. I'm so glad you could come," said Jean jumping from the rail and greeting them as they neared.

"I wouldn't miss getting a ride in a Revere. I hear it's the fastest car in America," Harold said, his excitement shone from his cheeks to the top of his shiny ears. "My brothers wanted to follow us down here just to see it but we told them no, didn't we, Francie?"

Harold had a new haircut and his hair was slicked back with Brilliantine oil. He must not have noticed that he'd rubbed some onto his ears as well, Jean silently observed.

"Your brothers. Fortunately I only had to remind them once that they had to get to church this morning. I noticed they didn't make early service like you did Harold," said Francie primly.

Harold beamed at her, not saying he'd waited down the block from her house that morning to see if she was walking to early morning Mass. Wee-hoo-wee-hoo, the sound of the Revere's horn crested the corner.

"Oh, there he is!" said Jean breathlessly, pressing her hands together and giving a little jump. The red roadster pulled up to the curb, top down, and Elden hopped out, leaving it running.

"Morning, girls. You look so nice today, Jean. Spiffy."

"Thank you, Elden," Jean blushed, her hands behind her back and skirt sashaying.

"Hey there, you must be Harry," Elden said, extending his hand and taking a step towards Harold. Standing side by side, Harold looked a foot shorter and a decade younger than Elden. Harold had never been called Harry, at least not since he'd been in short pants, but it had a solid ring to it – like one of the gang.

"And you're Elden no doubt. Can I call you Elden?"

"Sure. Elden. Just don't call me Ethel," Elden retorted. Harold laughed out loud.

"Okay, Ethel," joked Harold. Ethel was the latest term for a boy who preferred ... well, who bats for the other team, as the boys said. "And I believe you've met Francesca. You can call her Francie. We all do," Harold said, pointing to his girl.

"Pleased to see you again, Elden," said Francie picking up the edge of her skirt and giving a little curtsey.

"Friend of Jean's is a friend of mine," Elden said with a nod, flashing Jean a smile. "Get in, let's go! Gals, you can sit in the Struggle Buggy," said Elden, pointing to the back of the roadster.

"The what?" asked Jean.

"Struggle buggy, you know. The backseat. Pops calls it the struggle buggy when a boy's in there with a girl. He's so old fashioned. Says I caused him his worst nightmare once. I let a boy and a girl back there together. He'd warned me that I was just asking for trouble. He did get a call afterwards from the girl's father. Unhappy pappy, if you know what I mean."

"Oh, Elden!" both girls giggled in embarrassment.

"It was alright, Pops smoothed things over fine. He always does," Elden assured.

Jean felt a ripple of sadness. She couldn't help but think how fortunate Elden was to have such adoring parents, always there to protect him and make sure things turn out right.

"Hop in girls, but no struggling between you two, okay," he winked.

The girls giggled and situated themselves in the backseat, a wooden picnic basket between them. Jean peeked into the basket: bread, cheese, apples, grapes on the stem, a tablecloth, lemonade and four glasses. Her stomach rumbled and she smiled. It was the first time in days she had felt hungry. Elden had thought of everything.

The four drove through town and headed west on an open dirt

road. The city gave way to fields and the fence posts did fly by like matchsticks, just like Elden promised.

"Drive much, Harry?" asked Elden as they sped down the country road.

"Not much. Actually, not yet," Harold replied, his voice giving a squeak.

"Gotta give it a whirl today, you'll be lined up at the dealership in the morning for one of these gems," said Elden.

"Don't think I could, but it sure is nice," Harold said admiringly.

"Oh, I'll get you behind this wheel today, don't think I won't. Every man needs to know how to drive. This is the thing of the future, Harry."

"I'd try it!" piped in Francie, from the backseat. Jean looked at her like she'd sprouted a third eye. What had come over her? Francie didn't have an adventuresome bone in her body.

"Moxie, you got moxie, gal. We'll just see. Might happen today," volunteered Elden. Francie beamed, taking his words as high praise.

"Still in school, Harry?" asked Elden.

"Junior year. Westport High. You?"

"Wentworth. Left last year or so. Parents want me to go all the way through the Wentworth Military Academy there but 'No thanks' I said."

"Wentworth, eh? Impressive," said Harold. "Good set of businessmen come from there."

"Nah, it's just where the Whitcomb men go. Pops and his Pop went there so mother said something about it being my destiny," Elden laughed and Harold joined in.

"Wentworth boys are fast," whispered Francie to Jean. "Watch out for that." Jean nodded in silent reply.

For all the good those Wentworth boys did once they grew up, Francie wasn't wrong. Some were known for running wild when they could get away with it, but it never seemed to tarnish their reputations or the prestige of the medals on their uniforms.

"And Elden drives fast, too. Mother says boys who drive fast are looking for action, if you know what I mean," Francie whispered just loud enough for Jean to hear over the road noise. "She barely let me come until I told her Harold would take care of things if well, if ... you know, the Wentworth in Elden started coming out."

Jean just nodded, letting Francie's fretting wash over her without effect. Elden drove and drove and the wind whipped the girls' hair every which way, which didn't bother Jean a whit but caused Francie great consternation as she kept swiping hair out of her mouth.

Jean was glad to have the wind rushing through her hair, and making so much noise she didn't have to talk. She could just sit and watch the world flash by, thinking of all the possibilities that lay outside of the city, and not thinking about what she'd left behind.

She laid her head back on the leather headrest and let the sun bathe her cheeks. Elden made the world open up, created opportunities most girls only sighed about as they closed the cover of a magazine story. Jean felt now that maybe all things were possible, what with the sunshine, a boy, a fast car and a big world to explore together.

The boys took no notice of their girls as they commented on the countryside, farms, and fields. They'd driven almost an hour when Elden slowed the car and hooked a left down a narrow lane.

"Got to show Jean my favorite place today," Elden said to Harold. "Best spot in the world to put up your feet and let time pass by." He pulled the car off the road just before a gentle rise. "Barely on the map, but I sure love this place."

The girls were wordless, taking in the view. A lake stretched wide but you could see the shore on the other side, all green and dotted with flowers.

"See that path?" asked Elden of no one in particular, pointing to a three foot swath cut through tall weeds. "I cut a path here down to the lake this spring. Let's go take a look then we'll eat. Come on, Jean," he said opening the car door for her and Francie.

The four walked down the weedy dirt path to a clearing by the lake. Harold toted the picnic hamper and chose a picnic spot by the water's edge. The lake was clear and deep blue and a family of ducks paddled by.

Standing beside Elden, looking at the calm water, Jean was filled with a peaceful quiet and possibility that almost eclipsed her sense of loss. She tucked the little blue hanky in her pocket and tried to remember Abby's words, 'When the sun shines on you just so, you know then. You know they is okay. They is somewhere.' The sun warmed Jean's shoulders.

Sensing her melancholy, Elden looked down at Jean and smiled, knowing that to pull her in close would be too forward.

"Say, you want a lemonade?" called Harold, pulling the vacuum flask and glasses from the basket. Francie spread out the checkered tablecloth. They shared the picnic lunch and took turns throwing bread crumbs to the ducks, who quacked their appreciation. The boys lounged on their stomachs with elbows rested on the tablecloth. Elden pulled out a silver flask engraved with a scrolled letter W.

"Hit of hooch, Harry?" Elden offered as he unscrewed the top. Harold took the flask and looked up at Francie who gave a purposeful scowl.

"You'll be saying lots of Hail Marys, Harold," Francie whispered fiercely.

"Hail Mary full of grace," Harold said mockingly as he pretended to take a quick sip then playfully offered the flask to Francie.

Francie gasped and shoved the flask back at Harold, "Are you kidding me, Harold? You can't really think that I, I -- oh, forget it!" she said with a shake of her head.

Jean tried to ignore the exchange between her friends. The flask looked so elegant and she'd never seen anyone drink from one before, but she wasn't going to let on. She was grateful Francie and Harold hadn't made a terrible scene about it.

Francie whispered to Jean, "I told you Wentworth boys were fast," as Harold handed the flask back to Elden. Jean ignored her with a shrug, wanting no conflict.

Elden paid no attention to what had transpired between the three of them. He was on to the next thing already, skipping rocks at the lakeside. Harold joined him, getting one skip for each of Elden's three.

"Skip it straight, Harry. If you angle it just so it'll be perfect. Choose a flat stone and hold your arm back like this before you arc it and let go," Elden instructed as he demonstrated the technique.

"It's not that easy, you know," Harold complained.

"True. But it's the one thing you can do that feels right, exactly right, if you do it right," Elden said, pulling out his flask again.

Jean giggled at the boy's inane conversation – talking as if skipping rocks had some kind of science to it – and she turned to help Francie pack the picnic remainders into the hamper.

"Did you see him with that flask? See, I just knew the Wentworth in Elden would come out. Offering Harold a drink like that. Oh, I hate it when my mother is right," complained Francie as she sunk down on the picnic cloth, looking up at the blue sky.

"Francie, I know it. But do we have to talk about that now? He's brought us out here to enjoy the day, his special place. Let's just enjoy this moment and let it go. For me, okay?" Jean asked.

"For you, okay. It is positively paradise here," Francie confessed, her gaze on a passing cloud. "I can't remember a day so beautiful. Maybe I don't have to tell mother about the booze after all, do I?"

"What she doesn't know –" began Jean, but stopped herself, knowing Francie held no secrets from her mother. "It is all so perfect here, isn't it?" Jean felt a shadow pass over her. Elden. There, standing behind her.

"Perfect?" he asked. "You ain't seen nothing yet. Come with me, Jean. I'll show you perfect." Francie smiled and gave a little nod as if to nudge Jean along.

"I'll finish packing up and take things back to the car," offered Francie, sitting upright.

"Okay, show me perfect," Jean said, smiling up at Elden. He put his hand out and helped Jean to her feet.

"Hey, Harry, here are the keys, go give it a run. We're going for a walk," Elden called out, tossing the keys to the Revere to Harold.

"You sure?" Harold grinned widely, catching the keys in mid-air.

"Course I'm sure. Have fun. Got plenty of gas, too," Elden assured.

"Come on, Francie, can't hurt to run it down the dirt road!" said

Harold, his enthusiasm spilling out with the pace of his words. With that, Francie picked up the basket and the couple ran towards the car.

Jean and Elden walked west along the lakeshore hugging the shoreline until they came to a huge rock formation jutting six feet into the air. When Elden saw the rock he broke into a run and scaled it in two quick bounds.

"Come up here and have a seat," Elden invited. Jean watched her footing as she navigated the rock, trying to hold down the pleats of her skirt. When she was almost at the top Elden took her hand and guided her up.

"Sit, sit here," said Elden pointing to a scoop in the top of the rock. "That is just made for sitting," he said. "You've had just about the worst weeks a girl can have, Jean. And I'm sorry," Elden said with such a sincerity Jean was taken aback.

"Thank you, Elden. I'm about condolenced out though, just wrung out from all the sadness," Jean confessed, taking a seat beside him.

"That's why I wanted to show you this, this whole place. It takes my sadness away every time I come out here. Just look at that," Elden said gesturing out towards the water.

Jean looked out over the lake. This did have to be the prettiest place in the world. A willow tree hung over one side of the rock making dappled shade. A stand of wild lavender grew on the other side. Untamed honeysuckle vined its way across the far side of the big rock. The view was vast. She could see across the lake and beyond to little farmsteads far, far away.

"Listen, be still and just listen. Close your eyes," Elden urged. Jean shut her eyes and listened to the water hitting the shore. The slightest breeze brought the sweet aroma of honeysuckle mixed with lavender. The sun warmed her and she could feel every part of her relaxing.

Relaxation. It was a feeling she hadn't had in many months. Elden watched Jean as she closed her eyes and rested. He could sense her muscles untensing, her smile so genuine. He'd never been around a girl like Jean, a girl who had no sense of pretense, who wasn't looking to impress or cut up. This girl was different. Maybe even a forever kind of different.

"You feel it? We're really somewhere now, aren't we, Jean?" he asked.

"It's the most perfect spot in the world, Elden. The city seems so far away," Jean said, her voice dreamy with wonder. "How did you ever find this place?"

"Pops bought this land when I was just a kid, maybe five years old. On Saturdays we used to drive out here, him and me. We'd sit here and fish. But that was years and years ago. Then he started with the hotel. He's too busy now, so I come here by myself. He knows I come out here when I need to figure things out. When I feel ... you know," Elden explained. His voice trailed off as he ended the sentence, weighing his choice of words and finding none to measure the loss Jean surely felt herself.

"It's nice he lets you still come, I guess," said Jean, sensing his empathy.

"Oh, he doesn't let me. Heck, he just up and gave it to me about a year ago, more or less," said Elden gesturing in a circle. "Of course, that was when they thought I was going to take on responsibilities, go into the military academy. Had a lot on my mind then. Wentworth Military is a big step. Serious. I knew he and Mother wanted me to go on. I'd come out here and just think those first months. It's quiet. Sometimes I just need somewhere to be still. But, I guess he's right. I should step up and do more for his businesses. Maybe even go back there and get my commission."

"I don't know, Elden. You're smart and you could do just about anything you want. What's the rush? Wentworth isn't packing up and moving away or anything," said Jean, troubled by the thought that Elden might move away.

Elden looked at her intently. "That's right, Jean, it's not. I may tell my mother that next time she starts in on me." Jean was pleased she'd helped Elden again with his mother, just like she had done that first day they'd met, when she assured him he was anything but uncouth.

"Just being here is nice. It's so peaceful and if you listen close, it's like I can hear water, like it's falling," Jean observed.

"Oh, that's right," said Elden with a start. "I haven't shown you the very best part yet. Come see." He jumped down from the rock on the side opposite from where they'd come and offered his hand to help her down.

She followed his lead as he headed past the big willow tree, taking a barely broken pathway away from the water and down a marshy area so wet that tiny ferns were growing.

Jean tried to keep up but her pretty dancing shoes sunk into the soft mud. Looking down, her shoes were filled with globs of wetness.

Elden rushed ahead. She thought for a second of turning back to salvage what she could of her shoes. Instead, she pulled them off her feet and wiped them on the inside hem of her dress, getting as much of the muck off them as she could. They were the last present she ever got from her mama. The buttery leather cleaned easily, and she breathed a deep sigh of relief. She decided to walk barefoot rather than ruin them.

Up ahead, Elden noticed she was missing and called out, "It's okay. It's worth it."

He stopped and waited for her to catch up. When she got to his side, Jean realized Elden had been right – it was worth it.

Before them was a pond with a miniature waterfall, not more than three feet tall, with water rushing down its round rocks. The falling water created a gentle mist that sprayed onto the lily pond resting at the foot of the fall. Tiny purple flowers rimmed the pond's edge and the smell of honeysuckle was everywhere.

Elden took a seat at the edge of the waterfall and pulled off his shoes. He patted the spot next to him, "Come dip your toes. It'll make you laugh," he said.

Jean gently put her shoes on the grass and took a seat on a flat stone next to Elden.

"Oh, I've ruined those but good, haven't I?" asked Elden, looking at her shoes caked with mud. "I'm sorry. If you rinse them off I'll dry them with my sweater," he volunteered.

"Oh, no, no," said Jean, "I couldn't do that. These cost way less than your sweater did. It'll be fine." *Elden clearly doesn't do his own shopping. No one would sacrifice an expensive sweater for a pair of shoes, even if they meant the world to her.* She smiled up at him, wondering what it must be like to live in his world.

"This place feels magical, doesn't it?" he asked, with the enthusiasm of a little boy.

"Magical. Yes, it's all magical," agreed Jean her voice quiet as she took in the soft colors and sounds, unfamiliar but so inviting. She felt a tension release from her shoulders, tension she hadn't realized she was carrying until it was gone.

"Sure is. I'm going to build my house out here someday. This will be my backyard, and the lake will be my front. Can't you just see it?" said Elden.

"Too good to be true, Elden. That would be too good to be true, but I thought you liked the city," Jean replied.

"I do," Elden began, his voice dropping and jaw line tightening. "Like it a little too much sometimes. Need some place to clear my head. It'd be a perfect place to build a home, I've thought. I figure my parlor will be in the front, looking over the lake, and then I'll have a bedroom here in the back and - look there, there are my rabbits," Elden said with a laugh as he pointed to two brown rabbits sitting in a thicket of purple flowers at the pond's edge, "and off the bedroom will be a little porch with a swing so I can sit and just watch the bunnies every day."

"When I first came out here there was only one little bunny, alone, its big brown eyes all wide and scared. Then one day I came and there were two bunnies and neither one looked scared anymore. Last spring there was a whole flock of bunnies and those two bunnies were older, hopping all over trying to keep the babies herded up. Do bunnies come in flocks, do you think or is it herds? Anyhow, they're like a regular family now, I guess. Yeah, I'll be sitting on that porch swing, growing old, watching those bunnies someday," Elden said wistfully.

"You are too much, Elden," said Jean with a laugh, but she was secretly bothered that she could already envision herself sitting in that porch swing, curled up by his side.

"Too much?" asked Elden looking over at her. "I'm too much, really?" His brow was furrowed and Jean wondered if she said the wrong thing.

"No. Just enough. You're just enough Elden, and you sure have big plans," Jean cajoled.

"Got to plan ahead to get ahead, that's what Pops says. I guess he's right, but sometimes planning makes me tired. I just want to do. Not think about things too much," said Elden.

How can such a carefree boy carry around such big thoughts? Jean wondered silently. "I'm all for doing. There's time enough to plan. Plans are for adults. We're young, right?" Jean offered.

"You have me all figured out, don't you? No one has ever done that before," said Elden, leaning over to plant a kiss, a soft and gentle kiss, not one of those struggle buggy kisses he got from the other girls. He stopped himself, aware that rushing could somehow spoil everything. For once, he chose to be patient.

Jean could feel his warmth as he neared and then felt the sudden break as a small breeze rushed between them when Elden pulled suddenly back. Within her, a wave of nervousness had built and then just as suddenly dissipated. *Would I have returned the kiss? My first kiss?* Jean pushed the question away, knowing the consequences her answer could carry.

"Better get back to the kids," Elden said, taking his feet from the water and giving them a shake. Jean looked up at him, smiling.

"Here, I'll help you up," he said, offering Jean his hand.

"Thank you for sharing this with me, Elden. It's the prettiest place on earth." Jean stood, both relieved and disappointed that Elden had curbed his instincts. She braced herself against his arm, tugging on her soiled slippers before they walked back to the picnic spot in a contented silence. There was no sign of Harold and Francie down by the lake.

"Bet they're dusting off the tires. Let's go check."

As they neared the road, Jean was pleased to see Francie and

Harold standing by the car and not off on a jaunt. Francie didn't share Harold's smile. Her arms were crossed and Harold was tossing the keys in the air.

"Well, let's get in the wheels and go. Did you take 'er out for a spin?" Elden called out as they approached the roadster.

"It was smooth, so slick. It takes curves and wow, did we go!" said Harold.

"Maybe next time we'll get a lesson on how to start it up without jerking all over the place," said Francie, "and he almost ran off the road. Didn't let me drive even once."

"But next time I will, Francie. I promise," said Harold sounding genuinely remorseful.

Francie's mock irritation dissolved and she gave him a soft punch in the arm. Harold put his arm around her as she let out a giggle. Jean was relieved to see her friend so carefree.

The foursome piled back into the car and Harold conspicuously nudged Jean to the front so he could sit in the back with Francie.

"A little hiccup starting up is normal, right Harry?" asked Elden, as he put his foot on the gas giving the car a purposeful jerk.

"How it's done, that's how it's done," said Harold beaming. Harold reached out to Francie, who smiled, took his hand without a word and gave it a squeeze.

Elden drove the long way through town, stopping to toot his horn at a group of friends in the park and wave to another cluster gathered in front of the ice cream shop. Jean waved with him, unaware that she was being observed, judged.

When they got back to Jean's apartment building, Harold jumped out of the car.

"Thanks, Elden. Great to meet you. I can't wait to get home to tell my brothers all about your car. This was terrific!" he gushed. Elden laughed good-naturedly as he opened the door for Jean to make her exit.

"I had a great time today," Jean said wistfully

"Me, too," volunteered Francie, "That was the most fun I've had in ages! And please tell your cook thank you for the picnic."

"Sure. And, hey, I was thinking, let's go to the ballgame next weekend. Monarchs. The colored team. They're playing down at the stadium and they put on a good show. Don't mind going to our colored team's game, do you Harold? Girls? Pick you up here next Sunday, say at one?"

Jean's heart skipped a beat. A third date; they were an item. He was elegant and worldly and really from somewhere and now, a third date.

Jean didn't stop to consider that Elden hadn't asked if she was free or had other plans. She couldn't quite name the feelings that stirred from his presumptuousness. Was it flattery and enticement because he wanted to be with her? Or was it surprise from his boldness and the entitlement he carried always? Either way, she chose not to analyze it and was left with just the feeling, the physical, the deep thumping of her heart.

Jean shut her eyes, trying to still the pace of her heartbeat and squeeze out the thought that she could not run upstairs and share this moment with Mama.

"Course we would," said Harold, answering for the trio.

"See you then! Toodle-loo!" said Elden, hopping back in the car and pulling away from the curb.

Jean grabbed Francie's hand as the car disappeared from sight. She said breathlessly, "Can you believe it, Francie? Can you believe it?"

"Oh, Jean, he's the cat's meow!" Francie exclaimed then her voice dropped to a whisper as she leaned toward Jean, "And Harold, Harold held my hand all the way home."

Jean clutched her friend's hand, still warm from Harold's damp touch, and smiled, quietly imagining the possibility of someday holding Elden's hand in her own.

10

Sunday morning arrived and waking early, Jean lolled in bed thinking of all the changes in her life. Work eased the sadness and the ladies at the hotel were all so considerate.

The League Ladies had clucked over her, offering pats and words of condolence. Mrs. Velmar had brought in a loaf of crusty pumpernickel bread and pot of beet soup that she insisted Jean should take right home, rather than share with the staff in the break room. The kindnesses softened the hours at work, making them bearable, but still it reminded her of all she had lost.

It was the walk home each evening that was hard, the anticipation of the silence when she opened the apartment door and then the hardest part would come, nightfall. She missed her mama most of all in the dark of night and found herself talking aloud in the evening, telling the stories of the day, as if her mama could somehow still hear her.

Last night she'd told the story of Elden and the lakeside picnic. Saying all the words out loud made it seem like her Mama knew, and her Poppa, too.

In the light of day, Jean knew such things were silly, on the edge of foolish maybe, but it made her feel better all the same.

Jean pulled herself out of bed, brewed a quick cup of tea as she dressed, and headed out for a dose of Miss Abby's cure, sunshine.

Jean opened her door and was greeted by the kitten, who sat expectantly, mewing loudly. She had coaxed the little kitten into her apartment a few times with sweet milk and tidbits of meat and fish, but as soon as she'd open the door again, the kitten would leap away.

Jean hurried to pour the kitten a saucer of milk and put it on the hallway floor. The kitten backed away with a tiny hiss.

"Next time, kitty. After I go you'll have this milk and next time you'll remember me even better," she said teasingly and bounded down the stairs. Otis met her in the lobby, a newspaper folded under his arm.

"Beautiful Sunday morning here, Miss Jean. You back to work this week?" asked Otis as he opened the door to the apartment house, the lines around his eyes crinkling in the sunshine.

"Went back last week. Two days. It was hard, Otis. Everyone said the right things, but the words are –" Jean's voice faltered for a second.

"I know, Miss. I know," Otis said tenderly.

"And the League Ladies tried to help, saying condolences. But each 'I'm so sorry' and slow shake of their head made me think more about Mama. One lady took me into her arms and said she'd never had her own daughter and she'd look after me. But Otis, I don't even really know her, not really. Some of those League Ladies seem to have laid claim to me somehow," Jean said.

"They mean well. Those ladies lay claim to all kinds of things, Miss Jean and it always turns out for the best. They took up a shine to you, so James tells me. Just let them fuss over you. It'll do you good now," Otis assured. "We all want the best for you. Heart takes time to heal. We older people, we've seen it all. Hurts to see sadness in the young. You do your part so we won't worry, okay?"

"What's my part, Otis?" Jean finally found the words to ask what she had wanted to know for weeks. "What will make this better? Some nights I don't want to even come home, it's so quiet."

"Course it is, Miss Jean. And you shouldn't be alone so. Not good for a young girl. You see that Nowak girl, Francie, still?"

Jean nodded as Otis continued, "And you're getting out some, with the Whitcomb boy I hear?"

Jean wondered if it really was too soon to be going out and felt she owed Otis an explanation.

"Francie told me it was time, Otis. I thought it was too soon to have any fun, get out at all, but now I think Francie was right. Elden took me out to the country. Outside of the city, Otis. It was like walking away from my sadness for the afternoon."

"It's good for you then," Otis said, nodding his head.

"And he drove so fast and the wind whipped our hair. He showed me the lake and today we're going to see the Monarchs play. Can you believe it? I think Mama would be pleased. She liked the idea of Elden, I think," said Jean, remembering the smile on her mama's face as she'd described dinner at the Savoy Grill. "And today we'll go to the ballgame. Is James playing?" Jean asked, her words tumbling out as her excitement began to build.

"Well now, that is something. Yes, James plays today. We'll see you there maybe, Abby and I. And I imagine everyone will see you there," said Otis, patting the newspaper, under his arm. "So, you're seeing that Whitcomb boy again? His parents, are they going with you, too? Well, his father anyway?"

"Oh, I have no idea. I forget all about that chaperone thing. It seems so old fashioned," said Jean, biting her lip.

"Not somethin' to forget, Miss Jean. Not to forget that," Otis cautioned, unfolding the newspaper, open to the society page. "Not ever somethin' to forget," he finished, handing Jean the paper.

Jean read the headline out loud, "*Whitcomb Wanderings*. What's this, Otis? Are we in the paper! Oh, Mama would be so proud, Otis! So proud!"

Otis shut his eyes and shook his head back and forth slowly at her naiveté.

"Read on," he sighed.

"Which Whitcomb shared whispers with a wispy, raven-haired

beauty?" Jean read aloud. "I'm not wispy, am I? And raven-haired, now, I don't think so. It's definitely more brown than that. But maybe from a distance ... oh, wait. Oh, maybe this isn't so good," said Jean, dropping to take a seat on the front steps.

∼

*A*t the Whitcomb home, Mr. Whitcomb carefully put his coffee cup back on the saucer and silently turned the thin pages of the Sunday *Kansas City Star*, knowing better than to acknowledge his wife's presence before she'd had her Saturday night chaser, vodka with a splash of orange juice.

Katherine Whitcomb cinched the sash of her silk dressing gown, gingerly taking a chair at the breakfast table, her hand tremoring as she reached for the juice glass.

"My page," she said, teeth clenched.

Mr. Whitcomb raised one eyebrow as his wife brought the juice glass to her lips and then he peeled off the society news and handed it to her without a glance.

Mrs. Whitcomb grimaced. "A wispy creature this time? And you shared whispers? Really? Even I thought better of you," she said, her acerbic tone undisguised.

Wild-eyed, Mr. Whitcomb reached for the paper, hoping to plausibly deflect the accusation. The issue with that Cassandra Lee girl had just been taken care of, quietly, or so it had seemed. A little hush money and secure job should have taken care of her anyway. It certainly never should have made the society page again, for heaven's sake.

"Wispy? Wispy raven?" questioned Mr. Whitcomb, unable to hide his puzzled look. Elden entered the room and found his father leaning over the table, muttering to himself, his mother's face dark with a hungover fury.

"The society page is doing it again, Elden. 'Whitcombs Wanderings'. I just can't take this again," Mrs. Whitcomb intoned.

Elden reached over his father's outstretched arm and grabbed the page. "So, did I make the paper or was it you again this time, Pops?" Elden asked loudly.

"Must I be the only member of this family with a sense of decorum? Keep it in your pants and out of the paper. That's all I ask, gentlemen," she said, putting one hand to her temple as if to rub out her pounding headache. Mrs. Whitcomb shook her head and brought the orange juice to her parched lips.

Elden studied the society section, his brow furrowed. "Cripes! How did they already find out about Jean? Must have been that group at the ice cream parlor and we haven't even had a third date yet. Well, I guess they'll have a heyday with us going out again today," he chuckled.

Mr. Whitcomb let out a quiet sigh. The news was not about Cassandra Lee after all, his own dalliance that led to such scandal awhile back. "Have a new one, son?" he asked, obviously pleased he didn't have to jump to his own defense and battle his wife over the issue again.

"Jean. Oh, she's a fine girl. Simple. No pretenses. Not worried about the society page either," Elden scoffed, handing the paper back to his mother.

"Well, thank God it's not you again," Mrs. Whitcomb said, addressing her husband. She took the paper from Elden's hands, "And you, Elden, just don't screw up again. I hope she's a good girl this time, from a good family. That'd be something different. I just ask that you give me a break from the drama. The Good Lord knows I can't keep fixing the problems you two create," said Mrs. Whitcomb, pushing away from her empty glass and rising from the table.

~

After morning Mass, Francie hurried to Jean's. She knocked on the apartment door with one hand as she clutched in the other matching drop-waist dresses and little bows for their hair.

"Mother stayed up all night sewing them. Aren't they perfect?" Francie exclaimed as Jean opened the door. "And did you see the paper? People are talking about you and Elden already. Mother says its petty news but I think it's incredible."

"It is incredible. Elden is so kind and, sort of, I don't know, mature. He makes me feel safe," said Jean with a satisfied smile. She'd held Elden in her thoughts all week. At work, every time the elevator door opened she imagined he would be there, step in and take her in his arms. And now the day had finally come when she would see him again. She wanted everything to be perfect.

"The dresses are darling, Francie. We'll look dashing," Jean said as she turned over her shoes, checking for any remnants of dirt. She had scrubbed them carefully after the mud fiasco and deemed them immaculate.

At noon Harold knocked on the apartment door. He wore a white long-sleeved shirt, bow tie and pleated trousers.

"You look dreamy, Harold, just dreamy." said Francie, as she opened the door.

"You, too. You, too," he replied taking Francie's hand and giving her a twirl. "Hey, you, there, Miss Society Page, you're looking particularly wispy today," he joked. Jean blushed. The trio's merriment was cut short when they heard a distinctive car horn and dashed downstairs.

"Right on time, gang!" called Elden, "Top's down on the roadster." As they drove to the ballfield, Elden was full of talk but didn't say a word about the story in the newspaper and Jean thought it might be untoward to draw attention to it.

"Gals don't often go to these games, you know, but we won't sit with the colored. You know my Pops does sometimes. Just for the statement, he says. But that's not for us," Elden said, "No controversy today. Got a good team there, the Monarchs."

"I've never seen them play. Hear the Monarchs play good ball," said Harold. "I just play pickup games myself."

"Oh, Pops loves baseball. Loves the game. He and Mr. Donaldson have done a lot to support the team. They wouldn't have done a thing without a push from ole' Rube Foster." said Elden.

Everyone in town knew that Rube Foster was an excellent pitcher who had set up the Negro League in Kansas City. He had convinced a few wealthy businessmen that the Monarchs would be a winning team. His foresight and business sense were unparalleled.

"Of course, those League Ladies got their pantaloons in a stitch about it all, how it was progressive and good for the City to be forward-thinking. So they put their minds to getting investors and all. There were lots of reasons Pops decided to throw in his support, well, his dollars anyway," Elden explained.

"One of the League Ladies said the visiting teams should even stay in our hotel, but no one's ready for that yet," he continued.

It was true that all public accommodations in the city from the restaurants to the hotels, everything, were segregated. Some people thought it enough that colored men were allowed to play on the white team's ballfield and others boycotted the stadium when it came to be. But the stands seemed to be filled, mostly filled, despite the controversy.

"Team's got some good players. Going to attract a lot of people, Pops says," explained Elden.

"'Course not everybody thinks they should play on the white field," volunteered Harold.

"Oh, yeah, that was big news at first, wasn't it?" said Elden, "Got all the newspaper men weighing in on that one."

"Church people, too," said Harold, remembering the discussion around his own family's dinner table.

"Pops shut that talk down pretty quick though. No other place in the city made any sense and there's no money to build a colored stadium. Wouldn't pay for itself. Issue settled. Still, once in a while a rough-houser shows up at a game to make trouble. Or I make it myself, trouble that is," Elden laughed brusquely.

"Trying not to do that anymore. Pops says I gotta watch my temper. Just be aware. I don't want you to get caught off-guard if someone makes a tough remark. His people take care of things at the game though. He wants no trouble," Elden assured, unaware of the look Harold was giving the girls, as if to caution them.

Jean held her tongue but felt a trickle of dread crawling up her spine. Elden did take a drink or two, or three. Rumors were he drove like a 'lead-footed jackass,' one of the hotel workmen had said in the break room, and then there had been talk that he had gotten into more than one brawl. Jean had brushed aside those rumors as idle gossip, but now it was apparent they may have carried some truth.

Harold listened to Elden's talk about his father, the racial issues the city had faced when the Negro League came to town, and the trouble that ensued as the issues were debated around town, from the church pulpits to the countertops at the corner bars.

More than one fight had broken out when the social boundaries began to blur. Harold nodded his head, having heard all sides of the issue before.

People knew Elden's father pushed the social limits with his business decisions but only for the purposes of making a buck. Talk of Mr. Whitcomb's choices weren't uncommon, Harold knew. In his own house – his father was always going on about the have and the have-nots, the workers and the bourgeoisie, the plight of the workers, and the immigrant whites. Harold had learned to tune it out and nod politely when his father and older brothers started those conversations. He'd not yet seen a connection to his own life and all the talk seemed indulgent. It didn't change who had the money or who had to work and who got to own.

"Negro League started here in Kansas City just this year, didn't it?" asked Harold, wanting to keep the subject matter light.

"Sure did. Like I said, that was Rube Foster. Made that happen. Big man, lots of business sense. Acumen, Pops calls it. Now they'll get teams all over the country. The games are fun. Some have a show they put on before the game that the crowd thinks is pretty good too, with clowns. Some come out wearing grass skirts and bring out drums. Quite the show. Some people may come just for that. But it's insulting."

"I hope James isn't clowning today. I don't think that would seem right," said Jean, feeling a little pensive. She'd never given much thought to all the deep resentments some whites had and it made her uneasy to think about it on this pretty day.

"James? Oh, sure, James. He's a great player. Works as our doorman at the hotel," said Elden. "Good man. No, he's not a clown. Clowns, they play ball but not usually the first inning. James always bats first thing. No, the clowns, they're just for entertainment. Makes the crowd laugh; loosens them up. Pops said the whites probably wouldn't come without something like that. Too hard for some people to think of colored men as able, you know, as good as white athletes. Clowns break that ice, Pops says."

"Are there shows before the white games, too?" asked Jean naively, having never been to a colored or white teams' baseball game before.

"Gosh no," said Elden without hesitation. "Whites wouldn't pay to see professional white ballplayers act like clowns, making fools of themselves, now, would they?" he asked.

"Reckon not," said Harold, puzzling over this realization.

Jean had never thought of things that way but supposed that Elden and Harold were exactly right. Color did define much of life in the city. It explained Otis' formality, how he "Miss'ed" and "Ma'am'ed" herself and Mama, and didn't want to be seen as getting too familiar. It explained how Otis' words would get hushed if a white man approached the apartment house.

Jean had tried to talk to her mama about these things once, but her mama frowned and shook her head saying it was just the way things were and making a fuss wouldn't change it.

Elden pulled into the parking lot, a patch of dirt flooded with cars, and was waved right up front by a flagman. The Whitcombs apparently had parking spots reserved at the entrance.

Once at the gate, Elden just nodded to the ticket-taker who motioned for them to go on through the turnstile. No ticket, no problem. Jean shook her head as she watched the cavalier way Elden breezed past the ticket-taker. It made her feel uncomfortable, not acknowledging the man working there.

"Thank you," she said as she passed through the turnstile.

"No need to thank me. That family built this stadium. The boy can bring whoever he wants in here, so they tell me," said the worker, as he pulled a loose thread from his tattered jacket. "Makes no never mind to me."

Jean turned that thought over in her head. *Such entitlement,* she thought as she watched Elden striding up the ramp. *It doesn't seem quite right.*

The stadium was freshly painted and the lacquer smell lingered in the area. On the wall was a hand-painted sign with an arrow marked 'Whites Only' directing which way to go. The two couples made their way up the ramp and found seats. The pre-game entertainment was already underway, with clowns playing baseball and, like Elden had said, some wore skirts and beat on drums.

"How can they play baseball to a drumbeat like that? See, that man is throwing the ball every time the drum beats," observed Jean, awestruck.

"Practice. They must practice hours every day," said Harold.

"About every day. Most have other jobs they do, too. Colored teams don't pay enough for a full living yet," said Elden, "but it'll happen someday, Pops says. I say athletes are athletes. No reason white and colored should be different. Drink, Harry?" asked Elden, taking his flask out from his pocket.

Elden had made no attempt to hide his drinking. Harold took the offered flask but Francie gave Harold a scolding look. They may be at a ballgame, but rules were rules and it was still a Sunday, after all. Harold quickly handed the flask back to Elden.

"Not right for me, Elden. Man has to be the moral leader of his family and my dad said I need to start thinking that way," Harold said puffing out his chest and casting his eyes toward Francie. Elden followed his gaze.

"Family?" Elden whispered raising an eyebrow toward Francie.

"Maybe. If I do everything right, Dad says," Harold confided.

"Don't let me stand in the way of that then," Elden shrugged as he passed the flask to the men sitting behind them.

The men had their shirt sleeves rolled up and seemed to be overly relaxed even for mid-day on Sunday, having apparently partaken of a few beers of their own before the game.

Jean watched the interaction with care, relieved Elden didn't offer the flask to her. Francie observed what was going on and gave Jean a look with pursed lips. It was Francie's "he's going straight to Hell" look.

Jean disregarded both the look and the growing intoxication all around them but sensed she was seeing a pattern established. Elden was never without a flask and was so nonchalant about it as if he were above the laws barring liquor. Public, private, it made no difference to him. Somehow, to Elden, the rules seemed not to apply. Jean considered this for a moment.

Was it because he was rich and a Whitcomb, of the Kansas City Whitcombs, as he'd declared that day in the elevator, or was it because the liquor was a need, was somehow his anchor in the world?

Her thoughts were broken by the opening strands of the National Anthem played over the loud speaker. The crowd stood as the anthem played and the game began. Jean let the sounds of the opening of the game sweep away her thoughts and she concentrated on the game before her. Smack! The bat connected with the ball on the first pitch and James ran to first base and then second. The second batter made it to base and then James came across home plate.

"This is even more exciting than I thought it would be," Jean said to Elden.

"Gotta watch every minute. It goes so fast," said Elden, not taking his eyes off of the field. The next ball went into the stands, a long home run. Elden leaped to catch it, and all but grabbed it right out of the hand of a shirt-sleeved man behind them.

Elden's laughter rang through the stands, and Jean was happier than she had been since Mama's passing. Her happiness grew even bigger when Elden ceremoniously presented the baseball to her.

"Oh, thank you," she said breathlessly. "Thank you."

"Now you'll always remember this day," Elden said.

"I never could forget it, no matter what," Jean replied.

Jean looked around the half-full stadium. She spied Miss Abby sitting with Otis in the Colored Section nearby. She gave a vigorous wave, forgetting the social prohibitions on engaging a colored person in public.

Miss Abby was looking right at her but seemed to be clearly ignoring her. Jean waved again. Miss Abby put up one hand and started to wave back, but quickly dropped her hand as a veiled look came over her face. She shook her head twice at Jean who tilted her head, narrowed her eyes, and tried to figure out just what Miss Abby was communicating.

One of the shirt-sleeved men behind Jean called out "Girl's waving to colored folk. Got yourself a colored lover do you, Elden?"

Before Jean could turn around to see who had been so unforgivably rude, Elden hauled off and hit the man directly across the chin. The man fell back over his wooden seat and Elden jumped on top of him, fists flying.

~

Mr. Whitcomb had taken a seat in the stadium minutes before the game began. He sat further up in the stands where he could see the entire field and all of the seats. He had observed his son enter with a group, take a seat, and then begin his drinking.

"Another Whitcomb Whistlewetter," Mr. Whitcomb muttered under his breath, unable to stop himself from drawing the comparison between his wife and son as the society page had done last year.

Mr. Whitcomb trained his eyes back on his son, then studied the boy's companions. No question, Elden had found the naïve little elevator girl. Precisely the kind of girl his mother had this very morning cautioned against. Not from a good family. But maybe such a girl wouldn't be trouble. Like Cassandra Lee, she'd just be glad for a moment of a Whitcomb man's attention. Then she'd go quietly when Elden was through with her, never realizing she was entitled to a fuss.

Or maybe Elden wouldn't push this one aside so fast. This girl, the elevator operator, was a smart one, able to think on her feet, and she had undoubtedly come into favor with the League Ladies. But all of that would amount to nothing as far as his wife was concerned.

Knowing that mingling with the help so publicly would set his wife off for sure, Mr. Whitcomb surveyed the crowd for the Star's society page reporter. He breathed a sigh of relief when he found the man's seat vacant.

Mr. Whitcomb turned his attention back to the game but kept one eye on Elden and soon noticed the disruption that broke out in his boy's section. It wasn't the first time Elden had been at the center of a brawl, and most always it was of his own instigation.

With a single nod, Mr. Whitcomb called for his strongest two men, the enforcers. He gave them instructions and quickly dispatched them to quiet things down. Whitcomb's men attended all the home games, white and colored, and were responsible for crowd control. The men knew their orders - to settle disruptions as discreetly as possible. Any disruption, any bad publicity, and game revenues would fall. Then he'd have to re-argue just why it was acceptable for colored and white teams to share a stadium.

Everyone was worried about the social mixing of colored and white, but to the Whitcomb way of thinking, it was just a matter of commerce, dollars and sense. People could try to separate the race issue from the economics, but eventually, money always won out, Mr. Whitcomb reasoned.

Change meant dollars and the sooner people accepted it, the better. It wasn't a rationale everyone shared and often the ballgames were interrupted by liquored-up white boys. He had told his son, again and again, these were not his battles to fight. But, yet again, his son didn't have sense enough to stop himself, step out of the way of an oncoming fist.

Mr. Whitcomb's two security men wasted no time getting to the center of the fight. One hauled the offending man out. The other man made it clear to Elden, in no uncertain terms, that his presence was no longer required in the stadium.

"Go on, Elden. You've caused enough trouble here, again. Another fight. This time even your dad's suggested you leave. He said to tell you to 'keep that temper in check, dammit,'" said his dad's man, "And that's a quote."

Harold overheard the man and looked at the girls nervously. Before Harold could give Francie a word of warning, Elden dusted off his trousers, straightened his tie and shrugged his shoulders.

"Come on, let's get out of here, let's go somewhere," Elden called gruffly to the trio as he moved toward the stairs, rubbing his sore hand. Harold stood and motioned for the girls to follow.

Jean felt shame and emptiness forming a tight ball in the pit of her stomach and followed the group out. She knew better than to embarrass Abby and Otis in public and she had brought Elden to a terrible place of having to defend her behavior. But, his anger was not misplaced. He was right to stand up for her. *But did he have a temper and what did it mean 'another fight'?*

Jean took one look back as she ascended the stairs back into the stadium. She could feel the eyes of Abby and Otis burning through her. Francie, walking ahead of Jean, reached back and took her by the hand, saying nothing as their footsteps echoed on the concrete.

"Are you okay, Elden? Your hand is bleeding," Jean observed as they reached the car, her voice shaking.

"It's nothing. Forget it. Let's go somewhere," replied Elden.

"Go somewhere? After this? We're going home," Francie declared righteously. "We have no business in a place like this, men drinking and fighting. We know better, don't we, Harold?" Harold nodded. "And Jean, you too. Besides, we really do have to get back. I have to help with dinner tonight. Your parents are coming, aren't they, Harold?" Francie asked, changing the subject from the fray they'd experienced to something more civil.

Tonight was Francie's first dinner with her family and Harold's family. Francie's mother had shooed her out of the house early, knowing she'd fret and fuss.

"Sure, I'll drop you off at your place, Francie. You too, Harold. It's on the way to somewhere, right?" said Elden as he opened the glove box and retrieved a handkerchief to wrap his wounded hand. He held his hand out to Jean.

He needs me, Jean thought as she tenderly wrapped his hand, pulling the bandage taut to stop the bleeding. He smiled and took her hand in his, giving it a gentle squeeze. A heat rose from Jean's core as she held Elden's hand. He felt true and strong and had protected her today.

On the drive to Francie's house, Jean tried to lighten the atmosphere and pretty soon Harold and Elden were laughing as if nothing unusual had occurred, but the air was still thick with tension.

Francie sat with her arms folded across her chest, looking out the car window into the far distance, silent. No one spoke of the fight or whether Elden was right to react with his fists instead of words. Elden drove to Francie's house to drop her and Harold home first.

"Thank you, Elden. Sorry this didn't go quite as planned," said Harold as they pulled up to the front of Francie's house.

"Now, Jean, Mother asked that you come for dinner tonight. A full Sunday dinner. Six o'clock, okay?" said Francie. She pointedly did not extend the invitation to Elden.

"Wouldn't miss it," said Jean, knowing how important this dinner was to Francie. "I'll see you then. Tell your mother thank you," replied Jean, hoping to appease her friend.

"I'll have her back before six, Francie, don't you worry. We'll just take a drive," said Elden, "See you around, Harry!" Jean could see her girlfriend's jaw set in a silent fury at Elden's off-hand dismissal.

"Thanks, Elden. It would have been a great game, for sure," said Harold, politely as he turned away. Harold tucked his arm around Francie and walked her up the steps to her house. Jean watched them walk away. A perfect couple.

11

*A*fter turning off Francie's street, Elden seemed more himself, relaxed again. The tension was gone from his face and his jaw line wasn't as tight, Jean noticed.

"Sorry for what happened today. I just get so angry sometimes. People who are wrong acting like they know everything and that their way is right. But I shouldn't have gotten angry. There are places where people don't think that way, you know. Chicago, New York, Paris, somewhere like that, even some places here in the city," Elden said expansively.

"I should have known better."

"No. It's not a crime to be civil. To wave at a friend. People here are just backwards. It's not like Paris, Chicago. You know. Sophisticated."

Jean shook her head. She couldn't envision any city where there wasn't a racial divide, where the rules weren't etched in stone. She'd read about other cities, about Paris, with its beauty and art and riches.

Elden continued, "Chicago is a beaut'. Skyscrapers there are as tall as you can see. New York City is awake at all hours. There are restaurants with red carpets out front. And April, Paris was made for

April. There's a world to see out there, you know. It's not all small minded, tight rules. Or at least it shouldn't be."

Jean didn't know, not really. "I can't imagine," was all she could muster, her mind spinning with his ideas. Elden started to say more, about how people were just people all over the world, about how money seemed to muddle things up and create divisions for no good reason.

He looked at the sweet young woman sitting beside him and knew she wouldn't understand his words any more than his parents or his friends back at Wentworth did. But, he thought, maybe if he could bring her into his world, show her the one place where wealth and stature didn't matter, where the rules didn't apply and people could just be themselves.

"Can't go to Paris today. Today, though, we should go somewhere," Elden quipped.

"Somewhere? Kansas City is somewhere, isn't it?" she asked with a laugh.

"Yeah. Kansas City. Some call it Paris on the Plains with its big old fountains and all, but most of this town is nowhere. Tonight we're going somewhere, a place you'll never find and only I can show you," Elden said cryptically, "You'll see."

"You confound me, Elden. We're somewhere right now, 11th and Grand, in fact," said Jean, pointing to the street sign.

"Oh, we're somewhere now, but I know somewhere better. Just you wait," said Elden, enjoying his word game. He turned the car down an alley behind Grand Street where the workers entered the garment factories. It was all cobblestone and garbage bins, no people on a Sunday afternoon. On Sundays even the garment workers had the day off.

"Here we are, Somewhere!" Elden declared as he pulled the car in next to a brick building.

All Jean could see was a plain, gray door by a metal garbage bin. That door clearly led nowhere Jean wanted to go. Jean looked at Elden skeptically as he opened her car door and offered his hand.

For a second, Jean began to wonder if Elden was a bit daft. There were no other cars or people in sight. For a slight few seconds, Jean felt a mild panic as Elden approached the gray door and knocked twice. Jean stood behind him looking hesitantly up and down the empty street.

"Friend of Jake," Elden said tipping back his hat.

"Dame?" a male voice asked from behind the closed door.

"I vouch. She's with me, Alonzo," replied Elden.

The door opened and Elden motioned to Jean to follow him. They entered a hallway – long and dark, illuminated by a single bulb. A man stood by the open door but quickly shut it as they entered. He looked neither friendly nor particularly presentable, Jean observed.

"Yes, sir, sir, g'on back," the man said, lifting his chin in the direction of the hallway. It felt a little spooky walking into the darkness and a tingle of excitement edged down Jean's back as she followed Elden past the scruffy man.

At the end of the hallway on the right was a swinging door with a porthole window. Elden swung the door open wide to reveal a smoky, windowless room. Jean was surprised to see a crowd of people inside, a huge party in fact. There were a dozen tiny tables covered with glasses, half-filled and half-empty, and each table was crammed with three or four people.

A piano player sat at an old upright piano to the side. The dark air was thick and smoky. It was a bar, a bar like the ones that were raided and written up in the newspaper. Jean felt a wave of nausea race through her. The last thing she needed was to call Francie from a jail cell.

Jean reached out for Elden's hand, ready to ask him to take her home, but he was no longer by her side.

"Elden!" "Atta boy! Come on over." "Missed you last night." "Pick your poison, have a seat." Jean couldn't make out who all was talking, just faceless voices. Elden smiled, electrified by the attention.

"Somewhere. This is the best place in the whole city, don't you think?" Elden called to her, pride apparent as he looked at Jean expectantly. Elden looked at ease in the dimly lit bar, surrounded by noise and people of all walks of life. Jean's discomfort was growing.

"That's the name of this place? Somewhere?" asked Jean, taking a few steps forward to be by Elden's side. She felt unsteady, out of place, and didn't want to be left alone. *He'll protect me at least,* thought Jean glancing down at Elden's bandaged hand.

"Somewhere. That's it. What a gas, huh?" said Elden excitedly, "Have a seat. Let me get us some drinks."

Elden disappeared into the horde. Jean looked around at the massive crowd. There was a motley group of college boys, dressed in prep sweaters, a few rough men she definitely would have avoided on the street and a woman sitting alone and drinking fast.

Jean was fixated, watching the woman. She looked both lonely but oddly comfortable, at home in the dark bar. Jean shifted on her feet, feeling obvious standing alone in the crowd. She cast around for an empty seat and spied a chair next to the woman sitting all alone.

Jean tried to catch the woman's eye as if to ask if she could join her table. The woman noticed and gave a nod, tilting her head toward the empty chair. Jean was grateful for the silent offer and nervously smoothed her dress as she took a seat.

"Smoke?" said the woman offering Jean a pack of Camel cigarettes, her eyes a little unfocused.

There was a slight lilt to the woman's voice, but Jean couldn't quite place the accent. Jean thought for a minute and looked at the offered cigarette: three sins in one day – fighting, drinking, and smoking. Saint Peter would be erasing her name from his Good Book for sure. But would a refusal be rude? she wondered.

Carry yourself with dignity, Jean thought, recalling one of Mama's cardinal rules. Certainly Mama never imagined her little girl contemplating the nuances of dignity while standing in an illegal juke joint being offered a cigarette, Jean thought.

Jean really wasn't sure of the social protocols that applied in a speakeasy so, without a proper bearing on how to extricate herself quickly, she chose the path of least resistance.

"Sure," said Jean taking the cigarette, unlit.

Elden returned, smiling wide, with three tall glasses filled with crushed ice, clear liquid and a slice of lime. It smelled like a Christmas tree but looked like water.

"Water?" asked Jean, holding up the glass.

"Fire water," said Elden with a laugh. "One sip and you'll see why it's called it that." Jean held the glass gingerly, considering the options. She didn't want to seem like a prude, but drinking was wrong and illegal at that.

He made everything look so easy, so right. He had all the possibilities Jean had only dreamt of, and he was including her in those possibilities by entrusting her with the knowledge of Somewhere. Jean hesitated, uncertain what the right response should be.

Elden seemed oblivious to her dilemma. He seemed to be looking right at her but not seeing that she was quaking inside. Elden, who got everything he wanted so easily, looking at her with a mischievous grin, playfully daring her to be a part of his life. She put the glass to her lips and took a small sip. It burned her lips but wasn't totally putrid.

"Ah, see, not so bad. The next drink won't burn at all," said Elden. "People make such a fuss about the first time. Glad you're not one of those." Jean knew it was wrong to feel any pride in Elden's words but to have endorsement meant everything. Elden downed his glass and took up a second.

"Hey, let me introduce you around," he said. "I see you've met Collette."

"No, actually not," Jean replied.

"Collette, may I present Miss Virginia Ball. But she lets me call her Jean," Elden beamed.

Collette gave him a quizzical look. "Collette," said the woman pointing to herself with her cigarette. "Smoke, Elden?" she asked, offering the pack of cigarettes to Elden.

"Sure, kiddo," he said taking a cigarette and pulling a silver lighter from his pocket. Jean noticed it was engraved with the crest of the Empire Hotel. Did the Whitcombs have to set a mark on absolutely everything? she wondered.

Collette took the lighter from Elden. "Watch," Collette said to

Jean. She lit her cigarette, drew in the smoke and carefully blew a smoke ring into the air above her, "Now you," she said handing the lighter towards Jean.

"Here, doll, now just let me do that for you," said Elden giving Collette a frown and taking the lighter from her hand. Collette shrugged and picked up her half empty glass. "Another war injury there, Elden?" she asked, pointing to his injured hand.

"As they say, you should see the other guy," boasted Elden. Collette just shook her head. Jean disregarded the exchange, not wanting to remember the recklessness she'd seen in Elden just an hour before.

Jean looked around the room, soaking in the atmosphere – the music, the dusky air, the smell of gin. She felt her body starting to relax, first her shoulders then her back. She took another drink.

Sophistication, she thought. Yes, she felt quite sophisticated sitting with a drink and holding a smoldering cigarette. The smoke burned, the drink burned, but neither was a particularly unpleasant kind of heat. The smoke did hurt her throat though. She took several deep drinks from her glass. In no time, Jean's stomach felt queasy and then the room seemed to tilt.

"I think I'm, I think I'm -- " began Jean.

Before she could get out the word "unwell," Elden interrupted, "Hey, I'll be right back," he said, patting Jean on the back as he spotted a friend across the crowded bar. Jean was left alone with Collette.

"Not feeling great?" asked Collette, "Feeling a little green maybe?" Jean nodded limply.

"Did you eat today?" Collette asked, her head tilted in concern.

Jean shook her head no. She hadn't eaten since breakfast which had just been a slice of dry toast, then she'd been too excited thinking about the ballgame to bother to eat lunch.

"I'll order you something. Perry sells his barbecue right next door. Some good food will soak up that gin," offered Collette kindly. She called over a colored man, said something and handed him a quarter.

Jean sat, numb. She couldn't clear her head to focus on what was going on around her.

Within minutes a stack of sliced meat on white bread, all wrapped in butcher paper, was placed before her with a small red and white checkered cloth and glass of water. The sandwich was the best thing Jean had ever tasted – lean and smoky and warm. She ate every morsel then took a big gulp of the water. The room slowly stopped quivering.

"Thank you. That helps," she said to Collette as she wiped her fingers on the thin cloth. "What was that called again? And did you see where Elden went?"

"Elden? Oh, he won't be back for awhile. So that was your first barbecue, was it? It's one of the best things about this city, from what I can see. Perry sells it to the garment workers mainly but I like it too. So you feel better now?" Collette asked, as she reached up and rubbed Jean's back. Jean appreciated the sisterly touch and began to relax again.

"Thank you. I don't know what I would have done if you hadn't – " said Jean.

"Oh, it's nothing. Happened to me the first time when I didn't have sense enough to eat," said Collette, half-shuddering at the memory.

"Do you think Elden's ready to go?" Jean asked, looking around the room for her date. She spied Elden across the room. Someone was handing him another full glass and the piano player began to pound out a ragtime jazz. The center of the bar filled with couples doing a funny dance with their arms flapping and feet moving to the four/four beat.

"I think I'd better go," said Jean to Collette, as she rose to her feet.

"Oh, sit down. Don't bother. Elden hasn't even started his night," said Collette. "You dance?"

"Not like that," said Jean looking at the dancers. "I can foxtrot and all, but that's about it," replied Jean as she drank down the last of the gin.

"Got to learn the Charleston if you want to be with Elden. The piano player was teaching it here last week. He learned it from his brother. They play in the colored jazz clubs down on Vine. It's the next big thing." Collette stood up and took Jean's hand.

"Oh no, I couldn't," said Jean.

Collette looked over at Elden who was watching the two girls with a smile.

"I think you can," said Collette looking at Jean and then darting her eyes in Elden's direction. Jean turned and looked over at Elden. He was nodding his head yes, as if to say "Go on and try it." *Who am I to tell him no?* Jean thought. Collette led Jean to the makeshift dance floor and guided her through the steps.

"Doing fine. Just need a little instruction. Watch this," Collette said moving her feet to the four/four beat.

∾

Collette had watched the childlike woman since the minute Jean had entered the bar. She had quickly sized up the girl in the homemade cotton dress and knew this one would need to toughen up quick if she expected to run with Elden's crowd.

Collette had seen many young girls come, stay a few hours and leave either in a huff, for being objectified by Elden, or in tears, for the few never exposed to this kind of decadence. Elden couldn't see that they actually cared for him. Worse, on nights when he was really drinking, Elden couldn't see that it actually mattered. Those were the nights he got loud, looking for a fight. And those were the weeks when Mrs. Whitcomb would send over the maid four or five times for refills on the gin decanters. Collette had seen the pattern that Elden could not, or would not, see.

But then sometimes the tougher girls wouldn't leave in a huff. They were the girls who stayed and stayed, beyond their welcome. The ones who got sloppy and couldn't see that their play-value had long worn out.

Collette had seen some girls stay on weeks after the boys had plainly lost their interest. Those were the girls who grew deep circles under their eyes from long nights and cold gin, the ones who needed a nudge to go on.

Collette had been one of those girls, not with Elden, but with a boy long ago. And she'd made the wrong decision, had chosen not to leave.

Maybe she'd take this girl under her wing and Elden would finally commit to something, end the cycle of drinking and fights and the endless stream of pretty girls who meant nothing. Maybe she could help. That'd be something different.

"You got some rhythm," Collette observed, "Gonna hang here, you got to know how to move. And that dress, I can help. It'll never do. Hope you don't mind if I say so, but it looks like your mama dressed you today," Collette said, mincing no words.

The stranger's words were harsh, but Jean knew better than to show offense. "Elden likes this," Jean said. "He took me out for a picnic and my parents, well, they don't even know," she finished, having quickly sized up Collette and calculated how to impress. Jean bit her lip and tried to suppress the immediate guilt of betrayal she felt. How had she disrespected Mama so, so quickly?

"Yeah, parents, they don't matter here. Parents. They're something else. And of course you know about Elden's. He has his hands full with both of his," volunteered Collette.

"Oh, sure. I've met them. His mother, now she's something else," said Jean, relieved to find a diversion.

"Oh, yeah," said Collette, "His Papa makes the money and his Mama spends it up and drinks it down. She won't come in here, but you can bet her maid or her cook comes by for her refills three times a week. Five on her bad weeks."

Jean could easily envision Mrs. Whitcomb, the tippling Katherine, doing just that, but she couldn't think about that right now. The dancing was taking a toll. Her head was spinning as well as her stomach and a wave of nausea overtook her.

"I think I might retch," Jean said to Collette, stumbling to a full stop.

"You need some air. Come on," Collette said, heading Jean

towards the door. They walked out the swinging door and down the dark hallway.

"We'll be back," said Collette to the doorman, and together they exited through the grey door. Jean had forgotten it was the middle of the afternoon and the light made her feel worse.

"When you close that door you'd never guess what goes on behind there, would you?" asked Collette, still holding Jean by the arm as the door shut behind them. "Now let's walk."

Jean tried to get her bearings and make polite conversation as they started down the cobblestone alley.

"So, these are all over the city?" asked Jean, trying to focus on the here and now.

" 'Spect so, but you get your favorite where they know you. Gotta trust who's coming in that door. This one's not been busted yet, even though we're on the Kansas side of the line," said Collette by way of explanation.

Kansas City proper was divided at the State Line Road between the Missouri side and the Kansas side. Everyone knew that Prohibition laws on the Missouri side of State Line were enforced lightly, if ever.

The Kansas speakeasies were routinely raided with lots of fanfare - reporters taking notes, and photographers' flash bulbs going off.

"And Sundays are generally safe everywhere. Feds like to work a regular shift. Elden's people protect this place. Bet it costs a pretty penny, but you know the Whitcombs wouldn't do it if it didn't make money," said Collette, her accent unmistakable now.

"Speakeasies are easy money, as long as you have a good supply line, know the right people, and make nice with the authorities. You can count on the Whitcombs to do all of that," Collette laughed.

"So from your accent, I'm guessing you're not from Kansas City?" asked Jean, changing the topic.

"No, Paris," Collette replied matter of factly.

"Paris?" Jean asked, rolling the word across her tongue. The city she'd dreamed of each month. "I can't imagine ever wanting to leave Paris."

"My parents still live there, but things fell apart for us. I came over to live with my aunt. She doesn't care much what I do, as long as I can take care of her kids come Monday. She has six. Six kids. Imagine," said Collette with a roll of her eyes. "It's harder work than I expected, watching kids. How about you?"

"I work at the Empire. Elevator girl. It's where I met Elden," said Jean, her voice tinged with pride.

"Oh, that's how," said Collette, giving Jean an appraising look. "Smart girl. Now, about your dress, I was thinking we're the same size and I have one or two that just aren't my color. If you think you'll be coming here, can I have you take those for me?" Jean searched the girl's face for a clue behind her generosity as Collette continued.

"Just two, a baby blue and a green. Too pale for me. My mother sent them and they've got to go, all delicate and sweet. I thought of them right off when I saw you."

"But why? I hardly know you," Jean said in a hushed voice.

"You're with Elden and you're different. He needs different, see?" Collette began, her eyes growing serious. Jean silently nodded, not understanding. "I've been coming here a year. Seen him go from gregarious to sad. Real sad. He needs something. Sweet and delicate. And he doesn't seem to know it, but then tonight something was different. It's the first time he's introduced one of his girls with a real name. They've always been "Doll" or "Trixie," or some silly nonsense. The girls would laugh but they knew what he meant."

Jean nodded. Doll, Trixie, they were the monikers of the girls from the pulp magazines, the ones with the fringed skirts and bags stuffed with money. Everyone knew they weren't for real.

"I'm no doll," Jean offered, hoping Collette would continue, "and I can tell that you like Elden, too. You care for him?"

"Like a brother. He reminds me of my brother. But the bottle got him. My sweet little brother. We should have seen it. Stopped it. My parents, we couldn't even face each other after the funeral," Collette said, her eyes fixed on a middle distance. "God, I haven't told anyone that."

"It's terrible to lose someone. My mother. A few weeks ago," Jean said, her eyes edged with tears.

"Your mother? I'm sorry. And your father is --?" Collette asked.

"Gone too. It's too soon to know how to manage," Jean gulped back the tears as she shared a truth she'd felt but never spoken. Everything did feel different without Mama. It was like all the normal reference points were gone and Jean had to rethink everything.

"I'm so sorry. Someday it'll get better, but I know. It changes everything. At first, everything seems trivial. Then a few days later you wake up and the little things feel like the most important ones and it's like you're doing things again for the first time. You have to think about how to get out of bed, wash your face, pour a cup of tea. Grief. It throws off your balance," Collette explained and then gave her close cut bob a shake, letting the curls fall back into place. The two fell silent.

"Well, speaking of balance – you've got it. I saw you on the dance floor," she said putting an arm around Jean's shoulder as they turned to walk back towards the speakeasy.

"I've got no balance or rhythm," Jean laughed, grateful for the turn in their conversation.

"Well, Elden thought you were cute. I could tell. He was watching from across the room."

"Elden," Jean said remembering her date, "He's probably worried about me. We just left him in there alone."

"Oh, don't worry. Elden's never alone, but let's get you back inside. I imagine I know where he is. Follow me," said Collette as she gave a double knock on the metal door and repeated the words Elden had said, "Friend of Jake."

"Sure, Collette, like we all don't already know you," said the man with a guttural laugh as he pulled open the heavy door.

Collette flashed the man a piercing look, "Just come on with me," Collette said to Jean, taking her hand. Instead of turning right at the end of the narrow hallway, Collette put her hand up and slid aside a piece of wainscoting on the other side of the wall.

A flight of wooden steps appeared behind the hidden entrance.

They descended the stairs, going deep into a basement, first one flight, then two. Jean couldn't hear anything from above. They reached the bottom of the third flight of stairs. There was a long hallway, a tunnel that seemed to run for blocks and blocks. There appeared to be both no way in and no way out.

The two girls walked the tunnelway without talking, until Collette made a forty-five degree turn that put them in front of a black door that Jean would have completely missed.

"I've pulled Elden out of here many a night. Needs someone to prop him up when he gets out of hand. His friends just let him be, not wanting to spoil his fun. They can't see it's not real fun. Can't see where it might end, you know?"

Jean's face was pensive, as she thought about the poor choices Elden had obviously made in the past. "Don't look so scared," said Collette. "He's harmless when he's drunk like tonight. Happy and harmless tonight. Won't break any chairs or such." That thought about the chairs only compounded Jean's worries. Collette knocked once and then opened the door, not waiting for an invitation in.

The door opened into a large room lined with bottle-filled shelves and a large metal contraption with two tubes running out of it, a distiller. The still set in the far end of the room. In the center, seated at a round table, was Elden with two men in suits on either side of him. Collette had been correct. She knew right where to find Elden.

"Hey girls, look at that, you found me. You're regular gumshoes, aren't you? Tracking me down and all," said Elden expansively. Jean looked around the room with horrified curiosity.

"Oh, Jean. Right, this. All this," said Elden hesitating as he read her expression. "Well, you heard of bathtub gin? We make the real stuff, real gin here. Had some tonight, you did. Yup, this is made, right here," said Elden pointing to the giant distiller.

"Speakeasy above, still below. See, that's the evaporation coil, so it comes down there and voila! Booze. Made far enough away that you don't get the smell upstairs, you know. It has a vent right to the outside. 'Course you don't want to stand outside when that's in operation. Sure smells up the alley. Whets the garment workers appetite though," he ended with a chortle.

"You actually make gin? This place is a bootleg operation?" asked Jean, unable to contain her uneasiness. "I read about these in the paper."

First, just going into a speakeasy was breaking the law, then she'd learned Elden more than knew his way around a gin bottle, and now she was standing smack in the center of a full-blown distillery. It was the first time she was glad she didn't have to open her apartment door and face her mama. She'd have broken down and confessed every part of the evening, needing to clear her conscience and get her mama's reassurance.

"Hey, doll, sure. It's the only speakeasy in the city with its own operation. Total ownership of production - from grain to still to bottle. Cut out the middle man. Brilliant, isn't it?" Elden asked.

The two men sitting beside him said nothing and watched Elden silently, shifting in their seats, uncomfortable with their new visitors.

"Elden, we could go to jail just for being here," said Jean in a hushed whisper. One of the men rolled his eyes skyward and crossed his arms, tipping back his chair on its back legs.

"Whitcombs never go to jail, Jean. Don't worry. I own this," said Elden confidently. "Somewhere makes a fine gin. Distribute it all over town, the restaurants, the hotels. This stuff right here is a little raw," Elden said pointing to his glass, "Not aged out even a half day. Hey, I can get you a drink if you want to try it though."

"We'll take it from here, El," said one of the men rising from his chair. "You go on and take care of the ladies."

"Oh, good idea," said Elden with just a degree too much enthusiasm. "These are my dolls. 'Bout lost them in the dark upstairs. Came down this way - nope, you sure weren't down here and then I look up and there you are. Like Houdini."

With that Elden made himself laugh out loud. Jean knew it wasn't right but she couldn't help but think how cute he was when he laughed. She imagined that big laugh rolling out of him as a little boy.

He could even light up a moonshine room, she thought, but somehow it still felt all wrong.

"I'm going upstairs. You can take her out the back way, Elden. She's ready to go," said Collette gesturing towards Jean. "I hope I'll see you around here again." Collette reached out and gave Jean's hand a squeeze. "I'll drop by the Empire with those dresses, okay? Sweet and delicate." Jean nodded and gave a grateful smile.

Collette left them, closing the door firmly behind her. Jean saw no other way out. One of the rough-looking men then walked to a rack of bottles and slid it back from the wall. It opened to yet another passageway.

"Goes out back up by the alley. Our secret escape route," explained Elden. "Well, I'll see you, boys. You take care of the hotel deliveries, now, okay? And you'll pay the suits their due, right?"

"Sure thing, El," said one of the men, "We'll take care of all that. You go on."

Jean followed Elden without a look back at the illicit room. This was a place she'd rather forget. They walked up a narrow set of stairs and exited onto the alley, the daylight still so bright it made Jean wince. Somehow, it seemed that the sunshine should have vanished and they should skulk back in night mist, transitioning back slowly to the world and things that were pure and true.

It wasn't just the sunshine that seemed wrong. Jean hunched her shoulders, the guilt weighing on her. Guilt at being one of those girls, one of the drinking and smoking girls. This wasn't quite what she had in mind when she set out to be a modern girl. Something had gone all awry and she couldn't think of how to piece it all into its right place.

Elden took Jean by the hand as they navigated the cobblestones and that made her smile just a little, the tension easing from her shoulders. *Maybe I am his girl*, Jean thought. *He wouldn't share such a place, such a risk, with just any girl.* That thought hung silently in the air between them and Jean squeezed his hand a little, hoping for reassurance.

"You're a fun girl, Jean. Know how to live. And dance, too. I do love a girl who can dance. Saw you out there with Collette." He leaned over and whispered, "You know how to move."

Jean felt a stir from deep within her that felt dangerously attractive. She turned to Elden, trying to think of a witty retort, but her thoughts were broken by the sound of a distant church bell. Six rings. She counted each.

"Oh, I'm late. I've never missed a date with Francie. Could you drop me at her place?" asked Jean, her voice rising. How would she face Francie and her entire brood with alcohol on her breath? And she was sure she smelled of smoke, too. This was terrible. Francie's mother would never forgive her and, knowing her, would probably bar Francie from coming over, ever.

"No, no, we're not going there. Gin on your breath? Can't do that. My job is to get you home safe. That's my job," said Elden straightening his tie.

Jean was momentarily charmed. It warmed her to think he cared about keeping her safe. She wouldn't be welcome in the Nowak home tonight, not in this condition, Jean reasoned to herself. She'd explain everything to Francie tomorrow. Francie would surely understand, Jean thought hopefully, not wanting to give it much thought yet.

Elden started the car, giving it so much gas the engine raced loudly. Jean's fingers clutched the leather seat under her, worried now that he would drive too fast, his good judgment possibly washed away by the gin.

"You sure you can drive now?" Jean asked hesitantly, not knowing what the option might be if he said 'no', but almost certain this would lead to something bad altogether.

"Oh, don't look worried like that. I'm fine. Do it all the time, nothing to pull your face into a frown about," Elden assured. He drove the empty city streets without talking, making wide turns and seeming overly concentrated on the road before him. Jean could feel the danger of her decision to get into the car with him after he was drinking and silently swore she'd not do it again.

Nothing is worth this fear, she thought, foreseeing the consequences of one terrible mistake.

When they pulled up in front of her apartment building, Elden let go of the steering wheel and shot her a smile. "See, home in one piece," he laughed.

"This time, Elden. You could have killed us both, you know. We can't do that again," Jean said, drawing her first line with the boy who always got his way.

"I'd never hurt you," Elden assured as he opened her car door, "M'lady," he said with a deep bow. Jean laughed nervously and started to rise. She sat back down quickly. She began to realize that alcohol was perhaps potent.

Jean glanced around the sidewalk, hoping Otis and Abby were still out at the ballgame. Otis noticed everything.

"Elden, I think maybe all the city's old church ladies could be right, maybe gin is the devil's drink. I can't even get out of this car," she said, hiding her embarrassment behind her laughter.

"Oh, you get used to it. One drink doesn't even touch me anymore. You'll be fine," said Elden, helping her out of the car. "Let me walk you up." Jean hesitated.

A glimpse of her spare apartment may cause Elden's interest to waiver, she worried, her heart sinking. In her fog, she weighed that risk against navigating the stairs, three flights, alone and unsteady on her feet. The need for help won out.

"You can walk me to the third floor but that's it and it's only because you did this to me, Elden," Jean said, still nervous about what he would think when he saw the shabby lobby and tired stairwell. As he opened the front door they were smacked with the smell of boiled cabbage. Today's pierogies were cabbage, onion, and sausage. Delicious once they were encrusted in the soft dough.

"What died?" asked Elden loudly.

"Shhh, it's the Ivanovic's. She is a wondrous cook, but today she didn't salt the cabbage before she blanched it. Just don't breathe as you walk up the stairs," she said with a giggle.

Elden's return of laughter in response softened the worry she had that he may be making a judgment. They navigated up the stairway,

Elden's hand on the small of her back. Jean felt a warm ripple arc through her body at his touch.

As they reached the door to her apartment, Jean began to worry about what might come next, whether Elden's intentions needed to be reined in. She came to a full stop at the door and turned to face Elden, ready to bid him goodnight.

"Safely inside and then I go. Not before," Elden said protectively as he turned Jean around to face the door lock.

Jean smiled. *He does care. He really does,* she thought. She slipped off her necklace and fitted the key in the lock.

"Pretty necklace. Pretty necklace for a pretty girl," Elden observed, findings words that might keep the momentum of the evening going.

As she bent to turn the key, Jean's head began to throb.

"Well, I had a wonderful time," Jean said over her shoulder, hoping to cut off his avenue for chatter. She stood up straight and faced him, "And I want to thank you for a nice evening, overall."

"Somewhere is having music tomorrow. I can get you at five," Elden offered as he leaned in awkwardly for a kiss. He smelled of juniper.

"You're my girl, Jean," he whispered, pushing the apartment door slightly open.

Jean moved her head as she reached for the door, wanting to shelter him from the shabbiness of her life inside. The move evaded Elden's kiss.

"Elden! No, I can't let you in," Jean protested, the words coming out before she could reflect on what he had just said. Thinking quickly, she grabbed for the doorknob and pulled it half-closed. "The maid didn't come and you know a girl like me can't be cleaning up all by herself. It's a fright in there," she said, trying to sound delicate and still her pounding heart.

Elden put his hands on the door frame bracing himself and surrounding her with his strength, knowing he should say something charming.

"No, you can't. You're not a maid. You weren't made to clean. You were made for parties and dancing. I think you need a new pair of dancing slippers," Elden said.

He'd heard his father say that thing about dancing slippers whenever he needed something from, or needed to get out of a situation with, his mother. The effect was always the same. Mother would throw her arms around his dad, declare him a prince, and plant a big, sloppy kiss. It was sometimes an offer for shoes and a dress, or maybe a necklace, but that seemed a bit extravagant for this situation, Elden reasoned.

There was no such exclamation and sloppy kiss from Jean. Dancing shoes. Maybe those weren't magic words after all, Elden thought, a little bewildered. Instead Jean looked up at him with her bright green eyes that pierced him through with their innocence.

"Dancing slippers?" she asked, her eyes shining.

"And a dress, too. Go on down to Emery Bird tomorrow. Just tell the salesman to put it on my charge. No big deal and I am sorry about ruining your shoes the other day, too," Elden added.

Now there was no doubt in Jean's mind; Elden adored her. First it was the fancy dinner out, then the lakeshore picnic and sitting by the waterfall, then a ballgame and a secret juke joint fling, and now gifts from the best department store in town. This was beyond imagination. It had the making of forever.

"Really? A dress and shoes? I couldn't," Jean stuttered.

"Of course. It's what's needed. I expect no less. Five o'clock it is," Elden replied, his assurance unquestionable.

"So, I'll see you tomorrow at five, then?" she asked, ending the evening with a question.

"Five sharp. Wear something new. I'll really take you Somewhere," Elden said with a smile. "Pleasant dreams."

Elden's head was pounding but his heart felt light, as he headed down the stairs and back to the bar. He had done the right thing not to kiss her. Not yet.

Once the apartment door closed, Jean flung herself on the bed and pulled off her shoes, thrilled but guilty at the thought of having danced in such a place, wearing the shoes her mama had given her.

Mama. Her heart would have broken if she knew I was in a speakeasy, Jean reflected. *If Mama were here, she'd tell me what to do, what was right. I can't do this by myself. I don't know the rules for this.*

The drink, the smoke, the bar. It was all wrong, but somehow Elden had made it seem all right, acceptable. It was a world she had no idea about. Jean closed her eyes, wanting to take it all back, and yet wanting little to have changed. Wanting the impossible.

12

Jean woke up late to the sound of chirping birds fervently building a nest outside her window. She washed the thick feeling from her mouth with a gulp of tea and pulled a comb through her hair. She could hardly think straight and was grateful for not having to drag herself into the hotel to work. Having Sundays and Mondays off now had seemed unusual at first until she'd learned the rhythm of the hotel and how busy Saturdays were.

Jean put her hands to her temples, rubbing small circles. Her head ached and her mouth felt like cotton. Gin was a sneaky thing. No one told her it would make her feel so tired and empty.

Oh, no, Francie's going to kill me, Jean thought, remembering she'd missed the most important dinner Francie had ever planned. It was to have been the dinner that would announce, ever so subtly, that Harold and Francie were officially a couple. How could Francie ever forgive her for skipping Sunday dinner? Or maybe Francie would understand, would see that Elden was her own type of Harold? Either way, she needed to talk to Francie. Jean changed clothes and headed out to face her friend.

As she opened the door, she tripped on a dead mouse there at her feet. Beside it sat the kitten, looking proud.

"Oh, kitten!" Jean exclaimed, denying her instinct to grimace, "You got a present for me, did you? Now I know your name. You must be Orion, the hunter." She tried to hold back her revulsion at the sight of the dead mouse, because she could tell that the cat was offering her what he had to give.

"Thank you, Orion. My Orion," she said. The kitten tilted his head and began to lick his paws contentedly.

Jean felt a wave of sadness wash over her, as she remembered Mama's voice telling her the names of the constellations, as they had sat under the stars one night long ago. She shook herself free of the feeling and bent to pet Orion as she regarded the mouse offering. Orion meant no harm, she knew.

She went back and got a big piece of newspaper, and scooped up the mouse from in front of the door, pondering what to do with it. She didn't want to hurt the kitten's feelings by rejecting the gift, but she surely did not have a use for a dead mouse.

"Nature, red in tooth and claw," she said, remembering a poem that Mama had recited to her. After a moment, she put the mouse back in the hallway slightly away from the door. Orion seemed to understand. He grabbed up the mouse with dignity and then scampered down the hallway. Jean rolled up the soiled piece of newspaper and threw it away, and then washed her hands with the lavender soap her mama had loved best. She would have that scent, a little reminder of her mama, at least for part of the day.

"You're flying fast this morning," Otis said as she ran down the stairs. "Everything all right?"

"Yes. And, oh, I almost forgot," Jean said. "Wait here." She ran back upstairs and got the baseball that she'd caught at the Monarchs game. If not for Miss Abby and Otis, she would be even more alone in the world, and she had so little to offer anyone. She had planned to give the baseball to them as soon as she could because it would mean something special to them, too. It was what she had to give, after all.

"Here," she said awkwardly, thrusting the baseball into Otis's hands. "I want you to have this baseball, to remember the game. Elden caught it, but then things went bad, and I think it's better in your keeping than in mine."

"Why, thank you," Otis said, taking the ball with a smile and fitting his grip around the side seams. "My fast ball was never fast enough to catch James, but I sometimes caught him on my curve."

Jean's eyebrows arched in surprise. "You pitched to James? Truly?"

"Taught him how to hold a bat, too," Otis said with a nod, "Now look where all he's gone. And, I'm sure Miss Abby will be thrilled to have an original Kansas City Monarchs baseball, too. You sure you don't want to keep it, though?"

"I want you to have something, Otis, you and Miss Abby," Jean said. "If not for you, I never would have gotten that job as an elevator operator, and if not for Miss Abby, I couldn't have lived through Mama's passing. I want to give you something to thank you for all you've done for me."

"Why, we treat you the same way we'd treat anybody, Miss Jean," Otis said. "Neighbors help neighbors. It's nothing so special to help a neighbor."

"It's special to me, Otis, and I thank you and Miss Abby every day," Jean said.

"Well, then, you are welcome," Otis said. "It always makes our day to see you smile. You be careful with that Elden fellow, though, you hear? He might have a temper. You be careful. If you need anything, you know where we are."

"Yes, I do," Jean said. "Thank you."

Jean ran fast to Francie's house then and knocked furiously on Francie's door.

It's after nine on a Monday morning, surely they'll all be up, thought Jean. Francie opened the door dressed like a scullery maid, her hair tied up in a rag and her dress covered by a large apron. Before Francie had a chance to say good morning, Jean burst out an explanation.

"I couldn't make it last night. Tell your mother I'm so sorry." Not waiting for a response, Jean barreled on, "But come with me, he's taking me out tonight and he's buying me a new outfit today!"

"Tonight? It's Monday. Who goes out on a Monday night?" said Francie with an air of exasperation. "You know we don't go out on weeknights. Not ever. It's not right."

"Who goes out on Monday night? We do, Francie! We - you and me and Harold and Elden."

"No, we don't. We are not those people. Not me, not you, and certainly not Harold. Well, not me and not Harold anyway. I wash my hair on Monday nights, you know that, and church has girl's group. We're knitting blankets for the hospital." Francie was irritated, without question. "And how can you afford a new outfit anyway?" Francie asked plaintively.

"You have to come with me, Francie. I can't tell Elden no. You know that. He wants to take me out and he's buying me a new dress and dancing slippers just for tonight! Can you believe it? I am so lucky!" Jean said enthusiastically.

Francie looked at her, concern etched across her face. Elden drank and fought and drove too fast and her best friend didn't even seem concerned. All worried about clothes and impressions, swept up in the moment.

"Lucky? Lucky? He's one of those boys, Jean. The fast ones. Can't you see that? I mean, drinking is illegal last time I checked and he doesn't even care. It's like the rules don't apply. Is that what you want? He thinks his money can let him get away with anything," Francie whispered furiously, trying not to let her words carry into her house.

"He's spirited, it's true. But he likes me, Francie. He really likes me and he's so fun. And he wants to go out again. See?"

Francie's forehead crinkled with worry. Jean didn't look like herself. Her eyes darted, accentuating the darkness underneath.

"Oh, you wouldn't understand," Jean said crossing her arms.

"Well, go then, just go out with him and do all that, that, that stuff but don't count on me to approve. Harold and I can't go. And I can't go shopping today either. Mother has me cleaning the kitchen cabinets anyway," said Francie. She started to say something about the circles under Jean's eyes but stopped herself. She could tell that Jean wasn't in the mood to give explanations.

Jean was taken aback by Francie's intensity and judgment. She had never seen her friend so self-righteous and felt she needed to soften the exchange.

"Well, you make the prettiest little domestic I ever did see," said Jean, "but I'll definitely let you know what fancy little thing I end up getting."

"You're really going to see him again, aren't you? I can't stop you, can I?" asked Francie, placing her hand on her hip and shaking her head in disgust. Jean hung her head. Francie's approval had seemed important at first, but now she wasn't so sure.

"I've never had a boy who," she paused, "cared, you know," explained Jean. "He has everything, Francie, everything, and he likes me. I know he needs me, too. Can you see that?"

Francie sighed, her lips tightening into a scowl. "You're going to see him whether I say go or not, aren't you? Oh, Jean, you have to be careful. And buy yourself something sensible, okay? You know, something mother would approve of. Then I can borrow it," said Francie breaking into a smile and not wanting Jean's choice to date Elden to mark the end of their friendship.

"If you don't hate me for not knitting tonight then it's a deal," offered Jean.

"Sure thing," Francie replied, "Just make good choices, okay? Oh, give me a hug. I can't stay mad at you." Jean embraced Francie, and for a moment it felt like things might be okay between them.

"Well, au revoir, my sweet. Back to the scullery with you," Jean joked, relieved that she was forgiven as she headed down the porch steps.

"I'm serious. You be careful with Elden," Francie whispered and then shut the door without another word. Jean was halfway down the block before she realized she'd not even thought to ask about Francie's dinner with Harold's family. But it felt too late to turn back and ask.

∽

*A*cross town, Elden had stayed in his bedroom lolling about long enough so he knew he'd not have to face the scrutiny of his parents at the breakfast table. Wouldn't give Pops a chance to hound him about the speakeasy, asking all the annoying questions about the business end of things: Did you get in the supplies? How did the deliveries to the hotels go? Did the payments get made? All of them? Protection is assured for another month? Always the same nagging.

He pulled on a shirt and took a pair of freshly pressed pants off a wooden hangar, considering what he might do to pass the day, having no obligations, no worries. He thought about Jean. A nice girl. It was as if things were finally falling into place, he reflected as he walked downstairs.

The family butler greeted him in the library with a cup of coffee and the day's newspaper.

"Slight mention, again, sir," the man stated.

Elden took the coffee and eased himself into a wing backed chair. He opened the paper to the society page and shook his head, glad his parents weren't there to ask more questions.

~

*T*he burden of her choices weighed heavily as Jean walked towards Petticoat Lane. She passed the Empire Hotel and stopped abruptly at the sign on the shop next door: *Now Open -Lady Lydia's Salon* it read. Lydia, Mama's old friend from way back. She'd come to the service. Jean let out a sigh, welcoming the serendipity of coming upon Lydia when she so needed advice from someone like Mama, someone older who would understand.

"Hi, Lydia. How are things?" called Jean, opening the shop door, trying to make her voice sound casual.

"Jean! Oh, I have been thinking about you," said the stout little woman, beckoning Jean into the tiny shop. "You look every bit like your mama did at 17, don't you? Oh, she was a beauty back in high school and we were so close those years. I do miss your mama so," Lydia's voice trailed off. "But you, now, how are you? Getting out finally. I heard about the game yesterday. Guess you were with the Whitcomb boy."

This is a big city. How can gossip travel so fast? Jean wondered.

"What little bird was tweeting in your ear between yesterday noon and this morning, Lydia?" asked Jean a little more sharply than she intended.

Mama had told her that a girl's reputation could be ruined in one evening and spread through town by the time the milkman made his morning rounds. Maybe that wasn't far from the truth. Jean felt her stomach churn with worry.

In one evening she had certainly done almost all the forbidden things that tainted a girl's name: Drink, smoke, go to a secret bar, a speakeasy. What had she been thinking? People went to prison for such things, Jean worried.

"I heard it from James. He and I..." Lydia began, but stopped herself. "He heard from Miss Abby there'd been a ruckus. But, you know, I could've just read it in the paper." Lydia replied with nonchalance, her face giving away no judgment.

"The paper?" questioned Jean. *What if the society page wrote up everything about last night?*

"Have to wonder who in the city the Whitcombs have crossed lately. Paper isn't usually so pointed when it comes to a single family. Here you go," said Lydia opening the paper to the society page.

"See here? 'Seems a Whitcomb is playing the field,' is what it says. Not a bad picture of Elden there at the game and you in that cute dress beside him. Then it makes a note that certain enforcement efforts were needed at the game. Doesn't come out and say Elden was involved, but if you know Elden, then you can read between the lines," Lydia counseled.

Jean looked up at Lydia, registering the woman's look as one of genuine concern. Jean felt all of yesterday's events cause a tumble in her stomach. She quickly sat down on the manicurist's stool.

"You feel okay, Jean? You look a little woozy," observed Lydia.

"I'm all right. Don't worry about me. Elden's a good man. Really. He's not bad. Someone said something rude and he just wanted to put a stop to it. But do you have something for a headache?" asked Jean, rubbing her temple.

"Of course, just a minute, I'll get you an aspirin." Lydia walked to the back storeroom of her shop. Jean could hear her talking quietly to someone and recognized the other voice as belonging to James.

Could it be Lydia and James are – no, no, Jean couldn't think about that. Life was confusing enough all of a sudden.

Lydia returned with a Spartan aspirin tin and offered her two tablets. "I know that look, dear. Been there myself at your age. Let me get you some water, too. You have a seat now," Lydia said knowingly.

Jean could barely sit still, nervous that the story of the night before might spread. She distracted herself with the thought that Lydia, a white woman, might be dating the colored doorman. Jean gulped down the water when Lydia returned and swallowed the two aspirin.

"So I heard James," Jean began, "he's here, isn't he?" Jean gestured toward the storage room. Lydia's cheeks flushed as she nodded her head.

"Mama would be glad you're happy," Jean volunteered. "She always said you were a bit unconventional anyhow."

Lydia laughed. "Too true," she replied. "And you're right. It's James."

Jean looked on, hoping for an explanation. "I know your mama wouldn't judge me because James is colored and I'm white. Others say it's wrong, but he's the one I've been waiting for my whole life. I just never knew. Not until he walked in one day. Smiled. Asked for a drink of water," Lydia continued.

Jean shifted on her stool and looked intently at Lydia, whose eyes danced with the memory. "He'd forgotten his Thermos. It was blistering hot in that big doorman's suit he wears. When I handed him that cup and his hand brushed mine, it was like the earth stopped its rotating. It was just him and me in this tiny world. His eyes swallowed me up. I can't explain it. After that, I never even thought about the color of his skin. Well, not until he asked me to dinner."

"Dinner?" Jean questioned, knowing there was no place in the city that would let a colored man dine with a white woman.

"We had a picnic by the river because he was too worried to take me to a colored restaurant, which I understand," explained Lydia. "So we don't go out and that's fine. We have all we need, together." Lydia smiled, almost glowing with her recollections.

"And he provides well, has two jobs, doesn't he?" asked Jean.

"Plays ball for the Negro League, the Monarchs, and works at the Empire. Thanks to Mr. Whitcomb. For all Mr. Whitcomb may have done with the hotel maid, he's still done some things right," Lydia said.

Jean hadn't heard the hotel maid story but it didn't feel like the time to inquire. Things were different now that she was working. All the rules about social status, money, race, and women working had gotten jumbled around. It was as if everything was in a state of flux.

Maybe there was no right and wrong, contrary to what the sisters at St. Patrick's had taught. Jean furrowed her brow, pondering that thought and wondering what Mr. Whitcomb may have done with the hotel maid.

"You sure you're okay?" Lydia asked. "You look like you're carrying a burden."

"I'll be fine," Jean said handing the glass back. "Thanks for the aspirin. I've got to get on now. You let Miss Abby know she shouldn't worry a minute about me. Tell James, too."

"I will, honey. But you sit with me a minute. I want to know how you are doing. Your mama and I were dear friends in high school, then she married and you came along and I, well, I guess I wasn't the good friend I could have been. Got my life all tied up in knots for awhile. But it's smoothing out now, I have a business and I've found a good man, too. Calmed me down around the edges, finally. But enough about me. How are you?"

Jean smiled and her cheeks flushed She knew what Lydia meant about being calmed down around the edges due to the attentions of a good man.

"I know how it is. Made my way in the world at your age. Hard. It was hard. Your mama wouldn't want things hard for you. Glad you have a job, secure and all. Now, did she ever meet this Whitcomb boy, this Elden? How'd she feel about that?" Lydia asked, pointedly.

Jean wasn't ready to talk about Elden or Mama yet. "Oh, Lydia, don't worry about me. You're right. I'm fine, just fine. I'm working now. I'll be okay. Mama was so sick, frail. I couldn't get her around to meet Elden, but she knew about him. That he made me happy. I miss her, Lydia. She'd tell me what was right, what the rules are now," Jean said, finding words for the sad stirrings that had been in her heart for weeks. "I don't know what I'm going to do without her."

"She loved you with her whole heart. It'll be hard to adjust, I know, but you know you can come to me anytime, don't you? I know what it means to be seventeen and on your own."

"And things, they worked out for you?" asked Jean.

"Eventually. Things work out. They do. Not always the way you want them to, or expect them to, but they work out. And you have friends?" Lydia asked.

"Mama said every girl needs a friend during the growing up years," Jean said thinking of Francie and the look of disappointment on her face this morning. "But I guess sometimes even good friends grow apart."

"Sometimes they do," agreed Lydia, "but it doesn't take away what they had, that foundation. And work is good?" Lydia asked brightly.

"I like meeting people, learning about how they live, what they are doing. Sometimes I hear things even before it hits the newspaper. I think the League Ladies practically run that place though," Jean confided. "They're always coming in meeting about some program. If it's not whether the dairies are clean enough, it's whether there are enough fountains in the parks, or something about getting more women working. How they come up with these ideas, I don't know. But it keeps Mr. Whitcomb's hotel busy."

"Those League Ladies are a force, Jean. We can learn a lot from how they push their issues, make changes. Bless them for taking the time to think of others. Must be nice to have that kind of time, not have to work for your dollars," Lydia said, not unkindly.

"And, what about this boy, Jean? You be careful with this young man. Elden. He's a force, too, you know. Used to having everything, getting everything, wanting for nothing. On the easy side of the law. For now at least. You know what I'm saying?" Lydia asked.

Jean nodded, knowing there was more truth behind Lydia's words than she cared to acknowledge, or would want to share with anyone but Francie.

"Now, you can have yourself a good time with him, if you set the boundaries. Let him know where your edges are. You do know all about the he'ing and the she'ing, right?" asked Lydia.

"Of course," Jean blushed. Mama had filled her in on all the birds and the bees, as Mama called it. "It's not something I need to worry about. And I am not one for babies, Lydia. They cry and smell. No, I'm not ready for a family. I know what to do. But, I'd never. And we'd never. And Elden's not like that anyway," she said, adding the last sentence only to reassure herself.

"Honey, they're all like that. Give them a drink and it's mostly unstoppable. You ever need something, you come to me though, okay?" offered Lydia.

Jean looked at Lydia with a new-found respect. Maybe this older woman really did understand how things were. Things with Elden did seem almost unstoppable last night, as if they could spin out of control with just one more drink or the wrong turn of the steering wheel.

"I will. I promise," said Jean, leaning in with hopes of sharing just a little more, finding the tidbit of wisdom that would make it a little easier to handle Elden, and the booze, and the speakeasy.

As she opened her mouth to form the question, the shop door opened and a well-dressed woman walked in. The moment was gone as Lydia greeted the woman and waved her to the open nail station.

"Well, now, you think about what I said, Jean. I have to get busy now, but you come back anytime," Lydia offered.

"You do my nails someday, maybe?" asked Jean, hoping for a reason to return.

"Anytime. You come back and I'll do them," said Lydia as she rose and gave Jean a hug before turning to her customer.

Jean left the shop and hurried down to Petticoat Lane, making her way to the big department store. Her headache was subsiding, replaced by a building anticipation. To go into a big department store, something other than a mom-and-pop sundry shop, was an occasion.

Shopping trips were for the rich girls, the modern girls who flitted from picnics to parties. Jean and her mama had gotten so used to scraping by, making do and doing without, that the shops on Petticoat Lane had grown in Jean's mind to be something extraordinary, larger than life.

She opened the heavy metal and glass door to the EBT store and breathed in the lightly perfumed air. Taking a step inside, she looked around. Rows and rows of hats and scarves, all of silk and linen and tweed. Elegant.

The EBT was not yet filled with shoppers. The place was hers to browse. Shoes were on the first floor, but she couldn't choose those without knowing the dress. A rising feeling of expectation swelled inside Jean as she entered the elevator that would take her to the floor with women's dresses.

It was all even more exciting than she'd remembered when she'd first come here with her mama years before. The elevator man acknowledged her with a formal nod when he announced, "Third Floor, Finer Dresses." Jean thrilled at the word 'finer.' She gave the man a warm smile as she stepped out onto the marble floor.

Making her way to the dresses, with their whispers of silk and lace and chiffon, she was quickly greeted by the salesclerk, "And what can be done for you?" he asked.

"I'm here shopping on behalf of Mr. Whitcomb, Elden Whitcomb, today." Jean volunteered eagerly.

The shop clerk raised his eyebrows, "Oh, shopping for the Elden boy today, are we? Whitcombs are one of our best accounts."

What he didn't say was that the Whitcomb men had a veritable parade of girls who charged and the clerk had been instructed by the manager himself to accommodate whichever gal came in and used the Whitcomb's name. Same story, different girl.

Inevitably, the manager would then field a telephone call from Mrs. Whitcomb after the bill was mailed out. "Who is Cassandra Lee? Why did she charge to our account?" was her last call.

The manager had explained, "Miss Lee? Oh, Mrs. Whitcomb, let's have a look here. Hmmm…no, not a friend of your husband, I'm most certain. Yes, that's right. Your son. Another lady friend of your rascal Elden. Yes, ma'am," he'd lied.

The gals only seemed to come just once and then they'd be relegated to the growing list of the Whitcomb 'It Girls' of the moment. The clerk chose not to share those details with Jean.

The salesman took a careful look at the young girl before him and then selected three dresses he insisted had come in just within the last week. She chose a French silk shift dress in a drop waist with a delicate slip underneath. It draped low in the back, graceful and simple.

"Oh I definitely want this one," Jean said holding out the silk dress, "but I need it for tonight," she finished hopefully, her voice rising with expectation. She couldn't go out without a new dress. Elden was expecting it.

"Of course. Friend of Mr. Whitcomb, that's right. I'll have the alterations done on a rush, yes, ma'am," said the salesclerk.

"Really?" asked Jean.

"No problem at all. Anything for the Whitcombs, ma'am," he replied. "Now may I kindly suggest a lingerie fitting today? This dress requires a certain bodice. Those French women are all too small, too small indeed."

"No, no, I can't afford that," said Jean with a flush of embarrassment.

"But of course. EBT just shows it as a dress and fitting on the bill. We can sew the lingerie right into the bodice so it is part of the dress and won't show as a separate charge, of course," he explained. This was just how they worked such things. Fewer questions were ever asked that way.

It felt like a fairytale to Jean. The clerk was her personal fairy godmother. She gave a contented sigh as he escorted her to the third floor mezzanine and turned her and the dress over to a saleswoman in lingerie.

With little input from Jean, the saleswoman handed her hose, tap pants and a binding brassiere that was somehow backless.

"It's a Pierre Poiret," explained the saleslady, "Newest thing from Paris, holds everything in where it should be. So much easier than a corset. Those corsets should be outlawed someday soon, I swear," said the saleslady.

"You go put this on and we'll take a look. But I just don't see why all of a sudden the girls want to look like boys and hide their natural shape anyway. Girl like you with curves every which way wants to bind them up. Pity. We can crush them down and fit them into this dress if need be," said the clerk. Jean entered the dressing room and tried on the delicate underthings.

"So, what do you think?" The saleslady knocked and then entered the dressing room. Jean twirled in the little tap pants and brassiere, too excited to be embarrassed at standing in undergarments before the clerk.

"Perfect." Now here's a headband to match, the clerk said, businesslike, offering a slip of silk with a rosette to Jean. Jean put it on and smoothed her hair as she turned to the mirror, sure it would complete her modern look. She looked ridiculous, like a Christmas present pushed too far under the tree and forgotten.

"Too much," said the saleslady pulling it off Jean's head without finesse. "Maybe shoes, too?"

"Yes, dancing slippers, please," said Jean.

"Get dressed and I'll get you to Mr. Russell. He knows shoes better than anyone at Emery Bird. We'll get the dress in for alterations while you shop."

Jean changed back into her cotton dress and the saleslady led her down through the store to the shoe department.

"Your alterations should be done within the hour," said the lingerie saleslady once they reached the shoe department. "And this is Mr. Russell. He'll be assisting you today. We're looking for dancing slippers this morning, Mr. Russell, and please direct her to the fifth floor for pickup when you're done. This is on the Whitcomb account."

Mr. Russell made a quick assessment of just what he had before him. This girl needed some guidance. Her shoes were barely serviceable and not suitable for anything but puttering around the lawn.

"Dancing slippers?" he asked.

"Yes, please. Oh, those gold ones are lovely," said Jean taking a low-heeled shoe off the display shelf.

"Let me get you sized. That is a fine pair for dancing. All leather. Will wear well and last forever. A single pair of quality shoes can last a lot longer than the men who dance in and out of life, right?" said the portly salesman with a chuckle as he slipped her shoe off and measured her toe to heel.

Jean did not find any humor in his words. Elden would not be dancing out of her life, not now and not ever. *Silly shoe salesman*, she thought.

He came back with a pair of gold shoes that fit perfectly. When he put them on her feet she could just feel them filling her with dancing inspiration.

"I'll take them," said Jean.

"Let me wrap them up. You'll sign the slip and you can pick up the dress on the fifth floor. You come back when you need another pair. The black is always a good choice for next time," he offered, always looking to his next commission.

"Just sign the bottom of the slip, your name and then 'for Elden Whitcomb' and I'll send it to accounts receivable," he said offering the slip.

It was a tissue-thin piece of paper with a total of $36.75. Jean looked at the total and swallowed hard. That was more than three months of rent, but Elden had said to get a dress and slippers, she rationalized. Jean shut her eyes and signed, her discomfort unmistakable.

"Now don't give this another thought," the man said as he efficiently whisked the bill away, rolled it into a black case and then snapped its lock closed. "We tally up the Whitcomb charges and they pay each week. Just let me wrap these in something pretty for you," he said reaching for a roll of gold paper embossed with the Emery Bird Thayer monogram.

The man put the black case into a tube system and pressed a button. The case disappeared, magically transported throughout the building to the accounting office in the basement.

The salesman continued, "Sometimes the Whitcomb's delivery man comes by with the money. Other times it's just a check by mail. Quite the sophisticated set up they have. The rich, they just live differently from, from, uh, from me," he concluded awkwardly, glancing at Jean's worn shoes.

For a moment Jean felt deflated, like an imposter.

"Now, ma'am, up to the fifth floor with you," the man said regaining an obsequious demeanor.

Jean felt relief walking away from the man who had seen through her and her worries about the billing. By the time she'd been handed the new dress in its own special zippered bag, she was again filled with anticipation.

Several stories below, the little slip of paper with Jean's signature was making its way to the accounts receivable desk.

A young woman opened the black case and took out the slip. A bill for the Whitcombs, again. She looked it over carefully, her eyes taking in each word: a dress, a fitting, shoes, by Jean Ball for the Whitcomb account, $36.75. The Whitcombs. The name caused a clench in her chest.

She cast a glance down at her expanding belly and with a careful hand she carved the three into a perfect number eight: $86.75, and smiled. She heaved her ever-growing girth to walk the bill to the Invoice Desk; her name tag caught the light. It read "Cassandra Lee." Cassandra Lee. Mr. Whitcomb's most recent dalliance that had driven his wife back into the bottle, making her hands unsteady by the morning light.

Unaware of the pending drama she had just set into motion, Jean carried her packages home. As she neared the apartment building, worry crept into her mind.

Would Otis look askance upon all these fancy packages? Would he think her frivolous, spending the last of Mama's money or flitting away her own pay? Or would he know it was the boy, the Whitcomb family money? And which thought was worse?

Jean fretted over the possibilities but gratefully pushed them away when she saw no sign of either Otis or Abby in the building.

13

After a quick bowl of soup, Jean cleaned her dinner dishes and dried her hands well before unzipping the garment bag. The golden silk dress glimmered in the late afternoon light and Jean took in a quick breath as she slipped the dress from the satin hangar and glided it over her freshly crimped hair.

She took care not to pull a single silk thread. She was glad that she already had fed Orion, because the last thing she needed was to get something on this beautiful golden dress. She shut her eyes tight, wincing back a tear, wishing her mama could get just a glimpse of her. Her thought was interrupted by a knock on the door. He was early.

"You're the bee's knees, Jean, the bee's knees. You sparkle," Elden pronounced before Jean even had the door fully open.

Jean steadied her shaking hands on the firm oak door. She had never felt so appreciated and grateful, all mixed together. It was one thing to swell with pride and another to fill with thankfulness. Putting both of those feelings into the same moment was too sweet to bear. Elden smiled at her and everything felt right, completely right.

"It's a beautiful dress and you look so, so – magical," he said. "I can practically see the sunlight in your eyes, Jean." Elden seemed transfixed as Jean sashayed down the stairs where Otis stood waiting in the lobby. Jean gave Otis a broad smile as he opened the front door.

"You watch yourself, now. Pretty as a picture there. Be true to yourself, Miss Jean," Otis whispered. Jean gave a wistful look towards Elden as Otis walked ahead to open her car door. "Be careful, Miss. It's all I ask," he concluded, extracting a cigarette from his pocket.

Elden gave the roadster more gas as they headed out of town and down a dirt road towards the lake. As they neared a curve in the road he hit the accelerator with full speed and the tires screeched around the corner. Jean squealed as she grabbed the car door to avoid sliding into Elden's lap. Elden laughed, mistaking her fear for glee.

"Favorite thing to do at that spot. Gets the heart racing, doesn't it?" Elden laughed. Jean shot him a look of distress but he didn't notice.

"Elden. Do you ever think that you go too fast?" Jean asked, cautioning him against the readily apparent danger.

"Fast? That was nothing," Elden smiled, oblivious to her fear. "What's life if you're not living fast?" he asked rhetorically.

Maybe Mama was right, the rich do live differently. Maybe a sense of risk depends on money, on privilege, Jean thought and she didn't say anymore.

Elden pulled the car off the road near the lake. They walked hand in hand to the spot where they had picnicked with Francie and Harold and then continued on to the big rock.

Elden spread out a blanket so Jean wouldn't soil her dress. She pulled off her new golden slippers as Elden unscrewed his flask and took a deep drink. He offered Jean the heavy silver flask, "You?" he asked, holding it up.

She smiled back sweetly, "Oh, no, it got me the first time, remember? Do you know how bad that can make you feel? My head was filled with cotton afterwards. It was awful," she said, rubbing her temple and remembering the fuzzy thoughts that had clouded her judgment.

Elden put his arm around her, "Hair of the dog keeps it at bay. Keep drinking and you don't feel bad. It's when that alcohol leaves your body that trouble sets in. Hair of the dog. My dog's about bald because of it," Elden said with a laugh.

Jean couldn't help but laugh, too. She knew it was wrong but didn't want to offend, and he'd joked so sweetly.

"Ok, just one." She took a sip and choked back a cough. The smell, it did remind her of pine trees and Christmas. Christmas, her favorite holiday. "How does it get that smell, Elden? Reminds me of Christmas carols and Santa Claus."

"Juniper berries. Just like on an evergreen. Been around forever. Supposed to cure even bubonic plague, you know. Scientists are finding all kinds of medicinal uses for booze now that it's illegal," he said.

"How do you know so much, Elden? I feel I can say just about anything and you'll have a little fact, a little story about it," Jean said.

"I did my best not to absorb anything at Wentworth, but apparently some things just seeped into my brain without my knowing, I think."

"You can just admit that you're smart. I won't hold it against you, you know."

"You can hold anything you want against me," said Elden with an amorous gleam in his eye as he put his arm around her. "Look at that sunshine, Jean, barely peeking through the clouds. It reminds me of you. All cheerful, glowing," he said gently stroking her hair. "Something sweet and true, a constant."

Jean made a small movement away from Elden's touch. "Elden, I think maybe …" Jean began. "Well, let's take it slow."

Elden smiled. "Slow? Whitcombs don't do anything slow," he said, drawing one hand through his own dark hair. "Nobody makes a Whitcomb wait, that's what Pops says."

Jean blanched at his words and drew her soft smile into a pout.

Elden gave her a studied look. "Okay, for you, this time, I'll wait. For now. Guess I have something to work for?" Elden whispered, his voice playful. Jean could feel her heart beating loudly and she let out a nervous laugh as she considered her response.

"Maybe you should work for something. For a change," she said with a smile. "That seems fair. I work for everything. Don't really have much time to do anything else." She looked up at Elden expectantly and caught his questioning look. "But I'm not complaining. I really like my job and the hotel is extraordinary. And your father is --"

Jean stopped herself as she watched Elden's response. It was as if a cloud had covered Elden's face. "Yes, Mr. Whitcomb," said Elden, deflated. "It's a mess. He's doing his best to appear socially relevant. Kowtowing to the League Ladies, hoping he'll make a buck and that they'll finally accept mother. And mother -- don't get me started on her. She's a handful. Can't quite get over being from the wrong side of the tracks."

"Wrong side?" asked Jean.

"Her people were, well, let's just say they were not Whitcomb stock. Stockworkers maybe," Elden added. "Worked in the city stockyards from what I can piece together. Course no one in the family talks about that. Not directly. 'Crafty Croatians' my uncle said once. I don't know really. I've never met her side of the family."

"But she's, she's ... she's Mrs. Whitcomb. She carries herself as if...." said Jean, her voice wavering with astonishment.

"Lots of money buys lots of poise. Don't let that fool you," Elden said ruefully. "Booze can camouflage a lot, too. I think it fills up those places that love doesn't reach," he concluded philosophically, as he took another drink from the flask, seeing no irony between his words and actions.

"You think they don't have love?" Jean asked quietly, wonder what might go on between the elder Whitcombs.

"Not every marriage is about love," Elden mused. "Dad said once it's about duty. Then mom threw a gin bottle at him. Hit him square in the temple. He hasn't talked about it since," he said with a chagrined half-smile.

"It's like they haven't figured out that one thing, that one true thing that can hold them together. It's like skipping rocks, see?" Elden said bending down to pick up a stone. "I know if I can find the right stone, one that has a clean line, no bumps, and that if I can throw it straight and true, it'll sail across the water just perfect, skip and skip and skip, and last for eternity, sitting all still at the bottom of the lake. With them, it's like their stones are always imperfect and they keep blaming each other for it. Can't see beyond that, that the problem is within themselves," he said.

Jean looked at Elden, not quite understanding what he was trying to say, but knowing it was a truth that if she heard again, she might just grasp. She nodded in silent agreement, hoping he would continue.

"Everything's like that in our life. The Whitcomb life. I want to do what's right but what's right and wrong keeps changing on me. One day things seem black and white, there's a clear line. I can see what I'm supposed to do. Then everything changes and the lines blur. Take the ballgame last week," Elden said, skipping a rock that made just two skips before it plunged into the lake. "It failed, just like that, see?"

Jean was completely baffled by Elden's ramblings. "What do you mean, it failed -- the ballgame?"

"Black and white, clear lines. There wasn't any, you know. Like you, you felt bad watching the drumming before the show, right?" Elden asked.

Jean screwed her mouth into a frown. She hadn't ever said she'd felt bad and didn't want to acknowledge that to Elden who had tried to show her a nice time. "I felt funny about it, the men clowning out on the field," she said, quietly, "They shouldn't have to do that."

"Exactly. It didn't seem right somehow having grown men, good players, act like jungle savages, shouting and dancing in grass skirts. Because they're men. Strong, capable men. Ridiculous, right?" Elden asked.

"Right. I felt bad, um, funny, about that," Jean agreed.

"Of course you did. Everyone should have felt funny about it. But no one does. Like I said, whites would feel foolish watching white ballplayers put on a show about, I don't know – about say, singing cowboys on the wild plains, for example. It'd be stupid. But when it's the Monarchs team no one says a thing. So there are different rules for white and for colored men because having different rules makes us money."

Jean nodded. There were different rules. For white, for colored. For rich, for poor. For immigrants. In the city, there were different restaurants, different neighborhoods, different stores. Elden was correct but she couldn't figure out how this connected to his parents' marriage and money and clear lines and such. She looked up at Elden, questioningly.

"Maybe that's a bad example. Instead, let's take you. Yeah, that's good. Let's say that you needed a job, right? You work hard, are reliable, friendly, and overall just perfect, okay?" Elden said.

Jean smiled, relishing his choice of word. *Perfect. He thought that she was perfect, really and truly.*

"Okay. I understand that," she laughed. "So I'm perfect."

Elden touched her hand, "Yes. Perfect. And let's say that you're a good employee anyone should want to hire. That's a clear line, right? That's black and white. Hire/don't hire. So you hire, right? Get it?"

"Right," agreed Jean. She felt that Elden was leading her through some logical game, a maze that would probably end with a trick question. "That makes sense. I'm perfect, hire me." She smiled.

"No. Wrong. You're a girl. I can't hire you. Girls aren't supposed to have these jobs, these public jobs, big jobs, a man's job. So that choice to hire you isn't so black and white anymore. It'd be the right thing to hire you because you're perfect, but it's wrong to hire you. See, there's no clear line."

"But your father did hire me," said Jean, confused at his logic.

"Of course. It gets more complicated, doesn't it?" Elden said - enthused at the way his story was spinning out and how Jean was paying such close attention.

"So it's complicated, but in a good way because I get hired, right? How do you make that complication go away and make it okay to hire me?" Jean asked.

"Money. It's always money. So say our business doesn't hire girls. Certainly not married ladies or mothers. None of that," Elden said, shaking his head, "But then someone says, you hire that girl and I'll – I don't know – I'll ..." Elden narrowed his eyes, casting around for some consequence he couldn't quite name.

"I'll clean up the dairies and give your hotel clean milk for a year?" offered Jean, proud of being able to repeat something she'd overheard at work. Her friend, the old Rooster Tamer, said the League had found the hotel a good milk supplier through their dairy inspections.

"Oh, that's good, Jean. That's it," Elden said, reaching out to touch her shoulder. Jean blushed at the praise.

"So, then you go ahead and hire a girl, even though it's not exactly right by some people's way of thinking. But you do it to get something for yourself or your hotel, see?"

"So it's a clear line. It's good then. That's black and white to me," said Jean.

"No. Remember, most people say a lady shouldn't have a man's job. That's the rule."

"Well then it's a stupid rule," Jean replied, feeling a bit offended that someone would ever say she shouldn't work.

"Of course it's stupid, but everything was all black and white, right and wrong, and then it got all blurred and there was no straight line anymore." Elden's cheeks were flush with excitement as he continued. "See how things get muddled up?"

"I do see. And what I see is that you think a lot, don't you?" Jean asked.

"But you understand, right?" Elden asked, his blue eyes tender with hope. Jean nodded.

"When I talked about this at school the boys called me Witless. Witless Whitcomb. Crazy. Crazy, they said. Crazy to always try to fit things into right and wrong and draw a clear bright line, and when black and white rules needed changing, they hated it," Elden confided.

"At school it's what we did--figure out ways to blur the lines, for money mostly. They were always telling us the rules, right and wrong, showing us the clear lines that were to be followed. Then it'd get all fuzzy and blurred. And I'd get frustrated, get into trouble wanting things to be right and fair. Like, at the ballfield." Elden said. He leaned back on the soft grass and shut his eyes.

"How at the ballfield, Elden?" asked Jean, leaning over him and studying his face. He looked tense and worried. Just like at the ballfield. It had been a frightening moment, when she'd seen Elden's anger explode. When she'd seen what he was capable of, on a moment's notice, no less.

"You were right, right to stand up for me, protect me. You know that don't you?" Jean reassured.

"I know. But Jean, I just don't know what's right anymore," said Elden, opening his eyes. "But okay, okay, let's say that you have a friend, there at the ballfield. You wave to that friend, right?" he asked. Jean blushed, ashamed she'd broken the social rule. It wasn't right for a white woman to publicly acknowledge a colored person.

"Don't hang your head, Jean. It's okay. You see a friend and you wave," he said taking her chin in his hand and looking into her eyes, "You'd wave to Francie and Harold if you saw them, right?"

"Of course," Jean replied as Elden dropped his hand.

"Same thing with waving at Otis. It's okay to wave, if you follow the rule that you can wave at a friend," explained Elden.

"I know that's true. But then the man was wrong, the one who said that terrible thing. The one who can't see Otis for who he is," Jean said, frustrated at Elden's explanations.

"True, but then I did wrong by getting mad and hauling off and hitting that guy," confessed Elden. "He was stupid, but I shouldn't have hit him for being stupid," Elden said.

"You were protecting me, Elden. It's not wrong to protect someone," Jean offered.

"Oh I know that," said Elden. "It's not about you or that man. It's everything. See how things get muddled and fuzzy?" he asked. Jean nodded agreement. "I just want things to be right, predictable. You know. Smooth and straight and true," he concluded, laying back on the grass and studying the sunset.

"Of course you do," said Jean, stroking his hair. Elden's eyes shut and he finally looked at peace, at rest. Jean reached over and picked up a stone, a perfectly flat river rock and tucked it inside his hand so he could feel its smoothness without opening his eyes. Elden smiled as he stroked the stone.

"You're the first girl who's ever understood, truly understood me when I talk like this. I usually have to cover this all up, make a joke or pull a prank after I say these things, show people I'm just a 'Good Time' guy. They're more comfortable with that." He opened his eyes, tossed the little stone in the air and caught it.

Jean nodded. "Of course they are. Not everyone can carry around big thoughts in their head like you. It makes people uncomfortable. They don't like change or thinking things through."

"Here, you skip this one. Just try it. See how perfect this is?" he said as he turned the stone over in his hand and offered it to Jean.

"No, you skip it," Jean said.

"I can't. It's perfect. I'd ruin it. I always do," Elden replied, his voice dropping.

"You don't ruin things," Jean whispered. She gently slipped her hand into his and twined his fingers around the smooth stone. "You're perfect, see?"

Elden tenderly closed his fingers around the stone. "You're the only thing that's perfect. You keep it," he said tucking the stone into Jean's hand.

"For you. I'll keep it for you," she replied, slipping the smooth stone into her dress pocket.

She'd wait for the perfect moment to give it to him and watch him skim it smoothly over the water, skipping along, then gently falling into the water, somewhere quiet and still. They sat watching the sun drop slowly over the horizon. As the sky grew to a dusky pink, a breeze blew across the lake and Elden raised himself up on his elbows and smiled at Jean.

"Oh, enough about all that. I think too much out here. Evening's a-wasting," he said standing up abruptly and looking out over the water. "Let's go Somewhere. Monday nights, always find me there. Music's good and you Charleston, right? All the girls Charleston. Great music, yeah, you'll love it."

Elden was never at rest, Jean realized. It reminded her of something she'd learned back in school, - a scientific principle, a body in motion stays in motion until acted upon by an outside force. *I wonder how much force it would take to bring him to rest, let him find somewhere quiet and still,* she thought, studying Elden's profile.

The drive back to town was, like the drive out, anything but leisurely, but it built the excitement as they pulled into the alleyway entrance to Somewhere. Passing by the doorman was no longer intimidating. Elden even let her do the "Friend of Jake" bit and they laughed when she said it in her deepest tenor voice.

The bar was filled with people, music, and laughter. Collette called out to her as they entered, "Jean, back again I see. Thought I'd see you here again! I set those dresses aside. Next week, okay?"

They spent the evening dancing together while Elden joked with his friends and did whatever the men did in the backroom and downstairs. Jean no longer felt concerned when Elden disappeared and her worry about being in a bar, a place so clearly unlawful, seemed to lessen the longer she stayed.

14

And then the days blended into the nights. Jean worked the elevators during the day, bantering with the League Ladies about their exploits and plans, watching the business men come and go with their leather luggage and felt hats. She deftly averted her eyes from the men who showed up with the occasional woman in a short dress, the men who gave too much eye contact to be counted as respectable.

Opulence, power, intrigue, the future – the hotel housed it all and Jean felt a small part of something bigger.

Her nights were captivated by Elden and smoke and gin. Somewhere was becoming the most popular bar in town, filled with young adults, colored jazz musicians playing trumpets and saxophones better than anyone had ever heard, and dancers with feet that moved faster than the musical notes. Time moved quickly in the evenings and mornings came too early.

Jean would always catch a few hours sleep before having to get dressed for work, but the late nights were wearing and she hardly ever - no, never - saw Francie anymore.

The kitten, though, had grown into a plump cat, because Jean shared the delicious leftovers whenever Elden took her out to dinner, which was turning into their regular routine.

It was becoming an effort to keep pace with Elden and maintain a public composure each day at work, putting on a smile every Tuesday morning when the League Ladies convened in the rustle of their finery.

"So you're seeing the Whitcomb boy, are you?" asked one of the ladies as Jean pushed the elevator button for the third floor, shuttling them to their weekly meeting.

"How did you ---?" began Jean.

"It doesn't have to be printed in the paper for it to be known, Jean," scolded one of the ladies.

"Not that the paper doesn't do a thorough job on the Whitcombs, though," gossiped another.

"And we can see how Elden looks when he comes into his father's office, trying to focus on our projects and business. He's distracted. Last time he came in late he was all flush and out of breath....," the young League Lady giggled.

"Now, you stop there. You're not implying that ....," began the lady Jean had dubbed the Rooster Tamer, the one who had counseled Jean to avoid the rushing roosters of the world.

"You're not implying that our Jean is scandalous, are you?" the regal lady inquired.

"Not your girl, no Mrs. Parker. I'm sorry," said the youngest League Lady, chagrined. "I didn't mean..."

"Elden is a fine young man," Mrs. Hayward Parker instructed, "and Miss Jean, Miss Jean is our own. One of our own. Let's not forget that," Mrs. Parker counseled.

The women nodded in quiet agreement as the elevator bell chimed their arrival on the third floor. As the women exited, Jean put out her hand to the Rooster Tamer.

"Thank you, Mrs. Parker. I, I have been out with Elden. And he's dashing and lively, but he's a Whitcomb and it's just that, Elden is ...," Jean fumbled for the words.

Mrs. Parker stopped and stepped back into the elevator. "I know,

Jean. I know," counseled Mrs. Parker, giving Jean's hand a pat. "You remind me of myself, you know. My husband was a debonair young lawyer. My daddy was his tailor. Two different worlds. I know how it feels and what people say. Don't worry about that. I'll take care of things for you."

"I can't thank you enough, Mrs. Parker. I'm on my own now and a girl's reputation, well, Mama always said ..." Jean's voice trailed off. The thought of Mama could take her right back to that sad place.

"And she was right. She was most assuredly right," said Mrs. Parker. "You'll do her proud."

From down the hallway, a voice called, "Mrs. Parker, the meeting is coming to order."

Mrs. Parker took her leave with the final words, "Remember, I'm here if you need a friend."

Jean took comfort in the lady's kindness. *I do need a friend*, Jean thought. That's what is missing. Someone to share with, to talk with. Her steady confidantes, Mama and Francie, were gone. She never had time to dash over to Francie's for a catch up.

Maybe Elden was right, the right and the wrong here had gotten all blurry. Not like things had been, when Mama was alive and she'd had Francie. Francie. It was as if she and Francie, for the first time ever, were living in two different worlds.

I need Francie, Jean thought. She held that thought throughout the day.

On her lunch break, Jean walked gingerly down the stairs to the hotel basement and pushed open the door to the break room. There sat Mrs. Velmar, the woman who had been so imposing her first day on the job.

"Good afternoon, Mrs. Velmar. Beet soup today?" Jean asked.

"Zat right. You sandvich yourself?" Mrs. Velmar replied.

"Peanut butter. Again," Jean said with a smile, opening her lunch sack.

"Smiling. Yes, good but your face, your heart, not happy. I feel it, here," said Mrs. Velmar tapping her ample chest.

"Sad. I guess. I was thinking about my friend. My best friend. It's all different now, with the boys and all," Jean confessed.

"A boy? Pitter pat?" Mrs. Velmar nodded, patting her heart. "Yes, our talk, talk, talk time goes out vindows as boys come and the hearts go pitter pat, yes. No?"

Jean nodded. Mrs. Velmar had cut to the heart of it. Francie had found Harold. She had found Elden and suddenly the talk, talk, talk time, as Mrs. Velmar called it, had vanished.

"Talk time. That's what I need," Jean brightened as she took the last bite of her sandwich. "Talk time. Today. Thank you, Mrs. Velmar!"

Jean flung an arm around the Polish woman's neck and gave her a squeeze.

Mrs. Velmar laughed, "Oh, pitter pat!"

"Zat right," Jean replied realizing she never should have let the pitter pat come between herself and Francie. She owed it to Francie to fix that.

After work Jean walked straight to the Nowak house, hoping to catch Francie before the dinner hour. When no one answered the door, Jean took a seat on the porch swing and waited.

An evening breeze brought with it the scent of Mrs. Nowak's prized gardenias. Jean breathed in the sweet aroma, her thoughts on all that she had to tell Francie.

Surely Francie will be home soon. And within a few brief minutes she spied Francie and Harold coming down the walk, all smiles. Jean waved at them eagerly and called, "I'd hoped you'd be home soon, Francie." She tried not to show her disappointment that Francie didn't run to greet her. Instead, Harold and Francie walked in lock step up the wooden stairs to the porch.

"What a surprise, Jean," Francie said with a smile, taking Jean's hand in her own.

Harold said hello, but seemed formal and stilted as he spoke of the weather and the greenness of the lawn. Jean stood awkwardly on the porch, wishing Harold would leave. Nothing felt right about this.

Something was hanging in the air between them and Jean wasn't quite sure what it might be.

Finally, Francie burst forth with the question that had been nagging at her for weeks.

"You're still seeing him, aren't you?" Francie asked, squeezing Jean's hand.

Harold put his arm around Francie as he looked on pensively. Jean's heart sank. She swallowed hard and nodded in reply.

"He's trouble, Jean. We know about that bar. And he has a reputation, mother says, and then she said the Whitcombs always get what they want, whatever the cost. And I don't think she meant money," Francie cautioned, her head shaking back and forth.

"He really likes me, Francie. Truly. And I like him. It's not anything bad," Jean countered.

"But he's not like us. He's ..." Francie cast around for the right word. "He's too fast." Harold shook his head in agreement. Jean could feel her defenses rising. Harold was judging her, and making Francie turn away.

"He's not fast with me. He's different, sweet and he knows I'm not like that. It's a relief for him, I think," replied Jean. Harold did not try to hide the roll of his eyes. "You don't have to believe me if you don't want to, but I am just fine. Stop rolling your eyes, Harold."

"Be careful," said Francie. "Just be careful. We're just worried, aren't we, Harold?"

Harold nodded, his lips drawn tight into a frown.

"But we can still be friends, right, Francie?" Jean said, trying to keep the plea out of her question.

"Of course," Francie said with a note of hesitancy, but took that moment to drop Jean's hand. Jean noticed and saw that Francie had absently picked up the hem of her dress and was rolling it between her fingers. A remnant of how she'd dealt with stress when the nuns scolded her in primary school.

Jean could feel her own eyes filling with tears and she sat quickly down on the porch swing, trying to hide her emotions.

"Come on Francie, we have to go," Harold said, tugging at Francie's hand. "We're watching all the kids today so Francie's parents can have dinner with mine. Again," his voice was filled with pride. Francie blushed.

"They're getting along great, too, our parents," confided Francie.

"Nice," said Jean. "That's nice for you. Well, I guess I'll see you sometime, you two." Harold was already headed toward the front door, his discomfort apparent.

"Yeah, sometime. We'll see you sometime," said Harold as he opened the front door for Francie. Jean rose from the porch swing and gave Francie a quick embrace.

"Harold just wants us to do everything right, you know. He really is trying to make a good impression on mom and dad, I think," Francie whispered before turning to go into the house. "Wish us luck."

Jean watched the door close behind the couple and felt her stomach sink when Francie didn't turn to wave goodbye. Things had changed, irretrievably changed, between her and Francie. She wondered if it would ever be right again, and that question left her with an empty feeling. But Elden still adored her, Jean reminded herself. That would be enough. She held that thought tightly in her chest.

15

"Big night at Somewhere," Elden announced as he entered the elevator the next morning.

"And?" Jean asked coyly.

"And we'll go, you and me. Right?"

"Can we invite Francie and...."

"No, it's not something they would ... oh, c'mon, just say yes."

Elden's confidence was impermeable, something Jean found endearing but confounding all the same. *Of course I'll go,* Jean thought, *even though I'm short on sleep.* She had tossed on the thin mattress all night, worrying about Francie and how she was slipping away. A night out would get that off her mind at least.

"What time?"

"I'll pick you up at 7, okay?" Elden replied.

"Blue dress?" Jean asked, remembering Collette's generosity.

"The gold snazzy one tonight. Not sweet, okay?" Elden said slipping his arm around her waist just as the elevator chimed its arrival on the eighth floor.

"Your father's elevator bell saved my virtue just in time," Jean joked, pushing him gently out the door.

"This time," Elden said as he narrowed his eyes mysteriously.

"Seven on the dot then," Jean said, giving the brass door a firm pull shut.

~

The crowd was just filling out and music had started in full swing as Jean and Elden entered the bar. Collette was the first one on the dance floor and Jean joined her, as was their habit. Elden disappeared into a throng of boisterous young men.

Before the first set was over, Jean spied Elden emerging from the backroom looking serious, surprisingly sober, and with a fierceness of purpose in his eyes. Jean spotted him across the room and he wore a look she had never seen.

He crossed the dance floor and roughly took Jean's arm. "We go now. Don't look. Don't look back. Keep your head down. Just follow me. Collette, you go now, too." He had his jacket pulled back and Jean saw that his right hand was wrapped around a gun.

No one else in the room seemed to notice anything was amiss.

Collette called out, "Nighty, night, little lovebirds." Jean automatically turned back to wave goodbye.

Elden snapped her attention forward with a furtive hiss, "No. Just walk fast."

A chilling fear crawled up her spine. It was a time to do what she was told and not ask questions.

Elden pushed her through the door to the long hallway that snaked toward the alleyway entrance. He opened the panel that led to the secret stairway and the room with the still.

Just as the panel closed behind them they heard a burst of commotion. Federal agents. A raid. Shots were fired and there were voices and yelling.

Jean could hardly breathe. She suddenly felt very sober, knowing she should move quickly and not say a word. Elden didn't stop until they had made it to the room with the still and were out the back way to the alley.

"What happened?" asked Jean.

"Keep walking. We'll talk in the car," he replied.

Once in the safety of the car Jean looked at Elden and saw the wild in his eyes. He rambled incoherently, "Agents. Protection. Didn't pay protection on time. Again. My job. My only job. Dammit. Dammit," he said hitting the steering wheel fiercely.

"Alonzo tipped me off the feds were coming just now. Five minutes more and I could have cleared the place. Dammit," he said striking the steering wheel a second time.

Jean had no idea how to piece all of that together but could tell that whatever it was, there was no question that Elden felt it was his fault.

"Can I help?" she asked naively.

Elden looked at her blankly and then seemed to snap back, appreciating what Jean had seen and almost experienced.

"Don't think about this and whatever you do, don't mention this at the Empire. Let me get you home. Then I'll make it right, circle back and clean up," Elden said looking over at Jean whose mouth was starting to form a question. "No questions. I'll explain it all later. Don't worry. Everything's fine." Elden said emphatically.

"Not a word," said Jean putting a shaking finger up to her lips.

She was filled with dread about what she had seen, what had almost happened. And the gun. It was a brush too close with ruin. It could have changed everything.

She watched Elden carefully as he drove. He was controlled this time, extremely controlled, silent, eyes fixed on the road. As they pulled up to her building she knew she had to say something, let him know she was going to be okay. But Elden spoke first, words she never thought she'd hear.

"I'm sorry, Jean. You deserve better than me. I shouldn't have ever taken you to the bar. You're not that kind of girl and I knew it. I knew it. I knew I'd ruin everything. It's what I do," he said, leaning his head on the steering wheel, not meeting her eyes.

His words brought tears to Jean's eyes. She wanted to wrap her arms around him, reassure him it would be fine, that it would all work out, that they would always be together, even in times like this.

She couldn't find the words. Instead, Jean leaned over and kissed him gently on the cheek as she brushed his bangs out of his eyes and into place.

"I need you, Elden. I'll always be here," Jean whispered. Elden looked up at her, his eyes wet.

"I can't do this to you, Jean. I need to clean things up now. We'll talk later," he said.

"You'll do the right thing, Elden. I know you will," she assured, summoning a confidence she didn't quite feel.

Jean opened the car door and let herself out, then stood and watched as Elden pulled away. She walked slowly up the concrete stairs to the lobby, grateful to find it empty, the hallways quiet and marked only by the familiar smell of Mrs. Ivanovic's pierogies.

As Jean climbed the stairs, she suddenly felt tired, no, exhausted from all the questions of how this perfect man had gotten involved with such an imperfect place, something so illegal and dangerous. The questions swirled in her head and then landed like lead weights on her heart, pulling her down. She took the key from around her neck. As she fit the key in the lock her shoe brushed against something. A paper bag. Pierogies. Warm. Her heart flooded with gratitude.

Inside, she unwrapped the paper bag and pulled out two warm pierogies, wrapped in waxed paper. Comfort. She devoured the pillows of potato goodness, slipped off her shoes, and fell directly onto the bed. *What did I just get into?* she wondered. Then, in the fog just before sleep, she questioned, *Did I lock the door? Of course, I always do* and with that, she slept.

Across town, Elden's evening had only begun.

16

*A*fter watching Jean walk into her apartment building, Elden drove just down the block then pulled over to watch the light go on in Jean's third floor apartment. Jean was safe, he could breathe easier for that reason alone - but now he had work to do.

Elden pulled the Revere into the alley that led to Somewhere. The feds had cleared out and left a guard at the door. The guard, dressed in dungarees and a chambray shirt, was smoking a cigarette and leaning on the door. Definitely an hourly man, Elden assessed.

"Somethin' happen here tonight?" Elden asked as he approached the guard.

"Joint's closed tonight, mister. You know, the usual. Bust it up, shut it down. Probably be open again tomorrow."

"Paddy wagon come?" asked Elden casually.

"Nah," said the guard, taking a puff from his cigarette.

"Torn up pretty bad?" asked Elden.

"Nah, not bad," said the man.

"Any gunshots, anybody hurt?" Elden asked.

"Nah. Owner's some important guy. This was just for show. Heard he didn't pay his share, you know," said the guard as he ground the cigarette with his heel.

"So where can a man get a drink around here then?" asked Elden.

"Can't say. Can't say for sure, but I can tell you where they raided yesterday. I'm sure they're open," the man said with a rough laugh.

Elden laughed and clapped the man on the back. "Funny. You're funny. Hey, my name's Elden, Elden Whitcomb."

"Elden Whitcomb?" asked the man, a flash of recognition crossed the man's wrinkled face.

"Yes, sir. You know, I actually own this place," replied Elden with what appeared to be a confident smile. "Heard there was some trouble. Let me go in and pour you a tall one. You got a long night here."

"Shouldn't do that. Rules you know," said the man.

"Shouldn't maybe, but didn't say couldn't," observed Elden.

"Well, that's because I could. Ain't no one else comin' here tonight. I'm off duty at six in the mornin' anyhow. I'm in charge here," said the guard, jutting his thumb toward his chest.

"Yes, sir. Yes, you are," Elden nodded agreeably. "But the night's young, my man," said Elden, carefully putting his hand in his pants pocket and palming a ten dollar bill. He kept a sawbuck folded in his pocket for times like these.

"I'm sorry, I didn't catch your name there, my man," he said offering the guard a handshake, "Like I said, I'm Elden."

The man shook Elden's outstretched hand. "Ain't gonna tell you my name but you can call me Tony," said the guard. Elden's hand came back empty. Mission accomplished.

"Fifteen minutes. I'll give you fifteen minutes inside. Take a look around, see what you have to clean up, come right back. More than fifteen and I'll have to ring HQ," said Tony agreeably.

"Twist of lime with that tall one, Tony?" asked Elden.

"Yup," said the guard, opening the door just enough to let Elden pass.

Inside tables were overturned and broken barware was strewn across the floor. The bottles behind the bar were gone but they clearly hadn't searched for the stash. The piano bench was busted. Why did they have to go and do that? Elden thought. That was just spiteful. The rest, it was inventory. Inventory comes and goes – a piano bench, that was different. Damned Feds. But this wouldn't take much to fix.

Somewhere would be back open by mid-week for sure, after that payment is made, Elden thought. He knew better than to delegate protection delivery to someone else. His father had explained that the very first day Somewhere opened.

Elden recalled the conversation, his father's face set in its determination, his eyes trained on Elden's face with each word.

His father had explained the business, the connections, the Kansas City underground who took care of the speakeasies. Those who knew how to get things done and assure that the authorities look the other way.

There were people you just didn't wrong in this town, his father had said, and then he'd named the names. He told Elden how all of the Whitcomb businesses were run by the grace of those people, powerful people, people they had to keep content. He'd explained the consequences of having one of them lose that contentment. Consequences too horrid to imagine. And it had finally come to pass. Elden had neglected the payments one time too many.

Elden had been entrusted to take this business and keep it running, quietly, profitably running. And he'd blown it. True, it wasn't the first time, or even the second or the third that Elden had missed the weekly pay-off. But it was the last time now.

Elden could envision the look on his father's face when he heard the reason for the raid. He knew how his father would look– disappointed. It was the one look that cut Elden to the core. He could already hear his mother's spiteful diatribe - irresponsible, ungrateful, screw up. All words Elden had heard again and again over the years.

Maybe they were right. Maybe he needed structure in his life. Maybe he didn't know how to run a business and do what was needed. This might have to be the end of the line for Good Times Elden, he thought, as he picked up a broom.

Elden cleaned up what he could, swept the glass up from the floor and surveyed the walls for bullet holes. There were only two, both above the bar, more than seven feet up the wall. Those were wild shots, just for theatrical effect, undoubtedly.

Elden knew he had to let the family attorney know about this – maybe he'd call old Hayward even before talking to Pops, Elden thought. Hayward Parker, Esquire could fix anything. He'd bailed Elden out from the senior year pranks.

The seniors had a tradition of kidnapping the Dean of Student's horse and pet parrot every spring. The rules were simple: take the parrot from the Dean's office and secret away the horse from the riding stable. The duo had to stay together somewhere on school premises but each year the location had to be more outrageous than the year prior.

Elden had come up with a plan that eclipsed all the previous. Wentworth had a new cafeteria complete with a newfangled state-of-the-art walk-in freezer. They'd tethered the parrot to the freezer door using the band around its leg and coaxed the horse inside. His boys had arranged the deed for the wee hours of the morning so the old breakfast cook would find the pair. Hilarious. Legendary.

Who knew that the old horse had arthritis and would go almost lame like that? But it was the damned parrot that ratted him out by name.

"Witless Whitcomb, Witless Whitcomb," sang out the parrot, using the unfortunate nickname the staff had designated for Elden.

But just one call to Hayward and the Dean was patting Elden's back and calling him clever. Hayward had the means, knew how to work magic.

Hayward magic was definitely needed here, thought Elden ruefully as he swept the bits of broken glass into a dustpan and emptied it into the dustbin. It would all work out tomorrow. Now, it was late and there was nothing more to do, except fix that drink for the man standing guard.

In the backroom, Elden quickly located the gin stash kept hidden behind the shelves. It was enough hooch for a week's business, just in case. The stash also held a lock and key in the event of just such an occasion as this. He poured a double for Tony and took it and put the lock and key in his front pocket.

"For you, Tony," Elden said showing the guard the drink as he neared the front door, "if you let me put on this lock, okay? Can't leave the business open when you go off duty, you know."

"Course. That's how it's done," said the man, taking the offering. "Some send a goon over to change it out. Better to have you do it; you're a good man, and a personal bartender. Nice combination," said Tony raising his glass in Elden's direction.

Elden put a new lock on the hasp and clicked it shut. He had had enough for one night.

"I'd say nice to meet you, Tony, but it really wasn't," said Elden, not without kindness.

"Yeah, I hear that a lot," said Tony, "I hope we don't meet again."

"Me, too," said Elden. "No one else goes in tonight, all right?"

"Okay. Your rules. G'night," replied Tony, taking another drink.

With that, Elden headed back to his car. He wanted nothing more than to find Jean and hold her close. He needed comfort. So much had just come crashing down and much more would come crashing down tomorrow.

Jean had to have been scared out of her wits tonight, he thought. He felt guilty. He'd failed to protect her.

He would just drive over and see if he could explain a little about this part of his life, the part she knew nothing about. The part that scared him, kept him awake nights – the fact that his father skirted the edge of the law in all of his operations and had entrusted Elden to the secrets of getting business done. Elden had questioned whether doing business with the city's underground powerhouses and their enforcers was wise. His father had brusquely responded that he should not be 'naïve,' that he needed to 'be a man' and not worry so much. Then he'd made it clear that Elden was to take over his father's operations in every respect.

"You want to operate in this city, you talk to the men with the real power, you pay them their due," his father had bluntly explained.

Recalling the exchange, Elden knew that he owed Jean an explanation. He needed to tell her everything and then he'd let her make her own decision. Elden prayed she'd understand, and maybe even help him figure a way out, make it all better.

The light in Jean's apartment was still on when he drove by. I'll just go check on her, Elden thought, just for a minute.

He parked the car on a side street and walked to her apartment building. It was way too late for the doorman to be on duty and for that tiny mercy, he was grateful. That man watched everything and he cared too.

He was probably the one person who could influence Jean to walk away, Elden thought. The father-figure who had guided her in ways she probably didn't even realize. Elden could see that from the first time he'd come to call on Jean, how Otis had watched her closely and watched him even closer.

Elden walked up the three flights of steps and knocked gently on her door. No answer. He tried the door and it was unlocked. He opened it as quietly as he could. A flash of pepper-colored fur zoomed past him, and he leaped back. Then he laughed at himself; here he felt like such a big man, and he'd been frightened by a little cat.

He peered into the apartment. This place was even smaller and sadder than he'd ever envisioned. It had a tiny table and two wooden chairs by the window, a small chair by the chest of drawers, and a bedside table with a narrow bed, worn and tired. He'd never seen a home so spare, so lacking in any extra, devoid of even the smallest luxury.

'How the other half lived,' his mother would have sneered in her haughty way, refusing to see the humanity in anyone of reduced circumstance. He'd been raised with such falsehoods, so petty and empty. Elden's heart went out to Jean. This girl needed him even more than he'd realized.

He looked over at the bed. Jean was sleeping soundly. She looked like such a sweet angel, her face free of all tension, so peaceful and genuine. Suddenly he felt so old, so tired, exhausted to the core. She wouldn't mind if he just curled up beside her, Elden thought. He gently sat on the edge of the bed. It was soft and inviting. He'd only rest his head for a minute, he thought. He felt hot, and he flung his suit coat to the floor.

Jean awoke to a familiar smell. Elden. She definitely smelled Elden's cologne and juniper berries. She rolled over. He was lying there next to her, his suit on and hat resting on his chest. He let out a noisy snore. At first, Jean felt stricken and horrified at the idea of any man in her bed.

But, then again, it is Elden, she thought. She edged closer to him - he smelled good, so familiar. She felt so safe.

"Jean," he murmured sleepily, and he wrapped his arms around her.

He kissed her then, and she felt his strong hands sliding beneath her cotton nightgown. A shiver of delight went through her as he gently brushed a strand of hair from her eyes and kissed her on her neck, sliding his lips to her shoulder. She let him lead, just as he led when they danced together, and he lifted her above him.

Moonlight flooded the room in soft golden blue. Any thought that it could be wrong vanished as he enveloped her sweetness.

The next morning, she wouldn't think of the sharp twinge of pain or the gush of red that had stained her eyelet gown. Her whole body still tingled with the memory of that sweetness and safety, a blend more potent than any she ever had known. She didn't feel right using Mama's favorite lavender soap on the spot, so she put white salt on it and rinsed until the water ran clear.

17

The telephone rang in the offices of Parker, Benson & Partners, Attorneys at Law at eight a.m. sharp. Hayward Parker, coffee cup in hand, answered the phone, annoyed that his secretary was late.

It was the Whitcomb boy. Again. At least it wasn't the boy's father, Hayward thought. It's about time someone let Elden stand on his own two feet. Hayward listened to the Whitcomb boy tell his latest tale of legal entanglement, as Elden's words tumbled over themselves.

"Just some of that Hayward magic, okay?" Elden asked hopefully, but Hayward knew there was no magic dust to sprinkle on this latest situation. This wasn't going to be solved with a quick telephone call to a school dean filled with reminiscences of their own schoolboy antics.

"Probably little to be done here," said Hayward, "So don't get your hopes up on having this just go away. The agency has gotten serious about prosecuting and holding up examples. Old schoolmate of mine runs the local Bureau of Prohibition. He can be a tough one, but I'll do my best."

"Hayward, you've made bigger problems than this disappear," Elden cajoled.

"Let me make a call, Elden," Hayward concluded, making no promises. Hayward hung up the receiver and ruffled through the notecards on his desk, searching for the Bureau's telephone number. His friend answered on the second ring and Hayward explained the situation.

"Hayward, it's youth culture gone wrong," Hayward's friend replied. "You wouldn't believe what was toted out of Somewhere's holding bins. And the still. No, two stills. Makes the hooch right there. Quite the operation."

"No different from the raid down the street last month, right?" asked Hayward, his voice controlled and nonchalant.

"Different this time," said the agent. "This was high profile, Hayward. Sent from the top down. It's those damned kids. Agency directive is to crack down on Kansas City and Somewhere was a perfect target. Lots of young kids there, owned by a young kid. Coloreds and whites sometimes there together, too. You know what I'm saying. Hell, even the Savoy Grill is admitting women now, white women at least, but don't think that didn't hurt their business. Least for a time. What the hell is next?"

"Last time I checked being young, female, or even a colored isn't a high crime, least not in our city," offered Hayward, casting his eyes toward the ceiling.

"Let's not be naïve here. He's taken business from the established men's grills, Hayward. Yes, even the Savoy and, like I said, they were already hurting. This is generational. This youth thing, it won't just go away. Don't think that it will. The case is already assigned to a prosecutor — Charles Raltimer."

Hayward groaned at the mention of the name as his friend from the Prohibition Bureau continued, "Raltimer's not a man open to discussions, if you know what I mean."

Hayward had no doubt what his friend meant. More than one of Hayward's clients had a checkbook thicker than Hayward's legal ethics tome, and none of them ever made headway with Raltimer.

Hayward hung up the phone grimly and poured himself another cup of coffee. Breaking this news to the Whitcomb family would not be easy. They were used to paying for a result and getting one fast.

He hadn't failed Mr. Whitcomb yet, but this one was going to take some thought. With Mr. Whitcomb, it was always about the business, the money, the results. Hayward shook his head, thinking how all the meetings, the businesses, the money, had brought the Whitcombs wealth and status, but all of the material success had failed the one thing the Whitcombs had once loved the most, their son. Elden. He'd been a good boy, earnest, happy.

Hayward wanted to sit Mr. and Mrs. Whitcomb both down, tell them to look, really look, at the boy now. Lost, sad, drinking too much and driving too fast – everyone in town knew. But the Whitcombs didn't come to his office for personal guidance. And who was he, a man never a father himself, to pontificate about the right way to raise a son.

Hayward set aside these concerns of the heart, picked up the phone and dialed the Whitcomb's exchange. Mrs. Whitcomb answered and was sitting across the desk from Hayward Parker within the hour.

"Well, I'll make it go away, if you can't, Mr. Parker," said Mrs. Whitcomb, the crispness in her voice making no doubt of her ability. Hayward wasn't exactly sure what Mrs. Whitcomb had in mind, but her determination was unquestionable.

"You get me an appointment with this prosecutor Mr. Raltimer, today. And don't give me that look. I said today!" Katherine Whitcomb concluded, leaving Hayward no room for negotiation.

Hayward sighed. Mrs. Whitcomb was not to be reasoned with. There was no way Hayward could change either this woman's mind or the prosecutor's directive in this case.

"I will, ma'am but don't expect tears and a plea for mercy to make any difference. This man's a straight arrow. And leave your checkbook at home. If you try anything funny, this man will ruin your husband's reputation. Let's be clear on that," Hayward cautioned.

Hayward scheduled an appointment with the prosecutor for three p.m., knowing Mrs. Whitcomb's unorthodox meeting would amount to nothing. If she had arrangements to offer, Hayward knew they would have little to do with law and the procedure books and would rightfully be rejected out of hand. Katherine could just as well attend alone, sparing Hayward the embarrassment of witnessing her feeble attempt to sway the prosecutor.

~

"The boy is of legal age, he owns the place, and is guaranteed five years of jail time," the prosecutor explained to Mrs. Whitcomb, not sparing the harsh tone he felt for all the upstarts like Elden who were trying to wreak havoc on the city and established ways.

Hayward had explained to her that a commoner would face at least five years in prison for running an operation like Somewhere; she knew she could arrange better for Elden. It was ridiculous to think a little speakeasy could ruin a young man, a young man who had always paid out the share due and came from a good family; no, came from a very good family.

Mrs. Whitcomb sat across from the man who held her son's fate, looking him straight in the eye. She had carefully unfastened the top three buttons of her dress and gave every appearance of carelessness as she had taken her seat, absently hitching her skirt to expose her knee and beyond as she crossed her legs. She knew that a prosecutor could make things happen – both in his office and the courtroom and she knew middle-aged men well enough to predict his weakness.

The prosecutor was momentarily distracted as Mrs. Whitcomb fingered the hem of her skirt, creating the look of nervousness but placing her fingers with care. She uncrossed her legs and wrapped one foot around the chair leg.

When she had the man's full attention, she made a small sound in her throat and began, "Five years is a long time for a young man, and a Wentworth boy at that, sir. Wentworth boys, you know them, Mr. Raltimer. Bet you may have been one of them yourself once upon a time," Mrs. Whitcomb smiled modestly and dropped her eyes.

Katherine knew the prosecutor's history and that he had made Wentworth lore some twenty years before, all piss and vinegar. He was the one found toting a naked girl from the Catholic school across the commons on his own bare back.

The prosecutor looked at her, a bit of color rising in his cheeks, and offered up nothing other than a quiet, sanctimonious nod.

Mrs. Whitcomb let her breasts fall front and center as she leaned across the man's desk. "Look at that," she said breathlessly, pointing to the file folder open before him. She raised her eyes to check that the man's gaze had landed squarely on the gifts laid before him.

Her own eyes gleamed and with a captivating delay, she drummed her fingers on the open folder.

"You have discretion here, sir. That means we can be discreet," she said, leaning back in her chair and crossing and uncrossing her legs provocatively, "So worst case, and it's a naughty little case, would be, say, one year prison time, right? But we both know that Elden is a good boy. Oh, he has a wild streak," she said batting her eyes. "Comes by it honestly, you know," her voice dropping to a husky whisper. "And I do believe we have extenuating circumstances. What I'd like to do here is give you personal reasons why an alternative prosecution is proper."

Katherine absently fingered the necklace that dangled between her breasts.

The man's cheeks blazed and he reached up to loosen the tie that suddenly had grown too tight. This meeting was the kind of encounter he'd only daydreamed of during his government tenure. He was accustomed to pleas made by men in suits with their pockets stuffed with cash. What she was offering carried much more currency. He adjusted himself in his chair, making himself receptive to her every justification. She responded in kind, sharing every special circumstance and whispering the most important parts about the lengths she would attend to if leniency could only be shown. The prosecutor listened, watching Mrs. Whitcomb carefully as she pleaded her son's case.

This was the girl he'd grown up with, on the wrong side of town, the girl with the chestnut hair and curves. The girl he'd follow home from school, hoping she would glance back and catch him looking. The man doubted she even recalled him, even knew his name.

"He is such a good young man, truly he is," Mrs. Whitcomb explained. "We've had our problems. Elden takes things to heart. He's preoccupied, so much on his mind."

The prosecutor nodded. Elden's reputation was well known. He'd been a good student, affable, comfortable with adults and Wentworth boys alike, who all appreciated his predilection for practical jokes. But then came the booze and the women.

Women had always been the downfall of the Whitcomb men, the prosecutor recalled. First, it was Whitcomb Senior falling for the Croatian stockworker's daughter who sat before him now, fully displaying the wares that had won her a place in the Whitcomb family two decades before.

Then came the Senior's trouble with the hotel maid, Cassandra Lee, whose plight was whispered throughout the city's social clubs. Elden had followed in his father's steps from age fifteen on. Always with a new girl on his arm.

"I wasn't the mother I should have been," Katherine Whitcomb continued. "I was worried about things, all the time. You know the family I came from. I know you do. I remember, you know. You, with your one pair of tweed pants and a hickory wood slingshot in the back pocket. Like you, we had nothing. Nothing. Joining the Whitcomb family changed everything. I could feel how my life was always supposed to be. Like yours is now, too," she said glancing around the well-appointed office.

The man's heart quickened. She did remember him and he did understand. Katherine caught the slight smile that played on his lips and continued, "Elden doesn't know about that part, about me. The poverty. But he's always been fighting against something. Maybe it's the not knowing he's been fighting against, battling something he can sense but can't name. I don't know."

Katherine Whitcomb dropped her head to her chest and tears fell on her blouse. "I never wanted it to come to this. The boy has everything, had everything. He needs a second chance." She sniffled and raised her head. "I need to make it right. Give him a second chance, for my sake. Please?" The prosecutor shifted in his chair, his cheeks flush.

Mrs. Whitcomb studied his face. "I remember how you looked at me, followed me home. I remember," she said, letting her eyes soften ever so much as she raised her thick lashes and met his gaze. "I'll do anything if you can work this out. Anything. And we won't speak a word of it. I promise."

The man mulled over her words and silently considered the length she offered to attend to, perspiration gathering on his upper lip. He rose from his leather chair and locked his office door. This matter could be resolved amicably.

Mrs. Whitcomb was waiting at Hayward's office the next morning when Hayward rounded the corner from the elevator. She was pleased to report the leniency the prosecutor offered, after their meeting drew to a zippered close.

All charges would be dropped if the boy returned to Wentworth, received a commission and gave a guarantee of three years' military service. She explained that Wentworth would be pleased to have a Whitcomb rejoin its ranks and that the kind Mr. Raltimer had made a personal call to the dean to make the arrangements.

Mr. Hayward tilted his head, curious about how this had come about so quickly.

"Of course," Mrs. Whitcomb continued, "The dean had agreed that Elden was affable and polished, a good officer candidate. He promised that Elden would leave not only with a commission but friendships to last a lifetime, his position in the city's business community solidified. That prosecutor is an old friend, you know. We were childhood playmates. Like you say, connections never hurt, do they Hayward?" Mrs. Whitcomb smiled beatifically.

"All in all, that is one amazing agreement," said Hayward, who was not privy to the lengths Mrs. Whitcomb had gone to arrange the settlement. "Elden's a fortunate young man. Not every boy with his run of trouble gets a second chance at Wentworth – only boys like yours, with no complications. Good families."

"That's very kind of you to say, Mr. Parker. Elden may have had his little indiscretions, you know," volunteered Mrs. Whitcomb, "but those are behind him. One evening shouldn't ruin a boy's life."

"Yes, yes," Hayward agreed heartily. "What we have here is just a small run-in with regulations. Not serious. Now, I tell you, it's the run-in with the females that's limited more than one Wentworth man's future," Hayward cautioned, recalling more than a few of his classmates who'd created their own nine-month life sentences.

Mrs. Whitcomb knew that boys with obligations of the family kind couldn't enter or return to Wentworth. It was a place for the single men, the young men with futures to be shaped not those burdened with encumbrances that could cloud their judgment. Boys with poor judgment and encumbrances were not like her Elden. Those were the common boys who would just as soon work at the stockyards. Katherine tipped her nose upwards. Those kind of boys weren't meant to be Wentworth men. That would not be her Elden. Her Elden was a Whitcomb, and bred to be a Wentworth man, Katherine silently reassured herself.

"You're a persuasive woman, Mrs. Whitcomb. Don't know how you arranged this but you should be very proud of yourself," Hayward volunteered handily. "Like I said, Elden is very fortunate. Not every woman can change a federal prosecutor's mind once it's made up."

18

The words "she's a harlot," were out of Mrs. Whitcomb's mouth before Elden could say good afternoon.

It was the first week of October and Mrs. Whitcomb sat at her writing desk in the dark library, a stack of bills and a tall gin and tonic before her. She had just gone over the autumn bills and summoned Elden.

"Eighty-Seven Dollars for a dress? Elden, what did you dress this trollop in? Solid gold?"

"What are you even talking about?" asked Elden exasperated. Mother threw this kind of tizzy every quarter when she got it in her head to be Queen of the family finances. Usually her complaints were about some automobile bill or a bauble he'd purchased for a girl. It was always something.

"Elden, you have got to stop this. Eighty-Seven dollars for one of your girls, a new girl I expect. Trollop, strumpet, harlot, choose your word. Whatever she is cannot be hidden in an expensive dress," Mrs. Whitcomb said, waving a bill from Emery, Bird, Thayer in the air.

"You need to date that nice neighbor girl. She's from a good family, a League family, and she's a debutante. Stop chasing these loose skirts and settle down," Katherine Whitcomb instructed.

"Stop it, mother. You're being ugly. There must be some mistake. You always exaggerate," said Elden, crossing his arms reflexively.

"Oh, there's no mistaking this, Elden. Look for yourself," she said thrusting the bill in front of him.

She was right. There was no mistake. Eighty-Six dollars and Seventy-Five cents. That was nearly impossible, but there it was in black and white. Impossible, but unmistakable. Elden's heart sank.

"The League Ladies tell me you have set your cap for the damned elevator operator. In our hotel, for God's sake. The help, Elden. I assured them it wasn't true, not a grain of truth in that story. The Whitcomb men aren't like that, I said. One of the women laughed. Actually scoffed out loud at me when I said that," said Katherine, taking a long draw on her tumbler of gin.

"Ruined my lunch, that woman did. She thinks she's so much better than me with her Marshall Field & Company shoes, but she's not. And about those League Ladies, some of their daughters are interested in you, you know that don't you? It'd do your father some good if you'd date one. Just one. Don't queue them up and saunter down the line feeling up their fancy. This time just choose one. One. And not that one that looks like a horse, for God's sake. Maybe that little blonde. She'd be fine," said Katherine more to herself than to Elden.

Elden gave his mother a stern look, a look she was not accustomed to seeing from her son.

"I'm enjoying my time with Jean, mother. It doesn't matter that she's the elevator operator. She's real, she's sweet. She's trusting. This bill isn't her fault. It's mine. I didn't tell her there was a limit. I told her to buy whatever her heart desired. I'm sure the salesman overcharged her, too, because it's 'on account.' You know they're not careful about that. It won't happen again," Elden assured.

Katherine hid her disdain, waiting to choose her words as she picked up the half-empty tumbler and took a drink. Her son was not one to talk back. She needed to put a stop to it.

"Well, of course, it won't happen again. Don't even think that it can. The solution is quite simple. You won't see her again. Common,

Elden. She's one of those common girls from the hotel. An elevator operator will take anyone for a ride," she sneered.

"Stop it, Mother. That's terrible. You can't talk about her that way. Jean is more than that," protested Elden.

Jean had become more than that to Elden. She had taken him in her arms when he needed solace, had said all the words no one else had ever spoken so true – that he was strong and capable, that they'd build a future, would dip their toes in the pond by the waterfall and grow old on that back porch, together. She didn't talk about cars or dances, the event of the season or dresses. She was a serious girl and she was his, all his.

"You embarrass me, Elden. She'll never be more than one of the common girls," Mrs. Whitcomb said, continuing her confrontation. Elden rolled his eyes, which was easier than explaining the concept of real love to his mother after she'd had a few drinks.

"Be serious. You're never serious, Elden. If you were serious you would have finished at Wentworth the first time. You'd be a Captain by now. What are you doing instead? Playing with a little common girl. Spending our money. It has got to stop. People are talking. We have a station in life, in this city. Wipe that smirk off your face, Elden. It's not a practical joke, you know. We are a reflection of your father's success, his business. I shouldn't have to even say that anymore."

Elden's eyes narrowed. He knew how to end an ugly confrontation with his mother; it worked every time like a charm.

"You drink too much, Mother," said Elden taking the gin and tonic from her hand and walking out of the room. That ended the conversation. His mother would have no retort.

Elden's hands shook as he finished the drink and put the glass into the kitchen sink. Eighty-seven dollars was out of line, but his kitten, Jean, was worth every sweet penny. That it pissed off the lush was sheer bonus.

19

Jean hadn't felt like herself for several mornings. She knew she was coming down with something but slowly pulled on her clothes. Orion had slept in the little bed she'd made for him, fashioned from one of Mama's old flannel nightgowns. Jean couldn't stand to throw it away or bear the idea of wearing it, but it suited Orion just right.

"I'm glad you can't catch people sicknesses," Jean said, stroking his soft fur. "You are the perkiest, prettiest part of my mornings."

Orion didn't say anything. In the mornings, when she went to work, the cat made his own rounds of the building, keeping the mouse population under control. Sometimes he would be outside the building when she got home, but it always seemed like he felt ready to rest in his bed when she started toward her own.

Jean squared her shoulders and headed to work. The League Ladies were having a breakfast function and Mr. Whitcomb was meeting with representatives of the Negro League. The elevator would be busy. The Consumer League's chatter filled the lobby as Jean entered.

"How's our girl?" called out her favorite League lady, the Rooster Tamer, the one who had once smiled and introduced herself as

Michele. And then had quickly added in a regal voice, "Oh, I suppose I mean 'Mrs. Hayward Parker'." The kind lady had laughed and laughed and Jean could tell it was an intentional affectation. After that Jean always asked her how the roosters were doing and the lady seemed to enjoy the inside joke.

"Oh, Jean, you look peaked," Mrs. Parker said. "Are you feeling okay?"

"A little queasy today I think. Must have been something I ate," said Jean, brushing off her discomfort. She'd come to enjoy the banter of the League Ladies and appreciated when they spoke to her like an equal, not one of the help.

"If employers gave sick leave then you'd be able to stay home when you're sick. That might be the next issue we take up at the League. What do you think?" asked Mrs. Parker.

"I think you ladies can do whatever you put your minds to. The League is really something," said Jean.

Sick leave. That would be the day, Jean silently mused.

What she wouldn't give to be able to think such big thoughts and then put them to work. She smiled at Mrs. Parker then quickly grasped the back of a lobby chair as her knees began to give out from under her. She was suddenly overcome with the feeling of being both queasy and faint.

"You look like you should sit down," instructed Mrs. Parker, gesturing toward one of the velvet chairs, her head bent with concern.

"I'll take an early break today, but now I have to clock in," Jean replied, mustering a slight smile. She gingerly took soft steps across the lobby and down to the basement, making her way to the time clock.

"'Jean? Pretty morning, no?" bellowed Mrs. Velmar, greeting Jean as she punched in.

"Hello, Mrs. Velmar."

"Oh, hat look nice today. But you, you," said Mrs. Velmar, observing Jean's face closely, "you look tired codfish. Codfish left on the vindow. You sick?"

Jean grimaced at the thought of cod. "Mrs. Velmar, you have a way with the King's English. Tired codfish," she tried to laugh but couldn't. "No, I'm not sick. Tired. Really. Just tired."

Jean could hear Mrs. Velmar tut-tutting as she walked away.

Every jerk of the elevator brought a wave of nausea. By ten o'clock, Jean knew she needed some fresh air. She walked quickly through the lobby and stepped outside. The air was crisp and brown leaves swirled on the sidewalk. She spied James just leaving Lydia's shop next door.

That's it, Jean thought, *I'll visit Lydia and put my feet up just a minute.*

"Jean, come in. Haven't seen you in awhile. Read about you in the paper some though," Lydia said with a smile as she waved Jean to a nearby chair. Jean took a seat by the wall.

"I was thinking I should finally take you up on a manicure. I'm feeling downright ragged," Jean said referring to her nails.

Lydia tilted her head and studied Jean's face. "I'd say ragged is right. Something's not right with you?" Lydia asked kindly. Jean blushed. Lydia had seen more than Jean had anticipated.

Mama had always told me Lydia could see right through people, read their hearts. Maybe it's true, thought Jean.

"Jean, now don't you look at me that way, girl. You can't fool me," said Lydia. "I couldn't do this work if I couldn't read people, you know. Women come in every single day with heavy secrets in their hearts. All lookin' to lay down their burden. Some share a little, some a lot, then they can go back to what they're obligated to do. I listen," Lydia explained, tidying up her work table.

"Oh, you're a manicurist. You talk like you're some old priest," replied Jean, not bothering to hide her annoyance.

"It's true that I do the nails, but mainly I listen and watch. They say more with what can't be put into words than all the words they say. Okay, come sit here," Lydia said waving Jean up to the work table.

Jean took a seat at Lydia's table. She felt like all the air had been let out of her at once.

Lydia continued, "Now you, you ain't sayin' a word but my

listenin' ear hears a tale of a boy and a somethin', a thing too big for you to carry alone. I don't help the ladies that come in here. They share, but it's not my place to fix. No, it's not. But you, you're my different story. I'd do all I can to puzzle things out for you."

"Lydia, you sure have no shortage of words, like always," said Jean. "You're right, though, I'm in the thick of something. Something so thick I can't lift my feet out of it. So thick it's oozed around my toes and sealed up. I know I'm sick."

"Sick, stomach sick?" asked Lydia, inclining her head towards Jean.

"Yes, mornings are terrible and the elevator, up and down, down and up, just makes me sicker," said Jean, holding her stomach.

"You eat today?" asked Lydia.

"Tried to. Nothing stays down in the morning. Not any morning. I think I may be in a terrible shape. That's how Mama started, you know, after the cough," said Jean, her real worry apparent.

Lydia studied the woman-child sitting before here. All the signs were there. The truth could not be hidden for long.

"Jean, I have somethin' to say and I want you to listen real good now," counseled Lydia, quietly enunciating each word.

Jean sat very still and listened. She cried and was comforted by the nail shop owner, but her heart was filled with fear. When Lydia was finished talking, she pulled out a piece of note paper and wrote down the name of a doctor, a special tablet to start taking, and advice on the sickness and its cures. The last name on the list was Miss Abby's, a midwife, in case it all came to pass and the cures didn't work.

Wishing she could run home and curl up next to the one person she wanted most to tell, Jean cried. There was no Mama waiting at home. Lydia handed her a handkerchief. Wiping her tears, Jean folded the list carefully and decided her next stop would be to see Elden.

20

Elden knew there was no appropriate time to tell his parents he needed to wed the elevator operator. To even put that into a sentence, let alone manifest it into a reality, would bring the wrath of his mother and the hang of his father's head. But there would be no stopping this wedding, he had resolved.

Jean had come to him so teary-eyed, like a scared rabbit, bearing news that should have made her joyful.

"I'm going to have a baby," she whispered, her cheeks flushed in shame.

With those words, Elden felt, for the first time, that he could see before him a straight line, one impossible to blur. Jean was what he needed, he knew. She was different from the girls his mother thrust at him, the society girls, and she was different from Somewhere's barflies and flappers. Jean was truer, somehow, and she would be his girl, with or without his family's blessing.

They would be good parents, real parents. They wouldn't send their child off to school and then let him come home while they drank away the family holidays. He had the money to make a life for his wife and child and Jean had the tenderness to show him how to do it right. This was Elden's chance to set his mark in the world with the woman he loved.

Elden invited Jean to Christmas dinner and together they planned to share the news over dessert. Mother would never make a scene at a formal meal and it would catch the family enough off-guard that they would have to be pleasant, Elden reasoned. He hadn't shared that rationale with Jean. No, their conversation had been much less worrisome, Elden recalled.

"We'll tell them at Christmas dinner," Elden had said, sweeping Jean into an embrace as he entered her tiny apartment.

"A gift. It'll be our Christmas gift to them," Jean had replied, breathlessly. The fears and dread she'd carried for the past month as she recalled her mother's warnings about girls carrying the burdens of consequences had faded. Elden would stand by her, take care of the baby and her. Now she had no doubt.

"You're my gift. And now we have one together, too, for both of us," he had said, glancing at Jean's midsection. "Forever this baby will be our gift." Elden was caught up in the possibilities of being a father, hoping he'd find the fortitude to be a good husband, too. One able to push away from temptation and be faithful. They'd talked about the upcoming dinner, breaking the news to his parents, but had not yet set a firm date for the wedding. That would come soon, before the gossip could begin. He knew several of his pals had mysteriously large 'premature' babies and it never made the society news.

~

*J*ean dressed carefully for dinner at the Whitcombs. At first she couldn't imagine sitting through a dinner with Mr. Whitcomb and the imposing Katherine Whitcomb, not under any circumstance, but doing that while trying to hide her growing belly seemed well beyond possible.

Mr. Whitcomb had always been polite but formal when he encountered her in the elevator, never saying a word about his son or what had been splashed across the local paper.

But Mrs. Whitcomb, with her air of formality and haughty smile was impenetrable. She never acknowledged the help and Jean was too nervous to ever do more than say a quiet 'good afternoon' when she entered the elevator.

Jean couldn't help but wonder what dinner in the Whitcomb household might be like. Would Katherine be a carefree wife and mother inside the haven of her own home, or would she hold forth the image of the lady of the manor, and how would she treat the elevator operator come to dinner? Jean felt the butterflies building in her stomach as she selected her dress with the drop waist and donned her old flat slippers, the only shoes that still fit. Even her feet were growing. Jean felt absolutely huge.

Elden had become a fixture in the apartment building and everyone had let go of appearances. Mrs. Ivanovic kept an eye out and when he came to visit, she'd appear with a warm plate of pierogies for the couple to share. Otis no longer tutted and shook his head when Elden would pull up in his big car.

"Don't let him in there with you, alone," Miss Abby had cautioned the first time she'd seen Elden at Jean's door.

"I know, Abby. Don't fuss," Jean had assured. "He just doesn't want me to be running after him. Wants to pick me up like a gentleman does." Miss Abby had glowed upon hearing that comment.

"You deserve a gentleman, miss. You surely do," she'd said. "What does Miss Francie think of this? Haven't seen her around in some time."

Francie and Harold were always busy. Too busy. Jean worried about what Harold now thought of her. Jean's life had taken a turn. She'd broken all of the rules Francie held sacred. But Jean couldn't think about that now; there would be time enough after the wedding to make things right with Francie, Jean hoped.

Jean had just finished pulling the dress over her head and brushing back her hair when Elden knocked on the apartment door. She turned the lock and pulled the door open. There he stood, a light blue box, the color of a robin's egg, in his hand. Her heart raced.

Tiffany's. She'd seen ads for that kind of store in the magazines. Too fancy for even Kansas City.

"You're beautiful, Jean," Elden whispered as she opened the door wide.

"Stop it, Elden. I'm big as a milk cow and growing greater by the day. Can't even fit into my shoes," she said, lifting one foot playfully to show him. That little movement threw her off balance.

"Whoa there, Bessie-girl, you're going to end up on your keester," Elden laughed, offering her a steady hand.

"Let me sit for just a minute," Jean said edging to the bed, "get my bearing."

"This will make you feel better. I got you something, a little something. I know we said no presents, but you deserve just something little at least," Elden said, eagerly presenting her with the box.

"Elden, now we agreed -- " Jean began, but stopped as the pale blue box touched her hand. "Oh, this is the prettiest color, I can't imagine what's inside."

"Look and see. It's for forever, Jean, just like us," he promised. She carefully lifted the blue lid. Pearls, a string of perfect pearls lay nestled inside.

"Merry Christmas," he whispered.

"Elden, it's too much," she said, lifting the necklace from the box, her fingers shaking.

"No, not too much for you, Jean. You're my perfect pearl," said Elden with a smile.

"Let me take this necklace off," she said unhooking the jade necklace that had not left her neck for more than two years. She held her mother's necklace, her most precious possession, carefully.

"I want you to have this one, Elden," said Jean offering him the jade flower on the gold chain. "It was a gift from my Poppa to Mama on their wedding day. It means the world to me and so do you. We'll give it to the baby someday, ok? If it's a boy he can give it to his own wife and if it's a girl, well, she'll have something special from her daddy."

Elden took the necklace gently from Jean's hand. "I'll do it. I promise," he said giving her a tender kiss and slipping the necklace into his suit pocket.

"Help me put this on," she said carefully lifting the pearl necklace from its blue box. She turned back towards Elden, and deftly wrapped the long string of pearls twice around her neck. He fixed the clasp of the pearl necklace, delicately moving the wisps of her hair aside so as not to catch them.

"And now you're sure you're ready for mother? Father isn't much of an ogre, but Mother, she can be testy sometimes," said Elden.

"I'm ready," said Jean. "We can do this, can't we, Elden?" she asked, reaching for his hand.

"Together, we can," he replied, planting a gentle kiss on her cheek.

~

The Whitcomb's stately stone home was festooned with gold bows and bells and greenery wrapped around each column and banister. Elden had barely had time to take Jean's coat before Jean was greeted by Mr. Whitcomb.

"Happy Holidays. So kind of you to join us for Christmas dinner. This is a first, Elden bringing home a date for a family dinner. We were just saying this must be someone special, weren't we, dear? Are you coming, dear?" Mr. Whitcomb called out to Mrs. Whitcomb. "Now, can I get you a drink, Jeannie?"

"Jean, Pops. Her name is Jean," Elden said, shaking his head.

"Thank you. No. No drink, please. What a lovely home and I'm so honored to have been asked by Elden," replied Jean, taking in the grandeur of the foyer.

"Yes, well, he is our special boy," said Elden's mother entering the room with a grand sweep of her arm, "and he deserves only a very special girl."

Jean detected a slight slur in her words, but chose not to think about that. "Elden is very special," said Jean squeezing Elden's hand and giving him a sweet smile.

Elden's mother didn't reply, but spun on her heel and walked into the dining room.

"We'll do fine tonight, trust me," Elden whispered to Jean as he passed the squeeze back and led her into the dining room.

The table was set with white linen and enough glasses and silver that the Queen of England would be comfortable stopping in for tea, Jean thought. She had never in her life seen so much table service.

Which fork was the one to use first? Which glasses were hers? Oh, this had the makings of a disaster, Jean feared.

Mrs. Whitcomb had watched the girl's eyes go wide when she entered the room. This girl was a novice, no doubt.

"This is just a simple family dinner, dear. My, you do look so pale, like you've seen a ghost. I imagine your family has these all the time, well, at Christmas anyway," said Mrs. Whitcomb with more than a hint of arrogance, ignoring the scathing look Elden flashed her way.

"Jean's family is smaller than ours, mother. Not every family goes totally overboard for every holiday dinner, you know," Elden said curtly.

"And let's start with a drink, shall we?" said Mrs. Whitcomb casting a withering glance Elden's way and making a direct line to the bar.

"I believe you have already, mother," hissed Elden as he walked up behind his mother.

"Don't you start on me, El. I'm still bailing you out from that little problem with the Feds back in October. You owe me. No more booze talk. I get what I want tonight," Mrs. Whitcomb replied in a low tone through a clenched smile.

Elden knew he was seriously indebted to his mother for getting the most serious charges against him dropped and somehow working everything out with a substantial payment of cash. A fine they called it, but everyone knew she'd bought his way out of a jail sentence.

He'd accommodated her little jabs over the last few months, but tonight Elden knew he had to take a stand. He was confident he could manage a family, keep the bar going and have everything run smoothly.

"Just be civil, Mother. Not asking too much to be civil to Jean, is it? Is it?" he hissed back.

"Cool down, little El, cool down. Get her a drink and cool down. Get yourself one or two, too," said Mr. Whitcomb inconspicuously intervening.

"Jean can't drink, but I'll take a highball. Make it a double," said Elden.

"Can't drink? Like 'can't can't' or 'won't can't' because she's just too good to be around someone who takes a drink?" asked Mrs. Whitcomb haughtily.

"Can't, Mother," said Elden. "Jean's no prude. She has a delicate stomach lately if she drinks, if you must know. Strangest thing, sudden allergy almost," he finished, knowing it was a lie. Jean felt herself blush.

"A delicate stomach?" Mrs. Whitcomb asked, raising a brow. "Well, can't have that on my wool carpet. Cut off the tap for her, I say. Makes more for me," said Mrs. Whitcomb loosely.

Jean was relieved to hear the tinkle of a bell that Elden had said signified dinner.

"At Christmas, we always have a six course dinner starting with champagne and pear liqueur, served with a blue cheese pastry, of course," Mrs. Whitcomb explained, taking a seat at the table.

It was seeing a combination of the silver tray and the crystal liqueur glasses served by a wine butler that caused Jean to abandon all pretenses that she'd ever been served food this good, in this manner of luxury or of this quantity.

The pastry dishes were cleared and replaced with a roasted mushroom salad, offered with a German white wine.

At the sight of the salad plates, Jean began to worry that all of Mama's etiquette lessons had been for naught. Was it work on the forks from the outside in or inside out, she wondered, looking at the array of silver sitting before the bone china plate. It was opulence to excess, if there could be such a thing.

Jean glanced over at Elden who effortlessly picked up his outside fork and speared a lettuce leaf. She raised her eyes to him and smiled. *The rich just have too much silverware,* she thought ruefully.

No sooner was the salad finished than a large roasted turkey took center stage on the dining table, ferried in by aproned servers bearing "our time-honored accompaniments," as Mrs. Whitcomb called them.

Accompaniments. They were dishes Jean had never before seen: Celery root and potatoes mashed with horseradish, french green beans with baby shallots and a bread stuffing with oysters. A rosé wine service was poured with the main course. And, through it all, the servers stood to the side, at the ready to attend to any need.

Jean couldn't stop doing the math in her head: Five servants' time for four hours with preparation and clean up time plus the food itself, let alone all the plates and glasses they were going through. Extravagance was an understatement. She'd never seen such a thing.

Elden will need to scale back his expectations once we're married, she thought. *It's so wasteful, to have so much when other people have so little.* She thought of Miss Abby and Otis, and the Ivanovics, who made do with what they had and shared generously. Jean felt an edge of guilt as she picked up the silver spoon.

Extravagantly was a good description of how Mrs. Whitcomb was greeting each bottle of liquor that graced her setting. *Francie, and especially Harold, would have a fit,* Jean thought.

"Just a tad more, top it off now; why, yes, I'll take a refill," Mrs. Whitcomb said repeatedly.

Both Mr. Whitcomb and Elden had taken notice, trading looks across the table, but said nothing, hoping this would be one of her good drunks and not a nasty-tongued one that led to chaos and tears.

Jean was comfortably oblivious to the growing family dynamic and tension.

Jean pretended to take a drink of every beverage served, but her glass remained conspicuously full. She took a bit of every dish. It would be shameful to waste such indulgences, but the past few weeks she felt constantly full even when she wasn't eating.

Finally, it was dessert time. This was the time she and Elden had agreed would lead to telling Elden's parents that they were going to be married and that the elder Whitcombs would soon be grandparents.

Of course, the Whitcombs would be shocked at first, but they would embrace her and the baby. Elden had assured her there was no doubt of that.

On came dessert, a maple tart. Still, Elden sat silent.

Jean gave him an imploring look across the table that he interpreted as a sign of a full tummy. He patted his cummerbund and smiled back at her. Dessert was followed by the cheese course and red wine.

Where did rich people put all this food? wondered Jean. She looked across the table at Mrs. Whitcomb who was as thin as a whippet. *She must do an extensive exercise regimen every single day,* thought Jean, not realizing that some thinness can be brought by overuse of the bottle.

Mr. Whitcomb finally rang the butler for aperitifs and suggested they retire to the library. Maybe this was the time Elden had been waiting for, Jean thought hopefully.

In the library candles dimly flickered, a tinkle of music came from a Victor Victrola in the corner by the tiled fireplace that roared warmth into the room, and by the phonograph stood a single servant with a tray of glassware and a bottle. It was an intimate setting with a settee nestled by the fire next to two large chairs.

"Double for me," said Mrs. Whitcomb, taking a chair. Mr. Whitcomb nodded to the servant who settled the tray, opened the bottle and poured the brandy into tiny glasses.

"Double, why yes. It's Christmas, of course," replied the butler, pouring her a heavy double.

Jean and Elden took seats on the velvet settee. Mr. and Mrs. Whitcomb sat across from them in matching wing chairs.

"Now, Elden told me he has some news to share," said Mr. Whitcomb, opening the conversation.

"Oh, he's finally going to complete a commission at Wentworth, isn't he? It's about time now, isn't it?" asked Mrs. Whitcomb. "We are so excited for him, Jane. And I'm sure you are, too," she added sloppily.

"No, let me have my say, Mother, and her name is Jean," said Elden. "Now as you know, Jean and I are very close."

"Oh, no, no," blurted out Mrs. Whitcomb, fearing the words that would follow.

"Yes, and we will be marrying next month," Elden continued, looking first at his father and then his mother. Jean squeezed his hand and smiled.

"Holy Mother of God, save us! You will not!" Mrs. Whitcomb declared, sloshing her drink as she rose, "I forbid it. Forbid."

"It's not your choice," said Elden, putting his arm around Jean protectively. "I love her and she loves me."

"We're having your grandchild," blurted out Jean, her cheeks aflame. The secret was too big to carry and she felt certain that this news would sway the Whitcombs.

"What did she just say?" Mrs. Whitcomb hissed, "What did this girl just say? No grandchild of mine will be born to a common girl."

"I'll not have that, mother," said Elden, wanting to shelter Jean from his mother's acerbic tongue.

"Looks like you've had plenty of that already," Mrs. Whitcomb said snidely, pointing to Jean. "No, no, what it looks like is that someone's trying to set a place at the Whitcomb table using you as their meal ticket."

Jean was humiliated at the implication, stunned anyone could think such wicked thoughts about her feelings for Elden. Mrs. Whitcomb was on a tear now, "A child out of wedlock and you think it's yours? Are you stupid, Elden? It's not your baby. Why do you think it even could be? Remember what she charges?" Mrs. Whitcomb concluded, her hands waving as if she could pull that huge Emery Bird bill out of thin air.

Jean couldn't believe what she had just heard. She felt an anger rising from the core of her being. This woman was small and mean, thought Jean; she's never loved a single soul. Now this beady-eyed woman was implying she charged Elden for relations. Jean felt the rising heat of vengeful words.

"Charge? Charge what? What do you mean?" said Jean, ready to meet Mrs. Whitcomb's ire with her own.

"Charge. You charged. I know it," said Mrs. Whitcomb, referring to the Emery Bird Thayer bill. "Only a gold digger does that."

"Mother, you can't say that. You can't mean that. You've had a bit much of the Christmas sauce. You'll feel better about this tomorrow," said Elden, hoping to placate her a bit.

"You," Mrs. Whitcomb said standing up and pointing to Jean, "Get out. You are not a Whitcomb." She turned to address Elden directly, "She is not one of our kind."

Jean's body stiffened with anger. "You will not speak to me that way. I have every right to be here with Elden tonight and always. Don't I, Elden?" Jean asked turning defiantly towards Mrs. Whitcomb, knowing Elden would support her words and that this woman, so accustomed to having her own way, was treading upon her child's future.

With that, Mrs. Whitcomb met Jean's steely gaze, picked up her aperitif glass and threw it against the brick fireplace, making a resounding smash.

"Now, Mother," said Elden, "I fear you are drunk."

"Don't try to pull that on me, Elden. Your father and I can see what's happened here. We won't stand for it," Mrs. Whitcomb retorted.

Mr. Whitcomb volunteered nothing, took no sides. He sat silent staring at the fire. This wasn't the first time Elden had broken the family trust. Somehow this felt even more serious than the federal investigation of Somewhere and its ugly aftermath. Would Elden never get serious? Had he raised his boy to flit from one disastrous experience to the next? Mr. Whitcomb was deeply disappointed. This was something money couldn't fix. It was just drama and he had long ago resigned himself to let play out all the dramas between his wife and son.

"You and he won't stand for it? You'd better just sit down instead.

Get comfortable because I'll be around these next six months, as well as a lifetime of Christmases after," said Jean with a defiance that surprised herself. And the words kept tumbling out.

"And so will our baby, so just get yourself used to that idea. You 'won't stand for it,' really? Just take a chair and put your feet up," Jean concluded, wishing she could rein in her snide tone.

Jean ducked her head, her cheeks blazing. She'd broken one of Mama's cardinal rules: *Carry yourself with dignity.* She'd taken any semblance of dignity and dashed it right upon the Whitcomb's fine Turkish rug, speaking that way to her hostess, and future mother-in-law at that.

"I am not spoken to like that, Elden," said Mrs. Whitcomb, looking to her son for intervention. "You do not want me to respond."

Elden looked at these two women he loved so deeply. He had never seen Jean so fierce. It was a degree of fury he'd only ever seen in his mother. Perhaps these two women had more in common than he had understood. The thought weakened his spirit.

"You do not understand, Mother. We will discuss this tomorrow. We have to go now," said Elden turning to Jean.

Mrs. Whitcomb's tirade was still in full swing, her voice echoing off the library walls, "We'll cut you off, Elden. You even see her again, and we'll cut you off. Won't even hire you to run the elevator, Elden. You'll be on your own. Car's mine. You have nothing. Won't get the hotel, won't get the land. You won't get Somewhere. No, you'll get nowhere and you'll have nothing."

"I'll drive you home," said Elden, putting his arm around Jean.

"You leave this house and it's over Elden," said his mother, picking up a second brandy glass and throwing it against the library wall for emphasis. "You leave with her and it's over. You get nothing. We won't pay the fines. You'll go to jail."

"Stop it. That has nothing to do with this. It wasn't my fault Somewhere was raided. You will pay the fines. You must. Dad, tell her to be reasonable," Elden said pleadingly, his eyes wide.

Mr. Whitcomb was sitting in his tall-backed library chair stony-eyed. He looked up and said quietly, "We don't have conflict here,

Elden. This is not our way. I'm only now getting you out of your one mess. You will not lose your opportunity at Wentworth by wedding under these circumstances. No. Wentworth begins very soon and you will go. It's that or you'll face the consequences and you know what they are. End of discussion. Do not leave this house."

Elden's face went slack. His father had never spoken that way, had never set down an ultimatum. He could always be cajoled into whatever Elden wanted. To hear his father set down consequences was unprecedented.

With those authoritative words, Elden knew he had no choices, no real choices. The raid on Somewhere had undoubtedly been his own fault. He'd broken his father's trust and almost ruined one of the family's steady income streams. If his parents hadn't made things right, the consequences would have been severe. His father had offered to pay all the fines, under and over the table, if the charges levied against Elden were dropped.

All Elden had to do was promise to return to Wentworth for a short stint. He'd leave Wentworth as a commissioned officer and, with his father's pull, would be billeted in the Kansas City area, ready to take over the family business. His choice was to accept the terms his father laid out or end up in federal prison.

Elden digested what his father said. He could have no future at all, facing jail time, scraping out a life from nothing at all, and meeting his baby for the first time when his child was school-aged, or he could put in a brief stay at Wentworth and have a future he'd work out with Jean after that.

A plan began to gel in Elden's mind. He'd keep the family money if he chose Wentworth and let them think Jean was out of his life, just for a time. Surely she would understand – eventually.

"I'll get you home, Jean. It's a small setback here. I need a plan. I just need a new plan. They'll rethink it," said Elden quietly as he escorted Jean into the foyer. "I need to work things out here," he tried to explain, "We will be together; they just don't understand. I can't leave right now. I can't go until they understand and you can't stay. Our houseman will deliver you home. I love you. I love the baby. You know that. I'm sorry our Christmas ended like this." Elden took her shabby winter coat from the closet as his voice dropped to a whisper.

Jean's anger had dissolved into fear when she saw Elden reach into the closet for her coat. Nothing had turned out right and she gulped for air between words, "I thought they'd love me if you loved me. What happened?"

"They will, they will love you," Elden assured. "They just need to adjust. It took them by surprise, that's all." said Elden unsteadily.

"Okay, okay, okay," replied Jean, trying to give herself reassurance with each word, "I love you, Elden. I do love you," Jean said, expecting a gentle reply.

"I'll just ring the chauffeur. He's out back," said Elden, as he crossed the foyer, leaving Jean holding her thin coat. Jean knew the evening had gone awry for Elden, too, and she pushed his lack of reply from her mind.

Elden will make sure I get home safe and that's what matters now, she thought. She heard a car pull up outside as Elden returned to the foyer.

"I'll be over before midnight. Leave the door open, okay?" Elden whispered as he opened the front door at the soft knock from the waiting driver. "Take care of her," he said to the chauffeur who solemnly nodded.

"I'll leave the door open. You'll be the best Christmas gift I ever had," said Jean trying to make Elden smile.

Jean left her apartment door unlocked when she got home, washed her face, rinsed her dress and hung it to dry by the window, then climbed into bed. In the morning the apartment door was still unlocked. Elden had never come.

PART III

Character is destiny.

— Heraclitus

21

*E*lden did not show up to explain how things would turn out. He did not show up on New Year's Eve.

How could he not care? Jean wondered, eyes swollen with grief. *When we had so much together. A future. Had it all been a lie? A falsehood? And for what purpose, to show his parents something? Or was I just a dalliance, a plaything he's grown tired of and discarded?*

The questions weighed heavily on Jean and circled in her thoughts, always unanswered.

She began to think sharply about what it meant if Elden never appeared. The one thing that remained steady - no, the only thing that remained steady - was work. Getting up in the morning, putting on a smile, wholly forced but who was there to notice, really? And then going to work. The clunk of the arriving elevator signaled the start of a daily routine of up, down, and the limited range of phrases she had to share: Good Morning, Good Afternoon, Which Floor?, Yes, it's a lovely day, First time in the city? Lovely, just lovely.

The baby was kicking now, letting loose at inopportune moments as she tried to converse with the League Ladies in the elevator.

The League Ladies, Jean thought ruefully, worried about what they could be saying. She had made friends, and it felt like true friends, with one — Mrs. Parker.

Alone one afternoon in the elevator, Mrs. Parker had whispered to her, "A girl with a little problem is a girl who needs a friend, Jean. I want you to know I'll help any way I can."

Jean had blushed and smiled back at her, muttering a brief 'thank you', too embarrassed to confide the truth.

But as the evening light was fading, Jean sat alone in her apartment, finally ready to ask for help. She needed a friend. Never in her life had she wanted Mama more than in that minute. She tried to pray but in the silence, a sudden wave of panic washed over her.

She couldn't stand the loneliness. She washed her face with the lavender soap Mama had loved, breathing that sweet scent again. She combed her hair with Mama's comb.

The loneliness hit her, hard.

With a determined stride, Jean marched right out of her apartment and stomped up Francie's stoop. She wasn't about to let a little pride stand in the way of sharing it all with Francie.

Good-hearted, clear-thinking Francie would know what to do, and if she didn't know, she still would listen. If Francie judged her, so be it. Jean knew harshness never lasted long in Francie's heart.

Jean rapped sharply on the door, but no one answered. She knocked and knocked, but no one came. She kept knocking until the knuckles of her hand began to bleed. No one was home.

She squared her shoulders and turned back to the sidewalk. Maybe Francie wasn't home now, but she would be, and then they would talk until something started to make sense again.

Jean walked home slowly, and soon her head sagged low. She saw a bright yellow dandelion blooming, pushing up from a crack in the sidewalk, determined to blossom at all costs.

Back home Jean cast her eyes around the tiny apartment. Logically, she knew she had some savings now and food in the cupboard, but that would make do for weeks and months, a year maybe but not years and years. Not a child's lifetime. Not forever.

Jean sat at the small table by the window, unable to stop her legs from shaking as she pictured the years to come. She took a scrap of paper and pencil stub from the hat box and began to calculate how to live and raise a baby on ninety cents a day, forever.

Clothes. Food. Doctor bills. Medicine. School. Time. Tenderness. Attention. Laughter. Love. Yes, it would take money, and something more. It would take Elden. Elden.

How had he avoided her for weeks and weeks? Jean wondered.

Every time the elevator call button took her to the lobby floor, she would hold her breath, dreading and hoping that Elden would be waiting as the door opened. But no, he must be deliberately avoiding the hotel.

She'd not seen Elden at all and had seen Mr. Whitcomb only once in the elevator. He had stood stiffly, not even meeting her eyes. A business-like directive to take him to the top floor were his only words as he removed his hat and entered the elevator.

"Is Elden –," Jean had begun, her voice shaking. Mr. Whitcomb, holding his hat with both hands in front of him and turning it nervously around by its brim, had given her a sharp look. One almost imperceptible shake of his head seemed to answer her incomplete question and he offered nothing more.

Jean had gone so far as to ask Mrs. Velmar if she'd seen Elden, knew anything. Mrs. Velmar just clucked her tongue and shook her head, giving no hope for his whereabouts.

How could he just disappear? It wasn't fair and it wasn't right. Jean looked out of the apartment window at the fading light. It was Monday night. She knew where he would be.

Jean's worst fear was Elden had found another girl. She pushed the thought aside. It was time to figure things out for herself. She'd had enough waiting.

Something has got to change, thought Jean. She'd take matters into her own hands and figure out what Elden was up to and whether he could be counted on.

Jean waited until eight o'clock and then headed for the place Elden could be. He'd probably take her in his arms the moment she walked in. She knew she would forgive him these weeks of silence, if so.

Jean walked with deliberation down the alleyway that led to the speakeasy. She quelled her nerves as she knocked on the door to Somewhere.

There was no time for anxiety, no time to second guess. She needed help. She needed Elden.

~

"Friend of Jake," said Jean as she knocked on the gray door holding the secret entrance to Somewhere.

She entered the bar and the memories of their first night there came rushing back – how naïve she had been. She had had no idea there were places like Somewhere, places where women and men mingled and drank and danced, where coloreds and whites could share a dance floor, where music played all the time. Learning this and all that came after had changed everything.

Everything.

Forever.

The music was loud and the bar was full. She quickly found Collette in the crowd.

There was Collette doing her Charleston, filling up the dance floor. Collette looked up and seemed to have noticed Jean, but then looked away.

But would Elden even be here tonight? Jean wondered. She scanned the crowd, her eyes tearing from the smoke-filled room.

Yes, there was Elden, there in the corner. Drink in hand and two empty in front of him. Elden.

Jean moved quickly across the room, stopping just short of his table. Would he be glad to see her? Surprised? Yes, he'd be surprised, Jean realized.

Surprised alright, Jean thought, her heart sinking.

Surprised because his attention was occupied. A petite blonde in a new dress Jean had seen displayed at the EBT sashayed up to Elden's side.

Elden extended his arm and pulled the girl onto his lap. The girl tossed back her head and laughed, ending the laugh with a kiss on his cheek.

Jean could hear Elden and every word he said to the little blonde, "You are so beautiful. I saw you dancing out there. I do love a girl who can dance. Saw you out there with Collette." He whispered huskily, "You know how to move."

The same words he had said to Jean. The same inflection. The same smile. Then Elden leaned in and kissed the girl long and slow.

Jean knew with certainty it was over. It was done.

The callus that hardened on her heart grew thicker, impenetrable. Jean was enraged. As she moved to confront Elden she felt a hand on her shoulder.

"Well, now, look what the cat dragged in," Collette said with a forced smile as she spun Jean around away from Elden. "Don't know how that cat did it, you're so big. Now sit over here and get your breath before you do something stupid." Collette guided Jean to a booth in a dark corner.

"Collette, I've got to —" Jean said, her cheeks flush and eyes filled with urgency as she looked back to Elden who was stroking the tiny blonde's hair. There was no time to banter or for social posturing. She needed to get to Elden fast, before she lost her resolve.

"Stop. Just stop. Sit down. Your face is the color of fire and that can't be good for you or for the, the, you know," Collette stuttered. "I heard you were carrying, but I had no idea it would look like this. Are you sure you're okay? We'll get you some water." Collette gestured to the bartender.

"Carrying. Yes. With child. It's true. Does every single person in town know my business?" Jean asked, shaking her head.

As the bartender placed a cold glass of water in front of Jean, Collette volunteered her source: Mrs. Whitcomb.

"Witchy Whitcomb. She actually was in here one night, drunk as a sailor on shore leave, looking for Elden. She let it slip after I offered her a drink. She was disgusting drunk and, of course, Elden was nowhere to be found so then she was disgusting drunk and angry," Collette said scornfully.

Jean's eyes filled with tears.

"No, No," assured Collette, "Word's not all over town yet, it's okay. But, Jean, what are you going to do?"

Collette was one of the few women Jean felt she really knew, and chose to be honest with her.

"Elden. Look at him. I can't believe it. He's over there with another girl, Collette. The baby's due in a few months. I need Elden."

Jean, with that one sentence, felt all of her defenses fall. It was all she could do not to cry.

"Sure you do, baby," said Collette patting Jean's hand. "Elden needs Elden, too. He's doing the business here, but he's not good. He's in some real trouble. Serious. Police trouble."

Jean's eyes widened.

Collette dropped her voice low, "I heard he'd paid them off, but they came and bruised him up but good the day after Christmas. 'Bruised him up'. That's what Elden said. It was beyond that. His eye was black, his lip cut, and he couldn't move his arm for more than two weeks. They told him they'd be back, and soon."

Jean let out a gasp. Elden, hurt and in trouble, and dallying with someone else on top of it all.

"Now people say it won't be a bruising next time. In fact, if he survives the next one and they take him in, it could be prison," Collette continued.

"Not jail!" Jean exclaimed.

"Prison. Federal prison. But, he's a Whitcomb, so instead of that he's back off to Wentworth. For years," Collette concluded.

"Years?" Jean asked.

Collette nodded, "An eternity."

"I'm watching out for him, but he's torn up, too. Drinking too much, driving too fast, fighting with everybody. He can't help himself now. He's in no shape to help you," Collette cautioned. Jean felt her heart sink as the tears began to roll down her cheeks.

"Look over there at him, sitting with that girl," Collette continued. "That's a bit of nothing. She's a daughter of one of the League ladies. She won't last. One night and she'll be gone, back to tell her friends about her brush with the seedy side of the city. She's nothing to worry about. Oh my, he is drunk, isn't he?" she said gesturing to Elden, who had left the girl sitting alone at a table and was weaving out to the hallway, heading downstairs no doubt. Jean watched as he swayed into the darkness.

"But do you know what he said to her? He said she can move! What a traitor! He said that to me and this, this," Jean said, pointing to her belly.

"This is his baby. I have to be a mother. He has to be a father. It's only fair," Jean said, her voice breaking with defeat.

"He may even want to be a father, to be with you, but I don't see that he can. He'll go to the Big House if he doesn't pay up again. And he never pays the protection money. So now his parents say they'll take everything. They're making him go back to that school. Witchy Whitcomb cut some kind of deal with the prosecutor. He has no choice," replied Collette.

Jean stared at the water glass sitting in front of her. Beads of sweat had formed on the sides. She took a drink.

"He has no choice! He has no choice! Well, I have no choice either, Collette," Jean said.

"He's desperate, Jean. He sat me down after he'd had a few yesterday, and wanted to talk, 'get things clear with me,' he said. Said he can't provide for a family now. He got into bad trouble with the raid and all. His parents had to step in, pay up. His parents' money has a terrible hold," explained Collette. She looked intently at Jean.

"I know he must want you to be patient. He said if he gets his commission, then the parents give him everything. Everything. The hotel, a house. He'll get the bar back. He'll be set for life. His parents told him that," Collette explained.

"But he'll go to that place, get a commission in the Army and then go away and fight?" Jean asked, her eyes filled with tears, envisioning Elden lost on a battlefield far away.

"Jean, are you kidding? These boys, these boys like Elden, they get a commission, sure, but they don't fight. They run the city, here at home," Collette assured.

"I hear they get together and talk politics from time to time, but that's as close as any of them get to a battlefield," Collette explained. "Elden as a soldier? Never. His mother simply wouldn't allow it. Can you even imagine?" she joked.

Jean was numb wondering how this news of Elden had not circulated through the Empire's gossiping staff. She had heard no whispers of it from anyone, though she'd grown accustomed to conversations coming to a full stop at work whenever she came within earshot.

"He'll have everything but he won't have me. He won't have us," said Jean tearfully.

"Bet he's got some plan for that, doesn't he?" asked Collette.

"No. He doesn't. He doesn't like to plan. He told me that once," Jean replied shaking her head as she remembered their quiet talk by the little pond tucked back in the woods. "Where is he? I have to see him."

"He's down there, you know where," said Collette pointing back into the hallway entrance.

"I'm going down," Jean said with determination as she stood up from the table.

"It won't be what you expect, Jean. He's not ready. Don't do it. He's been drinking all day. All week. All month, really," said Collette reaching out for Jean, but it was too late.

Jean didn't have a clear idea of her own expectations anymore, let alone what Collette thought she might expect from Elden, but Jean had to know. She had to see Elden for herself. And, truthfully, Jean did hold a secret hope that just seeing her would bring Elden back to her.

She headed back towards the entrance and down the hidden stairway.

Collette was right. It wasn't the reunion Jean expected.

She found him down in the distilling room sitting with a ledger in front of him. He was more than one drink beyond drunk and had a drink in front of him. She barely recognized him. His face was puffy and pale.

Elden didn't seem surprised to see her. His eyes were blank.

"Elden?" Jean asked quietly, struggling to hold her voice steady, feeling her anger and righteousness melting away as she took in his vulnerable state. Elden shook his head.

He didn't hold her, didn't take her in his arms. It was as if he couldn't register who she was or why she was in front of him. She pleaded with him for an explanation of what had happened and why.

"The baby," she began and then dropped into the chair across from him, hoping to find a way to force him to make eye contact. "You didn't forget, right? You couldn't have forgotten. Me. The baby. You promised you'd come. I can't wait. I can't do this alone." Her voice broke, ending in a desperate plea.

"You're not alone. You'll never be alone. Trust me, Jean. I'll take care of things but I do what I have to do. You take good care of the baby. It'll work out," Elden slurred but kept his tone even and emotionless.

"'I do what I have to do'? What does that even mean, Elden? And you have to take care of the baby, take care of me. Things won't just 'work out'. This isn't something that just 'works out'. We need to find our own straight line. Do the right thing. We have to plan it out," said Jean, as her anger broke through her grief.

"It'll work out. I can't say any more. I've got to take care of things, of you, of everything. I can't go to prison. I saw you talking to Colette. She must have told you. I'll go to Wentworth and that's it. It's black and white. It's a straight line," he said, picking up the glass before him and taking a long drink, "I found my straight line." Jean's heart sank.

"Now go on. It's not safe here. The boys are coming for their tribute, their contribution, their bribe. That's what I do now, Jean. Like I said, it's black and white and now, here, it's all mixed up. It always will be. White has become black. I do what I have to do. Just go. This place isn't for you. I can't be here for you right now, but someday I will. I promise," Elden said as he finally met Jean's gaze.

His eyes were glazed, bloodshot, devoid of emotion. Jean rose from her chair, so angry her shoulders were shaking.

"You don't know what you're doing, Elden. There's a right and wrong here, and you're wrong. You can be here for me. You just choose not to be. You'll regret this, this going away, not knowing your child," she said, her acerbic tone surprising even herself.

Never leave someone in anger. Mama told me that. Jean pushed back that thought. Mama would understand. Jean turned her back on Elden. She couldn't hold back the tears as she ran back up the stairs and out past Somewhere's doorman. Elden did not even try to follow and that just compounded the hurt.

Outside, the glare from the streetlights pierced her eyes. Jean walked slowly back towards the apartment, taking the route that led her past Francie's house.

How could he have just sat there, in a stupor? Not embraced her, promising to make things right? It'll 'work out', he'd said, but his words meant nothing. There were no assurances, no talk of the future, no talk of being together. She was truly on her own.

As she neared the Nowak home she could hear boisterous laughter and music. A crowd was on Francie's front porch, her family and Harold's. Harold's many brothers had taken over the front lawn as well.

"Hey, Jean," shouted one of the brothers from the porch steps. "Glad you're here. Big news, isn't it?"

Jean sniffled back her tears. "Big news?" she repeated, hoping the question came out more of a statement.

"They haven't set the date yet, but her ring is sure pretty," the young man said. "She's right inside. Can't miss her. Look for the glint on her finger," he laughed.

"Thanks," Jean replied wiping her eyes with her sleeve as she pushed past the throng on the porch.

The living room was spilling over with members of the Nowak clan, from the wrinkled and cane-bearing to the tots in saggy diapers. Francie was seated beside Harold on the sofa, her hand clasped around his. It wasn't the glint on Francie's finger that first caught

Jean's attention. It was the softness, the tenderness, the love radiating from Harold as he looked at Francie.

"Jean!" trilled Francie as she rose from the sofa and threw her arms around her friend. "Can you believe it? We're engaged!" Francie thrust her ring finger towards Jean. Harold rose and stood proudly by Francie's side.

"My fiancé at last," he said as he put his arm around Francie's waist and pulled her close.

"Congratulations, you two. I didn't know," Jean said searching her friend's eyes for an explanation of how this had come to pass without Francie sharing the news.

"I put the note under your door a few hours ago. I'm so glad you're here. It was today after church he asked daddy for my hand, so I didn't know before," Francie volunteered. "I think he's had it planned for months though." Francie looked endearingly at Harold whose cheeks flushed as red as his hair.

"Had to get it all paid for first. The ring, you know. Won't have debt in our family. You ladies go ahead and talk. I'll check on how things are going outside," Harold said, dropping his voice into a deeper register as if to emphasize his position as the man of the house.

"And you're – well, you're – how are you?" Francie asked, looking at Jean intently after Harold had taken his leave.

"Big," said Jean looking at her growing belly.

"Oh, Jean, I can tell there's something wrong. You're sad. And, I know. Mother told me that just this morning. She heard it at church and I told her it was a vicious rumor. Then things with Harold got to be so –" Francie's voice trailed off and she looked down at her shoes. "I guess I haven't been a good friend, have I?"

"You're happy. I don't expect there's anything to be done for me anyway. I made this mess," Jean said, her heart twisting with grief as she recalled Elden's face, Elden's words.

"Mess? A baby's not a mess. No matter what Mother thinks about matrimony always coming first," Francie replied. "I love you, Jean. Now sit down and tell me everything. Quick before Mother comes over and pokes her nose between us. I can't imagine how she'll gloat over the rumors being true. I hate it when she's right about everything." Francie pulled Jean over to the sofa and bent her head in close.

Jean told her quickly what had happened, a brief version that ended with Elden leaving, not standing up to his responsibilities.

"Jean, it's terrible," Francie declared then put her hand swiftly to her lips, hoping her assessment hadn't offended. "He can't go to prison though. Then where would you be? I'm sure he loves you. He's making a hard choice."

"His family can figure things out with the law. No one would send a Whitcomb to Federal prison. He's not thinking straight. He's just not thinking of me. I know in his heart he's not. He wants a family, a quiet life, a home with me, with children. With me," Jean protested, wishing these things were all still true.

"But, you saw him tonight?" Francie asked.

"Right. But, tonight he was drunk, again. Just drunk," Jean confided.

"Don't mention him to Harold," Francie said scanning the room for her fiancé. "After seeing Elden at the ballpark, drinking, Harold has nothing good to say about him, and now that we're going to be married, he's gotten a little sanctimonious with me. I think he's trying to make a good impression with my parents." Francie rolled her eyes.

"Don't get me wrong, I agree with him about the drinking and all, but he says the Whitcombs are plain trouble. Then you with the baby and all, oh, Jean, I don't know what we're going to do," Francie fretted.

Jean took comfort in the fact that Francie was still referring to herself and Jean as "we."

"I know what we'll do. We'll still be friends. Harold will like the baby as much as we do," said Jean.

"Of course we will. I mean I don't know what we'll do. We. Harold and me. Mother says you can barely pray an illegitimate child out of purgatory, you know. And I know it's not the child's fault. I told her that, but she just told me to say more 'Hail Marys' for sassing. You know how she is. And Harold's all holier-than-thou about it," Francie said apologetically, patting Jean's hand. "I'll figure it out with them somehow."

"And, who do we have here?" asked a voice from across the room. "Why, Jean, how nice of you – " began Francie's mother but she stopped abruptly as she took in the sight of Jean starting to heave herself up from the sofa to greet her.

"Mary, Mother of God, bring salvation to this woman-child," Francie's mother prayed, loudly enough that conversations around the room stopped and heads turned to appraise the wayward waif being addressed.

Jean could barely contain her shame as Francie stood, taking Jean's hand as they rose from the sofa together.

"Jean and I are talking, Mother," Francie asserted. Jean's eyes widened. Francie never talked back to her mother.

"I have to go," Jean said, her voice barely a whisper. "I'm sorry, Francie."

"Mother," Francie said, "Jean has to go now. I'll walk her to the door. Then we'll cut the cake, okay? Could you get everyone into the dining room for me?" Francie intervened.

"I'm sorry," Francie whispered to Jean. "I told you she can be difficult. Now she's all wrought up about improper influences in my life and how to be a good wife. I can barely do a thing without her over my shoulder, criticizing. Advice, she calls it. Guidance. More like nagging and preaching. She's driving me bats."

Jean choked back the desire to share that she'd give anything to have her own mama back to give advice, guidance, and preaching.

Francie walked Jean down the front steps to the sidewalk. Jean drew in a deep breath as they passed Harold and his brothers. She smiled in their general direction to deflect any judgmental stares, but then quickly cast her eyes towards the twilight sky.

"Harold, round up the family and get them to the dining room. We'll cut the cake next, okay?" Francie called to Harold in a bright voice. Harold hastily beckoned to his brothers to follow him inside, leaving the girls alone on the lawn.

"I'm sorry about that, what Mother said. That must have felt terrible in there," Francie said.

"Everything feels terrible," Jean said, her eyes wet with tears. Francie wrapped her arms around Jean and pulled her in for a tight hug.

"I'll come over when I can. When I can get away from Harold and Mother. If one's not with me lately, the other one is. You are still at the Empire, right?"

"For now. No one lets pregnant women work, though," said Jean. It was true. A pregnant woman was rarely to be seen in public and certainly would not be working a real job. It just wasn't done.

"Make what money you can now though. I'll do what I can to help, but you'll need rent money for months. I do think Elden will come around. Be strong," counseled Francie, releasing Jean from the long hug. "I have to get back inside and cut the cake. Grandma spent all day making it. And --" Francie stopped. There was so much more to tell Jean. But not today. Francie embraced her friend again, not really wanting to leave.

"I'm glad you're happy. And tell Harold –" Jean's voice broke and she stopped before finishing the sentence.

"I'll tell Harold you're my friend and that's that, okay?" Francie reassured Jean with a pat.

"Get inside. Be happy," Jean said as she turned down the sidewalk for home.

As Jean walked, she formulated a plan. She knew what she had to do.

~

Jean met with Mr. Whitcomb in his office the next workday. He was surprised to receive her request for a meeting. Rumors had swirled that Jean had grown so large that she barely fit into the work uniform.

The week before, Mr. Green had even suggested sending her

down to Mrs. Velmar for a refitting, but that would have had the entire staff wagging their gums about his boy.

Mr. Whitcomb had explained to Mr. Green that Jean was simply very, very fortunate to still have a job with the hotel. He suggested that soon she could perhaps just go away quietly, as it was unsightly for the hotel to have an elevator worker with such girth.

When Jean's request came for a meeting, Mr. Whitcomb knew he'd ignored the situation as long as possible. His surprise to find her in his office at all doubled when he heard her request for a raise to two dollars a day, retroactive to October. Mr. Whitcomb was noticeably embarrassed by the request.

"October?" he questioned. Jean replied with two short sentences: "Baby's due in June. You do the math."

"I see," Randall Whitcomb replied tersely.

He stood and looked down into her eyes. Jean felt something flutter inside her, like a butterfly. Mr. Whitcomb crossed his arms and took a deep breath. Jean realized how much he looked like his son, Elden, with the same bright blue eyes.

"Jean, I hired you because you are smart, hard-working, and careful," he said. "I know you are a bright woman, and you will be able to see the sense of what needs to be done here."

"Sir?" she asked, confused. Summoning courage, Jean looked Mr. Whitcomb in the eye, "What needs to be done here is Elden and I need to marry."

"What? No. No, my wife, my wife," Mr. Whitcomb stuttered, "My wife has a doctor who will get rid of this little problem for us, in no time at all, and I will pay for everything. This can just go away, and you can keep your job."

Jean drew in a quick breath. "Never," she hissed. "Not now, not ever."

"It's simple they say, and afterward, we can go on as if nothing ever happened here. You'll get that pretty figure of yours back right away," Mr. Whitcomb said with a satisfied smile.

"You don't understand," she replied, putting her hands on her hips.

"It is safe, clean, no risks," he countered, oblivious to Jean's growing anger. "We will take care of this problem and never speak of it again. You can leave my son alone and I will see to it that you keep your job, with a raise in pay."

"You mean, if I . . . " Jean began, shaking her head.

"Of course," Mr. Whitcomb nodded. "Terminate this pregnancy. We've set the appointment for next week. A single girl with a child has no hope, no prospects. You know our Elden never will claim that child. It's best if we simply erase the stain and move on."

"Stain?" Jean repeated, her hands shaking. This man was deranged, she thought. This was her baby. Their baby. Jean put her hand to her throat. Suddenly the air seemed stuffy and stale, like her oxygen had been sucked away.

"You will have the best medical care in the city, of course, and I will give you a month of paid vacation time," Mr. Whitcomb said. "No Whitcomb will lay claim to a street-girl's urchin. It's better this way," Mr. Whitcomb concluded, taking out his pocket watch to check the hour.

Jean felt that flutter again, beneath her heart, and she gasped in surprise. She reached for a chair to steady herself. Mr. Whitcomb smiled, clearly misunderstanding.

"I know it's a generous offer, but I am a generous man. Young men make mistakes. This one can be forgiven if you will do the right thing and let us erase it all," Mr. Whitcomb said, snapping the pocket watch shut.

Jean began to shiver. She balled up her hand into a fist and clutched one hand with the other one so she wouldn't hit him.

"Are you all right? By all means, dear, sit down," Mr. Whitcomb said.

"Mr. Whitcomb, the baby moved," Jean said. "My baby moved inside." A joy filled her, unlike anything she had felt before. *Our baby*, she thought.

She impulsively reached for Mr. Whitcomb's hand to place it on her belly, so he could feel the baby kick, too. Realizing this was the man who just a moment ago had suggested something as egregious as taking away her only family, she pushed his hand away in disgust.

Mr. Whitcomb reached for his white cotton handkerchief and rubbed it across his hand as if scrubbing a stain.

"It's probably indigestion, dear. Too early for a child to move," he said.

Jean met his gaze with steely eyes and shook her head 'no.'

"I can see I've made my offer too late," he continued. Mr. Whitcomb turned toward the window and dismissed her with a wave of his hand, but Jean stood her ground.

"You ought to love this baby, even if you reject me now," she said boldly. "This baby will be your grandchild. Your family."

"That baby will be nothing to the Whitcomb family," he said sternly turning back towards Jean. "Katherine says she knows your type. I hired you to run an elevator, not to run after my son. If you weren't so stubborn, we could fix this."

"This baby is a gift," she said.

"Oh, my dear girl," Mr. Whitcomb said, his voice heavy. "Everyone makes mistakes."

"This baby is not a mistake," Jean said boldly. "This baby is a Whitcomb." Jean turned then and walked out of the office with her back straight and her head held high.

22

In the first paycheck after meeting with Mr. Whitcomb, Jean opened her pay envelope and saw that her wage had been doubled and the retroactive pay was included along with a handwritten note that read *"Gifting to you the generous sum of $75.00 for baby things from Emery Bird Thayer."* A wave of relief washed over her. She now made plenty of money each day and had a nest egg of nearly one hundred dollars, a small fortune. Seventy-five dollars would not outfit a baby for years, but it was something.

Jean paid her rent ahead three months and still had money to spare. She used the extra to stock the pantry and she bought a tin of Earl Grey tea, in honor of her mama. She splurged on extra meat tidbits for Orion and tried to push away the ironic question of whether this little tomcat would be the only man in her family now.

Jean knew what it felt like not to have a father growing up, but at least she had known that her father loved her, even though he had died so young. Jean's heart quivered in fear when she thought of all the feelings her baby would face, and she prayed again that Elden would come to his senses and love them both, especially this baby. She could not understand how anyone could fail to want to be part of a family.

Jean's arms already ached with longing to hold her baby. If she let someone else raise this baby, someone with money, then the baby never would know about her, or her mama. She wanted to be the one to teach her baby the letters of the alphabet, the names of the constellations.

It wouldn't be easy, if the baby's father didn't grow up fast, but letting go of this baby, growing steadily right there in the nest beneath her heart, felt impossible. Somehow, she would manage. She didn't have money, but she had friends.

Francie came to visit each Thursday after work, and plaited her hair into a French braid.

"What will you buy for the baby?" she asked one evening. "Babies need so many things."

"Francie, I'm scared," Jean replied.

"I'm here," Francie said. "And soon you'll have somebody beautiful in your arms, somebody who never will leave you and always will love you. Now, let's think. What do babies need?"

"What do babies need?" Jean asked. "Babies need parents. Babies need their fathers, and grandmas, and grandpas. Francie, I don't have any younger brothers and sisters. I never put a diaper on a baby, and there's nobody to show me anything. And what if it hurts, to have a baby?"

Francie sighed and hugged Jean close for a minute. "Have you heard from Elden?"

Jean nodded. "One letter. He hates it there. Says it's strict and he's muddled up about right and wrong and black and white. He said I should go to the EBT and put things on his account. He said he'd take care of whatever we needed," Jean said as her voice cracked, "But, he didn't say when he'd come back. He didn't say he loved me. Just that he was sorry."

Jean knew she had to be strong, but sometimes she felt so alone, even when her best friend was right there with her.

Francie drew her arms around Jean. "He loves you. And the baby. I just know it," Francie comforted. Jean shrugged; she couldn't change anything, but maybe she could do something right for her baby. Jean picked up a pen and a piece of cream-colored paper.

"Let's start making that list," she said.

The first day of spring arrived with a shiver, but was soon followed by blossoms. Jean was feeling well and not terribly, terribly huge. She had set aside this spring day for preparing for the baby.

She'd read the handwritten note from Mr. Whitcomb over and over, considering whether to take him up on his "generous" offer to outfit the baby's layette at the Emery Bird Thayer Dry Goods Store. After all, this was Elden's baby. This baby was a Whitcomb and deserved to be a Whitcomb. Elden liked nice things, and Elden knew nice things for the baby could be had at the Emery Bird store. Certainly Jean should charge a few items to Elden, lest he and his parents forget the child was coming.

She marched into EBT, head held high, and did not hesitate a second or let her voice quiver when she said she was charging to the Whitcomb account, for their new grandchild's layette.

The salesman's head whipped around at that pronouncement, to check out who was laying claim to be a Whitcomb daughter-in-law. This was a stretch for the It Girls who came in, by any measure, thought the salesman. This one looks great with child, he observed and he couldn't recall any other It Girls coming in lately to charge. Certainly none had ever come in carrying like this one was.

Jean didn't hesitate to pull out her list, "I'll take two flannel blankets for the baby, twenty diapers of the softest cotton you have, three cloths, two bibs, diaper pins, a pail, and clothes – yes, three t-shirts, two sleeper suits, one dressing gown, a bonnet and ...," Jean paused, looking around the store. "That, there, a pram. Yes, that one," Jean said with satisfaction, pointing to an elegant baby carriage sitting in the corner next to a beautiful wicker bassinet. "And the bassinet, of course," she concluded.

She folded the list, suddenly tired. It would all total more than the seventy-five dollars Mr. Whitcomb offered, Jean knew. But she had confidence a few dollars more would bring no retribution.

She couldn't find good grandparents at that store, or a father for her baby, but she could buy the best pram any baby ever had, and she would make sure that her baby went down the street in style.

Jean signed the tissue-thin billing slip with a tinge of pride, signing as a Whitcomb. $117.15 by Jean Ball for Elden Whitcomb. Plain as day. She would have taken it out on a billboard if she could. She'd print it in the *Kansas City Star* if she had enough money. She'd make up handbills and distribute them on the street: *The Whitcomb Family is pleased to announce that Elden Garfield and Virginia Ball Whitcomb are proud parents of a new baby.*

That little thought was unsatisfying, and it filled her with sadness, knowing public acknowledgment would not change the Whitcombs' feelings toward her or this sweet child.

The bill was put into a black case, snapped shut, and made its way through the tube to the desk of Miss Cassandra Lee.

Miss Lee was struck speechless as she perused the purchases. She, for once, had absolutely nothing she wanted to add to a Whitcomb bill, save for a quick turn of the pen that made $117 into $197.

Cassandra smirked. The items spoke for themselves. That was revenge itself, pure enough. She was envious she had not thought of this herself. All these beautiful things. Her Whitcomb child had never benefited from such an outfitting, but she could imagine the look on Mrs. Whitcomb's face when she saw that her own son was following in his father's footsteps. To turn the one into a nine, simple. And no one would ever know the difference.

Jean had the purchases packaged up and delivered to her apartment house. Otis was on duty when they arrived. "Shall I help carry all of these up?" Otis asked the delivery man.

"Sure would help. Lots going up to the third floor," the delivery man answered.

Jean was thrilled to get all the packages, but was overwhelmed by the work the unpacking entailed. Her delight turned to embarrassment when she saw Otis toting the pram up the stairs followed by a delivery man carrying the wicker bassinet.

Otis now knew for sure what she was facing. She had tried to hide it for months with her big coat and then her big springtime sweater. For the last several months, she had avoided even talking with Otis.

Otis had taken note and had been careful not to mention Jean's condition to James, Abby, or anyone else. But with the delivery of the big baby carriage and all, things had reached the point of no return. It did no one any good to continue the charade.

"May I send Abby up to give you a hand, Miss Jean? Maybe your friend Francie, too?" Otis asked kindly from the doorway. He still steadfastly refused to enter her apartment.

Jean looked at Otis, grateful for the offer. "That would be a real help, Otis. A real help. I'm struck down tired today."

"It's time for you to rest. You've done a lot of work this last winter, bigger work than any man could ever do," he said gently as he pulled shut the apartment door.

Miss Abby and then Francie arrived at her doorstep and together they unwrapped, folded and put away. They talked about babies and children.

Miss Abby seemed to know everything. She'd raised brothers and sisters, cousins and neighbor children and brought more than one baby into the world. Abby talked confidently about how to tell when a baby's coming, about how the baby will seem to drop and there's sometimes big swelling that happens just days before it's time.

"But, how will I know it's time?" asked Jean warily.

"Oh, you'll know, have no doubt. Keep an eye on your fingers and feet, too. They'll swell. And when your ankles look as round as a winter squash, it's probably about past time," joked Abby.

"I'm scared," said Jean. "I don't know how to do this, let alone take care of a baby. I don't know how to be a mother."

"You just remember every baby is a blessing," Francie said sweetly. "I told Mother and Harold I was coming over this afternoon. Harold said we'd say prayers about it and Mother said a few other things, you can imagine, but prayers, too. We light a candle for the baby every day. You know, I don't care what anyone says. I know you won't go to Hell because this is a blessing here," said Francie, confident of the Church's support of mothers and children.

"Ain't no Hell to go to," said Abby. "Hell is here on earth, what with the poor and hungry in the world. Babies, they're our hope. We'll all take good care of this child. Don't you worry, Miss Jean. My midwifery guild serves everyone. Any woman. Any race, creed, or color. Rich, or poor. We guild women, we know how to bring a child in, and I'd be honored to do that for you. Birth your baby right here at home. I'll take care of you the first few days after, get the baby nursing. I like to bring life. Like I told you before, I feel my own children close when I do such things."

Jean was comforted by her friends and their kind words, but knew that her own burdens extended beyond her growing belly. Her heart was heavy, regretting the huge bill she had just run up in Elden's name, knowing she had far exceeded even Mr. Whitcomb's so-called "generous" sum. Part of her wanted to package everything up, race back to the store, and make a gigantic return. She shoved that weak thought aside, resolute in her judgment to do whatever was needed to keep this baby safe.

23

Mrs. Whitcomb sat at her writing desk, reviewing the bills, her gin and tonic glass covered in a dewy film from the warm afternoon air.

She reached nervously for her glass and knocked it across the stack of bills. The drink spilled across the blotter paper and paperwork, landing on the floor with a crash.

She reached for the bill. That Emery Bird Thayer bill. Absolutely unacceptable.

She heard the front door open. Her Elden was home. A two hour visit from Wentworth. A surprise.

She had instructed the dean to have him waiting outside when the driver pulled up at the school gates and to give no hint as to the reason. She had envisioned his delightful smile when he saw the car. A visit home, even for an hour or two, would do him good, Katherine had calculated.

But this morning she had forgotten today was the day. That was happening more and more often. The forgetting. The terrible forgetting. Katherine pushed the thought aside. She would control this. That bill. Elden had gone one step too far this time.

"Elden!" Mrs. Whitcomb called sloppily, "Get in here. Bring a towel. And get me another drink."

"You called like an old fishwife, mother?" Elden asked as he entered the room, cloth in hand.

"Welcome home. Were you surprised? Now, look, you made me spill my drink. Why do you upset me so much?" she asked.

Elden raised one eyebrow at his mother. Father said she'd grown painfully ridiculous in recent weeks, with near-constant demands for a drink, for his attention, for whatever whim entered her alcohol-addled mind.

"I was outside, walking to the front door and by some conjurer's trick I reached in here and plunged your glass to the floor, yet again, did I?" Elden asked, not hiding his acerbic tone and contempt.

"Now, don't start with me. You know what you did," Mrs. Whitcomb quickly retorted picking up the stack of bills and giving them a shake. Droplets landed on Elden's hand as he wiped up the spill.

"Hmmm...what have I done this time? Something atrocious? Outrageous? Unforgivable no doubt? Again? So soon after doing all those other horrific things? How do you continue to breathe in and out mother, with a son like me?" Elden asked, sarcasm dripping from his words.

"Don't start on me. You know what you did. I told you to cut her off, so cut her off. I told you, and you didn't. You couldn't even be enough of a man to do that, could you? You always want a bright line, Elden. I gave you a bright line – do this one thing, I'd said. And you couldn't even do that," Mrs. Whitcomb declared, waving a wet bill in front of Elden.

Elden glimpsed the Emery Bird Thayer logo as the paper whizzed by him. He ripped the bill from his mother's hand. It was Jean's handwriting and read Jean Ball for Elden Whitcomb. Almost two hundred dollars. Elden let out a small sound and gulped back his words. Yes, he told her to take care of whatever the baby needed. And boy, she had.

Then Elden's thoughts raced. It was a lot of money, but it meant Jean would have what she needed to care for the baby. One hundred ninety-seven dollars. Yes, it was a huge sum. But necessary. Jean would only ever spend what was necessary.

Elden looked at his mother, her steely eyes cutting through him. He held his breath, thinking. It was a huge sum. This was not going to be forgivable and making it forgettable was impossible. Mrs. Whitcomb forgot little and forgave little else.

"You didn't earn a dime of this, Elden. It's not for you to say whether she gets a cent," said Mrs. Whitcomb, cold sober. "I won't have a common streetgirl spending our money. She is not one of us. You can't love her or that child of hers. You'll have nothing if you don't cut her off. Nothing. You choose us, Elden. You will always choose us."

Elden's father, hearing the commotion, had entered the darkened library, a fresh gin and tonic in hand. He handed it to his wife.

"Be quiet, Katherine. I gave her the money," Randall Whitcomb said quietly.

"You? You?" screeched Katherine. "You wouldn't dare."

Elden let out a rush of air. Never had he been so grateful for his father's words.

"I did. She's having a baby, Katherine. For God's sake. Our grandchild. I can't make the situation go away, but it's not wrong to ease her burden. Don't mention it again," Mr. Whitcomb instructed.

Katherine glared at her husband, "She is not to become one of us. That child is not one of us. The girl's done this just to trap our son. It's clear as the summer sky that's what's she done."

"That's not true," Elden protested. "It was, it was – it was my mistake, mother. It was all me. Jean is good and fresh and true. Her heart is as clear as the summer sky. This was my mistake."

"Your mistake? Your mistake was not having the sense to take care of Somewhere, make the payments, keep the protection paid up. That was your mistake, Elden," said Mrs. Whitcomb. "We're still cleaning up that mess. You know what you have to do now to make it right at least."

"Wentworth isn't for me. You know that, mother. They try to tell you they're teaching you right and wrong, the way it is and the way it shouldn't be. But, it's not what I'm learning," Elden said, his cheeks flush.

"I'm learning how to get by, how to make money, make people think you like them when you can barely tolerate their sight. It's fake. It's all fraud. Respect authority they say, but we know people are lying and cheating and paying bribes. I can't stand it," Elden protested.

"You're so immature, Elden. That's not how it is. You're learning about business, that's all. Things aren't black and white, the lines are not always clear. You don't know what I had to do to get your charges dropped. You don't know what it took out of me," Mrs. Whitcomb said, her voice rich with venom.

"No, there is no black and white. You do what you have to do to keep your place in this society. It's time you learned that and just grew up," Mrs. Whitcomb concluded, turning her back to Elden as she settled in with her accounting ledger. "You've ruined our short time together, Elden. How could you?"

"Elden, we've taken care of the department store bill. The girl has what she needs. Now you do as your mother says. It's not a choice, it's a requirement. No one will do business with a man whose son has gone to prison. Gone to prison for not having enough common sense to take care of business. No, you can't afford to botch this. We can't afford it," Mr. Whitcomb said.

Elden picked up his mother's full gin glass from the writing desk and set it down, empty.

Jean, I have to see Jean, he thought. Little did he know that his father had taken Jean's fate into his own hands just days before.

～

Jean was too big to work, too big to fit into the elevator. First, it was the staff in the break room and then it was a few of the newer League Ladies in the lobby and meeting rooms who had begun to talk.

On the last day of May, Jean was summoned to Mr. Whitcomb's

office. Mr. Whitcomb was not in the office, but there stood his secretary, Mr. Green, looking serious.

Mr. Whitcomb had been very clear with his secretary. The girl was to go. Today. What Mr. Whitcomb didn't share with Mr. Green was what had happened to make this so. Mr. Whitcomb's secretary knew none of what had happened in the Whitcomb's home, but only that his orders were to terminate a position.

"Your services are no longer needed, Miss Ball. Mr. Whitcomb asked that I give you this," he said handing her an envelope.

"I know," said Jean quietly.

Pregnant women didn't work. Not at a hotel, not anywhere. It simply wasn't done. Jean had known this day would come, but she still wasn't prepared for this sinking, trembling feeling.

"Turn your uniform in today."

"Yes, sir," she said in a low voice, unable to summon the indignity she felt.

"Now," said the secretary with finality.

Jean opened the envelope. Five twenty dollar bills. No note, no words. Jean's eyes filled with tears.

"Can I see Mr. Whitcomb?"

"No, he's not taking appointments today. Just go."

Jean turned and headed for the laundry room to turn in her uniform.

"All done today?" asked Mrs. Velmar, needle and thread in hand.

"All done. For always," Jean said, her eyes wet with tears.

"Nie! Don't say 'for always.' Nie!" said Mrs. Velmar, reaching out to touch Jean's cheek with heartfelt tenderness. "Rest. For baby, rest. You'll come back."

"Rest. Rest won't pay the bills," said Jean ruefully as she turned and walked out of the laundry room.

∼

"Otis, I need to see Jean," Elden called out as he pulled his long convertible up to the apartment building.

"Well, sir, she's out right now," Otis replied. "Been taking walks. Been doing what she can to keep moving what with all the changes coming."

"Does she, will she, do you think she'll see me?" Elden asked as he jumped from the car, his words coming out in a rush. "I've been away so long."

"Oh, I'd guess she'll see you, but say - look there. Those men might want to see you first," Otis replied nodding his head. Elden turned.

Two police officers had their eyes trained on Elden, their faces scowled and one reached for his beat stick.

"Oh, no, it's them," Elden hissed. The police officers. The ones he'd failed to pay off. The ones who were to have kept Somewhere open. "Tell Jean, tell her," Elden began.

"Right, but you best go. Go, fast," Otis whispered as the uniformed men neared, "Go." But, Elden was not quick enough.

Otis watched in fear as the two men shoved Elden into the backseat of the convertible and one of the officers took the wheel. The car screeched as it pulled away from the curb. A blur of color and noise.

"Tell her I . . ." Elden's voice called out as the car turned the corner. Then the street went quiet.

"May God have mercy," Otis whispered, turning his eyes to the heavens.

24

Jean felt the labor start fast. When the first contractions came, Jean thought she was going to die, turn toes up and die, it hurt so bad. Orion heard Jean cry out, and scampered down the hallway.

It was all Jean could do to make her way down all the stairs to Miss Abby's door.

"The baby, something's wrong," was all Jean said.

Abby assessed the situation quickly. Nothing wrong at all. The baby was definitely coming, but likely not soon. No water broke. No blood yet, observed Abby, just a baby making its way and taking its time.

"We'll get you upstairs, Otis and me. Nothing to worry about here," assured Abby.

"Otis, yes. Otis. Tell him to go to James," Jean insisted, "Please tell James. He can get Elden for me. Elden wants to be here. I know he does. Otis told me he came a few days ago. To see us. To see me."

Jean stumbled as they helped her up the stairs. Miss Abby motioned for Otis to go as they got to Jean's door and instructed, "You get us water, hot and cold, and the birthing towels. Then you stay within the distance in case I need help here."

Miss Abby had birthed children throughout the city and knew the job that was to come. Sometimes it was easy and quick, but then sometimes, things took a turn. It was always good to keep help within shouting distance, at least until she got a sense of things.

"You got some time now. Pains will come and go and feel like a giant squeeze and you can't get your breath. Don't get the panic goin' when that happens. Just wait it out. Let me get you a cool towel now," Abby said calmly.

"I need Elden, Miss Abby. He needs to be here," insisted Jean.

"Ain't no man in here while I'm here. Ain't no man comin' through that door while your hither and yon is spread out across this bed. This part of livin's not for a man," explained Abby as she wiped Jean's brow.

"No. Right after. He needs to see our little boy as soon as he can," said Jean, and her voice broke.

"Don't think about that now. A little boy? This child may well be a girl, Jean. You're not carrying it low like for a boy. Girl is what you need here, anyway," said Abby matter-of-factly.

"A girl? Oh, maybe, but a boy, he'd have to love a boy. A boy could follow him around, play ball, go to the lake. It'll be our son. He won't turn us away then, I know it," said Jean.

"Real men don't turn away any child, but don't be fooled. We know some men ain't real men, that's for sure," said Abby.

"Don't ever say that about Elden," Jean snapped feverishly. "He'll be here. I know he'll want to be here."

"You settle here. I'll make you a tea 'fore that next pain comes. And of course now, I'd never say a bad thing about a fine man like Mr. Whitcomb," replied Abby.

"Okay, okay then. Yes, tea would be good," said Jean. "I still have some of Mama's Earl Grey tea. Oh, I want my Mama. It hurts! My mouth's so dry."

"Dry 'cuz you're breathin' so hard it pushes all the water out. But, you'll be fine. This is all just fine, just right," assured Abby.

Abby studied the little girl from across the room. Women at this point, all women, need to think things will turn out like a fairy tale, all princes and castles. This is no time for a talk about reality. Clearly, this girl didn't know the stories about the Whitcomb men.

Midwives, they talked, talked among themselves. The stories were told that the rich Mr. Whitcomb himself had a mistress who'd lost a baby a few years back and that the gal had sunk into a sadness even fancy jewelry couldn't cure.

And then the story circulated lately that he'd seduced one of the Empire's own maids, and that she and the baby had been taken care of by the League Ladies, quietly given a respectable job at a local department store. The League Ladies even arranged for her to have an apartment suitable for raising a child.

Rumor had been that Katherine Whitcomb had come sniffing around the midwifery guild looking for help for the girl, though it was not help she really wanted. Hinted that the baby might not live through the delivery, and that would just be one of the tragedies to be taken care of quietly. She'd pulled out her fancy purse and flashed a real hundred dollar bill at one of the young midwives.

It was true that some midwives would make things happen like that, take care of unexpected problems. Mrs. Whitcomb had gone to the wrong midwife guild for that.

Abby's guild, and even their apprentices, took an oath among themselves to treat every new baby like a gift, a blessing.

Each meeting they'd read the verses of Exodus about midwives Shiphrah and Puah refusing to slay the Hebrews first-born sons, though it defied the powerful Pharaoh who ordered it be done. None of Abby's guild would question God's destiny. But, these were things not to be shared with Jean, Abby knew, not today and not ever. A midwife's judgment and discretion were paramount. Not a midwife's business to gossip or advise on men or in-laws, only the babies and the mother.

"Here's your tea now, not too hot. Now, you stop gritting those teeth first," said Abby seeing the grimace on Jean's face. "Don't you push yet. Not time. Drink this down. Strong and no sweet in it either. No need to sugar-coat this baby. She'll be sweet enough."

Abby held fast to the belief that the words that were said and things that were taken in a birthing room manifested itself for the child, even though it was a belief that young midwife apprentices seemed to scorn anymore. Some of them wouldn't even put a knife under the birthing bed to cut the pain - such were the changes in young people these days.

"This child will be strong like this tea and loved like no other child you know," Abby said with assurance.

"Elden will love this baby, I know," said Jean.

"And you'll love this child. Even if times are hard, this child will be the one that saves you, Jean. Remember that," Abby said.

"You know, I've seen women weep when their child's born, all a fearin' about how to raise a child, maybe their second or third child, or sometimes they cry because they're alone. They all worried out. But, you never know which child may be the one that saves you, sent by God to hold your own self up when times too hard," explained Abby. "Sent to hold your hand when you have no strength yourself."

Jean listened and her thoughts went back to her own mama, the tenderness, how it felt to brush back her hair and lay a cool rag on her forehead, the gift of the time they had together. Love and caring and kindness, without thought to the result, the outcome. And how Mama had tended to her, taught her the right from the wrong, the rules that would make life easier. She would do that, for a baby. And, like caring for Mama, it would turn out to be a gift.

She felt like bursting at the revelation, releasing the wellspring of joy she knew she would have with this child. And, just as quickly Jean was filled with a sense of contentment and resolve at what was to come.

"I can do it, Abby. I can be a good mother. My mama taught me how. And we won't have hard times. We're going to have a house, a little house, with a yard and a fence so he'll run and play and Elden will get him a dog. Every boy needs a dog," said Jean, envisioning the way things would be.

"Happy thoughts, nice thoughts," said Abby looking to reassure, making no promises.

"Is Otis telling James now? James can send word for Elden," said

Jean. "I know Elden will come when he hears the baby's coming. I know he will. He will."

"Oh Otis, he won't leave that door 'til I tell him. He's right outside there now," said Abby pointing to the apartment door.

"Otis, get Elden. Tell James to find him. Elden needs to come soon," shouted Jean, hoping she was loud enough to be heard through the door.

"We have at least two hours now. Poppa, you can go on now, send word and find James if you can. It's okay," called out Abby, knowing Jean would not relax without the thought that Elden may come.

"Yes, ladies," called Otis, "I'm going right now. I'll find James. He'll know how to get ahold of Elden."

Otis stood outside the door recalling Elden being driven away by the men who had been filled with such fury. He'd not told Jean that part.

That Elden couldn't come felt like a certainty to Otis. He was, undoubtedly, far away, probably locked up. And a birthing room was no place for a man, never would be, but Otis headed down the stairs and over to the hotel. He'd get word to him at the least.

"When can Elden come in?" asked Jean.

"Men can see the baby first, but can't see the mother 'til she got herself together," Abby explained. "I find men, most men, don't think with words like you and me, you know. Men remember what they see. Their brains what like a movie house I think sometimes. Just different from us. See their wife all wrought out and sweaty, tired from the birth, and that picture in their head now. We'd see that and it'd not be the whole picture for you and me. Now don't think that means a man isn't a complicated thing with the complex things in their head. Just means the man believes what he sees is true and that it's the whole picture, when the real thing may be layered up with something else," said Abby.

"I know. They're different, aren't they? Not always good with the complications," agreed Jean.

"Some girls learn that from watching their poppas with their mamas. Not every poppa can sort through the muddle of raising children, dealing with things of the heart that children need. Most can't, truth be told. Mama has to be the heart watcher, the real caretaker, I think. You're fortunate, you know, your mama was like that. She did a fine job of raising you herself. She'd be proud here of how you been managing things," replied Abby.

Jean smiled, remembering the sweet moments she'd shared with her mama, two girls making their way.

"Will it be hard to raise a boy? I hadn't really thought about that," said Jean.

"Get your heart off that boy idea. This is gonna be a girl child for sure. I have no doubt," Abby said definitively.

"Stop it. You don't know. What would Elden do with a girl-baby?" asked Jean, exasperated at the idea she wouldn't be giving him a little boy to carry on the Whitcomb name.

This child had all her hopes on a son. Abby had seen it so many times, especially with the unmarried girls – thinking a son would make everything right. Almost backward.

"Listen to this, Jean. You just remember that girl babies bring out the care-taking part of a man. Man made to take care of the female, like a lion take care of his pride. So you best hope for a girl if you're worried about Elden," cautioned Abby.

"Of course he'd love a girl, too, like he loves me," said Jean, white now with pain.

"Let me check you. Could be nearer time than we thought. Yes, baby's crowning now, head coming first like it should be. Everything is just like it should be," said Abby, so quietly that it sounded like a prayer.

It was a gentle birth and quick. The child gulped for air and gave a tiny cry. The baby came out with a caul and covered in a thin film. Abby knew it was the mark of a female who'd grow up to be wise, knowing things others couldn't sense, seeing things invisible to the eye.

"You have yourself a daughter, Jean. A perfect little girl to add to Elden's pride," said Abby.

"I'll hold her," offered Jean.

"Let me clean her up a bit. She's a lucky child, special child. Born here with a caul, a sign of a strong woman. A woman of second sight," said Abby.

She wiped the baby tenderly and laid her on Jean's chest.

"Now, you stroke her cheek. See her perfect mouth open and shut? You stroke her foot. See that curl up? That's good. Now take her little palm, one hand at a time. Tickle your finger across. Yes, just like that. That's good. See those precious fingers close right up like that? Sign that she's gonna be a fast little thinker. Take after her mama, right?" said Abby explaining all the ways to measure for a healthy baby.

"She's perfect," said Jean.

Jean touched her fingertip to her baby's perfect rosebud mouth. The little lips puckered into a kiss. She counted the baby's ten fingers, and carefully contemplated the black button of the umbilical cord.

"My baby," Jean whispered. "My very own little girl."

She held her daughter close to her heart.

"Your daddy won't be able to help but love you," she whispered. "You are Ella, after Elden. Ella means beautiful fairy, like you. Welcome to the world, Ella. We have a little family, but we are big in love. Francie will be your chosen auntie, and we have a kitty cat."

She looked hopefully at Abby.

"Can Elden see her now?"

"No, no man in here yet. I don't care if it's the President himself who knocks on that door. We need to get you and that baby presentable. You just did the most important work of a woman's life. Time to let you rest and I'll clean up the baby in just a minute. You two rest here now. I need to use the indoor plumbing. You'll be fine here for a minute," said Abby.

Abby stepped into the hallway and pulled the door closed behind her. She knew the next few minutes were important to the mother and child, just to have a few quiet moments before the world intruded forever.

Abby smiled in relief to see Otis waiting in the hallway, leaning back with his eyes shut.

"Healthy?" Otis asked without opening his eyes.

"Just fine. Jean, too," replied Abby.

"God bless," he said softly, opening his eyes and taking his daughter's hand in his own. "Grown up to be such a kind woman, Abby. Your mother would be so proud of you today. You make our family proud."

"Daddy, I wish Jean had a daddy like you. She's gonna need somebody. But, I know this baby girl will be a gift for her," said Abby.

Otis cast his eyes downward at their clasped hands, "This girl, her baby," he said forming the words slowly, "we'll do right by them. Feels like she has no one but us now. Reminds me so of our little Katie." One tear rolled gently down Otis' cheek.

"Katie. Sister Katie. First time you've said her name in years, Daddy," Abby whispered. "She was just 17, too. We may never understand why the Good Lord took her and her baby home."

Otis nodded and wiped his cheek. "I still search the Good Book each day for an answer."

"We'll do right by this girl. For her memory," Abby said, her voice a husky whisper. "You find Elden?"

"Yes. The boy won't come today, for sure. Bottle got him now, says James, and he got quite a beating from some men he owed. He's in no condition," explained Otis.

Abby shook her head and patted her father's hand. There was nothing more to say.

She walked down the hallway to the bathroom, washed her hands and filled the basin with tepid water. She'd bathe the baby and let Jean rest.

Abby said the Prayer of Life she recited after each birth, to thank God for the work done, and to give strength to the mother who had embarked upon a journey that would never end.

She dried her hands on the towel and headed back into the apartment.

∽

*I*nside the apartment, Jean held the baby and felt the little heart beating in rhythm with her own. She'd never considered how little this baby would be, how warm the tiny breaths would feel when they touched Jean's cheek. She thought about her own Mama and remembered what it felt like to touch a person with no air. *Now I'll never have to remember that day again,* Jean thought.

Jean whispered to the baby, "We're a family. I'm your mama and you are my girl, forever. I call you Ella after your daddy, Elden. And you're named Virginia, after me. Virginia Ella Whitcomb. I have the whole world to show you, Ella. It's a big exciting world out there and you're going to love it. We'll see everything together. There are big cities, like here where we live, and lots of farms and a sparkling lake that your daddy loves. That's where we fell in love, too. There's so much to see. We're going to be so happy. I'll always love you, Ella. You'll always be my girl. Always."

Abby had overheard most of Jean's little speech of hope and wishes and couldn't help but smile. "Sometimes God grants prayers quick like," Abby whispered to herself.

"Let me bathe her up now. I'll put her in a diaper and then show you how we swaddle a baby. Here's some tea. You drink it all now and sleep," said Abby.

Jean felt a tired like she'd never had before come over her. "But, you wake me when Elden comes, okay?" she asked.

"Sure will, honey. I sure will," said Abby as she pulled a clean cover over Jean.

Jean felt the comfort of Abby's touch and shut her eyes. She slept a dreamless, hard sleep. When she woke it was all dark outside. Miss Abby sat in a chair pulled next to the bed. Baby Ella was bundled in a blanket tied around Miss Abby's chest, both were sleeping soundly with heavy breaths. Jean was sore and it hurt to move. She couldn't even try to get out of bed and instead rolled to her side, not allowing herself to give a single thought to Elden's whereabouts. Sleep quickly found her again.

In all the commotion, they had left the door slightly ajar, and Jean didn't see Francie as she peeked quickly into the room. Jean didn't know that her best friend had stepped through the doorway and gently kissed her forehead.

"Elden?" Jean murmured.

Francie unfolded the soft baby quilt she'd made for the newborn and draped it across the sleeping new mother. She knew Jean would cherish the Victorian Crazy Quilt with every seam embellished with fancy hand stitching, embroidered with birds, butterflies, and even a little cat. Francie's mother had helped her make it, lacing prayers among the stitches. Francie said a quiet prayer for her best friend's well-being as she tiptoed out the door.

25

Elden woke up, his head pounding. His face was bruised, ribs ached from where they'd been kicked until his stomach felt like jelly. He'd surely be dead if it weren't for Alonzo. The bouncer from Somewhere. He'd found Elden in the alley, bloodied, hanging out of the backseat of the Revere.

His father had been on the phone all night cleaning up the mess with City Hall, with the Chief of Police. No, no jail. Wentworth was an absolute obligation now, not an option. How would he do that and take care of a wife and child? Who could even help him answer that question?

Elden knew of only one man who had ever faced his dilemma, only one man he could turn to for the right advice. One man who had made a thing like this work -- his father.

Elden pulled the pillow over his head and let out a groan. How could he even face his father today? First things first, an aspirin – or three, then a dose of reality.

"Hey, Grandpa, how are you doing this fine morning?" asked Elden jovially. His father was seated in the dining room drinking his coffee and reading the newspaper.

"Morning? It's after eleven, Elden. Some night, I hear. Ass over teacups in the alley, hear tell. I've put everything on the line to get your name cleared, son. Now will you just grow up?" asked Mr. Whitcomb.

"That's actually what I wanted to talk about," said Elden, clearing his throat.

Mr. Whitcomb braced himself for another roust from his son – of all the reasons why he didn't need to go back to the academy, how he could figure out a different deal with the prosecutor, and how, by the way, he could sure use some cash. It had all grown beyond tiresome.

"It's Jean, Pops. The baby's going to be coming. I don't know when, but soon," said Elden, taking a seat at the table and rubbing his head.

"That's unfortunate for her. Not your problem, son," said Mr. Whitcomb, choosing his words carefully and trying not to register the anger rising in his chest.

"Of course it's my problem. It's our baby," replied Elden, looking at his father with disbelief.

"There will always be girls like Jean, Elden. They're not your problem," Mr. Whitcomb responded. "We have money to take care of these things, son."

Some two decades before, Mr. Whitcomb had awakened with a headache like Elden's, and he had made a rash decision, a decision to do the right thing. The moral thing. He had offered his hand in marriage and Elden had been raised as a Whitcomb from the start. Of course, his own parents were shamed. Katherine was not a girl they had ever pictured for their son - a stockyard man's child and a Croatian from Strawberry Hill at that. A girl who didn't know a salad fork from a fish fork.

It had been a summer dalliance culminating in a walk by the river. Four months later she'd appeared at the Whitcombs' door. He'd done the right thing and it still didn't make things right. If things were right, she wouldn't crawl into the bottle of solace. His wife would have made friends with the League Ladies, he wouldn't have had to take a mistress, and their son wouldn't have failed.

There were things Mr. Whitcomb long ago gave up trying to make right. Making money under the guise of righting social wrongs was easier.

"Jean isn't a 'problem,'" said Elden.

"Do I give you advice, Elden?" asked his father.

"No. Mother does."

"Do I support your decisions?"

"More than Mother."

"So today if I give you advice, then you'd listen?"

"Of course, Dad."

"What if I directly told you what to do?"

"I'd do it," said Elden knowing his father had never once been direct like that.

"Then listen because I will only say this once," said his father. "You've had fun, a lot of good times these last few years. Right?" asked Mr. Whitcomb.

Elden nodded warily.

"I understand you care for this girl and her child. That's admirable," his father continued.

"Right," said Elden, not lifting his eyes.

"And I've given you opportunities. We've taken care of all your little problems, more than you even know. I gave you a business to run. Running Somewhere wasn't that difficult now, was it, Elden? And you ran it all the way towards federal prison. You got distracted. Took your eye off the ball, again. Didn't have follow-through. You're too old for this. Do you know what I'm saying?" he asked.

"I guess," said Elden, shifting uncomfortably in his chair.

"This isn't about guessing, Elden. It's time to straighten up and take your place in society. In our society, we don't sleep with the help, Elden. We are Whitcombs," concluded Mr. Whitcomb.

Elden sat silent, not wanting to confront his father's hypocrisy, but unable to hold himself back.

"Am I right, son?" he asked.

"Right. Unless it's a maid at the Empire Hotel," said Elden, needing to take the conversation to the one sad thing they had in common.

Mr. Whitcomb looked caught. He gulped silently, taking a moment to gather his words. "How did you know?"

"Everyone knows, Father," Elden said contemptuously.

"A dalliance. It was wrong. Wrong for me and the girl. Wrong for your mother and all that she'd worked for, hoped for, in her life," Mr. Whitcomb confessed.

"But you did it just the same," Elden accused.

"It was wrong. You know it changed things for us. You've seen what it's done to your mother. I live with that every day. It was a mistake and you need to learn from my mistakes. There are expectations for us. I had to learn that the hard way. My son won't," Mr. Whitcomb replied.

"But the baby's mine, and I love her," Elden responded.

"No. You can't. You will lift up the workers, not bed them down. Take care of them and they'll take care of our business. I've taught you that, by words if not always by example. You must do better than I have done. If we do well, they do well, but do not forget your place in this equation," Mr. Whitcomb instructed. "You cannot lift them up if you are sitting among them. You lose your place, then you lose our standing."

Elden looked at the man sitting in front of him. Disgusting, he thought. This weak man is beyond contempt, talking with such callousness about people as if they were chattel. He blurs the lines between right and wrong again, just for the money, just for the social standing. Always his parents blurred the lines and it always came down to the money, thought Elden.

Unaware of Elden's growing disgust, Mr. Whitcomb continued, "I was lucky to have that put behind me, thanks to the League Lady who got Miss Cassandra Lee a placement elsewhere."

"It cost me dearly for them to keep that quiet. Had to hire an elevator girl to show them how progressive, equality-minded, I was. Had to give them their meeting rooms for free, throw them a big party to raise their money," Mr. Whitcomb continued. "I paid dearly for my little mistake and they won't step in for us another time, you know."

"Pops, it's a baby here. And Jean. It's not a hotel chambermaid I seduced on a slow day at the office," Elden jabbed, happy to see his father's face turn scarlet.

"Do not judge what I do. I have built everything you have. Everything you see. And we'll take it away if you go to prison. Disinherit is an unfortunate word, but it is precisely what will be done. Your mother and I can't risk all that we have because of your mistake. She couldn't hold her head up if you don't do the right thing here."

"And what is the right thing? Really, what is the right thing? Tell me, because I feel we have differing views on this, Pops," Elden said, putting his head in his hands and rubbing his temples.

"You know what you have to do. You will be running the hotel, owning all that land around it, this house, the summer home. Elden, it's all yours when you go back to Wentworth. All of it. We've gone over this before. I'll just say it this time: You will be a millionaire three times over in a very short few years. And then you can do anything. You will have everything. Probably even this girl and the child then, if you really want. Or you go to the girl now and you go to jail. You'd have nothing. I'll even take away that bar, Somewhere. You'd have nothing and she'd have nothing."

Elden stood, stricken, uncertain. He could not imagine a life without money or comforts, or a life in prison. He started rationalizing, thinking that maybe, in a couple of years, he could find his way back to Jean and begin again. She could forgive him, and he would have all the comforts to offer her and the baby then. Otherwise, what would they have together? He would be a penniless man in prison, and he knew himself well enough to see that he had no skills for surviving that life.

Elden rubbed his eyes, wishing he could erase every misstep, every mistake.

"The car comes for you in fifteen minutes," Mr. Whitcomb said.

"You're going to the Academy. Your mother has sacrificed more for you than you ever will know, and I have, too. You will not disappoint us now. And no, you have no choice. We packed your bags last night. They're in the front closet." Mr. Whitcomb stood, folded the newspaper and left the room. There was nothing more to be said.

26

Jean gathered the baby into her arms and nestled into the bed beside her. She and Ella slept, surrounded by all the things the Whitcombs' money had bought. Her initial regret about charging the costs of all the baby's things had dissipated completely. The abundance of new things made her feel almost safe sometimes, and she needed that feeling.

The baby would need a father, grandparents, family – but for now, a pretty pram and playthings could be her connection to the family she might never know.

Orion purred from his perch in the cat bed made from her mama's flannel nightgown. Jean felt the heaviness of the baby in her arms. Somehow, her life had become a patchwork quilt, pieced together with prayers for the binding. Jean had no idea what might come next. She learned long ago that food didn't just appear by magic, and the landlord didn't get paid with promises. She could count on no one but herself.

As the days passed, Jean tried to stave off a rising panic over what may happen in the future. There was no prospect of working at the hotel again. She had applied for work at the EBT, at another hotel, at the sundry shop. Nothing.

She'd talked with Lydia, but the nail shop didn't have business enough to offer her work. Even though she hadn't said so in as many words, Lydia kept a low profile in the community and didn't want to risk offending the Whitcombs, either. She didn't want to risk any harm to James or to his reputation.

Francie had thought Jean could be a nanny for some rich person through church, but that opportunity never materialized, and Jean couldn't help but wonder if it might be because the church folks didn't take well to having an unwed mother in charge of their children's care. Besides, as Jean was beginning to realize in these short months with baby Ella, other people's babies and children were definitely not for her. It took all her courage to stay strong when Ella cried, and she couldn't imagine what it would be like if the children belonged to someone else.

Jean took out her pay envelope and counted the dollars, worrying over each one. She remembered how Mama had counted the same dollars, again and again, and for the first time, she understood what her mother must have felt.

Ten dollars needed for the next rent. She needed to budget with care, but she always included a few pennies for tidbits of meat for the cat, and a little cream from time to time.

I need to find work, just anything, Jean thought. Her final safety net, Francie and all the Nowaks, felt elusive, remote. Francie's mother was clear that she believed a sin had been committed and had raised most of her children to agree.

Francie had explained how her mother was praying the rosary for Jean every day, glossing over the part about her mother saying Jean could be going straight to Hell, not even Purgatory, for her misdeeds. Francie had to sneak away from her mother in order to visit.

Jean pulled back a sniffle. Feeling sad wouldn't help, and it wasn't as if she were really alone, with the near constant visits from Miss Abby who never stopped her fretting and busywork around the tiny apartment. Miss Abby had taken to saying, "just to check on things for a piece" as she opened the apartment door.

Jean heard the apartment door creak open and put a quick hand to her face to wipe away the tears.

"You are getting outside," Abby declared, filling the apartment with light as she lifted the window sash. The warm spring air rushed in carrying a hint of lilac. "Eight weeks old already. Let's call this Ella's first visiting day," offered Abby, picking up the sweet bundle from the bed. "Who wouldn't want to see this sweet bundle of baby-ness? Now get on out of here today and let me take this laundry. I'll wash it up while you two are gone."

Abby picked up the dirty diapers from the bedside table and bustled back down the stairs. Every time Miss Abby burst into the apartment, she was on some sort of mission – to feed Jean, check Ella's diaper, just tidy up, pick up the laundry, bring a tidbit to Orion. She was a dynamo of good intentions. It wore Jean out to watch her bustle about.

So much easier just to lay in bed and feel sorry for myself, Jean often thought.

"I guess we're going out today, Ella," said Jean to the baby.

New mothers were often cautioned to keep their babies indoors for months for fear of the croup and such, but Abby was right. Jean shouldn't stay cooped up one more second, all worn down and sad.

Jean dressed the baby in her cutest outfit, a little seersucker pinafore covered in white and yellow daisies, a gift from Abby. It was Ella's only little girl outfit. She would have picked out more frilly dresses at the EBT had she known she would be graced with a girl child. Jean double diapered the baby and put her in a pair of matching bloomers.

This is the prettiest, sweetest baby in the whole world. I should feel grateful. She held Ella close and breathed in deep. The baby smelled of everything good and pure Jean had ever known, but even that couldn't edge out her sadness. *Elden would have loved Ella,* Jean thought, *just loved her.*

She quickly pushed the thought of all that Elden was missing, and had not done right, out of her mind. It would just bring her back to that sad place, that place that kept her laying in bed, not wanting to move, and it reminded her of that first week. That first week that was so hard. Jean had laid in the bed crying, unsure how to care for this child. But, that was weeks ago. She needed to shake off that sadness.

Today is a day for getting outside and remembering there is life all around. Miss Abby is right.

Abby was coming up from the basement when Jean brought Ella into the lobby.

"Well, look who's finally out and about. You look like a fine mother, Miz Jean. Ella is a most beautiful child, just look at her," Abby admired.

Abby had spent hours washing and diapering and tending to the little one the first weeks while the girl had just lain about and cried. She had secretly worried Jean would be like some young mother cats who walked away from their mewing kittens, too little themselves to care for their young. Today Abby felt relief when she saw Jean was beaming down at the tiny bundle that held the baby. Maybe Jean was going to be all right.

Jean gently laid the baby in the big pram that she kept in the apartment house lobby, and headed to a nearby park. She took a seat on a wooden bench and nudged the pram back and forth to settle the baby, her mind on puzzling out options for their future. She was coming up blank.

No work meant no money. No money meant no home. No home, no food. No food. Her thoughts stopped on that. She had to keep up her strength, to be able to feed little Ella, but she had lost her appetite. She no longer felt any pleasure in tasting; it was one more thing she had to do to take care of her baby. How would she ever care for Ella?

Jean's worries were interrupted by a tangle of commotion in the south end of the park. A nanny was raising her voice to three little children who had decided throwing rocks at one another was loads more fun than playing tag.

"And I'll take you over my knee right here if you don't stop it! I don't care what your mother said!" hollered the nanny.

That is one woman who should find herself a new line of work, thought Jean. But the voice had a familiar lilt to it. Collette, a woman in clear need of a diversion.

"Oh, let them just kill one another. What do we care?" Jean called out to Collette in her biggest voice.

"What?" Collette replied, turning her head in the direction of a possible kindred spirit.

"What do we care, really?" Jean said, offering a smile and wave.

"You!" said Collette, "Look at you sitting there with your perfectly well-behaved child. Did you see my heathens? Beating on each other like Cain and Abel."

Collette smiled as she approached Jean's quiet bench. She looked pert and strong in a plain blue frock, buttoned at the shoulders and concealing all her curves.

"Come sit. Let the kids wreak havoc on the world. You tell their mama they were acting out Bible stories today in the park. Their mama won't ask any questions after hearing that good news," joked Jean.

Collette let out a laugh. "Jean, I have just had it with this taking care of these kids. They're terrors – night and day. And look at that," she said turning her gaze to little Ella. "This one's not a terror at all, is she?"

"I guess she's a good baby. Only one I know, so I'm not exactly sure."

"You sure dress her nice. You do that on an elevator operator's wage?"

"I've got no wage now. Mr. Whitcomb let me go before the baby came. Money's going to run out someday. But, how about you? You doing okay?"

"I'm sorry, Jean. That's awful. You don't want to do what I do. I hate watching these kids. I stay up late and then have to put up with this during the day," Collette said, gesturing to a ball of three hollering children tumbling across the park, fists making contact with flesh on each turn.

"Well, what are we going to do about that?" asked Jean.

"Don't tell anyone, but I'm going to quit," Collette said, her voice husky with glee. "I have a new job at night and it makes good money so I don't need these ingrates any more. I figure I'll stay at their house and just pay a little rent. Then she can hire someone who actually likes these brats."

"You have another job? Pays well?"

"Dime a dance. I get a nickel every minute and a half. Why if I danced for an hour I'd have almost two dollars."

"Two dollars in an hour? That's not possible at all, Collette. What are you talking about?"

"Taxi dancing they call it."

"Taxi dancing?"

"Sure, ever notice that men can't dance, or think they can dance but shouldn't be dancing, or can dance but can't find a girl who can keep up?"

"All kinds of men in this world," Jean nodded.

"There's a dance hall needing 'dance instructors.' That's what they call us. Instructors. Now, don't get me wrong, most of the men don't take to instruction," Collette laughed. "They just want to be dancing with a pretty girl. Voilà, c'est moi!"

Collette stood and gave an exaggerated curtsey. "I guess they call it taxi-dancing because you pay to dance like you pay for a taxi-ride. If you don't like the looks of one fare, you wait for another. But, who waits, right? It's money."

"And they pay you to – to just dance?" asked Jean, raising one eyebrow at how doubtful that sounded.

"No, they pay the house, the dance hall manager, and he gives them a ticket. One ticket costs a dime and a man gets ninety whole seconds of prime dancing time with me, or another girl, for the men with poorer judgment. I get half that and half of all the drinks I sell. I made three dollars and fifty cents last night, in just five hours. It's like a miracle, that kind of money. Do you know what I can do with three dollars?"

"Three dollars, in one night? You're joking. I need a job bad, and quick. Do you think ..." Jean's voice trailed off as she looked down at Ella.

"The dance hall is always looking for girls. I guess now that Elden is –" Collette stopped herself, embarrassed. "Just come on down. It's 18th and Vine. Miss Simone's Dance Studio."

Apparently everyone knows about Elden and they're all afraid to tell me, Jean thought. "He's really with someone else, isn't he?" Jean asked.

Collette shrugged. "He's Elden. So, who knows for sure, right?"

Jean could feel a chill, a steely cold, come over her. Maybe it was true and nothing mattered now.

"Thank you, Collette. I do like to dance and you'll teach me more steps, right? I owe you big if this works out," said Jean a little too brightly, putting on her best face.

It would get her nowhere to let Collette see her sad, confirming Elden's betrayal. Ella started to fuss.

"Time for Ella's nap now. I'll see you tonight. Miss Simone's, right? 18th and Vine?"

Collette nodded. "Ask for Simon. He owns the place. Named it Simone's because it sounded fancier and it suited him. He's a real Ethel. Go around three when he's setting up. I don't get there until eight. *Bon chance, mon amie!* And best you forget about Elden for now. He's got to figure things out," Collette counseled.

~

The dance studio was not what Jean had envisioned. She'd expected an elegant ballroom with a wall of mirrors and tall ceilings where the girls would wear their hair swept up and don silk dresses. Instead, the room was smoky and dark. Its polished hardwood floors and lone chandelier gave only a passing nod to elegance and were eclipsed by the smells of hair cream, stale beer and a sadly familiar wisp of junipers.

Jean eased Ella's pram into a dim corner and said a silent prayer that the baby would be still for just a few minutes. She looked around the large room.

No, a ballroom it was not. A serving bar stretched along the wall of the short end of the dance floor and five or six bare wooden tables lined one wall. Padded chairs were scattered around the tables and in no particular order throughout the room. A tiny man in his shirt sleeves was wiping down the tables and emptying ashtrays into a battered coffee can.

"Excuse me, are you Simon?" asked Jean, summoning her city manners.

"Yes, Simon of Simone's, missy. How can I help you?" replied the man, flipping the cleaning rag over his shoulder and sticking his fanny out into a curtsey. Jean suppressed a giggle.

"I understand from my friend Collette you are looking for instructors," said Jean.

"Collette? Oh, sure, Collette. She's a lot of fun," said Simon.

"I can dance," Jean began earnestly.

Simon cocked an eyebrow and put his hands on his hips, "I don't care if you can dance, honey. Show me your legs."

Jean's cheeks flushed. No one had ever spoken with her so frankly, but this mouse of a man looked positively harmless. She lifted the hem of her skirt a bare inch and gave her toe a point.

"Hmmm, awfully young, aren't you?"

"No, I take care of myself."

"That yours?" Simon asked, pointing to the pram in the corner.

"Yes," said Jean without apology or explanation.

"Parents aren't going to storm in here one night and haul you out?" he asked.

"No. I can guarantee that won't happen." Jean suppressed the urge to say more. She swallowed her words and concluded, "I'll be no liability, no trouble, as long as I get paid."

"Well, it's dime a dance but, of course, you get three cents of that."

"I'll take half."

"Hmmmpphhff, well, but drinks, now drinks, for those you get twenty-five percent."

"I'll take half and we have a deal."

"Start tomorrow?"

"What time?"

"Eight. Come any night around eight."

"No. Nine thirty. I can work late, but can't be here before 9:30." The latest Ella had gone to sleep had been 9:15. That would give her time to get the baby settled for the night and then walk downtown to the studio.

Simon squinted his eyes and gave the girl a once over. This gal looked sweet but apparently was a tough one. Few of the girls ever tried to set their own terms – just took what was offered and were glad to have it.

"Have it your way. The place will be busy by then. A few rules – you pay for your own drinks. Buddy's the bartender and he keeps track, and no koochyhoo on work time. If I say you're out, you're out. And dress nice," he said.

Jean looked down at her cotton sweater and simple dress, the one she'd worn so many months ago on the picnic to the lake.

"What you have on is fine," said Simon, noticing her unspoken question, "If you smile and make nice no one will care anyway. Any questions?"

"No, sir. Wait, one. I'm paid every night, right?"

"Yeah, finish a shift you get paid. Buddy keeps track and I sell the tickets. Work eight to midnight, paid at twelve thirty. If you work midnight to two, paid by two thirty. I try to close up by two. Found that nothing good happens after two in the morning. Oh, and if you help clean up after closing, it's an extra nickel."

"Ok. I'll see you tomorrow night. And I'll get paid then, right?"

"If you earn it. Got to learn the ropes. Don't think you'll dance off with a bankroll in one night, girly," said Simon, turning back to his table wiping with a swish of his towel.

"Of course not, of course. Thank you, Simon," said Jean as she retrieved the pram from the corner. Ella had, thankfully, slept right through.

"What's your name, girl?" Simon called out as Jean was leaving.

"Jean Ball, well, Virginia Mae Ball, of the 'life's a ball' Balls," she said cavalierly. "Everyone calls me Jean," she called over her shoulder as she made her way out the door with the long pram.

27

As the sun set, Jean slipped the golden silk dress over her head. Her fingernail caught on the fine silk, tearing a line along the length of the skirt. Jean grimaced as she examined the rip and then donned her dancing slippers with resignation. She put a hand up to smooth her hair. Her hair. It would never do. Too old-fashioned to still have long hair. All the girls had bobs now.

Jean reached for the scissors, her Mama's good sewing scissors, and walked down the hall to the shared bath. A wave of sadness swept through her as she cut her hair into a modern bob.

What about this feels liberating to so many girls? And what would Mama have thought? Jean wondered, knowing she had just shed what her Mama called a girl's crowning glory.

She finger-curled her locks into gentle waves as she fought back tears, and looked in the mirror. Gone. It was done.

Jean's hands shook as she gathered the fallen locks and scooped them into the trash. She could hear Ella giving a gentle coo from down the hall and hurried back to the bassinet. Reaching in, she hugged Ella close. She could feel the safe pitter-pat against her own heart. This was no time for regret.

After a good feeding and fresh diaper, Ella fell right to sleep. Abby said she would be right in at 9 p.m., where was she?

Jean raced to Miss Abby's downstairs knocking hard. Miss Abby answered, "I'm on my way up now. I'll take care of her. Don't worry," Abby assured. "Pretty hair, Jean. Quite a change."

Jean's hands quaked as she patted down her curls. "I know. I know, but it's just hair. And my Ella, she's so little, and I can't leave her, and I need . . . " Jean's eyes filled with tears.

"You go now. I'll take care of Ella and feed that furball Orion too," Abby replied, "Go."

"I'll be home soon, Miss Abby."

"Go," Miss Abby said, asking no questions. Jean could hear Abby's prayers beginning before she'd even closed the door.

Collette greeted Jean as she entered the dance hall. "Oh, I was hoping you would come. Come on over, I'll get you a drink." Collette said as she headed for the bar at the back of the room.

"No thanks, I'm fine," Jean declined. She had no intention of drinking and positioned herself against a wall. She watched the other girls closely and tried to figure out why one was asked to dance over another who stood alone. It didn't seem to have any relation to their ability. Collette sidled up to her, drink in hand.

"You're hunching up your shoulders like you're going into battle, Jean. Relax. Now, look around the room. Smile. Not like that. I said smile. Show your teeth. No, you look like you're a grizzly ready to pounce on your prey. The trick is to relax your upper lip. See? That's better. Now, look over there," said Collette, pointing to a cluster of men in the corner. "There are some regulars here. They'll ask you to dance. Just loosen up. I think you need a drink."

"Can't drink. Baby's nursing. A friend told me that wasn't good for the baby," said Jean trying to relax her shoulders.

Abby had been the one to school Jean on the gentle art of nursing, which was neither gentle nor felt like an art. But, that was only the beginning. Then Abby had sat Jean down and gone over all the things Jean should and couldn't eat because of the baby. The list of all the couldn'ts was longer than the list of coulds: no peanut butter, cabbage, cauliflower, onions, beer, hard alcohol, tomatoes, oranges, grapefruit, and chocolate. Without peanut butter, Jean had learned to subsist on toast and an occasional egg. Not even tomato soup, for heaven's sake. It was almost unbearable.

"Oh, the baby. My gosh, I forgot. What are you doing with Ella tonight?" asked Collette. Jean was embarrassed to admit what she'd done. Left her with a sitter. Jean pushed away her worry.

"Oh, my Ella, she's sleeping. A friend is with her and I left after she fell asleep. She's fine," Jean quietly confessed, her cheeks aflame with guilt.

"Wish I could do that with the brood I watch. Have someone else watch them. You're lucky," said Collette wistfully. Jean only nodded and pushed away the thought of precious baby Ella, hoping she was still wrapped up warmly, sleeping blissfully.

∽

*E*lla startled when Abby entered the apartment. Abby quickly gathered Ella from the bassinet. The child was wet, just wet. She pulled the diaper off. Her fanny was blister-red, chaffed, covered in a rash. Diaper rash.

Abby took the wet diaper off and swaddled the baby in a towel and together they ventured back downstairs. She rustled in her cupboard for cornstarch and a length of cotton cloth.

Abby cut a square of fabric and filled it with cornstarch, then cut another strip of fabric to pull the packet up tight. She then made up a sugar teat to comfort the child. Abby's own mother had made many of these and had taught her that if you poured a tablespoon of sugar into a cotton cloth, tied it tight, and wet it down, the baby could suck on it through the cloth and would settle down. It was a handy trick she passed on to all her apprentices and it should stop the baby's crying through the night.

Abby patted the cornstarch on Ella's backside, then picked her up and held the sugar teat to the baby's lips. The baby's cries fell to a whimper and then tapered off. Abby returned the baby to the bassinet, all diapered, but this time cooing and just closing her little eyes.

~

By 10:30 Jean had survived her first two dances – one with a geriatric man who spoke not a single word of English but knew the foxtrot, and another man who didn't know a foxtrot from a fox den. Then she spied a familiar man standing in the corner by himself swaying to the music. It was a man she'd seen at the hotel. She vividly recalled him, booze glass held aloft, her very first night at the Empire, the night of the big League party.

"How's business these days?" Jean asked, as the man approached her.

"Business?" asked the man, eyeing her directly.

"Dairy business, right? I remember you from the Empire," explained Jean. "You were with the Consumer League ladies the night of the big party."

"Oh that, yeah, well, that was something," he paused and gave Jean a quick once over, unable to recollect much of that evening long ago. "You were there that night, eh?"

"I was. The Empire. It was a sight to see," said Jean, looking to boost his confidence a bit. "Dancing tonight?"

"Oh, I don't know a thing about dancing," said the man, suddenly timid.

"I'll show you the Charleston," Jean offered as the fast music began.

Jean felt good dancing. It had been a long time since she'd felt her body was her own.

By the end of the second time through the dance, the man still didn't have the arm movements figured out and rather resembled a drowning man out on the dance floor. He was simply hopeless.

"That tuckered me out. I bet you're thirsty, too," she said, wanting a break.

"I sure could use another beer," said the man. "How about you?"

"No, not for me. Let's just get you one," said Jean. "No need to spend money on me."

With the third beer down and who knows how many before that, the man's tongue began to loosen.

"So, business. You asked about business. I'm in the dairy business myself. Made friends with those Consumer League ladies and am doing just fine. Got myself on their White List of Authorized Dairies. Got myself barns full of cows now. Now, enough work talk. How about a dance?"

Jean cocked her head. Slow music, close-dancing music. She turned away from the man and made a face, revolted at the idea of the man touching her on the dance floor.

"Oh, now, don't get shy on me," the man said in a ragged low voice as he reached for Jean's waist.

His voice, his tone, his leer, it all made Jean suddenly feel dirty. Dirty and cheap. *Carry yourself with dignity*, Mama had instructed. She was doing anything but that. She cast her eyes around the room, searching for Collette.

"Well, I think my dance card's full now," said Jean, mustering her tattered dignity. This man was an affront to women and she needed to get away from him, and fast.

"How about I get you another cold drink," said Jean conjuring up every ounce of sugar-sweetness she could muster, as she planned her escape.

"Sure, doll. A drink. Here's a quarter. Kind of you, doll," said the man, his smile eager and anxious. Jean made her way to the back of the room and edged up to the bar.

"Two drinks?" the bartender asked. "You're new here. You can let the men buy you a drink, if you want. But, if you drink up yourself, then you really don't make money. A girl can get herself into trouble," he cautioned, pointing to Collette.

He was right. Collette was never without a drink in her hand and a man on her arm the entire night. Jean turned away, not wanting to witness the depth to which her friend had sunk. She shook her head at the bartender, disgusted with the entire premise of the establishment.

"One beer, for that sorry excuse for a man over there," Jean said gesturing to the man who was watching her with hungry, beady eyes.

"Be careful with that one," the bartender cautioned as he placed a frothy glass in front of Jean.

"Oh, don't worry. I'm not staying. And, can you tell that one," Jean said pointing to Collette, "tell her I had to go, okay? And then send that drink over to the man with the empty grin there, would you please?"

"Not staying? Well, good for you. Good to see a girl here who knows her own mind for once," said the bartender, "But, you know, there's no pay if you leave."

Jean looked the man squarely in the eye. "You're better than that. You can pay me. You need to pay me," Jean instructed the bartender. The man raised his eyebrow, registering her determination.

"You're right. I should, whether it's policy or not," the man said, pulling dollars from his register. "Now, go. Get on out of here. It's no place for a nice girl, you know."

Jean didn't even wait for the man's sentence to end before she was heading toward the exit, dollars in hand.

Jean walked the twelve blocks home, thinking over the evening and what some women would do for money to survive. There was unquestionably more going on in the dance hall and its backrooms than a simple foxtrot.

Jean was filled with disgust and felt soiled, to the core dirty, for the first time ever. She never wanted to become one of those girls, not ever.

What would her daughter think, growing up with a mother like that? *Her daughter.* Jean missed Ella. How would she ever work, have a paying job, and have enough time with the baby? It was too hard to be away from the precious girl.

Her thoughts collided into a pile of sadness, hopelessness, as Jean traipsed the long flight of steps to her apartment. She mourned the loss of Elden, Mama, her childhood, and she feared her uncertain future.

Sometimes when Ella cried, Jean cried right alongside her. And Jean couldn't stop the nagging fears. Even giving the baby a bath in the big bathtub was a nightmare of scary possibilities. Jean worried about everything. 'What if I slip, what if she squirms in the water and I let her go accidentally?' She knew such thoughts were silly, borne of sleep deprivation and being bone-tired and edgy.

Other mothers had troubles, too, but they also had someone there to help pay the bills, rub her feet, laugh with her, cry with her, hold the baby, or carry a bag of food in the apartment.

Some days she felt like she would split in half if she had to take one more step carrying anything, even her own weight. She thought ruefully that it was lucky she only could afford one bag of groceries at a time, because carrying a baby and a bag of groceries already felt almost impossible.

She had to do everything that any new mother had to do, and she had to do most of it alone, but for Orion, who watched her placidly from his sweet perch. Orion never seemed perturbed by the chaos and occasional howls of the baby. He seemed to take everything in stride. Jean wished she could face her days and nights with that kind of equanimity.

Jean's eyes flooded with tears as she entered the apartment building. It was all so hard.

"Jean, she was perfect," Miss Abby said as Jean entered the apartment. "Look how she's asleep there. Now give me a hug. You look like you've had a hard evening," Abby observed scanning Jean's face.

"I hated it, Abby. It was a dance hall and I was to be an instructor, but it wasn't like that at all. I missed Ella. It just felt so wrong," Jean confessed.

"It's okay. Ella's fine. Not every job is the right one," Abby assured. "I'll make you some tea. You rest."

"Thank you, Abby. You're a true friend. I'll be okay. Truly," Jean assured.

After Abby took her leave, Jean stood by the bassinet. There was

Ella, her precious baby, sleeping. Breathing softly in and out with a smile on her pink lips, lying right where Jean had left her. Jean quietly checked the diaper. The baby wasn't even wet.

Ella really is a perfect baby, Jean thought, grateful that, for once, the baby didn't need a thing. She fell in love all over again with her baby, the only person with her night after night, the only lifelong love she had left in the world.

Jean had her moments, but she really cherished her child, those perfect shell pink fingernails, that tiny rosebud mouth. She felt determined to be a good mother, like her own Mama.

Jean changed into her bedclothes. She hung her dress, the stench from the seedy dance hall's smoke clung to the fibers of her clothes. Her stomach roiled with revulsion - the smoke, the liquor, the clawing men and desperate women.

She shook her head, thinking of Collette and how she'd soured, somehow. The youthful exuberance from their first meeting at Somewhere months ago had been replaced by a clinging desperation fueled by alcohol and a desire to impress the men. No, Simone's dance studio held no allure, and certainly no future.

Jean laid down on the bed and curled Ella into her arms. She listened to her baby's heartbeat, and remembered the joy she'd felt when she first realized she had carried two hearts in her own body.

She took a ferocious vow, then and there, to protect this little one from all harm, even the harm of her own hopeless fears. She had to survive, somehow. Another life depended on her, and on her alone.

Jean woke up to Ella wailing, all hungry and wet. Morning light was just peeking through the curtains.

After nursing Ella, Jean changed the diaper. A white paste was creased across the baby's fanny. She drew her finger through it. What was that? Did it come from Ella? She rubbed it on her hand. Cornstarch. Yes, Francie had once told Jean that she'd always use cornstarch on her baby sister's diaper rash.

Who would have . . . and how? Jean wondered. The answer came to her in a flash. She picked up Ella and dashed out the door and down the three flights of stairs.

"Miss Abby, Miss Abby," Jean knocked on Abby's door with an urgency, "Can I borrow some cornstarch?"

Abby opened the apartment door. "At this hour?" Miss Abby questioned. "Everything okay?"

"The baby. Ella. She has a rash and I didn't know what to do and you, you know what to do," Jean continued, her voice near breaking.

"Cornstarch. Reckon I do have some of that. You wait here." Abby returned with the little cornstarch puff she made. "Now let me show you how you make one, honey," said Abby kindly, unfolding a square of fabric. Jean watched every step with care.

"I'm pleased you'd come down here, Miss Jean. I was just thinking more about you and that child. Thinking that a girl your age needs to get out some. I surely don't mind to watch the baby more. I miss my own little ones, you know. I like to watch that child. Feels almost like a favor to me and Otis," Abby said.

Abby didn't say more or ask Jean about her hair or why the new job requiring such a fancy dress had gone so very poorly. There were some things known without saying.

28

"Nice day to get outside, before it gets too hot. You going for a mother-daughter stroll?" asked Abby the next morning. She was pleased to see Jean taking the initiative to get Ella out of the apartment.

"I thought we might go visiting today," said Jean, trying hard to keep her voice even and her demeanor light. She'd been fretting all morning about the dance hall and then about money or, rather, the lack of money.

She had taken out her wrinkled pay envelope that morning and counted and recounted. She knew exactly how her mother had felt, the gnawing worry. She had meticulously stowed all of the coins and bills, regretting the times she'd resented shuttling the envelope to and fro for Mama. Jean forced a smile at Miss Abby's sunny expression.

"Now you have an extra diaper?" asked Abby, aware that Jean sometimes hadn't the most practical sense about taking care of an infant and could always benefit from a reminder.

"I double diapered her so I can take one off and still have another," said Jean, feeling smart.

"Well, I never, I --," Abby began, then caught herself. "How clever. I expect that'll do just fine. She eating?"

Abby pulled back the thin pink blanket covering the baby's head. Jean felt that the baby was constantly eating, puckering up her lips and looking for milk every minute.

"All the time. Just all the time," answered Jean.

"You drink lots of water now, you hear?" instructed Abby.

"Yes, ma'am. I do."

"Now you go on and show off that baby," said Abby, shooing Jean away with a smile.

Jean walked through the streets toward Francie's house. Francie dashed off her porch and swooped for a quick hug, admiring Ella.

"I wish I could walk with you, but Harold and I are off to . . . " began Francie. "Oh, your hair! Jean, it's so pretty."

"Thanks, I did it myself the other day. And, I know you're busy. It's all right," Jean replied, trying to give a convincing smile.

"Oh, look at that pretty little Ella," Francie said. "She looks the picture of you, Jean. She is the most beautiful little girl in the whole world."

"We're fine," Jean said, a little too quickly.

"I know you are," Francie said reassuringly. "Of course you are."

"That quilt you made for her sure keeps her cozy, too," Jean said. "Now, run along to Harold. We can catch up later."

Francie gave Jean a quick hug and Jean pushed the pram past the house and along the city sidewalk toward Petticoat Lane.

Jean hesitated as she neared the Empire hotel, but held her head high as she passed the entrance, her hands shaking. She gripped the pram tighter. It would be okay. She'd go visit Lydia at her shop. Yes, she'd been remiss in not introducing Lydia to Ella.

As she opened the door to the salon, she spied Mrs. Hayward Parker sitting on one of the stools having her nails done.

"Well, hello, Miss," Mrs. Parker greeted Jean.

"Precious child. Come in. What little bundle do you have there?" Lydia sounded as if she'd burst with excitement.

"Meet Virginia Ella Whitcomb," said Jean, emphasizing the last name for Mrs. Parker's benefit. "I call her Ella of course, after her father."

"Precious," said Lydia.

"Whitcomb, is it? Ella Whitcomb, you say?" asked Mrs. Parker, her question reflecting no ill judgment. "Very nice."

"Yes," Jean said, uncertain about how her sophisticated friend may really feel. "Not by law, but it's the name she should have."

"You two have met?" asked Lydia looking from Jean to Mrs. Parker and back to Jean.

"At the Empire. Ages ago. She gave me good advice about what to do if a big rooster ever rushes you. Looks like I didn't quite take that advice, though," Jean said as she looked down at Ella.

Mrs. Parker laughed. "Sometimes we see those roosters coming and just get mesmerized and can't move out of the way, I guess."

Lydia smiled, "Oh, let me hold your little girl, Jean. She is just splendid. And your hair, so modern."

Jean proudly held Ella up so Lydia and Mrs. Parker could see her glorious child.

"She's a good girl," said Jean, "sleeps through the night, too."

"Nice outfit, too," said Mrs. Parker. Jean wondered if she'd heard about her charging escapade on the Whitcomb's EBT account.

"She deserves all the best, of course," said Jean.

"May I hold her?" Lydia asked Jean. "You don't mind if your nails take an extra minute or two do you, ma'am?" she said to Mrs. Parker. "I'd like to show this little one to James, he's in the back."

Mrs. Parker gave a kind smile and a nod of her head. "You go on," she said. "Jean and I have some catching up to do. Sit down by me, Jean," Mrs. Parker said gesturing to the leather-topped stool beside her.

After Lydia had disappeared into the backroom, a murmur of voices followed. Mrs. Parker cleared her throat.

"Colored and white are separate in this city," she began. Jean nodded. "Can't see that will ever change, in my lifetime anyway. But, I know we can't choose where love comes to roost, can we? I know that's true, though some disagree with me." Mrs. Parker gave Jean an appraising look.

"I can't see that love is ever wrong. I'm not in a position to judge, either," Jean agreed. "It's good to see Lydia happy and James is a real man, a good man."

"You're not at the Empire any longer, I hear? Haven't heard tell, which is unusual," inquired Mrs. Parker, "but I wouldn't be at all surprised if they let you go. Mr. Whitcomb is not yet as progressive as he needs to be."

"Right. Mr. Whitcomb did let me go. I guess it was an embarrassment to keep me on. Married women don't work, of course, and I guess unmarried ones like me aren't supposed to either. It makes no sense, those rules. I need work more than anyone now," Jean said.

"We're trying to do something about that, you know," said Mrs. Parker. "The League is. Getting women into jobs that pay a living wage is important. Whether they're married or not. It shouldn't make a lick of difference. Businesses need to be smart and create opportunities not limit them."

Jean sat quietly, wishing the League Ladies and their big ideas could reach down and create a solution for her.

"There are things that happen that you can't anticipate in life. All of us League Ladies know that – whether it's a birth or a death or some financial misfortune. Women have to be able to stand on their own two feet, make their own way in the world. We don't think work is only for the young women, the women without obligations," Mrs. Parker continued.

"But, who hires someone like me? It'd be a scandal, I think. I've applied everywhere in town already. No luck." Jean shook her head sadly.

"Do you type?"

"No, but I know shorthand. Gregg's shorthand. And I write well," Jean offered.

"Oh, that's very good. Shorthand's quite a marketable skill," Mrs. Parker said, her eyes lighting up with the news. "And we've started a typing school, at the League offices. We have one student starting the first Monday of next month. You can come too. We think that our ladies who complete the typing school will be hired right up by the local paper, the *Kansas City Star*. The newspaper needs good workers who won't cost too much. They're in a hot competition with the other newspaper in town. Need to cut overhead and they can pay women less than men. Can't change that. Not yet. But, it would be an income," Mrs. Parker explained. "Would you consider coming to our headquarters and learning to type?"

Jean nodded her head eagerly, scarcely believing her good fortune.

"And you can bring Ella. She'll behave during your classes and you'll be right there if she needs you. All of us understand about raising a baby," Mrs. Parker said kindly.

"Could I really? How much does it cost, this class? Do I pay by the day or the week?" Jean asked, wanting to get the facts before she let her hopes be raised.

"No charge, Jean. It's the League. It's what we do, trying to move things along. Civic good we call it. It takes awhile for us all to agree on a project, but once we decide as a group, there's no stopping us. The money just rolls in somehow. Sometimes from unexpected places," Mrs. Parker said.

"I'd be, I'd be . . ." Jean's voice faltered, taking in the kindness being offered and trying to find the words that measured to the gratitude in her heart, "grateful. I'd be grateful," she said, her voice breaking.

Jean had lain awake many nights, holding the baby, thinking, praying, trying to come up with the one thing that might save her and Ella. And Mrs. Parker had just plunked it right down in front of her, without fanfare, without even being asked.

Jean let the tears cascade down her cheeks. *Maybe the League Ladies could change things, little by little,* Jean thought.

Jean recalled Mrs. Parker's words from months ago, "a girl in trouble is a girl who needs a friend," and she remembered how afraid she had been to approach Mrs. Parker for help, and she'd been there ready to help all along.

"Don't, don't. No tears, no tears," Mrs. Parker said reaching over the manicure table to pull a tissue from a pile and offer it to Jean, "This is a time for celebration, for joy. You have a beautiful child, a bright future. Truly you do. I know you're not afraid of hard work. Not shy about working around all kinds of people, even men. You're different from most girls, Jean."

Jean sniffled back her tears. "You're so kind. Why me?" she asked.

"Why you? Well, we're not so unlike, you and me. Stepping out, getting involved with a man some people think is better than you. I did that too. This man, this Elden, he's not better than you. He's just a man, a weak man. And you've paid the price for that weakness. You made choices I think I would have made in your circumstance. Now dry those tears and tell me what's really going on, Jean."

Jean wiped her eyes and clutched the tissue in her hand. "I'm grateful for an opportunity, but I don't deserve it. I've done so much wrong. My baby doesn't have a father. I almost lost my best friend over this, you know. I broke all the rules," whispered Jean.

Mrs. Parker sat silently for a minute and then said in a soft voice, "People pass judgment on people because it's easier than looking at things through and through. Like Lydia and James. Like you and the baby. It's easier to say it's wrong than to say the social rules need to change."

"And you know all about Lydia and James?" Jean said.

"Honey, everyone who knows Lydia knows how much she cares about a certain Monarch baseball player, and you know she never misses a game," Mrs. Parker said. "I only pray that she will learn to be a little less open and honest with some of the people who might not understand. I worry for that girl, Jean, but I worry more for her man. In these days, he's the one taking the risk. The KKK here on the Missouri side ---" she began, and then her voice trailed off and jaw tightened.

Jean knew she was right, to the core right. Lydia and James could have real trouble, and James was the one taking the biggest risk. He had to hide his feelings for Lydia in order to save his life. The natural joy of a woman in love, wanting to call the man's name from every rooftop, would have to be kept quiet if James was going to survive in this city.

Mrs. Parker continued, "And you. Women sometimes have to go it alone. Not every man has what it takes to be a father anyway."

"I know that's true," Jean said.

"Most women don't figure it out until a child is almost out of diapers and they've done all the care taking, diaper changing, meal-making, doing all the scurry around behind-the-scenes-work, for years," Mrs. Parker said.

"Taking care of the mother, that's what a father can be good for. But, honestly, some men can't even do that well," Mrs. Parker said, patting Jean's hand. "You, you're strong, and this will make you stronger. You don't need a man to raise this child. Never think that you do. All you need is a roof over your head for shelter and a little money for food, clothes. This is about survival. From here on, it's not about how you feel or wish things were or how they could have been. We can't change any of that."

Jean nodded, her eyes filled with tears, remembering how her own mama had to go it alone, too.

"And don't go reading magazines or sappy stories," Mrs. Parker counseled, pointing to a pile of Lydia's pulp magazines with their tales of lost romance. "None of that will help you. You focus on today and tomorrow. The next day will take care of itself."

Mrs. Parker wanted to find a way to reassure Jean, but she got quiet as Lydia re-entered the room. Lydia grinned from ear to ear and waggled her ears at the baby. Jean never could figure out how Lydia managed to make her ears wiggle that way.

"The Monarchs have a ten-game winning streak," Lydia said brightly. "Did you hear, Jean?"

"I'm proud of them," Jean replied. "And James still leads off batting, doesn't he?"

"You know he does," Lydia said. "He leads the Monarchs in home runs, too. I wish I could tell everybody in this world how proud I feel to know him."

"Someday times will change," Mrs. Hayward said.

"Yes, but will it be soon enough?" Lydia asked. "Sometimes I wonder if someday ever will come. True love deserves respect. We ought to be able to walk proudly down the street, heads held high, side by side, hand in hand, not skulking into corners, in shadows, hiding from other people's hatred. Love deserves celebration."

"I know that's true," Jean said. "Well, at least I know other people say it's true."

"Oh, Jean, I didn't mean to trample your feelings, there," Lydia said. "I know you have your own rough row to hoe."

"I do," Jean agreed. "You're lucky to have love and someone who stands by you, even if you have to keep it hidden. Your man risks everything to love you, and my man won't even risk a frown on his mother's face. I'm going to raise my daughter to be better to other people than her father ever was."

"Yes, you will. Now could you take this girl from me, Jean? She's wet. I do nails. I don't do wet," the rotund woman said, holding baby Ella out from her smock.

Even when Jean was at her saddest, Lydia could figure out how to make her smile. Jean took Ella in her arms and peeled off the diaper.

"I know you're right, Mrs. Parker. I got into this and it's mine to see through," she said. "I'll focus on today, and what I need today is a paper sack for this diaper."

"That's my girl. The here and now. That's what's important," said Mrs. Parker.

"I'll get you a bag," Lydia offered as she walked to the cash register and rummaged behind the counter for a paper sack. She handed it to Jean as she sat down and began inspecting Mrs. Parker's nails.

"'Spect I should tell her now, don't you, Mrs. Parker?" Lydia asked cryptically.

"Good a time as any, I think," Mrs. Parker replied as Jean's curiosity grew. Lydia picked up her nail file and began to shape Mrs. Parker's near-perfect nails.

"Well, so you want news about the Whitcombs, Jean? Do you really want to hear?" Lydia asked, scrutinizing Jean's face for an unspoken answer.

"Yes," Jean said quietly, "I do. About Elden. You know that's part of the reason why I came today. I figured James would have told you something."

Lydia rubbed cream into Mrs. Parker's hands and began, "Well, James has been busy with the Monarchs, but he's working overtime, too. My James told me that Mrs. Whitcomb's gone off on a big bender, can't even get her lipstick on straight and raises her voice to everybody, even the hotel desk clerks."

"Public like that, so anyone could hear?" Jean asked, her eyes widening. Lydia nodded.

"The desk clerk told me he heard Mr. Whitcomb back in his office with Mrs. Whitcomb actually say to her, 'Katherine, you're no different than Jean ever was,' and then he heard all this glass breaking and cussing like no one's ever heard inside that lobby," Lydia continued.

Mrs. Parker nodded. "I heard tell of that, too," Mrs. Parker added, "Just an unseemly amount of noise."

"Then Mrs. Whitcomb flew out of there screaming that she was changing the locks and he was not welcome to darken her door. It was just like one of those penny pulp magazines, all passion and drama and yelling. So now Mr. Whitcomb just lets her do what she wants. He's spending most nights over at the hotel," Lydia concluded, raising an eyebrow to Jean.

"He said she's no different than me, really?" Jean asked, her eyes wide with disbelief. "I think we're completely different," she said with a shake of her head.

"No, Mrs. Whitcomb is nothing like you, Jean," Mrs. Parker intoned. "Integrity is something she discarded long ago. Once gone, it cannot be restored, you know."

"And, did James say something about anyone else?" Jean asked hesitantly, her thoughts on Elden.

Lydia pursed her lips tight as if she were considering something important.

"Well, Elden smashed up his car a few weeks back. He's away at that school and, apparently, took off one night. Headed back here they say. Three sheets to the wind," Lydia offered, her voice low.

"He's one who really shouldn't get behind the wheel in the wee hours. He knows better, but he's not thinking straight, of course," Lydia continued.

"And then there's the money. After the raid, his father had to pay thousands. Thousands, well into the five digits, to get Elden out of that mess. Sent him off with no notice, they say. That's why you haven't heard from him. People say the boy really had no choice," Lydia finished.

"No, he had no choice. It's true. The government has cracked down on the liquor trafficking and Somewhere was a target, no doubt. Even money couldn't fix this," added Mrs. Parker.

Jean squeezed the baby tight to her chest and said nothing. There was always a choice, and Elden had made his choice quite clear.

"I know this might hurt you to hear, but you embrace the facts and you move on. That's how we do it," said Mrs. Parker. "You be strong and build your own future."

"That's how I'll do it," Jean said, her jaw set. "I'll be moving on, on from him. Not that I have a choice."

She rose from the small stool, having heard quite enough. Inside, the thought of Elden's choice lit a rage deep inside her. He truly had chosen his parents' lifestyle and money instead of her and the baby. Jean fought to maintain her composure and chose her next words carefully.

"Well, Lydia, Mrs. Parker, I'd better get Ella on home," she said. "I'll be back sometime though. Tell James I appreciate the news and I'll be all right. We'll be all right, I mean," Jean said in a stilted voice as she picked up the baby. There was no place to go but home.

"Wait, Jean. No polish today, Lydia. I'd rather walk with Jean. Maybe even get to hold that little baby myself," said Mrs. Parker as she drew a dollar bill from her purse. "You keep the change. I'll come by next week for my polish, okay?"

Lydia bade them goodbye as they left the shop. Jean saw her smooth the dollar bill, and she waved to Lydia with a small smile.

"I'm sorry for the news about Elden," said Mrs. Parker as they stepped onto Petticoat Lane. "He has the weakness for the drink, and that started all of his troubles."

"Yes," Jean murmured.

"You just put that aside. You're a lucky woman, really," said Mrs. Parker. "A child is a blessing. I could never have one myself. Might I hold her?"

"Of course," said Jean, flattered that this lady would even be seen with her out in public. She felt glad, too, that she had wrapped her baby in the beautiful, soft baby quilt that Francie had made for the baby.

Mrs. Parker folded the quilt down from around Ella's tiny face, and Ella gave a gurgle of delight as the woman reached to take her.

"Beautiful baby. Mr. Parker, my husband - Hayward Parker - and I, we did always think we'd be blessed with a child. Years went by and I saw that sometimes God makes other plans. So I started my League work and I do my church things. He has his law practice, so I guess our life is as full as it is meant to be. Frees me up to do other things is what I tell my friends. Like the dairy inspections. Are you feeding her good milk from our White List?" asked Mrs. Parker. "You are now, aren't you?"

Jean hesitated. She was weary of all the ups and downs of feeding the baby and would have given most anything to have fresh milk delivered, but it was not feasible. Jean's pay envelope was getting thinner by the week.

"Not exactly, ma'am," she replied quietly.

"Not exactly sounds like exactly not to me," Mrs. Parker said resolutely. "Now where are we headed today?"

"Stover building. On Eighth," Jean replied. Jean nodded toward the intersection and took a sideways glance at this society lady would dare be seen in public with her, an unwed mother.

Mrs. Parker, however, gave no hint that her choice to walk with Jean and the baby was untoward and to Jean's delight the conversation didn't lag.

The lady was full of stories of the League Ladies' latest antics and how they were casting around for a new cause once the dairies were straightened up to their satisfaction. The typing school idea had come about after the ladies made a long list of all the local businesses where they or their husbands had contacts and then they'd narrowed that list to the ones that could afford to pay well and take a financial risk, she explained.

"We wanted good jobs for young women, someplace where their innate abilities could shine and they wouldn't be judged by the hem of their skirts or scuff on their shoes," she explained.

Jean grew wide-eyed, wondering how Mrs. Parker had learned to cut to the heart of things so. She smiled at the older woman who continued talking about her husband, the long hours he kept at his law practice, her church community, her dreams for the city.

Jean relished the adult companionship and let the words, all the words about everything other than Elden and the Whitcombs, wash over her. It lightened Jean's heart to think of other things and the walk went quickly.

"This is our home, third floor," said Jean as they arrived at the apartment building.

"What a lovely building and, most important of all, what a lovely child. Thank you for sharing Ella for a moment," said Mrs. Parker. "We'll see you at the typing school, first Monday of next month. Our headquarters are right off Petticoat Lane, around the corner from the Emery Bird, you know."

"I know. I can't thank you enough, Mrs. Parker." Jean took Ella from the lady's arms.

"I'll look forward to seeing you and little Ella then," said the woman with a wave at the baby, who cooed a goodbye.

As she walked away, Mrs. Parker made a mental note to follow up on Jean and Miss Ella, no matter what the Whitcombs would say or do.

The Whitcomb boy had created an issue yet again, but this was one that could be made right. She'd get Jean through the typing school and settled in at a good job at the newspaper, but that was only part of what needed to be done.

Jean wasn't the first girl whose reputation the Whitcombs had sullied. Mrs. Parker puzzled over the possibilities as she continued down the street. She had never used her husband's influence or profession for her own personal gain and wouldn't start today. But, Hayward Parker was the Whitcomb's attorney and she knew her husband could help make things happen. She had seen it many times before. Elden had a habit of needing Hayward's skills to fix any number of problems and make things happen the Whitcomb way.

Mrs. Parker began to envision a possibility for her Hayward to make things turn out right for Jean.

The next morning Otis delivered a bottle of fresh milk to Jean's door. He knocked gently and handed it through the door when Jean answered.

"What's this for, Otis?" Jean asked, taking the chilled bottle from him.

"Don't know, Miss. Milkman just said it was for a baby named Ella," he replied.

Ella drank the milk greedily, and Orion got a little sip, too. The bottles of milk began arriving regularly, three times a week. No note, no letter, no bill. It was only the first of a few things Mrs. Hayward Parker was going to set right.

29

In the passage of a single month, autumn had come. The trees were barren and the air was crisp with the hint of winter. Jean's envelope of money dwindled steadily. She'd heard nothing more from Elden. It was as if he had vanished from the Earth, as if he was gone all together.

A chill had set in to Jean like she'd never felt before, a cold and clear understanding of what life was to be, along with the realization that she was truly alone and forever responsible for this child.

At least the baby is doing well, thought Jean. Ella could eat solid food now and slept long stretches during the day. A good napper, Abby called it. Jean was grateful for the nap hours, two hours every afternoon, like clockwork.

The baby even slept two full nights in a row, from nine to six, and that alone brought Jean relief. Before that the days had started to blend into the nights and it was in the nights that Jean let her mind set to the worries. She had nothing, no job, nothing that would sustain them. She counted the days until the first Monday of the month when the typing school opened.

Maybe I can get a good job, take Mrs. Parker up on her offer, she thought.

When Monday morning came Jean summoned all of her courage as she bundled the baby and walked to the League headquarters to join the typing class.

The League office was bustling with important women on a mission of some sorts.

"Jean! You've come. I was just saying to the ladies that we were counting on you. Just in time, too. We'll start the typing class in a few minutes and Mr. Bosco from the Kansas City Star is coming by to check on our students. He has an opening for a girl, a smart girl, in his Classifieds department. Wants someone with sense who can help with the want ads, the typing, you know," Mrs. Parker said in a rush. Jean had never before seen Mrs. Parker flush with excitement.

Jean nodded as she looked expectantly around the room, an office. An office with something extra. Two baby cribs were lined up against the far wall. Two desks with typewriters were positioned nearby. She took off her winter coat and Mrs. Parker hung it in the front closet as Jean unwrapped baby Ella, setting the child free from three layers of cotton blankets.

Jean tucked Ella into the crib with a fresh bottle of milk and took a seat at the open desk, across from a wisp of a girl wearing an Emery Bird Thayer smock.

Jean watched as the girl rolled a white piece of paper into the machine and she followed suit. Jean studied the keyboard. The placement of the keys instinctively made sense to her. Typing. It was like thinking with your fingers. Reading.

Typing is like reading in your mind and making the words dance through your fingers, she thought, taking naturally to the task at hand. The first lesson was easy. Yes, the quick brown fox jumped high over the lazy sleeping dog's back.

After the instructor called for a break, Jean turned to the thin girl in the smock.

"I'm Jean. Jean Ball," she said to the brunette at the desk next to hers. "And that's Ella," she said pointing to the baby's crib.

"I'm Cassandra. Cassandra Lee. I'm not sure about this," said the girl scrutinizing the Underwood keyboard with a loud sigh. "Working at the EBT is so much easier than thinking about this idiot brown fox. But, I need to make more money to raise my boy." The young woman pointed to the crib across the room.

"That's Tommy in the crib. Thomas. Thomas Whitcomb. Not that his father knows his last name, though." Cassandra said, the words catching in her throat.

"Whitcomb?" asked Jean, taking in a sharp breath. It couldn't be. Jean's chest tightened and she feared the breath she'd just taken would be her last. "Not Elden. Not Elden Whitcomb, is it? The father?" she asked, dreading the words that may come next.

"No. Randall Whitcomb. The one that owns the Empire. The great Mr. Whitcomb. Not that boy of his. No, Mr. Whitcomb himself. Of course, his wife, Katherine, forbids me from telling people. Even him. And she got me a job at the EBT to keep me quiet, but I won't keep quiet," Cassandra said, her hostility palpable such that it filled the air with venom. "I'll make my own way and they can just be damned. I'm telling everyone until the word gets back to him directly."

"Mr. Whitcomb? He's the baby's father, you're certain then?" Jean asked, flooded with relief.

"One and the same. So smooth, so kind, so ... so filled with lies. I take it you know him?" Cassandra asked. Jean nodded.

"Well, he told me that his Katherine didn't understand him. Said she loved her booze more than him. Said he needed someone, someone kind. Someone like me. All a lie," Cassandra continued. "He needed the thought of me, not me. Then when it hit the newspaper, just a hint of me being seen with him, it was over. All over," Cassandra said, her voice trailing off. "But, it was too late. Sweet little Thomas Whitcomb was already on the way."

"I think Ella's daddy just wanted the thought of me, too. It was Elden, the son," Jean confided, her voice a whisper as her eyes grew misty. She shook her dark curls, trying to retain her composure.

"I can't believe we're both here because of the Whitcombs. Do you think they know?" Jean asked, nodding over at the League Ladies clustered at a meeting table in the next room, "It can't just be a coincidence, you know."

"Could be," Cassandra shrugged. "I got a note, signed by a Mrs. Hayward Parker of some ladies group, sent down to my desk at the EBT inviting me to come learn to type. It said I might get a better paying job if I learned a skill. Don't know her. Don't know a thing about these League Ladies, really. They seem real sure of themselves though."

"I met some of them when I worked at the Empire. They held their meetings there all the time, every week at least and always had some grand scheme to make the city better. That's where I met Elden, too," Jean offered.

"I was a chambermaid there at the Empire until -," Cassandra began, her voice breaking, "until Mr. Whitcomb chased me around one of the hotel rooms one too many times." Cassandra gave a rueful smile.

"It was supposed to be forever. At least that's what he said and I was stupid enough to believe him," she ended as her voice cracked. "They did nothing for me and I, I did something terrible because of it." Cassandra's face fell as she made that confession.

The girl looked like she was about to cry and she gulped in a breath of air as if to push the tears back down.

Jean knew the part about doing something terrible. She thought back on her evening at Simone's Dance Studio, how she'd almost made a choice that would feel irreversible.

"Don't feel bad for whatever you did. You were sad, scared. I know how that feels. I've done terrible things since, too," Jean confided.

"No, I did something terrible. To you, I think. I didn't know," Cassandra stumbled over the words.

"Me? You did something terrible to me?" Jean asked, puzzled and a little worried the girl was perhaps touched, unhinged. "But, I don't know you."

"The EBT. It was you. You charged to the Whitcomb account. The expensive dress and shoes and all the baby things. You. For this ba- the ba – the baby," Cassandra stuttered, pointing to Ella's crib.

"How do you know that?" Jean asked, her cheeks reddening. "It was wrong because I bought so much, but I was desperate and so scared," Jean confessed. "But, how could you know about all that?"

"I, I, I'm downstairs. I work in Accounts Receivable. I saw them, the charge slips, and I, I, I made them pay. I, oh, they have to have been so mad at you. I'm sorry," Cassandra explained.

"Why mad? Elden said I could sign, well - mostly," Jean said, recalling how much she'd spent.

"I did something. Terrible. For revenge. I wanted to make them pay for ignoring our son. He was a Whitcomb whether they'd acknowledge it or not. I changed your bills, your charges. I was mad so I turned all of them into something bigger, more expensive. Thirty-six became eighty-six and the baby things, oh that was worse. One hundred seventeen. Oh, I did something very bad. I made it one hundred ninety-seven. And they must have thought that you, you ... oh, this is terrible," Cassandra said, her voice shaking.

Jean's mouth flew open. She was mortified as the realization of the girl's deed sunk in.

"Elden never told me. He must have thought – oh," Jean stopped herself. *A gold digger, a Doll, a Trixie – but he never said a word.*

"I'm sorry. It was wrong, petty, mean of me. I didn't think about – I would never have if I'd have known. I was sad, so sad, you know and Randall and I, it was supposed to be us, forever. Forever he said ... " Cassandra's voice trailed off.

Jean looked at the distressed young mother sitting before her. It would do no good to berate her. All that was in the past and it wouldn't change what had happened, how it had happened. It wouldn't make Elden strong and straight and true.

"That was a lot of money," Jean said. "But, Elden told me it would be him and me forever, too. He said it was love. He told me he wanted things all straight and true, he said. Told me he always wanted to do things the right way, but it was a lie. He really wanted things easy, his way. Uncomplicated. And, he's gone now," whispered Jean as the typing instructor re-entered the room. "They didn't love us."

"They didn't. The rich are like that, you know," said Cassandra, repositioning her fingers on the keyboard, relieved to have been absolved of her misdeeds.

~

*J*ean completed the typing course in three brief weeks and tried to hold her new friend, of sorts, Cassandra Lee, at a distance. It was nothing like her real friendship with Francie.

She and Cassandra skimmed the surface of friendship, with talk of babies and diapers and grocery sales, but Cassandra's words always turned back to bitterness. Jean knew not to broach things that truly mattered – integrity, truth, beliefs. She could see for the first time that some people needed to be held apart, something she'd never do with Francie.

When the typing class ended, the *Kansas City Star* offered Jean work five days a week. Within a month she'd grown bored typing the want ads-- always neatly separated into two columns: "Jobs" and "Jobs for Women."

She asked her boss for something more and he assigned her to the society page. *The society page*, Jean thought, recalling the titillating headlines that held the ability to devastate.

It felt good, right, to soften the edges of the sharpest stories, put in a gentle word or two when the observations seemed too harsh.

On Jean's lunch hour, Miss Abby would usually bring the baby to the park near the newspaper office and they'd sit side-by-side on a bench, eating sandwiches while Jean read the headlines aloud to Miss Abby. On Fridays, Francie would join them, after running her weekly errands.

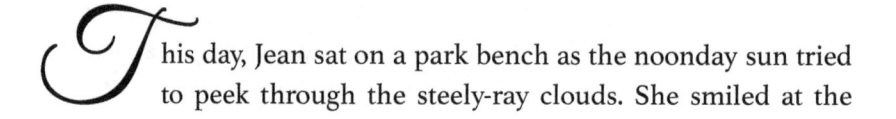

~

*T*his day, Jean sat on a park bench as the noonday sun tried to peek through the steely-ray clouds. She smiled at the sight of Abby crossing the park towards her, Ella's little pram leading the way. Miss Abby's eyes were extra sad-like and heavy.

"Something's wrong, Miss Abby. Is it Otis?" Jean asked, with a sudden fear that the older man may have slipped away.

Miss Abby shook her head. "No, not Otis. No good way to share this news," Abby began her voice cracking, "James came over just now and told us. There was an accident. Bad, bad, too."

Jean stopped listening, knowing the words that would come next. James telling Otis and Abby of an accident, Abby searching her out. It could only be one thing.

"If it's Elden, don't say another word, Abby. Don't tell me," bargained Jean. Abby reached out her hand and put it gently over Jean's.

"We can't know the plans for us in this world, Jean," offered Abby, "If we knew we'd not be able to live through every day. I'm sorry. I'm sorry."

Jean looked at her searchingly as she went on, "It was an accident. That fancy car. Drove it fast down a country road, round a curve out by some lake nearby. If maybe you hear he had some to drink then that won't surprise you," said Abby, knowing there was no easy way for Jean to hear what had to be told.

Jean stood up in a panic. She started to run but there was no place to go. Her hands shook as she turned back and reached for the pram.

"I have to go home," said Jean shakily. "It's not true. He's going to get better. He's coming for Ella and for me. He said he'd be back."

"Jean, listen to what I've said. He's gone. The service is next week, ten-thirty on Tuesday. Country Club Christian Church," said Abby softly.

Elden. She always knew he would come back to her, always. He'd figure things out and come back and she'd let him. Elden. Gone. It wasn't possible. It couldn't be true. Tears streamed down her face.

"Abby, the last time I saw him, I shouted at him," Jean said. "My mama always told me never to leave anyone in anger, and I left him in anger, and now it never will be better. It never, never will be better."

"Blessed be Elden. He's with his Maker now. He didn't suffer, they say. Gone quick. They say he'll look fine. Them Whitcombs always have an open service, what for people to take one last goodbye. You brace yourself for that if you go to the service. I'll walk you home now. Otis made a telephone call to the Kansas City Star, explained you needed the afternoon off and tomorrow," offered Abby, gently taking the pram. "Come home now. We'll say our prayers."

Back at the apartment, Jean couldn't sit still. Her thoughts were scattered, filled with questions and fear, not yet stuck on the jagged edges of memory. That would come later.

What to do? What to do? She could only think of survival. *Elden is never coming back now. I have to see him again*, Jean thought. The service, Tuesday morning at Country Club Christian Church.

I have to see him, she thought. *I'll go and then see that it's not true, that he's really okay.*

Ella began to cry. Jean looked over at her baby. The thought came to her, little Ella would never know Elden. Never. Their baby would never have a poppa or learn the things a daughter should learn from her poppa. Jean's arms shook as she picked up the baby. Her sadness and fear dissolved into a pocket of anger.

The selfish man went out and got himself killed when he could have been here with us. Now there's nothing to ever keep the baby safe. No one who can care for her but me.

The sky darkened, night fell and Jean struggled to go about the baby's nightly routine, dressing the baby for sleep, changing the diaper, one last feeding. It felt wrong to go through the regular steps of life on a night like this.

Jean laid down beside Ella, seeking comfort in her warmth together, side by side, and still the tears came.

"It's you and me for keeps, now, Ella," she said. "You and me, we will do fine things, when you grow up. You can ride a pony, and we will look at the stars together. Nobody can take the starlight away from us, no matter how poor we are. No one can take away the sound of the robins singing in the trees. I'll teach you all about the birds, and the alphabet, and we'll take walks together. I have you, and you have me."

Sleep did not come and Jean sat through the night, her mind racing with possibilities of how life would be now. The world felt cold, unsteady. She recited prayers until her throat felt like a dry husk. And, still, she felt no comfort.

She watched Ella so quiet, blissful and unknowing of the hardships to come. Jean had nothing to give this child. As morning dawned, Jean grasped for a sense of something normal. Something to make Ella safe, at least for a time.

The Whitcomb's. The EBT charge account. She'd make sure Ella would have everything she needed to be safe and warm. She'd get her everything that a poppa would if he was here and then they'd go to Elden's service. Jean knew she had to go, that she needed to go, just for herself.

She counted the hours until the shops on Petticoat Lane opened and then she bundled up the baby in a double wrap of blankets and strode down the street, making a direct line to EBT's children's department – sizes 1 year, 18 months, 2 years, 3 years, 4 years, winter coats in each size, shoes in 4 sizes, socks the baby could grow into, pajamas in each size, a dress, no, two dresses, there, that would be enough, thought Jean frantically. All Jean needed was enough, just to have enough. Enough, and a funeral dress.

In the ready-to-wear she found for herself, an inexpensive navy dress that covered her knees and a veiled cap that would cover her eyes. Presentable, respectable even.

Better to underdress than overdress, Jean thought, recalling another of Mama's rules. Mama. Elden now and Mama, too.

Jean swept away the wave of sadness, the thought of Mama and Elden together, meeting at last. It was too much.

She signed the charge slip, "Jean Ball for Elden Whitcomb" and the salesclerk didn't question it. Jean took the mourning dress and one outfit for Ella from the purchases and arranged for the packages to be delivered separately.

Night came. Sleep didn't. Jean rose at Ella's first morning cry and took her time dressing the baby just so. She dressed Ella in navy, so they would have matching outfits. No one would have to ask who belonged with this baby.

In a fit of fancy, she twisted a navy ribbon into a tiny collar for the cat. Then she opened a small, cedar box that had belonged to Mama, and took out the lace collar that her mama had made with tender care. It gave a look of elegance to her simple dress, and that lace meant family love.

With Ella on her hip, Jean walked to the church. It was the city's newest church, an impressive building with three great spires, an arched doorway and a massive bell tower made of stone. Jean stood across the street, watching, waiting.

First, there were Elden's parents, and then crowds of others streamed in behind them. And Colette, broken, a handkerchief to her face. Then a group of ill-dressed men, rougher men, from Somewhere no doubt. Then the group from the very first day at the park so long ago, Elden's boyhood friends.

Anyone of them could have been in that car, in that wreck, thought Jean. They all drove like fools and carried flasks that never saw the bottom of empty. But, no, those boys, they had been the lucky ones. Elden had crashed, alone on the road going out to the lake. Too late at night to drive that road in the dark, thought Jean. She pictured the very curve that he would always take too fast, too dangerously fast.

Jean felt someone just behind her and turned. Otis. "Saw you standing here, Miss Jean. I 'spect you have to pay your respects now," he said with a nod. "I'd do the same in your place."

"I'm scared, Otis. Scared to go and scared not to. But, I have to see him again. He can't really be gone."

"I spoke to Miss Abby yesterday when I heard the news, you know. She knows I'm here. Said to tell you not to hesitate. You deserve to walk into that church. Said you deserved to walk down that same aisle as his bride and today you deserve to walk down that aisle like you're his widow with his child."

Jean nodded and held back her tears.

"You hold that baby. Take her slow so she's not afraid, too. He's laid out there, up front. You brace yourself for that right now. You go, pay your respects." Otis paused, reflecting. "Didn't 'spect it'd turn out this way. He didn't 'spect it would either. More than you know, he didn't think you and he and Ella would end up like this. James told me that."

Jean hesitated. Otis spoke with a certainty, like James had been held in Elden's confidence about all nature of things.

"Prepare yourself now before you go in," cautioned Otis. "You are presenting here, Jean. You are a fine young woman and you're presenting today for yourself and your family. Let the Whitcombs see. Let them all see. Hold yourself tall and they'll know what you're doin' is true. Miss Abby, she said to give you this advice."

"You're right, Otis. Thank you. I will do this," said Jean.

"You'll have no regret, Miss Jean," said Otis.

Jean already knew the weight of a final regret. Her soul wore down when she recalled her words the last time she saw Elden. She didn't have room in her heart to carry more regrets. She understood it was better to measure words, good and bad, by what your heart could truly bear. From here on she would do what needed to be done and say what needed to be said. Life was too uncertain for regrets.

Without another word to Otis, she stepped off the sidewalk and crossed to the church. She took each stair resolutely, knowing what would come next.

"I'll be off to the side in the Colored Section if you need me," Otis called to her. Jean turned and gave him a solemn smile. *A good man, straight and true*, she thought.

Jean opened the door to the church. The foyer was simple, understated, but the sanctuary was ornate, all oak and stained glass with a rose window. The Whitcombs had given quite a bit to the church and had their own pew up front.

As Jean stepped into the sanctuary, in the center aisle, she could almost envision what should have been. There, Elden would have stood beside the minister, smiling in his dark wedding suit, waiting for her. She would have swept quickly toward him, the train of her bridal gown delicately brushing the church floor. The church would have been filled, filled with the same faces here today, the ones who would witness them wed. But, it was not to be. Not ever. Jean shook the vision from her head and looked around the church.

She drew in a steadying breath. At the end of the aisle, Elden was waiting, but the wait was for a final goodbye.

Jean pulled Ella tight to her chest. The walk down the aisle was the longest walk she'd ever taken. She could hear the low murmur that drifted through each pew as she passed. She couldn't bring her eyes to the open casket until she was right in front. The minister stood just to the side, dressed in his vestments. He clearly didn't know her as anyone other than a respectful mourner. The pastor took her arm when he saw her knees buckling.

"Thank you," she whispered to the pastor as she held her footing and shifted Ella from her hip around to her front.

Jean turned to face the man she had loved, who had given her baby Ella, but left so much unsaid and undone. She had rebuked him, a regret she would carry forever. Elden, his hair so thick and dark and beautiful, looked at peace, at rest. Jean gently whispered in Ella's ear, her voice breaking, "It's your poppa, Ella. That's your poppa." An unmistakable clarity crossed the minister's face, as he watched Jean with careful attention.

"I'll let you find a pew now, ma'am. Please have a seat, and we'll begin," he said with formality, directing Jean toward the aisle.

Jean, holding tight to Ella, turned back to face the congregation. Steeling herself against what she might see in those faces, Jean walked to the pew with the engraved plaque "Whitcomb Family" affixed. She carefully took a seat and felt the dagger stare of Mrs. Whitcomb seated just down from her.

Jean settled Ella on her lap. She could feel the eyes of judgment on her, but she knew that today she would carry no regret.

As the service began Jean heard the rustle of a crinoline skirt coming down the aisle. Francie scooted in the pew beside her and tenderly held out her arms, offering to hold baby Ella. Francie's mother sat down next, giving Jean's arm a reassuring pat and turning her head to meet Mrs. Whitcomb's eyes.

30

"Miss Jean, you and Miss Ella had visitors today," said Otis one afternoon as Jean returned home. "Francie came over. With her mother. Left a pound cake and tin of that Earl Grey tea here for you. Francie, now, she looked real happy. Told me you were to come to dinner on Friday next. Then another lady came. Real different from Francie. She didn't look so happy herself. Left a calling card for you and asked that you telephone. Said it was important. 'Of vital importance,' she said."

"Who was it?" asked Jean.

"Here's the card. 'Katherine Whitcomb' it reads," he replied, stubbing out his cigarette before reaching into his shirt pocket to hand the card to Jean. Jean's hands shook and the card dropped to the sidewalk. Otis bent and picked it up, offering it back.

"It was the Whitcombs, yes ma'am. Her and him. He wore a suit. Their driver waited right here. Nice man, the driver," said Otis.

"Did you talk to him?" Jean asked.

"Well, I could have right off told them you weren't home. I knew you were not in, but those kind of people want to check everything for themselves. Also, gave me an opportunity to talk with their man. Drivers hear so much, you know," said Otis.

"You sent them up? They both walked all the way to the third floor?" questioned Jean, imagining the judgment they must have felt as they climbed each stair and took in Mrs. Ivanovic's cooking today, the aroma of turnips and good mutton fat.

"That's right. Took them plenty long, so I was congenial with their driver for a time," replied Otis.

"And?" asked Jean impatiently.

"And I hear that 'Mrs. Whitcomb's heart's like an open wound since her boy gone,' so he said. I said 'I 'spect you would know that empty-well feeling yourself.' He nodded. He liked the boy, Elden. Knew him from a toddler. Said Mr. Whitcomb is empty too, all buried in business. He said their boy Elden was full of surprises and gave them the surprise of their life. I didn't have time to ask if that was because of what happened in the end there, or if it was something else." said Otis.

"But, did he say what they wanted?" Jean interrupted.

"Driver said it's the baby they're worried up about now. Claiming now it's their flesh and blood, too. Guess we shouldn't be surprised," said Otis.

"Like they even cared before," said Jean with an edge of bitterness.

"No, I see as how they didn't give this baby a thought for a long time. Now, the driver said they'd be back. Said they won't let this just go by. I might suggest you consider meeting with them on your own terms, Miss Jean," Otis said, pulling himself up tall and looking her straight in the eye.

"You're the mama here. You make them come to you. Stand firm, like Mary did by her son. Good Book tells us all we need to know about how a mother do for her child."

Jean wasn't sure how Otis' Good Book would lend itself to fixing this situation – what with its judgments about harlots and illegitimate children being barred from heaven extending out ten generations, but this was no time to raise philosophical questions.

"You call them, Jean. Call and see if they want to help or if they just want to help themselves. Use the telephone in the hallway there," advised Otis.

Jean's hands shook as she dialed the telephone, remembering how Mrs. Whitcomb had called her a street girl, and how the Whitcombs had kept her from marrying their son.

As her fingers dialed the last number, she was struck by a realization. That, maybe, just maybe, she might not be the only one with regrets about Elden.

"We need to have a good talk, in person," Mrs. Whitcomb said. "I don't understand these silly things. These telephones. I can't hear right with them."

"What is it that you needed from me?" Jean asked tensely.

"My dear, it's time for me to ask what you need from me, and from us," Mrs. Whitcomb said. "We have an offer for you that we must discuss face to face. You must need so much."

Jean felt her heart melt. The loss of Elden was too much. A tear rolled down her cheek, "I miss him. I can't do this alone," she confided.

"No, it's all just too much for a girl," agreed Mrs. Whitcomb. "We would like to help. We have been so remiss in not coming to you sooner. I just can't even hold a thought in my head since Elden – oh, I just can't even --," and then her voice trailed off.

"Please come by on Sunday," offered Jean.

"Yes, after church. Of course. Two o'clock then?" replied Mrs. Whitcomb.

"Please. That will be nice," said Jean.

～

On Sunday, Jean opened the apartment window to let in fresh air, wiped down the table, and filled the kettle with water. She cleaned her teacups so they would be ready. She'd offer them both tea. None for herself because there were only two cups, but they wouldn't notice such a thing. They couldn't imagine such a life.

"She's a beautiful, healthy baby. We're so fortunate," gushed Mrs.

Whitcomb as she entered the apartment. She scooped up the baby and shook the wrinkles out of Ella's lace dress.

Mrs. Whitcomb's enthusiasm left a tin taste in Jean's mouth, an acid burn. Mr. Whitcomb had said not a word. He looked somber, vacant.

"You should hold her, dear," said Mrs. Whitcomb to her husband. The shake of his head in response was definitive. This man was not a baby-person, of that there could be no doubt. Mrs. Whitcomb clutched the baby and wound her fingers through the lace dress. It looked to Jean like spiders crawling though and it gave her a chill, imagining things like that.

"Please, do have a seat. May I get you each a cup of tea?" asked Jean politely. "I have nice Earl Grey."

The Whitcombs each took a chair by the little table and both declined the tea.

"Oh no, no need to bother," said Mrs. Whitcomb, taking in the shabbiness of the surroundings and no doubt questioning how her own flesh and blood could ever have found such a girl in such a place even remotely appealing.

"You know we're here to talk about this precious baby, our Ella," said Mrs. Whitcomb.

"I know," said Jean softly as she stood by the table, steadying herself for what was to come. "You didn't seem to think of her as your Ella when she was born, but she does have some nice things from the store. I want to thank you for that."

"We can provide all the best for her. You do realize that, don't you? And she'll need so much. A girl needs a good nanny and a proper education. We will give her that, and help you get on your feet and set a new course."

"That's so very kind of you. After Elden, well, the accident, I didn't think we'd hear from you. It's been a long time," began Jean.

"It took time to get things in order of course," explained Mrs. Whitcomb.

"So now you want to, well, you want to see Ella, and have holidays, and be her grandparents?" asked Jean.

"Dear no, no nothing like that. She's our girl. Look at her. She's a Whitcomb through and through. I saw it the minute I came in here. She's just like our Elden. She's our girl," said Mrs. Whitcomb, patting Ella's back softly.

"My girl. She's my girl," said Jean possessively.

"Just consider what Elden would want for her. We can give her all that. You just sign these papers we've had drawn up. Give her the papers now," Mrs. Whitcomb instructed her husband.

Mr. Whitcomb had said not a word. He took a fountain pen out of his pocket, opened the folder that he had laid on the table, and pushed the papers and pen across toward Jean.

Panic gripped Jean's heart as she read the cold words. The papers terminated Jean's parental rights and gave all rights exclusively to the Whitcombs.

"Sign? Sign away Ella? You want to take her?" asked Jean, her eyes widened with fear.

"Raise her, dear. Raise her right, of course," said Mrs. Whitcomb. "You'll go back to school, a boarding school in the East with the Whitcomb family as your benefactor. You'll have a fresh start and nothing will ever be said about your unfortunate status here. You'll have a whole new life. It's best for you and for Ella. Ella will never know. We'll protect her from this illegitimacy. Such a thing can ruin a girl. Ruin her."

Mrs. Whitcomb knew firsthand the hazards of a wrong choice. She had married the man, borne the child, and still would never be a true Whitcomb. If she had only known that then. No girl in Jean's position could say no to this offer. An offer Mrs. Whitcomb herself would not have refused had it been made decades before. The waif standing before her would have no choice but to acquiesce.

Jean's mind raced. Elden was gone and now Ella would be gone. This couple who had failed their own son would be the only parents Ella would know. They wanted to take away everything, everything Jean had. She couldn't leave Ella with them and go away forever. Babies need a mama, someone to protect them and always be somewhere to go home to. Jean could be such a mama, she knew it because the alternative was to be nothing. To be alone. The feeling of being alone would be thick, palpable. It made the air in Jean's lungs feel like concrete. Jean had to get these people away from Ella and fast.

"Simply sign and that will be that," Mrs. Whitcomb said. "Ella's future will be secure."

"Why do you want to take Ella away from me? You could be her grandparents, and I will be her mother. You could help me raise her," Jean said.

"Nonsense," Mrs. Whitcomb replied tersely.

"What is it that you want here?"

Mrs. Whitcomb's eyes gleamed with what could have been tears, and she said, "That baby, this Ella, is the last we have of our son, Elden. She is all we have left of him. You don't understand. We can raise her as a Whitcomb, remove the taint of the streets from her, and make her a lady. Something you never could do. It's what Elden would want for us."

Jean looked at the couple in disbelief, her mind racing. It was not what Elden would have wanted. Never, Jean knew. Quickly, Jean devised a plan. A plan that would begin with a firm 'No. Never. Never in a million years.'

"Here, let me see those papers," said Jean pretending to look over the stack of words as she pressed down her panic. "I need to take a closer look. It looks like a lot to read, doesn't it?" she said with a false smile, hoping it hid the fierce flash of anger coursing through her.

Jean caught Mr. Whitcomb's eye and she saw him gulp as he registered her look of fierce determination.

She stole a glance at Mrs. Whitcomb from the corner of her eye. Oblivious. Mrs. Whitcomb was running her fingers through Ella's soft wisps of hair, then stopped suddenly and wrinkled her nose.

Excellent timing, Ella. "Let me get that diaper changed now. I'll need to read these papers, too, I guess. It's too much to think on all at once," Jean said. "Here, let me take the baby and I'll just be right back."

"Take your time. We'll wait. Won't we, dear?" said Mrs. Whitcomb, smiling at her husband. Mr. Whitcomb gazed out the window, not offering a reply.

Jean took the baby as if to head to the bathroom for a change. Instead, she set off down the stairs to find Otis.

Otis was standing in front of the apartment building chatting with a man in a long black car. She opened the door to the apartment building, stepping outside with the child.

"Otis," she called, "Otis, I can't. They want. And I just can't. I will tell them 'No' because I won't. Not ever," Jean said in a jumble as tears started down her cheeks.

"Miss, what can I do? You alright now? Ella alright?" he asked, putting his hand on Jean's shoulder and turning her away from the automobile.

"Help me get them out of here. They want the baby. They want me to sign papers and they'll take Ella away. I just won't," said Jean.

Otis sheltered Jean and the baby and said in a low voice, "Okay now, okay. You could get them to leave but, please, let me fix this. Let me fix this. I expect I can explain you are now indisposed and ask if I may kindly escort them downstairs. Would that help?" asked Otis, "And you go see Miss Abby right now. Even if they're mad, they won't go to a colored person's apartment."

"Yes, yes, please, that's good. That's good. If I said what I need to say, it would be unchristian, Otis. Yes, I'll be with Abby, and I'll go into her bathroom with Ella. I'll lock the door. And we won't come out for anything," Jean said, clutching Ella to her chest.

"Let's you and I walk to Abby's door together then," said Otis. He turned back to the driver in the waiting automobile, "It was nice to speak with you today, sir. I would guess we may not have this opportunity again," Otis concluded with a nod.

The man replied with a knowing smile, "Your lips to God's ears, Otis."

Otis and Jean walked down the steps to Abby's and were greeted by the comforting smile of the woman who had brought Ella into this world.

"You come in now, you're safe here," Abby assured, as Jean spilled out the story.

Otis straightened his shoulders and walked up the stairs to Jean's apartment, steady resolve in every step. The door was open and he could see the Whitcombs shifting with discomfort at the small table.

Otis cleared his throat. "Miss Jean seems a bit upset. She didn't say why, but I would guess she has some things on her mind. Sometimes a woman needs time, is what my wife always said. God rest her soul," explained Otis gently as he lowered his eyes.

"We'll go then," said Mr. Whitcomb, uttering his only words during the entire visit.

Mrs. Whitcomb looked at her husband. His face was locked with a look of determination she had not seen in years. He rose from the table and put his hand on the back of Mrs. Whitcomb's chair.

"Well, yes, we'll go, but you give her these papers," said Mrs. Whitcomb, her voice twittering like a nervous bird.

Mrs. Whitcomb rose from her seat as Mr. Whitcomb pressed his hand to her back and directed her to the door.

"And you tell her she will sign them and have the child sent to our house with them. That will be the end of things. Tell her that's how it's to be done," Mrs. Whitcomb called as her husband shepherded her into the hallway.

"I will give her those papers and I will say those very words to her, just like you did here," assured Otis. He would be certain to emphasis that one particular sentence about how signing the papers would surely 'be the end of things.'

~

Jean heard the apartment door close and several feet shuffle down the stairs. She clutched the baby close and silently vowed to never let her go, not even if they broke down the door this very minute. Her grip on baby Ella loosened as the footsteps passed away. Ella let out a whimper and Jean looked down at her girl.

The whiff of a diaper due for a change was unmistakable. And this baby needed a bath. It was time. Miss Abby nodded and opened the door to the bathroom.

Jean started the bath water, warm not hot, tugged the lace dress from over Ella's head, and peeled off the diaper. She gently put the baby into the water.

When Ella's bottom slid into the water, a smile broke across her baby face. The baby sat up straight and brought her two hands down into the water at once. Droplets sprayed all around little Ella. The baby splashed her hands up and down, up and down.

Water flew and Ella laughed. Ella laughed and laughed.

Jean had never seen such pure joy. She leaned over and kissed her laughing baby then unfolded a soft washcloth, took the bar of Ivory soap, and began to wash her child.

Miss Abby heard the water running and the warm coo of Ella's voice. The child would be fine. Right fine after all, Abby thought, as she said a silent prayer of thanks.

31

Mr. Hayward Parker adjusted his tie in the mirror as he watched his wife apply her lipstick.

"So today's the day," he said. "I've got the Whitcomb estate, Elden's affairs, all tied up. Took longer than I thought to sell that speakeasy. Finally got the auction receipts finalized. It's all public now."

"You're right. It certainly took long enough, didn't it, Hayward?" Mrs. Parker asked.

"Well, I was surprised that his own father was the high bidder. Hadn't expected that, the way Katherine tries to keep control of his affairs. I'll tell Jean all that in due time. She'll be surprised to know Randall, now, only wants the best for her and the child."

"Randall is a changed man, a good man. Like Elden. And, when Elden left some of the money to the League to build the training center for unwed mothers, and Randall matched it, I know that sent Katherine right over the edge. But, look what a difference it's made already," said Mrs. Parker with a satisfactory smile.

"The boy was smart. Smarter than anyone ever gave him credit for. He knew right from wrong, and made things right. Atoned for the sins of the father, as they say. Not something every man can stand up and do. He had a good heart," Hayward Parker said, recalling his final meeting with Elden.

"So, you've made an appointment to see Jean then? She didn't say a word about it to me. I saw her just last week. And, you know how much the *Kansas City Star* likes her work?" asked Mrs. Parker.

"Do they now?" Mr. Hayward asked, unsurprised that his wife's little project was already a success.

"Yes, and she'll have a newspaper job as long as she needs it, or as long as she wants it, I should say. She's smart, careful, and they told me she has a real eye for editing that society page," Mrs. Parker gushed. "They'll be promoting her to reporter soon, you know. She doesn't know yet, but she'll cover the labor movement and the League news, too," Mrs. Parker shared, her eyes dancing.

"So, Hayward, you know I'd like to go with you today. I can support Jean through this. I expect this will be quite a shock for her," Mrs. Parker offered.

"No, this is mine to handle. You can take care of her tomorrow, you know. We discussed this," asserted Mr. Parker.

∽

Mr. Parker pulled the car up to the front curb of the apartment house.

"Appointment to see Miss Jean, I hear?" Otis asked courteously as he opened Mr. Parker's door.

"Yes, sir," said Mr. Parker.

"She mentioned that. A little nervous, she is. Now, I told her it's not about taking the baby. That's done with. She'll be okay, won't she?" Otis asked, not bothering to hide his own anxiety about the girl's well-being.

"She'll be fine. It's not about the baby, I promise. She'll be just fine," Mr. Parker assured. "She's fortunate to have your concern."

Otis blushed. It was true that Miss Jean had always been like a daughter to him, someone who needed looking after, someone to care for.

"Good, good, then. She's on the third floor. Just past that mutton smell. You'll know which one I mean," Otis said.

Jean answered the door on the first knock. "Hello, Jean. I'm Hayward Parker, here for our appointment. Don't look frightened now. It's not about the baby. I know what Mrs. Whitcomb tried to do. It wasn't right. I'm here to make things right for you, and for your daughter. For Ella."

Jean took a deep breath and stepped back from the door, letting the attorney inside. "Please, come in. I've made us some tea. The baby's sleeping, but we won't wake her," she said.

Carry yourself with dignity, she thought as she tried to still her quaking hands and pour the tea.

"Thank you, Miss," said Hayward as he took the saucer and cup from Jean and pulled a chair up to the table. "Please sit down, too. This is about Elden. Don't let the papers here intimidate you."

Jean took a chair across from Mr. Parker as he continued, choosing his words with care, "Elden was a good man, had a good heart. There was a time he did not take care of business matters. Then, after your baby was born, he took care of one matter, one important matter."

Hayward paused. Jean held her breath. It was more than she could bear remembering. Tears filled her eyes.

"I know he passed so unexpectedly," Hayward acknowledged softly.

Jean nodded and gathered her composure, taking a sip of tea as she studied the man's eyes. She had no idea what this man was talking about. He didn't seem crazy, but you never knew. His words weren't making sense to her.

"His estate was not insubstantial, however, he wasn't to come into his share of the family trust and other holdings until he finished at Wentworth or reached age thirty, whichever came first. He did, though, own a little land and an establishment called Somewhere, a bar. A secret tavern. Probably was even a secret to a nice girl like you. But, the land you may know. It's his lakeshore property," Hayward continued.

Jean hadn't thought of that little lake in months. In fact, she had shut that place out of her mind completely until now. It was too hard to think of the place where Elden had opened his heart to her and spoke to her of their future, of right and wrong, and porch swings.

"I know it. Yes. I remember," said Jean, reluctant to follow the conversation's lead.

She recalled a picnic, the sunshine, a huge rock, wildflowers, and then a waterfall, a magical, beautiful waterfall, and conversations about truth and bright lines, and family, and love. She recalled his story of the little family of rabbits he'd seen grow up and grow old together. Jean's heart felt like it was all crushing in, again, and her eyes grew wet, remembering the one place where Elden had been hers, really and truly and only, hers.

Hayward cleared his throat, bringing Jean back to the present day. "Well, it's about what he wanted and what he owned," Hayward said, taking an envelope out of his shirt pocket.

He carefully opened the envelope, took out a piece of parchment paper and began to read. "I will read to you what he wrote, just how he wrote it."

"To Virginia Mae Ball, my Jean, I deed to you the property on Springfield Lake, including that big boulder I pulled you up on our first date." Hayward read. His eyes crinkled around the edges and grew misty. "You remember this place Jean. It is my special place, with the waterfall. I deed this all to you, with its improvements, to have and to hold in your name alone, forever more."

Hayward stopped reading and looked up. Jean didn't say a word and Hayward wondered if she understood fully what the words meant.

"There's more, though it's not technically legal, of course, but the law tells me I need to tell you this as it's written. So, I'll just read it now," said Hayward. He cleared his throat and continued.

"I need to think of you, you and our baby, both of you, as being somewhere still, no matter what happens with my family, or me, or what may happen in your lives, and our life together. I know I may not be with you on this day. There's been some trouble and I need to clear it up. I have to go away for awhile and there's a chance it could be prison. For now, it looks like it's Wentworth and if that works out, I'll be back. But, the way things are going, I feel more than ever I need to prepare for not being here for you. That scares me, Jean, and I don't know how to make it right. They gave me a clear line. I'd lose you if I didn't go to the Academy. I'd lose everything, they said. Federal prison, for years. And, I want you to have everything. Please know that I'll be with you when I can. As soon as I can. Forever."

Jean was flooded with memories of things she had said, and words she had never said, her hopes and regret. Tears rolled down her cheeks and Hayward handed her his linen handkerchief. Her breath came in rasping waves. Her head felt light and she felt as if she were disconnected from her body.

Hayward continued reading, "I know how hard my parents are when it comes to us. They don't understand. My mother doesn't want to understand. She doesn't want to remember she was once from the other side of the city. She makes things too hard. Pops, he's better, but he makes things hard too, and it's always for the business. But, life doesn't have to be hard. I want to make things easy for us. For you. Always. I want you to have a home. I'm breaking ground on the home today, this week. I'll pay as I go and see what I can build for us. Circumstances mean this could be simple, or if I've done well, then it's grand. I sketched it all out and we'll just see what I can do."

Jean couldn't register what was being said. Could this be true? Had Elden loved and cared so deeply? Across the room, Ella let out a low coo. Yes, Elden loved them.

Hayward continued reading, "I hope you love it. I'll build our home, Jean, until everything is just right. And all the lines are straight and true. I know things aren't the way they should be right now, but if I do this, then I know where to picture you. I can hold you in my mind's eye and see you in this house. I feel it now. I love you, Jean, and I love the baby. My Ella. I love you both. Forever. You are mine."

Jean broke into sobs. Hayward put a hand on her shoulder.

"Should I continue?" he asked. Jean nodded.

"Please. Tell me everything. He really loved us. I need to know everything," she said.

Hayward's voice slowed as he explained that the home was built to the specifications Elden had drawn up.

"He contracted for construction of the house almost immediately and started pulling money out of Somewhere, his tavern, to do it. It was all his money so his parents couldn't say a word, though they threatened to take it away. I heard tell that he'd leave the Academy and drive out there, sometimes twice a day, sometimes at night, to check on things. Tried to do what was right by everyone, and it was tearing him apart they say," Hayward explained.

"I didn't know," she began, her voice faltering. "How could I have not known? Why didn't he tell us?" Jean asked, gesturing to Ella.

"He wanted to do everything just right. He didn't want you to know, not until it was done. Had everything arranged so you'd be notified the day the place was done, furnished, key in hand. Ready for you and Ella. He was clear about that. But then, well, you know what happened," Hayward said, his voice dropping.

Jean put her hands to her face. It was all too much. Her shoulders heaved as she sobbed.

"Just breathe, Miss Ball. Just breathe," counseled Hayward. "It's alright now. From now on, everything is all right. We can't bring him back, but we can honor his wishes."

"We'd drafted out his Last Will and Testament when he came up with all these plans. I'd counseled him to do it, of course. We both knew what his mother would have done if he hadn't written things out in black and white. Put a stop to all of it, if she could have. His father, though, he would have understood. I'm now sure of that." Jean nodded as Hayward Parker continued.

"His mother was mad, beyond mad, you know. Insane with grief at first, and then rage-mad for months after Elden passed. She tried every means she could to stop the liquidation of Somewhere, the tavern Elden owned, so that the proceeds would not go toward this. Didn't want to give you any reason to think you could care for Elden's child on your own. She fought especially hard after you, Jean, refused to give up the baby to her and Mr. Whitcomb. She was crazy mad after that. Not the legal term, of course, but crazy mad just the same," explained Hayward. "I know what she tried to do, with Ella. I didn't represent them in that. It wasn't right, you know."

Jean sat quietly, remembering, reflecting on what had almost happened to her baby. Their baby. She had never told anyone except Otis and Abby about the day the Whitcombs appeared at her door and demanded Ella.

Mr. Whitcomb had looked sad, like he'd been dragged all the way up each stair and then been propped in front of her door. Mrs. Whitcomb was perfectly coiffed and virulent. They'd made every promise about Ella's future if Jean would only sign the papers. Mrs. Whitcomb produced a tall stack of legal documents and an ink pen.

"Mr. Whitcomb finally put an end to the legal proceedings, against his wife's wishes," Hayward explained, "and the home was finally finished, then furnished. He bought Somewhere, all the remaining assets of the tavern, at the auction to make sure there was money for everything to be done right here. Kept his men bidding up the price higher and higher. Quite a spectacle."

Jean nodded. "It's impossible to think my Elden did this. Impossible. How did I not know? And his father? His father helped, afterwards, after Elden ..." Jean's voice broke.

"Passing so young, it was the one thing he hadn't planned. We went over everything, everything he wanted for you and for his baby. He kept saying, 'a home. We want a home.' He'd didn't mean just land or a house, it was something more to him. You'll see," Hayward said, his voice full of assurance.

Jean put her head down to the table and sobbed.

~

*H*ayward gave the girl a moment to compose herself and stepped into the apartment house hallway. It was all more than he expected. He'd forgotten the true weight of it all in the clutter of documents and words and process. Leaning against the wall, he shut his eyes.

He well-remembered the meeting with Elden. The meeting request had come about from an unusual source. His wife. She had never made a professional request of her husband. She'd always respected his professional boundaries, except this once.

She had seen the baby on the street with Jean and had come home that night and asked – no, demanded - that Hayward call Elden in for a discussion and to draw up some legal papers, an estate plan. She said Elden had responsibilities and told her husband that she could sense where he may be headed.

Hayward knew to trust his wife's instincts, so he had called Elden and asked if he had thought of the future. The boy sounded relieved to get the call.

Hayward sat Elden down and told him the way things could be done. Should be done.

During the meeting, Elden talked for two hours, articulating the future he wanted for himself and a girl he called "Jean."

Then Elden had said the girl's full name, Virginia Mae Ball and Hayward took notice. He'd known the young woman's father, a good man, many years before. Integrity. Kind. A spirit of service. Tragic to have lost him in the War, Hayward had silently reflected.

Hayward listened closely to Elden, taking careful notes and then he had sent Elden away, asking him to consider things for the next week and to come back later to review the specifics.

A week to the day, Elden was back in Hayward's office, stone cold sober and adamant. Elden was of legal age and a property owner. He knew now his responsibilities, his moral obligations. Hayward was more than obliging to help Elden fulfill his duties, and he drew up the papers.

Elden's affairs would have been simple to close up, had it not been for his mother's wrangling over the sale of Elden's business, the bar. She'd challenged every court filing mandating the sale, so desperate was she to hold on to any part of her son. But that had all been resolved and Jean would be the rightful owner of the home now, free and clear.

Only one tiny detail remained - the transmittal of a package from Elden. Elden had brought the envelope to Hayward's office the day the legal documents were signed. He'd made Hayward promise to keep its contents confidential and keep the envelope safe and away from his parents. Elden said he needed to give it all to Jean someday – that it was letters Elden had written to baby Ella and Jean, but had never sent, and a necklace, a jade flower dangling from a gold chain.

The package waited for her in the house, on the table overlooking the lake. Those were things for later.

~

Hayward knocked gently on Jean's door. She'd had time enough to dry her tears by now.

With the baby in one arm, Jean opened the door. He studied the woman who had captured his client's heart. She was a young woman now, stronger and more confident than he'd anticipated.

And she had now the look of dawning realization, of the opportunity Elden had created and had intended to share.

"He thought that I would be living out there first, didn't he – living there, Ella and me, waiting for him. And then he'd come to us, right?" Jean asked, already sensing the answer.

Hayward nodded his head. "But, please, don't think about that now. Just take the keys," he said handing her a large brass key dangling from a rich maroon tassel. I think you'll like the place and everything in it is yours, free and clear. My job is just to file papers with the probate court and make everything final. I'll take you two out now, if you'll let me. I'll drive your car."

"Car? You can't drive my car. I don't have one," Jean gulped, still trying to absorb all that had just happened. Her mind was racing. What had Elden been thinking, not to let her know about all of this? What had his parents done to keep him so scared and silent, she wondered. Had he really loved her and Ella after all?

"Yes, right. Well, that's the other thing. The car. He was very specific about the car you were to have. He wanted you to have one like his, only yellow. The color of sunshine, he said. It's outside. I took the liberty of driving it over," Hayward explained. A smile spread across his face as he watched Jean's eyes widen again in disbelief.

"But, I don't drive," she said in a barely audible whisper, her eyes wet with tears.

"You'll learn how. My wife said she'd like to teach you. She's a terror now that she's driving. Just loves it. You'll have to learn now that you'll be living out in the country, at that lake. Have to get to town for your work, you know," Hayward said.

"Can we go now?" Jean asked, her eyes filled with eager anticipation. It was all too much.

"Right now. Otis is waiting to open the car door, I'm sure," Hayward said.

Jean gathered Ella, her blanket and a bottle of milk. "Take a bag of overnight things. I think you'll want to stay there tonight, once you see the place. I'll take the car home and my wife will drive it over in the morning to start your lessons. I'll meet you downstairs in a moment."

"Yes. But, wait. I don't think I can leave here for good. Otis and Abby, they're like my family," Jean said. "I won't have to lose them to accept this gift, will I? Oh, I can't wait to tell Francie! I can't lose any more people, you see. I need them. Ella needs them."

Hayward nodded. "You don't need to lose anyone ever again," he said. "Now, I'll be downstairs."

Jean looked around the small apartment, remembering all the years she'd spent with her mother, building a tiny life, a happy life together.

She packed a satchel of necessities, confident she'd be back soon and uncertain about where she was headed.

Jean took one last look at the tiny apartment and walked back to the bedside table. She gently took the blue handkerchief from the tabletop and put it into her pocket, patting it twice. She picked up

Ella and together they hurried down the stairs where she was greeted by Otis' wide smile.

"I expect that man loved you true after all, Miss Jean," said Otis as he opened the apartment building door and led her to the yellow Revere convertible. "Yes, I expect he was a real man through and through."

Jean reached an arm around Otis and brushed his cheek with a tiny kiss before sliding into the front seat.

~

*H*ayward Parker drove through the countryside, explaining who owned what land and how much. Jean let his words rush over her as she clutched Ella to her chest, murmuring words of comfort.

The white clapboard cottage had a wide front porch that wrapped around the house. Wicker furniture with pinstripe cushions adorned the porch, making the entry inviting.

The interior of the home was designed with equal care. There was a large kitchen with a deck that overlooked the water. A screened porch protected the kitchen entrance from the driveway. And the kitchen was ready to be used. Even the pantry was stocked. The cupboards brimmed with everything they needed - from china and silver to tea, sweet biscuits, tinned food and dry goods.

Jean, with the baby in her arms, wandered through the spacious rooms, taking in the splendor and plush furnishings – all the details in place. The baby bassinet was placed strategically in the master bedroom. Ella's own bedroom was adjacent for when the baby grew big enough for sleeping apart from Jean.

Jean was speechless as she marveled at the home's every feature. She opened a closet door and found a stack of perfectly pressed linen sheets and brand new cotton towels. Hayward followed her from room to room, waiting for the moment to say more.

"My wife is Mrs. Parker, you know, with the Consumer League," Hayward began, "she's fond of you. Has been from that first day you caught her splattered in mud from that dairy business. Never had a girl of our own, you know. Talks about you all the time."

Jean turned and looked at him with wide eyes. All the pieces were falling in to place. Mrs. Hayward Parker, of course. Michele Parker.

"You won't mind if she comes by tomorrow? She'll take you into work until you get used to that fancy car."

"Honored. I'd be honored, sir," Jean said, unable to quell her astonishment at this turn of events, the kindness of the Parkers, the luxurious appointments of the home and, most of all, Elden's love, his deep abiding love.

Jean was brimming with dozens of questions. Maybe Mrs. Parker could tell her tomorrow. Yes, she'd brew a pot of tea in her perfect kitchen and ask her Rooster Tamer to explain everything over sweet biscuits.

Ella cooed in her arms as Jean's eyes filled with tears of joy, of relief, of regret, of loss, of heartbreak.

"One more place for you to see, then I'll go. It's something Elden said to be sure to show you," Hayward said quietly as he led her toward the back of the house.

Jean knew she was truly home the minute Mr. Parker opened the heavy French doors that led to a covered veranda off the backyard. Stepping stones led through the expansive green lawn dotted with flowerbeds.

"Designed this himself. Said you'd recognize the view from over there, where he put up the swing," Hayward said gesturing to a white porch swing that hung on the far side of the veranda.

Jean, Ella still gurgling happily in her arms, walked toward the porch swing, her heart melting, filled with love and loss. She sat down gently on the swing as it began to sway.

From the swing she could just see the waterfall and little pond where she and Elden dipped their toes that first day together.

Elden finally had done what he could for them. He had brought them home to a safe haven for their daughter. For herself. It was in that place, when the sun shone just right, she could feel his presence.

EPILOGUE

At age four, Ella was an explorer. No part of the little house was left untouched.

She knew the smoothness of the fireplace tile, the cold clean finish on the foyer's marble floor, the rich smell of the library with its tall shelves filled with leather-bound books, the warmth of the oak butcher block in her cozy, light-filled kitchen.

It all made her feel happy and safe, especially the way her mama would walk through the house in the morning, pulling open the curtains as she sang silly little songs to herself, or to Orion, her kitty cat.

Sometimes her friends Mr. Otis and Miss Abby would visit, or Harry and Mrs. Francie, who kept promising to teach her to sew and brought her a pretty Bible with pictures and stories and everything.

And when Mrs. Parker came with all those laughing ladies, the house sure did fill up. And it felt like a party the day mama got her big job reporting on those 'ployment things.

The best days were when Miss Lydia visited, though, with Mr. James and once he brought her a baseball. She liked to hold the ball in her hands, but when she tossed it up in the air it came down too hard on her head one time, and then her mama made her put it away until she was a big girl.

To distract Ella from the disappointment of the withdrawn ball, Mr. James showed her how he could skip rocks on the water. Her mama tried to teach her to skip stones all summer and she had grown frustrated that every stone sank with nary a single skip.

Ella had struggled but couldn't find the words to explain to her mother what was wrong. She knew if she found the right stone, the best stone, everything would be right, in its place, always.

It wasn't fair that Mama's rocks skittered like bugs across the water, but hers all sank. And she figured James could skip stones so well because he played baseball. The baseball!

Ella started looking for that baseball, determined to find it. She could teach herself how to throw, and then her mama would feel so proud of her. And then, Ella imagined, James would stand up tall and laugh, and tussle her hair like he does.

Ella adjusted the strap on her blue jean overalls, tugging it back onto her shoulder and shoving her tiny hands into the deep overall pockets.

Where haven't I looked? she wondered, looking around the hallway and considering the options that may lay behind the wood paneled doors.

Mama's room. That pretty cedar box under her bed. Mama would have hid that 'ole 'hit me on the head' ball somewhere far away.

Mama had never told her anyplace was off limits, forbidden, but she'd never actually offered Ella a look inside the satin wonderland that must hold all of her most favorite things.

Ella pushed open the door to her mama's bedroom and took in the muted colors of the restful space, with its chocolate brown pillows and pale green walls. The room reminded her of the thicket of tall trees where she and Mama would picnic down by the big lake.

Ella flopped onto her belly in front of her mama's big bed, comforted by her soft landing on the Turkish rug. She wiggled her hand way underneath the bedskirt until she felt the side of the cedar box, cool and smooth. Yes, it was the perfect size to hide that ball.

Ella scooted the box along the oak floor until it peeked out at her from underneath the edge of the bed. She hitched a little finger underneath the lid's edge and giggled as it slid easily off, exposing what surely were her mama's best treasures. She took a deep breath in, the smell reminded her of trees and dark woods.

Ella's sea green eyes landed first on a pile of papers all covered in long boring words. Not treasure at all, and no baseball. Then she saw a necklace, all pearly and light. Ella sucked in her breath. It looked too special to even touch.

Then Ella's eyes alit on a stone. One perfect, smooth gray stone. It was exactly what Ella had been waiting for, hoping for, searching for, forever.

Ella picked up the stone and caressed each side. She held it to her soft cheek, feeling its smooth perfection and then she carefully slipped it into her front pocket where it lay nestled next to her happily beating heart. She could feel the soft pitter-pat resonate against the stone. Her stone. The one she had imagined always existed, if she could only find it.

Ella raced out of the bedroom and down the hall to the back entryway. The French doors leading to the porch opened with a satisfying thunk, the sound echoing through the house.

Ella's little bare feet flew down the wooden steps and along the stepping stones that led to her pond. To her private spot where she thought her very best thoughts and from where she could most always see her family of brown baby bunnies. To the spot where her mama sat at this very moment reading some boring 'gazine.

Ella stood close to her mama and proudly pulled the stone from her chest pocket. She turned it over and over in her warm, tanned hands. Ella took in a deep breath and smiled. She looked out across the blue, blue pond, the water perfectly still.

"What do you have there, Miss Ella?" Jean asked, putting down the *Ladies Home Journal* and reaching for the stone. "Oh," she said as she touched its smooth surface. Memories flooded through her. She could feel Elden's very presence beside her, as if all of time had stopped.

Ella smiled innocently up at her mama as she fitted the stone into her throwing hand just so and pulled back her arm at just the right angle.

Ella's little arm came forward in a perfect arc as she released the stone from her grasp. One clear line, smooth and straight and true. The stone that lay hidden for years skipped, again and again across the water, free.

"I do it, I do it!" Ella hollered with glee, her little feet stamping the soft earth. Ella pointed to the water and flashed a big, bold smile at her mama. Jean's eyes followed to where Ella pointed.

Forever the stone flew across the surface, skimming the line of water just so until it settled quietly into the great deep pond, landing somewhere perfect and still.

READING GROUP GUIDE
SOMEWHERE STILL

If you enjoyed *Somewhere Still*, please consider leaving a review on Amazon.com. Reviews are very important to authors and have a strong impact on book sales. Denitta reads each one and would appreciate hearing from you. To sign up for news about Denitta's appearances and new releases, sign up to receive her newsletter at www.denitta.com.

QUESTIONS TO CONSIDER

1. Jean ventures out to explore the city's newest hotel knowing she needs a means to support herself. The stakes are high and her safety net is virtually nonexistence. What might that have felt like in the 1920s? What were your feelings when you had that responsibility? How strong was your safety net?

2. The society women of 1920s Kansas City were organized into social clubs, like the Consumer League, dedicated to bettering society. They assured dairies were hygienic. Yes, they really had White Lists for dairies and the Kansas City Consumer League ladies were inspectors.

This women's group really captured my heart. They supported beautification efforts throughout the city and its parks. They took over the State Legislature one day to advocate for their causes. What was Jean's impression of these women? Do you see this type of collective action in our own cities and towns today? Why or why not?

3. The loss of a parent is devastating. Jean's mama seeks to impart wisdom and rules on Jean, knowing the end might be near. Was Jean ready? How did her understanding of her mama's rules evolve? And, did they always apply? What can we, as parents, do to prepare for endings?

4. The Whitcomb's business judgments appear to be influenced not by right and wrong or even the common social mores of the day. At times, they appear forward thinking, as in their support for desegregation of the ball park and hiring Jean to do a man's job. Other times, as Elden reflects on right and wrong, black and white, and clear lines, we see maybe decisions were made for economic, rather than social or cultural reasons. How much does profit play into Mr. Whitcomb's decisions? And, does it matter?

5. Mrs. Whitcomb was not all that she put on airs to be. How is it she identified with, yet shunned Jean, and why? And how does her treatment of Jean compare to Mrs. Parker's treatment, who herself was a tailor's daughter who "married up"?

6. Cassandra Lee's momentary decision to change Jean's Emery Bird Thayer bill had unknowable and unintended consequences that may have influenced Jean and Elden's relationship. Have you experienced this kind of ripple effect of a quick action or inaction?

7. Jean finds strength and refuge in her relationship with Abby, who knew of death and of birth, with a deep faith. How does their friendship help Jean transform? What does it mean to support without proselytizing?

8. Did you think the ending was appropriate? What are your hopes for Jean and Ella? What do you suppose the Depression Era brings?

∼

If you enjoyed the book, please leave a review on Amazon.com. Reviews are important to authors and I'd be delighted to hear from you.

Visit www.denitta.com to sign up for the *Somewhere* series newsletter and learn more about the places and events that inspired *Somewhere Still*.

You may want to read more about Prohibition in this novel's historical companion, *Prohibition Cocktails*, available on Amazon, Barnes & Noble, and at independent bookstores.

ABOUT THE AUTHOR

Denitta Ward, author of the *Somewhere* series, writes historical and contemporary fiction from the foothills of the Rocky Mountains. After decades of writing legal briefs and contracts, she picked up her pen and decided to finally write the stories she really wanted to tell - about young women discovering their own resilience in times of transition.

Somewhere Still, written as a Mother's Day gift, captures a society in transition and a town near to her heart as a backdrop for this story of the price of love, the hurts that are slowest to heal, and a certain kind of infinite redemption found when women band together across race and class.

Denitta is a member of the Women's Fiction Writers Association, the Historical Novel Society, and Rocky Mountain Fiction Writers. She is an alumni of Georgetown University Law and the University of Kansas.

Sign up for Denitta's Somewhere series newsletter at
www.denitta.com

ACKNOWLEDGMENTS

Writing is a solo activity, but a book comes into being only with a web of support nurturing it along. This was so true for *Somewhere Still*.

Thank you to Patricia Ray, my mother, for her inspiration and instilling me in the love of reading from an early age. Thank you to Kent, Alex, and Olivia, who supported my writing moments with care and feeding, as well as long patience when I headed to the mountains for writing weekends.

Once formed, the book became so much better through the edits of Kiesa Kay, and then suggestions from my agent, Elaine Spencer, and a talented set of first readers: Laurie, Michele, Mary, Gwen, Marybeth, Lori, Rebecca, Tonda, Chris, Fran G., Mindy, and Debbie. A special thanks to Fran Katnik for meticulous line edits. Lisa Manifold of Rocky Mountain Fictions Writers held my hand along the publishing path - thank you, Lisa. And, Welbourne Press.

I also have much gratitude towards John C. Sease, Jr. who took gentle care reviewing for unconscious bias. For that, I am grateful and in awe at the sensitive review, deep professionalism, and tenderness of his comments.

Finally, thank you to all who read this book for indulging me in bringing the story of Jean and Elden to life.

ALSO BY DENITTA WARD

PROHIBITION COCKTAILS

Prohibition Cocktails reveals the history, secrets, and recipes of 21 of the most popular drinks of the Roaring Twenties, when the rules were clear and made to be broken. From 1920-1933 the U.S. banned liquor and the cocktail culture flourished.

Try the sweet Mary Pickford to the startling Monkey Gland. Captured here are the best recipes and secrets of the era's 21 most captivating cocktails, along with a Roaring '20s party-planning guide.

Prohibition Cocktails is the historical companion to *Somewhere Still*. Enjoy the sneak peek that follows here - a sampling of the stories and recipes. Available at Amazon.com, Barnes & Noble, and independent bookstores.

For news of Denitta's next book release and appearance schedule, sign up for her Newsletter at www.denitta.com.